BEST
OF THE SOUTH

BEST
OF THE SOUTH

From Ten Years of *New Stories from the South*
edited by Shannon Ravenel

Selected and Introduced by
Anne Tyler

Algonquin Books of Chapel Hill / *1996*

Published by
ALGONQUIN BOOKS OF CHAPEL HILL
Post Office Box 2225
Chapel Hill, North Carolina 27515-2225

a division of
WORKMAN PUBLISHING
708 Broadway
New York, New York 10003

For permission to reprint stories in this volume, grateful acknowledgment is made to the holders of copyright, publishers, or representatives named on page 425, which constitutes an extension of the copyright page.

Library of Congress Cataloging-in-Publication Data
Best of the South : from ten years of New stories from the South, edited by Shannon Ravenel / selected and introduced by Anne Tyler.
    p. cm.
   ISBN 1-56512-128-7
   1. Short stories, American—Southern States.   2. Southern States—Social life and customs—Fiction.   I. Tyler, Anne.   II. New stories from the South.
   PS551.B38   1996
   813'.0108975—dc20   95-45857
                                                  CIP

10 9 8 7 6 5 4 3 2 1
First Edition

CONTENTS

INTRODUCTION

The Southern town where I spent my teens had a tree-shaded square at its heart, with a statue of a Confederate soldier standing guard on his pedestal and small shops lining the streets all around. You could watch a movie at the movie house for fifty cents, eat a pit-cooked-barbecue sandwich at the five-and-dime, and buy clothes in a department store where the clerk was addressed as Miss Mildred.

The tree-shaded square still exists, of course, but no longer would you take it for the heart of town. Life in Raleigh, North Carolina, seems to have moved in an outward direction, toward the gigantic, streamlined malls with their salad-bar restaurants and their multiplex cinemas. And I assume that teenagers in Raleigh— like teenagers in Detroit or Philadelphia—watch music videos on MTV, eat hamburgers at McDonald's, and buy jeans at the Gap.

Still, whenever I speak with anyone who happens to come from that area, I fancy I notice something distinctive in the style of our conversation—something warmer, more ambling, than what I have grown accustomed to since I moved away. I realize this may be wishful thinking. Americans everywhere, I suspect, cling to the hope that this country still has identifiable regions, in spite of all the changes wrought by modern times.

My own hope has resurfaced with each annual volume of *New*

Stories from the South. There are ten such volumes so far, covering the years from 1986 to 1995 and containing a total of 163 short stories hand-picked by Shannon Ravenel. Her selections range from tragic to comic, from experimental to conventional; but they're always of top quality, which won't surprise her many admirers. As past editor of *The Best American Short Stories*, Shannon Ravenel holds uncontested the title of Guardian Angel of the Short Story Form. Moreover, she is Southern herself—born and raised in the Carolinas, living there to this day. What better person, then, to shed light on the issue of "Southernness" in literature?

That there *is* an issue most people will agree. Traditionally, Southern writing is expected to be Southern in its very bones, defined not just by the happenstance of the author's origins but by a yeasty prose style, a strong relationship with the past, and a feeling for place. A real Southern story (the theory goes) remains Southern even if you change the name of the locale from Nashville to Boston, the name of the hero from Billy Bob to Kevin. The question is, does this still hold true today?

I thought about that question a lot, while I was choosing twenty favorites from a decade's worth of *New Stories from the South*.

To call this collection the "best" of the series is in part misleading, because so many different considerations weighed in: which story works well with which other stories, how many of a given type of story a single volume can support, and, inescapably, what my own personal prejudices may be. Not once did I base a decision on how Southern the writing was (although I did exclude, with the greatest regret, a few authors whose home states I classified instead as Western or Midwestern). Just for fun, however, I sat back when I'd finished and asked myself, of each choice, "Could this story have come only from the South and nowhere else?"

By my calculations, the answer was a definite "yes" in eight cases. Rick Bass's "The Watch" qualifies in the most concrete sense: it is so geographically grounded, its swampy, steamy setting so intrinsic to the plot, that it couldn't have happened anyplace except the deepest South. Padgett Powell's "The Winnowing of Mrs. Schuping" is suffused with a similar setting—and let's not forget (who could possibly forget?) that extremely Southern good-old-boy sheriff.

Barry Hannah's "Nicodemus Bluff" juxtaposes a hard-drinking, nonhunting "hunting trip" with a fierce awareness of race and class divisions—both of which can occur elsewhere, surely, but not in quite this combination. And Patricia Lear's "After Memphis" studies the torn-up-by-the-roots feeling of a Southern child moved North—a child who, in addition, is lovingly urged toward what I consider a particularly Old Southern attitude of feminine passivity.

Reginald McKnight's "The Kind of Light That Shines on Texas" bears chilling witness to a different Old Southern attitude in its depiction of three black students submerged and barely breathing in a white classroom. The same can be said for Melanie Sumner's "My Other Life," with its funny, pathetically well-meaning parents trying their best not to notice that their daughter has fallen in love with a Senegalese native. And Bob Shacochis's "Where Pelham Fell" richly testifies to the Southern view that the Civil War (or what one of my teachers used to call "The War for Southern Independence") happened about a week ago.

Don't assume, though, that the Old South is the only South there is. Tony Earley's "Charlotte" is so modern that its hero runs a fern bar, and yet it has a resoundingly Southern ring to it—not just because of the gum-snapping, we-all style of the narrative, but also because one of its central characters happens to be the very Southern city of Charlotte, North Carolina.

Nine other stories, while they could conceivably have come from elsewhere, possess at least a Southern flavor. Sometimes it's a matter of tone. In "The Rain of Terror," Frank Manley hilariously demonstrates the tape-recorder ear for dialogue that Southern writers possess in such abundance. (Is it that they've listened more, from an earlier age? Or is it that there's more to listen *to*—more colorful, quotable conversation?) Lee Smith's is an especially faithful ear; her "Intensive Care" is as riveting as a gossip session with your neighbor over the backyard fence.

The beautifully grave voice of the child who's digging his way through the Delta in Lewis Nordan's "A Hank of Hair, a Piece of Bone" seems to float across the air of the room you're reading in. Equally audible is Madison Smartt Bell's "Customs of the Country," which employs a certain quiet, uninflected style of Southern speech that can hit you in the chest without a bit of warning. And when the title character in Marly Swick's "Heart" says she "felt real special" after her father left and her mother went crazy, I knew that the author (an iffy case, geographically speaking, on account of a peripatetic childhood) had made the best possible use of her sojourn in Georgia.

Other times, it's a matter of character. In Leon Driskell's finely observed "Martha Jean," the heroine blends almost holy sweetness with an iron backbone—a combination instantly recognizable to anyone who's attended Youth Group in a Southern church. Mary Hood's "After Moore" shows us the Southern woman as she often really is: feisty and outrageous, had-it-up-to-here, the diametrical opposite of the wilted-magnolia type many Northerners envision. You'll find a younger version in Nanci Kincaid's "This Is Not the Picture Show," along with—a bonus—one of those mysterious, dangerous, back-of-the-classroom country boys that send shivers up a Southern girl's spine. And the heroine of Edward Jones's stunning "Marie" turns an unmistakably Southern eye upon Washington, D.C., which (Northern though it may be by Civil War standards) draws much of its atmosphere from its large population of African-Americans transplanted from the South.

Finally, we're left with three stories that could have been relocated without altering their essential natures—and without making them any less wonderful. The barge in James Lee Burke's electric "Water People" could have navigated some body of water other than a bay in the Gulf of Mexico. The real setting of Richard

Bausch's "Letter to the Lady of the House" is the complete, small universe of a working marriage, no matter what latitude or even what hemisphere the couple lives in. And Mark Richard's "The Birds for Christmas" slashes its irrepressible young heroes into our memories without once stepping outside the four walls of a hospital ward in an unspecified city.

That gives us seventeen stories out of twenty that show a clear connection to their region—eight of those inextricably so. Is this an unusually high percentage? Is it higher than what you'd find in, say, a collection from New England?

I don't for one moment imagine that the South holds a monopoly on what used to be called "local color." Anyone who's encountered Carolyn Chute's Egypt, Maine, or Richard Russo's Mohawk, New York, knows there are other parts of this country that lend themselves as well to vivid characterization. And I think the series could legitimately have been called *New Stories from the South* even if its only defining quality was that its contributors had spent some portion of their lives below the Mason-Dixon line—regardless of whether the stories themselves reflected the fact.

But I do feel that, more often than not, the South exerts a gentle but pervasive influence on the substance of the fiction produced there. Three factors may account for this. First, the Southern accent, which continues to hold its own against even the non-accent of national TV, sets up a kind of music that makes most snatches of dialogue as seductively reproducible as jump-rope rhymes. Second, the Southern approach toward narrative (not just "what happened" but "whom it happened to," as in, "Now, first you need to know that Uncle Jimmy was the type of person who . . .") affects the path and pace of the plot. And third, there's the Southern sense of belonging to a group—the feeling, often, that it's "we" telling the story rather than "I." Heaven knows, this trait is not unique to the South, but in combination with the accent and the narrative style it makes for something that *is* unique, I truly do believe. There were moments, reading these stories, when I felt I was listening to a modern version of a lovely, mournful Greek chorus. It struck me as mournful even when a story was killingly funny, because always in the back of my mind was the thought: *Don't go! Don't change! Don't slip away completely!*

And maybe it won't, if we're lucky.

Anne Tyler
Baltimore, Maryland
1995

BEST
OF THE SOUTH

1986

Leon V. Driskell

MARTHA JEAN

Leon Driskell, who died in 1995 at the age of sixty-two, taught for many years at the University of Louisville. For all those years he also led "Leon's Group" of writers, to whom he was endlessly available, as reader, friend, colleague. He has left behind only a single book of his own fiction, Passing Through *(1983). "Martha Jean," which appeared a few years later, was to be part of a book about growing up in his home state of Georgia. His mastery of characterization is never more evident than in this portrait of a girl "always proving something, being fun so that everybody could see how fun it was to be a Christian."*

A good many years back, when I was a kid trying to grow up down South, all of the soft drink companies took to giving prizes for numbers they put inside the bottlecaps. That was before you could buy just about anything you wanted to drink in an aluminum can with a snap top and throw away the can when you were done. That goes to show you about how many years ago what I am going to tell happened.

If you wanted to try and win a prize, you had to gouge out the number that was between the metal top of the cap and a thin pad of rubbery, or cork stuff. Sometimes you had to have a special card to paste all your numbers on, kind of like bingo. One company had what they called Magic Numbers, and if you got one of the good numbers you got a prize just for sending it off to that company's district office. Some of the prizes were things like an electric can opener, which nobody would want unless they had a heap of cans to open. Other prizes were worth a considerable amount of money.

Some of them were worth cash, and those were the ones Martha Jean was after.

Not that she wouldn't have taken a can opener or anything else she happened to win, but she was out for big prizes and for a special reason. Cash would have suited her best, but she would find a way to use anything she got. Every little bit helps, she said. That was her way, and still is.

Martha Jean is a girl I grew up with but never thought much about until our last year in school. If you lived where I did, in the town of Whitehall, Georgia, as I did then and still do, you didn't have much choice but to grow up with just about everybody in the county who happened to be born about the time you were.

There wasn't much to Whitehall except the people, and not many of them. Whitehall has grown a lot since then, but we still do not have what you would call a population explosion: town is maybe five stores, a restaurant, and a movie theater. In addition to which we have three churches, not counting the Jehovah's Witness Church, which was then in a lady's basement and is now in that same lady's attic. All the churches are Protestant except for the one they call backdoor-Catholic and that nobody much goes to.

Back then, we had just two kinds of schools to go to, white and colored, separate like they said but equal. So Martha Jean and I grew up together and went to the same schools but not to the same church.

Martha Jean wasn't what anybody would call ugly. They just didn't think much about how she looked. I know I didn't. She was not the kind of girl you would think about kissing or holding hands with. She had what all the girls called "a good personality"; other girls, the ones who secretly disliked her, called her "sweet." They said it the way they would say that a little bitty diamond in a so-called friend's engagement ring was "sweet."

For a long time none of us boys noticed her personality any more than we noticed that she had violet-colored eyes and curly brown hair which she kept pinned down and half the time under a kerchief. If anybody had asked me about Martha Jean I would probably have said that she was good and would be a missionary or something when she got older. If I had known about nuns, I would have guessed that she might become one of them.

Knowing how good Martha Jean was didn't make us like her. Mostly we boys didn't dislike her, but we regarded her as a nuisance. Sometimes one of us would go by to see some girl we thought we liked and there would be Martha Jean spending the night. Had it been almost any other girl any of us knew, we could say, "Hey, I know this boy I'll call, and we'll all go to ride and maybe stop at Uppy's and get some onion rings and a Nu-Grape." But any friend you had wouldn't be caught dead riding around with Martha Jean, and if he would, he wouldn't be your friend.

Those nights, Martha Jean would have this awful glitter about her. You could tell she knew she was in the way and did not know what to do about it. It never occurred to us boys that we were maybe in the way. Martha Jean would talk a mile a minute, and you'd sit there in the girl's living room, or maybe on her porch depending on the season, and you'd wish Martha Jean would say excuse me and get herself lost. You'd look hard at the other girl, who would frown and shake her head and try to carry on nonsense with Martha Jean, but you could tell she would like to be rid of Martha Jean as much as you would. Martha Jean never let on, but she knew too.

What was wrong with Martha Jean was not how she looked or even that we boys knew better than to try and touch her or fool around any. Everybody could tell that Martha Jean had a purpose in everything she did, even when she was cutting up and trying to make everybody laugh. She was always proving something, being fun so that everybody could see how much fun it was to be a Christian. Everybody I knew could tell the difference between really having fun and having fun to show that they could do it.

Martha Jean probably never had any fun in her whole life, though she talked lots about Joy, which I take to be different from fun.

Parents liked for their daughters to be around Martha Jean, for she was both serious and, from the parents' point of view, fun; she was a kind of model. She did not wear makeup, and she taught Sunday School at the Church of Christ and went away summers to work at some church camp or another. She was probably a great swimmer, but I bet she did that for Jesus too. She went to a different camp every summer, for, though she could sell almost any camp director the first time, they thought hard about having her back two summers in a row.

Martha Jean knew every game and joke in the book, but when she got done with them, they might as well have stayed in the book. You know the kind of books I mean. She was always reading things like "Object Lessons for Intermediates," and "True Fellowship," and "Stories of Faith." Later, she took to reading books like "The Christian Home."

I have watched Martha Jean read books like that, and I know she was not doing it for fun. She was dead serious, and when she tried out the games and jokes she had studied up on, she just naturally made people feel like they were in church or something. The more she glittered at you and tried to make you have fun, the more you felt solemn and serious. That was just how Martha Jean was.

Everybody knew she planned to go away to Columbia Bible College after high school and get a degree, maybe two or three, in what she called Christian Education. You could not ask Martha Jean how she was doing without getting a full report on what she had lately learned about Christian Education.

The way Martha Jean talked about Christian Education made me shiver. She meant it when she said she was *thrilled* or *excited* about it. You could tell she was going to be hell on wheels once she got ready to start teaching in earnest. She was just trying out on those kids down at the Church of Christ and on us at the Whitehall High School.

Well, Martha Jean was one of the commencement speakers at our high school graduation, and everybody wondered which of the girls' spend-the-night parties she was going to afterwards. All the boys wanted the girls they were with to go to another party, for we did not think Martha Jean was likely to approve of what all went on. It was the custom for the boys to drive back and forth from one girl's house to another's. The girls would slip out to see certain boys, even after all the girls were supposed to be in bed. Sometimes a whole gang of girls and boys would pile into the cars and go away and do crazy things like singing and dancing in front of a teacher's house, or eating pickles in the cemetery.

Nobody could imagine Martha Jean slipping out to go riding or anything else, and nobody wanted to spend more time on graduation night with her than they had to. You can just bet that if Martha Jean could, she would have everybody, boys *and* girls, sitting around playing the games she had worked up special for the occasion. It was hard to tell which would be worse, doing what Martha Jean would regard as fun or hurting her feelings by refusing.

It may not be the same everywhere, but in Whitehall, where we grew up, all the boys in the graduating class would ask some girl to walk down the aisle at commencement exercises with them. There was always a girl or two left over, sometimes more, and they always paired off and walked down the aisle together. The boys naturally liked this practice; we never thought that we could be the ones left out, and neither had the girls. At about Christmas, the girls in the senior class began to realize that they might be the ones left out. If they did not have steady boyfriends, they would start being extra nice to anybody they thought might ask them to walk down the aisle.

There was a saying that you always walked down the aisle twice with the same person, which made girls think it was romantic for a boy to ask them to walk down the aisle. The saying really meant that you would go down the aisle twice, once at rehearsal and again at the exercises. Still, even if a girl didn't like a particular boy very much, she would start to think about him different if he asked her to walk with him at graduation. Graduation and marriage seemed almost equally significant then, and it would occur to boys as well as girls that they just might marry the person they walked down the aisle with on graduation night. The odds were for it.

About a dozen of us planned to go to college, and we knew that three of us would most likely be picked as graduation speakers. Our pictures would be in the county newspaper, and we would get to sit on the front row, no matter what our names began with. Mostly, the same ones of us who were officers of practically everything and honor graduates would be the ones nominated as speakers. The way the speakers were selected was that the school principal and the teachers all had a meeting and made their pick first. Then the senior class got to vote on the five they had picked.

I was going to the state university, and, though I didn't count Columbia Bible College as being the same, I knew that Martha Jean might be one of the speakers along with me and Henry Elder. As it turned out, my name did show up on the list the teachers picked, and I got busy right away planning my speech. Once I made it by the teachers (especially Mrs. Schneider, the librarian), I thought I had it made. Anyhow, I did not think I had to worry about Martha Jean beating me out, so I voted for her — though in second place. It was the first time I ever voted for myself, and I lost.

The way Henry Elder and I figured it is that everybody thought we were sure to be speakers, so they voted for Martha Jean either first or second. The balance of us got the scattered votes. Nobody had expected Martha Jean to be elected, but we knew she would make exactly the kind of speech everybody expected to hear, and she did.

After the election, which took place late in April, everybody began to worry about who would walk down the aisle with Martha Jean. Naturally, she did not have a boyfriend. Everybody agreed that it would look funny for a speaker to walk down the aisle with another girl. Generally, the girls walking together were put back on the back row so they wouldn't show up much, but you couldn't put a speaker on the back row.

I had spent most of my senior year being in love with a sophomore drum majorette named Juanita Langley, but I obviously could not walk down the aisle with somebody who was not even graduating. Besides, Juanita had suddenly taken an interest in a truck driver she met at a Coca-Cola stand during halftime at the State Football Tournament. Though the driver had a wife and

what Juanita called three and a half children, she later quit school
to ride with him back and forth to Birmingham.

Commencement was on a Friday, the eighth of June, and by the
time I got over not being elected a speaker and got around to asking first one girl and then another to walk down the aisle with me,
they had all said yes to somebody else. I had thought all along I
could walk down the aisle with just about anybody I asked, but all
the girls knew I would probably go off after the graduation exercises to be with Juanita. My stock had slipped some too because I
had not been elected a speaker. I made a list of everybody graduating and who I knew, or thought, everybody had paired off with.
Nobody much was left, and I began to think of ways I could miss
graduation completely.

There was this one goon in our class that nobody had anything
to do with unless they couldn't help it. He was a real oddball,
whose father was a one-legged carpenter, which of course he
couldn't help. A week or two before time for graduation rehearsal,
I had this awful thought. What if I ended up at graduation without anybody to walk with, and all the girls, even the ones I didn't
want to walk with anyhow, were all paired off, and I ended up
walking down the aisle with old Lowell?

It would be the first time in the history of Whitehall High
School that two boys had to walk down the aisle together. That
would be what everybody would remember me by.

I didn't even bother to check with the one or two girls whose
names I had written down as "possibilities." I knew one certain
bet, and I lit out for Martha Jean's house. I half expected to get
there and find Lowell had beaten me to it.

For a minute, I thought Martha Jean would not do it.

As soon as her mother had left us alone, I asked her. She stared
at me hard and then looked away.

"Well," she said. That word sounded like the *amen* to a prayer
the way Martha Jean said it. "Well, Katie and I —" Katie was this
girl almost as bad as Lowell. Her only supposed friend in the
world was Martha Jean, and everybody said that even Martha Jean

had a hard time being nice to her. I about died to think that it might get out that I had gone so far as to ask Martha Jean to walk with me and she had turned me down for Katie. I'd end up with Lowell anyhow, or, if I was lucky, with some girl about twice as awful as Katie, though that would take some doing.

"Martha Jean," I began, and then I couldn't say any more. I kept wishing I knew her better and had been nicer, so I could go ahead and beg. She fiddled with her new class ring, and I could tell she was thinking hard about me and what I had asked her.

"I'll do anything," I said finally, not quite knowing what I meant I would do. She looked at me in a way that made me sorry I had said it; she looked like she really pitied me, and I realized she knew without my telling her why I had come roaring into her house. I started to tell her to forget it, that I would try to break my leg or preferably my neck, or catch Something Awful so I could spend June 8 in the hospital. I didn't do it though; I sat there waiting for her to decide.

"Well, Jim," she said. She begins nearly every sentence with *well,* which seems a small thing but gets irritating after awhile. "Well," she says, "if it means so much to you, I will."

I knew I had won, but I wasn't certain what.

Graduation night was terrible, and I don't even want to talk about it. Juanita, as I was soon to learn, was stringing me along so she could make her family think she was with me when, in fact, she was with her truck driver at a motor court called The Blue Pines. So, Juanita got mad that I was walking down the aisle with Martha Jean and made me promise I would take Martha Jean home, or somewhere, by eleven so I could come to her house. I said I would do it, for I did not know that Juanita meant to have me drive her to the Blue Pines Cafe where her boyfriend would be waiting. I didn't mind getting rid of Martha Jean early, and I had an idea that our disappearing early was not going to break anybody else's heart.

Half the people in my class thought I had been noble to ask Martha Jean to walk down the aisle with me, thus preventing her having to walk with another girl. They kept giving me these pitying looks and trying to be jolly. The other half thought I had asked Martha Jean so I could sit on the front row though I had not been elected to speak. No matter which side they took, nobody wanted to be around me long at a time on graduation night. To make it worse, Martha Jean had got Katie and Lowell together, and we double-dated.

To top it all off, Juanita's truck driver, whose name turned out to be Ed Greenway, kept buying me beers at the Blue Pines Cafe, and I was dumb enough and gloomy enough to drink them. Wouldn't you know I would get sick, and Ed had to lug me to the toilet to throw up. The odor made me twice as sick, and so Ed had to help me back past Juanita and out to my car. Juanita was simpering and shaking her head the way older women do when children get into trouble. For the next hour or two, Ed kept coming out to rouse me where I was half sitting, half lying on the front seat. He brought me coffee, and once Juanita came and peeped in and sniffed. I mumbled something to her and she went back in the cafe.

I had meant to hate Ed, and there I was depending on him and saying "Thanks, Ed, thanks" every other minute. I even said thank you when he came out a few minutes later and offered to take Juanita home for me. I didn't even say good night to Juanita, for I did not intend to call her again and I doubted she would call me.

Two or three nights later, the telephone rings and my mother answers it and calls me to the phone in her supersweet voice and gives me this knowing look. I had hoped it might be Juanita so I could tell her she had the wrong number and hang up, but my mother's look let me know it was probably somebody I did not want to talk to. It was Martha Jean, so naturally my mother, who normally does not approve of girls calling up boys, thought it was just great.

Martha Jean said she had a proposal for me, and I nearly choked. She wanted to see me the next day, or, if possible, that night. I chose the next day, thinking that nobody seeing me going into her house in broad daylight could possibly think I was having a second date with her. I had been thinking lots about that saying that you will walk down the aisle with the same person twice, for Martha Jean had been sick and could not go to the rehearsal.

I didn't think I ever wanted to see Martha Jean again, but I could not think of any good reason not to go to her house the next day. She had said she would like for me to "drop by," and I started to tell her that she knew as well as I did that you could not live much further from one another than we did and still be in the same small town. Anyhow, I went.

When I got to the door, I could see Martha Jean sitting at her desk, which took up half of one wall and which I could see through the window at the top of the front door was mostly dedicated to Christian Education. I rang the bell and Mrs. Foley let me in, though she had to come all the way from the back of the house and Martha Jean was sitting just ten steps from the door.

When I saw Mrs. Foley tiptoeing down the hall to let me in, I thought, "By God, she has even got her own mother thinking it's church time — on a Tuesday afternoon in her own house." Mrs. Foley did not exactly whisper, but I had to strain to hear what she was telling me. She said Martha Jean was studying so she would be ahead in her courses at the junior college at Carrolton that summer, which she was taking so she would be ahead when she went to Columbia Bible College.

Martha Jean had not looked around when I rang or when I came in, but now she closed her book and looked back at me almost as if she was surprised to see I was on time. She looked at her watch, as if to calculate how much time she could take off and not miss too much.

I began to smart a little at that, for it was not what I had expected. I thought she would be waiting at the door for me. Her mother tiptoed out. She hunched her shoulders up and poked her neck forward every step she took, and I could tell tiptoeing had got to be a habit with her.

I sat down where Martha Jean told me to, and she began the conversation right to the point.

"You acted as if it was important for me to walk down the aisle with you," she said. "And I did it."

She said that last as if it was to her credit, almost as if she had made some sacrifice for me, which was not the way I saw it at all. I started to tell her, but thought better of it.

"You said you'd do anything," Martha Jean said.

I nodded, and she went on.

"Katie had meant to help me," she said, "but now she's mad at me, I guess you'll have to do."

I knew she thought it was my fault Katie was mad, though I wondered why Katie had not let on she was mad on graduation night, if my walking down the aisle with Martha Jean was the trouble. Martha Jean frowned a little, and I knew she was thinking some of what I was thinking and I wondered if she knew some of the reasons people said I had asked her to walk with me. Then she seemed to soften up some. She almost smiled.

"If Katie gets over it — me walking down the aisle with you, I mean — we can get twice as many."

"Twice as many what?" I asked.

"Bottlecaps," she snapped as if I hadn't been keeping up.

She told me her plans. She intended to win all the prizes she could in the bottlecap contests, and use the cash proceeds to fully equip a recreation center in the Church of Christ basement. If there was anything left over, she might use some of it to help defray her expenses in learning Christian Education. (I swear that's the word she used — *defray*.)

"After all," Martha Jean says, beginning to glitter a little, "it's all for the same goal." I knew better than to ask her what goal she meant.

I stood up and rattled my car keys in my pocket.

"What exactly do you want *me* to do?" I asked, trying to stop feeling sorry for Martha Jean as I had begun to do. It seemed to me like Martha Jean talked about going to Columbia Bible College but did not really expect ever to get there. I decided that probably her daddy did not have the money to pay, and she had not got a scholarship as I had done. I had made a promise, though I did not know she would hold me to it, and I meant to keep it.

What Martha Jean wanted me to do was to use my car and go twice a week to a bunch of cafes and restaurants she had already contacted and get the bottlecaps out of the little boxes under the openers. The way Martha Jean had led up to it, I expected it to be harder.

"I added a few places to the list when Katie backed out," she confessed. "There are some places you wouldn't ask a girl to go." She waited a minute and then added, "Even for the Lord." I shivered and nodded. I thought I would rather go to all that trouble for Martha Jean than for the Lord, though the truth was I would just as soon not do it at all.

"After you make all your stops," she instructed, all business now, "you bring the bottlecaps here and we'll gouge out the numbers and put all the prize winners in a special pile, and I'll write off for them to send me the prizes. What we don't need, we'll sell and use the money to buy what we do need."

Martha Jean was so thrilled about what we were going to do for the Lord that what she was saying almost made sense. I did not think she'd need many stamps to write off for prizes and I hated to see her building up for a big disappointment. I guess she could tell I was cool to her idea, so she says, "If there's something you especially want, Jim, you can have it." That was like Martha Jean, and I said thank you, though I doubted she would win anything I wanted.

A minute later she cut her eyes toward her desk and I took the hint and tiptoed out. She was reading again before I got off the porch.

I began that same week. Martha Jean gave me two gunnysacks to put all the bottlecaps in and I went everywhere she told me, though I did feel a perfect idiot carrying a gunnysack into the Elks Club and the American Legion and places like that. I drove past the Blue Pines Cafe twice before I got up nerve to go in, but, fortunately, neither Ed nor Juanita was there. I had one of the bags nearly full when I got to Martha Jean's house.

"Where's the other one?" she says as soon as she sees me.

"This is all," I tell her. She frowned and led me back to the porch where we were going to gouge out the numbers. I knew she thought I had somehow failed.

She began gouging right off and I watched how quick and easy she did it. I could tell she'd had considerable experience. All the time she was gouging, she was thinking.

"Wednesday is a bad day," she said. "We'll have to change the collection day, but do you know where some of these places put their garbage?"

"In the garbage can," I say sarcastically, for I know already what she's about to ask me to do.

"Fine," she smiles. "While I work on these, you go back and see if you can't find the ones they threw away. There's no telling what wonderful prizes are sitting in garbage cans going to waste." I told her there was no telling what kind of nasty stuff I would have to root through to get all those lovely prizes, but she hardly listened to me.

"You won't have to do that again," she said, "for you're going to go on Friday and Monday from now on, especially to those places Katie couldn't go."

I started to tell her that the places Katie couldn't go to mostly made their money selling beer and illegal whiskey and that the beer companies and the bootleggers do not need to give people prizes for what they sell. I didn't have the heart to say any of that, for I had this funny feeling I would end up scrounging around in garbage cans no matter what I said.

When I got back to Martha Jean's house the second time, I had maybe four or five hundred more bottlecaps. She was still gouging and from the look on her face I could tell she had not come up with any winners.

She brushed her hair back from her face and said, "You sure this is all you got?" It sounded like she thought maybe I had held out all the winners, but I knew she was tired and sad she hadn't already got a ping-pong table or something for the church basement.

I dumped the new bottlecaps out on the table for her to see and sat down and started gouging.

This went on for over a month. Twice a week I'd go around with my gunnysacks and deliver them to Martha Jean's. I became real well acquainted with the help at some of the most regularly raided joints in the county. At first I did not want to tell these characters that I was collecting bottlecaps to try and outfit a recreation center in a church basement. When I did, they began to take an interest and sometimes gouged out the numbers for me when they didn't have anything else to do. I was sure they gouged them out without even checking to see if the numbers were good ones, but Martha Jean was not so sure. Sometimes, if the bartenders and dishwashers had not had any time to gouge out bottlecaps, one of them would come to where I was emptying the bottlecap containers and stand around, looking mad for a minute or two. Then they would stick a crumpled-up dollar bill, or sometimes a five, at me, and mumble something about maybe this would help.

When I took the bottlecaps to Martha Jean, I would always give her the money first, all smoothed out and neat. She would mist up and say, "Even if we do not win anything, Jim, we are doing some good." It turned out she thought we were *helping* the people who gave me those dollars. I didn't quite understand, for it seemed to me *they* were the ones doing good. I did not try to explain that to Martha Jean.

I would nearly always try to help Martha Jean gouge out the numbers to see if we had won anything, but this made her nervous. She thought I might throw away a winning number, or gouge into one so hard she would not be able to read it. Sometimes she looked as if she might start to cry. Still, she never suggested we should give up, and neither did I.

In the middle of gouging out a thousand or more bottlecaps and checking to see that she still had not won anything worth mentioning, she would say, "Jim, how do you feel about a pool table in a church? Don't you think we should have one?"

I told her a recreation center would be nothing at all without at least one pool table, and we should most definitely have one if we could get it. I felt funny about saying "we," for I was not a member of her church and hadn't any intention of ever going down to its basement if I could help it. After a conversation like that, she would gouge away faster than ever, and if pure spunk could have come up with a pool table she would have had a dozen of them.

Toward the end of summer, I was dragging. It seemed summer hadn't been summer at all, and I wondered where those long, carefree days I used to know had gone. Martha Jean would not admit she was tired too. She had finished her courses at the junior college, and from what I could see she was not doing anything now but gouging bottlecaps. Once or twice, I started to ask her to ride along with me when I did the collecting, but I decided Martha Jean would not like sitting out front at places like the Blue Pines Cafe.

Katie was helping some now, and I learned that she and old Lowell were going out together regularly. Lowell was helping his father build houses, and I thought that maybe between them they might make a passable carpenter. A bunch of Martha Jean's Sunday School students were going all over town asking the women who answered the door to save their bottlecaps for Martha Jean. When Martha Jean won an electric mixer, the newspaper carried an article about her and what she was hoping to do. People began to drive up and ring the doorbell and hand Martha Jean a sack full of bottlecaps. Martha Jean always asked them to come in, but they would edge away and she would call out "God bless you" when she saw they were really leaving.

Martha Jean said that our testimony was having a good effect, and I told her I would appreciate it more if the folks who dumped their bottlecaps on her front porch would gouge out the numbers and leave her the winners. That way, I said, they would know what they were giving away.

Martha Jean took it as a personal victory when we won a prize from some of those bottlecaps left on her front porch. The prize — a year's supply of one of the drinks — wasn't much, but Martha Jean got excited about it. She even wrote to the company and suggested that they should supply the church with drinks for all its social functions.

"That's two prizes, Jim," she said. "The third will be the big one." She was almost hysterical and kept saying the same thing over and over: "The third will be the big one."

To make her stop, I grabbed her and whirled her around. I hadn't meant to pick her up, but she was light as anything and I spun around and around with her held up against me.

"Sure it does," I yelled. "This changes our luck for sure."

When I put her down, she looked at me funny but she did not seem mad or anything.

It was almost time for me to leave to go to college, and I knew Martha Jean would be looking for a job and that Columbia Bible College was going to have to wait for awhile. To make myself feel better about how unfair it was that I could go off to college and Martha Jean couldn't, I told her I thought she ought to use all the prizes she had won, or might win, to help her pay for studying Christian Education. As I expected, she said no to that. She had set out to equip a recreation center and that would have to come first.

She wrote me at the university that fall, and more than halfway suggested I should go around and collect bottlecaps to bring home with me at Thanksgiving and Christmas. I could tell that she had not even thought of giving up yet, and I wrote her back that I was staying at school for Thanksgiving because of the big football game. I didn't mention Christmas, for I hoped that by then she would have given up.

When I came home for Christmas, Martha Jean's daddy was sick and I only saw her once. She didn't mention the bottlecaps until I asked about them. She said she was way behind with gouging them out, for people still brought her bags full of them and, now it was cold weather, she had no place to work without disturbing her daddy. She had been doing some typing at home, but that bothered her daddy too, so she was about to get busy and find herself a job.

About February, I got this letter at school that was so damn cheerful I couldn't stand it. Martha Jean wrote that her daddy was in the hospital and that he was much more comfortable there, and she was getting caught up with the bottlecaps. It was like she didn't even care about winning any longer; she just wanted to keep up.

She said she had got a good job as secretary at a lumber company. "I am plane board," she wrote. "Get it?"

She went on to say that she collected the bottlecaps out of the cold-drink machine in her office and that the men who drove the lumber trucks picked up bottlecaps at all the places they stopped. "Everybody has been so sweet," she wrote.

She said she had won an electric hairdryer since she last saw me, and I wondered if she had kept it or sold it. I wouldn't put it past her to give the hairdryer to the church as she had done with the electric mixer. (I could not think of anyone needing to dry their hair at church, unless, of course, they had just been baptized, but that wouldn't make any difference to Martha Jean. She would put it there even if nobody ever used it.)

After I read that letter, I got to thinking how rich Martha Jean would be if she had been paid even fifty cents an hour, which was the rate of pay back then for babysitters, for all the time she had put in gouging bottlecaps. She would be about ready to retire if she had been doing anything worthwhile. I began to hate the sight of a drink machine, for I felt guilty if I did not stop and get the bottlecaps for Martha Jean and I felt silly if I did.

I could not answer Martha Jean's letter. I had nothing to tell her but the one thing I knew she would not listen to. Which was to give up. While I was still trying to answer that letter, I got a second one, and then my mother wrote me to say that Martha Jean's daddy had died and it looked as if she would be working at the lumberyard the rest of her days to pay off the hospital and funeral bills.

I knew I had to write Martha Jean, but I did not know what to say to her. I worried about not writing, and every time I thought about her I got this heavy guilty feeling. Nothing was any fun anymore. I could not go to a party and see a girl drinking a Coca-Cola without thinking of Martha Jean on that dingy back porch of hers gouging out bottlecaps and working the rest of her life to pay off doctors and undertakers. Once or twice, I got to feeling so bad I would go out late at night and fill up my briefcase with bottlecaps. I would come back to my dormitory room and gouge out all the caps to see if I could win a prize for Martha Jean.

When I went home for spring holiday I called the lumber company and Martha Jean answered the phone. From the sound of her, you would have thought she was on top of the world. That made me feel so bad I asked if I could come by and pick her up after work and drive her home. She sounded glad about that and said she had something to show me at her house. I thought it would be something she had won, and I hated the prospect of pretending to think it was great.

I got to the lumber company just before five o'clock and went in for Martha Jean. We shook hands very solemnly, though I do not think I had ever shook hands with a girl my age before. I could tell everybody in the office thought the world and all of Martha Jean and that they were hanging around to see if they thought I was good enough for her.

Old Mr. Rossiter came out from behind the glass cage that was his private office. He said he was coming out to inspect Martha Jean's young man. He talked like he thought I was taking Martha Jean out on a date, and I wanted to explain to him about Martha Jean and me, but then I couldn't decide what to say.

I held Martha Jean's coat for her, and somebody said it looked like a shower. I looked outside real quick, for I had left the top down on my car. Martha Jean blushed and said April showers would bring May flowers, and everybody laughed. You could trust Martha Jean to think of something like that and never think about the rain ruining my car seats. Mr. Rossiter said that April showers also bring June weddings, and everybody but me laughed again.

"You behave yourself," Martha Jean said. She tossed her head as if maybe there was some truth in what he said, and I wished I had never called her up at all.

Because I could not think of much else to say when we got in the car, I asked if she wanted to stop anywhere before I took her home. She shook her head, and I asked if she would maybe like to stop and get something to eat.

"I'd love to," she said real quick, "but if we do that it will be too late for me to show you what it is I said I wanted to show you. It's out back."

Without much thinking, I said, "Okay, we'll go out to eat after we've been by your house."

"If you want to, James," she said. I looked at her quick, for she had never called me James before, always Jim. She was sitting straight up and staring out the windshield ahead.

In a minute she said that she wouldn't want to be too late getting home without letting her mother know where she was. I asked if she could not call her mother, and she said no. They had probably taken out the telephone to save the money. I was feeling about as bad by then as when I got her first letter.

Martha Jean began talking a blue streak when we hit her front porch. I guess it was to let her mother know she was home and had company, or maybe it was to let her mother know she was having a good time. We went into the living room, where Martha Jean's desk was still loaded down with books, and I had hardly sat down (in the same chair I sat in the first time there) before I had to get up again because Martha Jean's mother came in to say hello.

As soon as I saw Mrs. Foley, I knew why Martha Jean had to be so cheerful all the time. Her mother looked like she had cried until she had no more tears, but none of the tears had helped her any. I would not have known her had she not been tiptoeing.

I guess she knew how bad she looked, for she had tried to fix up a little when she realized Martha Jean had company. She had a big blot of rouge on each cheek, and she had turned up the edges of her mouth with a little bit of lipstick. She made me think of that clown in a movie I had seen with Juanita; he was always singing "I'm laughing on the outside, crying on the inside."

"Jim," she says, turning her mouth upward in an even bigger smile, "I haven't seen you in ages. Not since —"

She trailed off, and it was not hard for me to guess that she was thinking she hadn't seen me since her husband died. Martha Jean was smiling and trying to encourage me to say something, but I didn't know anything to say.

Martha Jean pipes up, "Not since James went off to college, Mama."

"That's right," Mrs. Foley agreed. "And do you like your teachers, Jim?" She was clouding up again, possibly thinking about how Martha Jean had counted on going off to Columbia Bible College but hadn't been able to go.

I talked awhile about my teachers and even made up one or two. Finally, Mrs. Foley said she would go and finish up supper and I should stay and eat with them. I knew I had to say something quick so I could get out of there. I was about to die I was feeling so sorry for Martha Jean and her mama. I don't know which made me feel worse, the old lady breaking down every other minute or Martha Jean chirping away like she was Queen for a Day.

I said it would be too much trouble for Mrs. Foley to cook for me without any notice, and I thought maybe Martha Jean and I had better hurry so we could get something to eat in town before time for the early movie. I had not mentioned a movie before, but neither Martha Jean nor her mama looked surprised.

I remembered all of a sudden that Mr. and Mrs. Foley and Martha Jean did not use to think very highly of people going to the movies, and I wondered if I had said the wrong thing. I said quick, "Or, if you don't want to go to the movie, Martha Jean, we can do something else." Which was silly of me, for everybody knows there is nothing else to do in Whitehall on a date but go to a movie.

I had not meant to do it, but there I was going out on a date with Martha Jean Foley.

Martha Jean said she would love to go to the movie, but then she settled right down to entertain me and her mama as if she had all night. She talked about everybody she had seen, or spoken to on the telephone, at the lumber company that day. She made everything that had happened sound so funny that Mrs. Foley and I sat there in that dusky room staring at Martha Jean as if she was one of the Wonders of the World.

Once or twice, Martha Jean made her mama laugh, and I could tell that that tickled her, but then Mrs. Foley would get sad again. She would laugh and then she'd look like laughing had made her think of when she used to be happy and she'd cloud up again. Still, Martha Jean had said no more about what it was she had wanted to show me.

I stood up and told them that we could still make the late movie, if Martha Jean didn't mind staying out later, but that unless we got started we would miss supper or the movie, or maybe both.

"Goodness," says Martha Jean, "time flies when you're having fun." And she began to glitter a little.

"It's about dark already," I hinted, and Martha Jean shot a look at her mother.

"Mama," she says softlike, "we're going out the back door. I want to show James what we've made." Her mother nodded, almost as solemn and serious as Martha Jean had sounded.

After a minute, Martha Jean added, "James helped. Without James, we might not have done it." I could not imagine what she was talking about.

I saw it as soon as we got to the back door. Martha Jean had gone ahead of me, and Mrs. Foley followed me. I stopped short at what I saw, and Mrs. Foley nearly ran me down.

Toward the back of the yard were eight or ten big trees with the last light of day showing through them. Just in front of the trees, and sticking up almost even with the lowest branches of the trees, was what Martha Jean wanted to show me. It was glittering in what light was left, and its shadow fell on Martha Jean when she turned and smiled back at me as if to say, "Look what I have done."

It was a twenty-foot cross made out of strips of lumber and covered all over with bottlecaps of all kinds. That is what made it glitter, thousands and thousands of bottlecaps. I did not know what to say. I felt as I had the one time I went inside a Catholic church and saw all those candles glittering up front and reflecting in the silver candlesticks and other things.

"It's not a recreation center," Martha Jean says in a funny, high voice. "But I decided to use all those bottlecaps and all our work. I wanted them to go to a good use, not go back to the garbage heap." She was smiling and looking desperately sad all at the same time, and I wanted to run to her and touch her or say something to tell her what she had done was good.

That backyard felt like a church, and Mrs. Foley and I were the congregation. Martha Jean looked small and almost helpless, but she also looked as if she wanted to understand why she had done what she had done. I was so overwhelmed that if I had known then how to genuflect, I would have done it although Martha Jean would have disapproved.

"Mr. Rossiter let me have the lumber free," Martha Jean said in a quiet voice. It was almost as if she was a wife trying to explain some extravagance to her husband. "I drew up the plans," she went on, "and some of the drivers put the pieces together and brought them out here. I decided to do it when I first knew things weren't going to happen the way I had planned them."

She turned back toward the cross and seemed almost to be talking to it. "I didn't know how I was going to do it," she said, "but I had the idea ages and ages ago. Getting a job at a lumber company wasn't my idea either, but there it is."

She turned back to me. Her mother had gone quietly back to the house. "I knew," she said, "ages and ages ago." I nodded as if Martha Jean was revealing some mystery to me. I went to the cross and touched the bottlecaps.

"I see," I said. "I see."

"It's sunk in concrete," Martha Jean said, giving it a good hard tug to show me how steady it was. "It's there for keeps. I nailed the bottlecaps at the highest parts before we set it up, but Mama and I got impatient so we sunk it in concrete and every day I nail a few more on."

"Yes," I said, and Martha Jean smiled as if I had said the perfect thing.

"The back's not finished yet," she told me. "Only the front."

I walked behind the cross and into the dark shade of the trees. I smelled the spring growth and became conscious of the sounds of crickets and birds in the trees. Nobody could see the back of the cross unless they came through the woods, and Martha Jean had nailed bottlecaps only at the very top of the cross. Down low, you could still see the rough grain of the wood.

"With the stepladder, I can reach the top," Martha Jean told me, "and now the days are getting longer, I'll nail more on than I have this winter."

Martha Jean showed up gray in the dark against the light her mother had turned on. I stood in the dark watching her and knowing she could not see me except as a shadow behind the cross. Listening to her that way was like hearing somebody's confession, as I had seen priests do in the movies. But I didn't know why Martha Jean Foley should confess to me.

She went on: "I still gouge out the tops of most of them before I nail them up," she said, "but some of the companies have stopped their contests by now. Those things come and go, you know."

"Most things do," I said. "Most things come and go." I felt paralyzed, and Martha Jean's face when she turned it a certain way shimmered. I seemed to have lost control of myself, but I did not regret losing what I had never understood anyhow.

"I told Mama," Martha Jean confided, "that it would be good if I could go ahead and nail up all the rest of the bottlecaps on the cross without wondering what I would find inside if I gouged them, but she said I had worked too hard for a recreation center to give up." She was smiling. "It wouldn't be giving up at all," she said.

"Sometimes, I nail up one without looking to see if it is worth a prize. It's kind of like an offering — you don't know what it's worth, but it's all you have."

I stepped out, and without meaning to do it, I took Martha

Jean's hand in mine. "You mustn't do that," I said. "He doesn't want that. He wants you to give yourself a chance." I am not, and was not, sure who He was, or is, or how I knew what I said was true, but I believed it. And still do.

Martha Jean looked at me as if she believed what I had said too. I took her other hand and we stood there in front of that giant cross, not looking at each other but looking at It.

I felt as if I had stood up at church and testified. I also felt the need to say something practical.

"While I'm home, we'll finish the cross," I promised. "We'll gouge out the rest of the bottlecaps before I nail them on, and if that's not enough I'll get some more." I laughed and said that while I was nailing up the bottlecaps, Martha Jean could write off for all the prizes we would win.

Martha Jean said nothing, and I said, "Okay, Martha Jean? Okay?" It sounded as if I was begging her.

"If you want to, James," she said, "we'll do it."

That night after the movie, we gouged out bottlecaps. The next night we stayed home and ate sandwiches and did the same. None of the numbers were worth prizes, but we kept at it as if the next one would make up for all the rest. It seemed like old times, and that I had spent my life gouging out bottlecaps. I did not think I could tell my parents what Martha Jean and I were doing.

The next day, which was Saturday, I finished nailing on the bottlecaps, and I took some pictures of Martha Jean and her mother in front of the cross. Since the next day was my last day at home, I said I would drive Martha Jean and her mother to church. Afterwards, Martha Jean took me down and showed me the basement where she wanted to put the recreation center. I went home to have Easter lunch with my own family, and the excuse I gave was that I had lots to do to get ready to drive back to the university. I didn't have all that much to do, though, and the last thing I did before I drove out of town was to take my gunnysacks (which I found in the garage) and fill one of them up with bottlecaps and leave it on Martha Jean's porch.

The next night, somebody yelled up to me in my dormitory room that I had a long-distance call in the lobby and to come quick.

I thought, "My God, first Martha Jean's daddy and now mine." I was sure I would find out my daddy was sick or dead.

I ran down the steps and grabbed the phone, and the operator asked me my name and said, "Sixty cents for the first three minutes, please." My throat unstopped then, so I could breathe and talk, for I knew it was not my mother calling from a pay phone.

It was Martha Jean and she was laughing and crying and jabbering all at once, and I couldn't tell what she was talking about. At first, I thought something awful had happened, and then she settled down enough I could understand some of what she was saying.

"I ran straight out of the house to call and tell you, James," she said. "Mama doesn't even know yet. All I said was 'I'll be right back.'"

Before I knew it, I was laughing too and saying, "Come on, Martha Jean, come on and tell me."

I knew we had won something, and from how happy she sounded, it had to be something big — like a pool table, maybe. The more I laughed, the more settled and serious she got.

She cleared her throat and said, "Your faith did it, James, your faith did it."

I began to tighten up inside and didn't want to laugh anymore, for I didn't think faith had anything to do with it, and, besides, it was just exactly like Martha Jean to try and give all the credit for something she had done to somebody else. I did not want her to give the credit to me, for I did not think I could live up to it, or escape from it either.

The telephone connection wasn't too good, and everything I said rang back in my ears. I felt as I had felt in Martha Jean's backyard, when I saw the Cross. I felt like I was listening in on somebody else's conversation.

"What is it, Martha Jean? What did we win? What?"

"Nothing for the recreation center, but it's one of the biggest prizes." She laughed again, and I thought maybe Martha Jean was beginning to have fun. I hoped so, for I wanted to stop having to worry about her all the time.

"Great," I said. I listened to that word echo in the telephone and went on. "We'll sell it and buy what you need for the recreation center — or maybe we'll just haul off and send you to Columbia Bible College."

I hoped we could get it over with quick. I was losing interest now Martha Jean had finally won something big. Maybe she could be happy now and stop pretending everything was great when it wasn't. She would have her recreation center and her cross, and maybe I could have some peace of mind. I had blisters on my hands from all that gouging and hammering I had done, and I wondered what on earth had made me do it. When my friends at school asked me what I had done during the spring holiday, I didn't know what to tell them.

From then on, I had to strain to hear Martha Jean. My hands were sweating and cramped from holding the phone so close and hard. Martha Jean sounded different now, and I could not tell if she was still happy or about to cry. What she said was this:

"If you want to, we'll get the money for it, Jim, but what we have won — is a trip for two to Bermuda."

"For two?" I asked, and then softer: "For two?"

Martha Jean whispered, "Yes, for two." The operator came in and was saying our time was up, and I said I'd better come home that weekend so we could talk. Martha Jean asked me if I was thinking about coming Friday or Saturday. I said Friday, for we had a lot to decide. And then we hung up.

On the way back to my room, I stopped at the Coke machine and felt in the box under the opener. I guess I did that from force of habit. It was almost empty, and I went on upstairs to my room wondering how on earth I had gone and fallen in love with Martha Jean Foley.

1987

Mary Hood

AFTER MOORE

Following two widely acclaimed short story collections, Mary Hood's first novel,
Familiar Heat, *was published last year. It has been said that Hood's stories are so
rich in character and situation and insight that they might well have been novels
themselves were it not for her compactness. Certainly the experience of reading
"After Moore" is a remarkably full one, and the world created inside its premise—
how can this marriage do anything but fail?—is as wide and deep as any novel's.*

I

Rhonda could divide her whole life into *before* and *after*
Moore. She was fifteen when they met, and thirty now.
She had gone to the Buckhorn Club with a carload of older friends
and a fake I.D. in her pocket just in case. Moore, a manufacturer's
rep, had been standing alone at the bar, thirtyish, glancing indif-
ferently around, looking familiar. Her friends kept daring her, and
after a few beers Rhonda threaded through the crowd to ask him:
"You think you're Ted Turner or something?"
It is true he cultivated the likeness, in style and posture, the neat
silver-shot mustache, the careless curve of gold around his lean
wrist, the insolence: his calculating, damn-all eyes focused always
on the inner, driving dream. Because she had been searching so
long for her mysteriously lost father, a trucker, she thought she
preferred men rougher, blue collar, not white silk, monogrammed.
For his part, he knew he was dancing with danger. Still, or perhaps

because of that, Moore drew her to him, so close he could reach around her, slip his hands into the back pockets of her jeans, and ask: "You ever wear a dress, jailbait?" They were slow-dancing, legs between, not toe-to-toe.

"I take my pants off sometimes," Rhonda said. She was pretty fast for fifteen, but not fast enough. That was when and how it began, with her wanting someone, and him wanting anyone. Love was all they knew to call it.

"My problem is I'm a romantic," Moore said.

"I guess I still love him, but so what?" Rhonda told the counselor. They had sought professional help toward the bitter end. The family counselor listened and listened.

"I got married when I was fifteen," Rhonda explained. "A case of *had to.* . . . Three babies in five years, tell me what chance I had?" And Moore with such ingrained tastes and habits—sitting for barbershop shaves, manicures, spitshines on his Italian shoes. "What he paid out in tips would've kept all three babies in Pampers," Rhonda grieved, "except he didn't believe in throwaway diapers, said it was throwing away money." But he couldn't stand to be around when she laundered cloth diapers, either, and when it rained—before she bought her dryer at a yard sale—and she had to hang them indoors on strings all over the house, and the steam rose as she ironed them dry, Moore would leave. "He just doesn't have the stomach for baby business," Rhonda said.

Moore said, "I never hit her. If she says I did, she's lying."

"He had this *list*," she told the counselor. "A scorecard. All the women he's had." She found it the day Chip and Scott ran away.

The boys had made up their beds to look as though they were still asleep in them, body-shaping the pillows, arranging the sheets. They slipped out the window and dropped to the sour bare ground, not to be missed for hours. When Moore slept in on Saturdays, the duplex had to stay holy dark, Sabbath still, and no cartoons. "Boring," the boys remembered. Rhonda made sure there were always library books around, but Chip and Scott weren't readers then. They saw the window as a good way out. "We had a loose screen," Scott told the counselor.

"You've got a loose screw," Chip told Scott. He didn't see getting friendly with the counselor, who had classified him, already, as a "tough case." Chip lay low in his chair, legs spraddled, heels dug in, arms behind his head as he gazed at the ceiling tiles. He was the one most like Moore.

Corey said, "We had fun."

Scott said, "Not you. You were a baby in the crib. Just Chip and me."

Corey told the counselor, "Chip's the oldest."

"*Numero uno*," Chip agreed. The boys were talking to the counselor on their own, by themselves. Rhonda and Moore sat in the waiting room.

"It wasn't *running away*," Scott explained. "We were just goofing around."

Corey said, "I bet Mom yelled."

"Mom's okay," Scott said.

Corey agreed. "I like her *extremely*. I guess I love her."

Chip said, "Oh boy."

"Moore came after us," Scott said. It had been years but the shock and awe were still fresh.

"God yes," Chip said. "He gave us Sam Hell all the way home." And it is true that Moore had stripped off his belt and leathered their bare legs right up the stairs and into the apartment.

"It was summer," Scott said. "No Six Flags that year, no nothing."

"They thought you were kidnapped," Corey said, in that slow way he had, as though truth were a matter of diction. "Mom worries about dumb stuff," he told the counselor. "During tornado season she writes our names on our legs in Magic Marker . . ."

"And we have to wear seat belts," Scott added.

"And keep the car doors locked *at all times*."

"That was because of Moore trying to snatch us that time and go to California, but that's okay now," Chip said. "He was just drunk."

"We call him Moore because that's his name," Corey explained. "He says, 'Is *Son* your name? Well *Daddy*'s not mine. . . .'"

"He tells the waitresses we're his brothers," Chip said.

"He belted us because he thought we ripped off his wallet," Scott said. "That was why."

"Which we damn well did not," Chip pointed out.

Rhonda had found it in the laundry box, in Moore's jogging pants pocket, where he'd left it. "That's when it hit the fan," Rhonda said. She had looked through the contents, not spying, "just exercising a wifely prerogative," and behind the side window, with his driver's license and Honest Face, there had been the record of his conquests, a little book with names and dates.

"I was number seventy-eight," Rhonda said. Not the last one on the list by any means.

When the family counselor spoke to them one-on-one, they talked freely enough, but when they gathered as a group again, reconvening in the semicircled chairs, a cagey silence fell. The counselor, thus at bay, tested their solidarity, fired shots into it, harking for ricochet or echo. Were they closed against each other, or him? He left the room, to see. In the hall, he listened. There was nothing to overhear but their unbroken, patient, absolute silences, each with its own truth, as though they were dumb books on a shelf. He did not necessarily know how to open them, to read them to each other.

"It can't all be up to *me*," he warned, going back in, as they looked up, hoping it would be easy, or over soon.

II

Moore had said, "All right, then, let's split," more than once when the bills and grievances piled up on Rhonda's heart and she made suggestions. Moore called it "nagging." Sometimes Moore did leave them, not just on business. Perhaps after a fight, always after a payday. He'd be back, though, sooner or later.

"A man like Moore can be gone a week or so and then whistle

on back home like he's been out for a haircut," Rhonda said. "In the meantime, he'll never stop to drop his lucky quarter into a phone and call collect to say he's still alive and itching." On a moment's notice he'd fly to Vegas, the Bahamas, Atlantic City, anywhere he could gamble. He never took his family.

"We'd cramp his style," Rhonda said. "He's the sort of man that needs more than one woman."

Moore had been the one to say, "Let's split, then," but in all those years Rhonda had been the one who had actually walked out with full intentions of never coming back. The first time had been early on, while Chip was still an only child, in that rocky beginning year, long before Rhonda discovered that she was number 78, Rosalind was number 122, and Moore was still counting. Rhonda took Chip and drove away, rode as far as she could till she ran out of gas. She had no money, and the only thing in her pocket besides Chip's pacifier was the fake I.D. she had used to get into the clubs. Her learner's permit had expired while she was on the maternity ward.

When she had burned up all the gas, she nosed the coasting station wagon over the berm and into a ditch, and ran the battery down with the dome light and radio. This was a side road heading generally toward Alabama, and not much traffic passed. She told the ones who stopped she was fine, didn't need help. When things got dark and quiet, she and the baby slept. It was good weather that time, so they were fairly comfortable. By morning Moore had had the state patrol track them down. They had to be towed out.

"God, he loved that Volvo," Rhonda said.

The only other time she had left him, she had learned better than to take his wheels. She walked, rolling Chip along in the stroller. Scott, baby number two, was due in three months. Rhonda headed for the church.

"You know, just to hide out," Rhonda explained' "till I could figure what to do next. The last place he'd look." She didn't count on its being locked. It was raining so she pushed the baby back on down the road to Starvin' Marvin's and bought a cup of coffee. She gave the baby her nondairy creamer, loaded her cup with sugar, and nursed the steam till the rain let up. Then she headed on home.

"Moore don't know about that time," Rhonda said. "He never even missed us."

She said, "Don't expect me to be fair. The kids love him. Ask them. They think he's Jesus Christ, Santa Claus, and Rambo all rolled into one. But you ask me, I'll give you an earful. I'll try for facts, but I can't help my feelings."

She said, "Between jobs he'd get so low he'd cry." Moore was always jumping to a better job, and when the glamour wore off, he'd jump again, sometimes with no place to land.

"I've only been fired three times for my temper," Moore said. "The real reason is I drink a little sometimes. But I never lost a client or a sale. When I did, I made it up on the next one. They've got no kick! Anywhere I go I can get a top job in one day. You kidding? My résumé's solid gold. People like me. They remember me. They trust me."

"He has a bad habit of talking up to his bosses," Rhonda said. "Says all men are created equal and he isn't in the goddamned Marines any more and don't have to call no S.O.B. *sir*."

"I've got an 'attitude,'" Moore said.

One layoff with him home underfoot every day, Rhonda took up gardening. "I got a real kick out of digging in the dirt. Anything, just to stay out of his reach. If he wasn't yelling at me and the kids, he was wanting to talk, as in 'Lay down, I think I love you. We didn't need any more rug rats!'"

She made a beautiful garden that year. There was even time for a pumpkin vine to bear fruit. She trained it around a little cage of rabbit fence filled with zinnias. "Pretty as a quilt," she said. "I'd go out there and rake leaves, pull weeds, plant stuff for spring. . . . You have to look ahead, put out a little hope, even if you rent." They were always moving. They rented their furniture and TV.

"Someday I'm going to have my own place, great big yard. Put down roots a mile deep. My house is going to suffer, but that yard'll look like a dream come true. I'm tired of praising other women's glads!"

She and her babies would stay outdoors till moonlight, working, enjoying the air, steering clear of Moore's moods. She was still a teenager herself, more like their babysitter than their mother. They played in the leaves, piling them, jumping in, scattering them around by the armloads. "The way Moore spends money," Rhonda said. "Fast as he can rake it in."

He never did without anything nice he could owe for. "You've got to go into debt to get ahead," he'd tell Rhonda. But somehow they never could get enough ahead to put a down payment on a house of their own.

"According to *Woman's Day*," Rhonda said, "what married couples argue about most is m-o-n-e-y." She had showed Moore that article about credit counseling, with the local phone number already looked up. He threw the magazine out the window.

"Not down, but *up*," Rhonda explained. "I guess it's still on the roof, educating the pigeons."

But he did agree to open a savings account, salt a little away for the boys. "The school says they all test way above average and Scott's maybe a genius," Rhonda told the counselor. "I figure we owe them more than life. I *know* we do. What's life if there's no future in it? What did my parents ever hope for me?"

With the opening of the savings account, and the balance slowly growing, Rhonda had begun to feel that they were on their way. Then that fall the tax bill came.

"See, we rent," Rhonda told the counselor. "No property taxes on that. But here was this bill for taxes on a lot in Breezewater Estates! Waterfront high-dollar location." Rhonda couldn't believe it. Since it was near her birthday, she guessed that Moore had meant it to be a surprise. She didn't want to wait. "I tooled up that day, while the kids were still in school, just to sneak a peek. Wouldn't you?"

She drove along hoping for a shade tree or two. "An oak," she decided. "If there wasn't one, we'd plant an acorn. There was plenty of time for it to grow." But when she got there, there was no oak, just pines and a trailer. "Not a house trailer, but a little bitty camper," Rhonda said. No one was home. "But there was sexy laundry of the female persuasion dripping on the line," Rhonda said. Patio lamps shaped like ice-cream cones, a barbecue cooker on wheels, and a name on the mail in the mailbox: *Rosalind*.

"I won't say her last name," Rhonda said. "Why blame her? She'd be as shocked to learn about me as I was to learn about her."

Rhonda laughed. "I knew it wouldn't last either. Maybe not past first frost. That trailer had 'Summer Romance' and 'Temporary Insanity' and 'Repossess' written all over it."

Rosalind was Moore's 122nd true love.

"That's how Moore is," Rhonda said. "He can't help it."

She had driven straight home in her Fury, a rattling old clunker she never washed, believing that the dirt helped hold it together. "I could poke my finger through the rust," she said, "but not the mud." Moore hated the whole idea of that car. She had had to cut a few budgetary corners to achieve it — buying it from Moore's father at his auto-salvage yard — and from spare parts made its fenders whole again, though of unmatching colors. She paid cash, like any customer off the street.

"No favors," she told her father-in-law. "Except don't tell Moore."

For six months she kept the car a secret, parking it down the block. But when they moved away from there, she had to explain it to Moore when the car showed up on their new street. It wasn't the sort of car you can overlook. She told him his father had made her a deal on it, for two hundred dollars. Actually, she had paid three-fifty, but the extra had gone for transmission seals, retreads, and a new battery. The muffler was shot and the car blew smoke, rumbled and shook in idle, and when she gave it some gas, the U-joint clunked.

"You're a goddamn redneck," Moore had yelled, over the racket. "I don't want to see that car in my driveway!" He stood between her and his leased BMW.

"Like rust was contagious," Rhonda said.

All the way home from discovering Rosalind's little trailer Rhonda thought up ways to pay Moore back for the rotten surprise, for using up their savings to make another woman happy. She considered cutting off the sleeves of his cashmere sweaters, or filling his shoes with dog mess. He was particular about his shoes. "He'll pay out more for one pair than he gives me for a week's groceries."

Moore said, "I'd rather go without lunch for a month than walk on crappy leather."

"He threw the slippers the boys bought him for Christmas in the fireplace. J.C. Penney, not junk! They burned. I couldn't even take them back for credit on our revolving charge," Rhonda said.

"In my line of life," Moore said, "you have to impress people into respecting you. I don't mean pimp flash. I mean class. What people can *see*: tailoring, jewelry, gloves, car. . . . Look at my hands, like a surgeon's. And I've got a great smile. A fair country voice too; I could've been a singer. I could've been a lot of things; that's why I can sell: I have sympathy. I'm a great listener."

Rhonda said, "I don't know why I wasted my breath arguing with him when he came home that night. And the funny thing is, we didn't really argue about Rosalind at all. We argued about money. So I guess *Woman's Day* is pretty much on the ball."

Moore had said, "That bank account was my money. I earned it."

Rhonda said, "I earned it too."

Moore said, "Housekeeping?" with a mean look around the kitchen: greasy dishes piled in the cold suds, laundry heaped on the dining table for sorting, and no supper underway.

Thus the stage was set for the final argument, with shots fired.

III

Corey, their aim-to-please baby, the one they all called Mister Personality now he was nine, told the counselor, "Mom tried to kill Moore, so he left."

Chip said, "In your ear, Corey," but Corey didn't take the warning, just went right on, adding:

"It was Moore's gun. He had to buy another one. She stole it and kept it. It's on top of the refrigerator in the cake box."

"It's not loaded," Chip said.

"That's what Moore said," Scott pointed out. "Then pow! pow! pow!"

"She only fired twice," Chip said. He had watched, the bedroom door open a pajama button wide, his left eye taking it all in, from the first slug Rhonda fired into the shag rug between Moore's ankles to the way the taillights looked as Moore headed west.

"I probably shouldn't have drunk those three strawberry daiquiris made with Campbell's tomato soup," Rhonda said, with her wild, unrueful laugh, "but we were out of frozen strawberries." She was a good shot, even when hammered with vodka. That was exactly where she had aimed. She raised the gun a little, between Moore's knees and belt buckle. "Dead center," she warned. "Don't dare me."

When she and Moore had gone to the firing range so he could teach her how to handle a gun, her scores had been sharpshooter quality. His were not.

"An off day," he had said. "Too much caffeine." He didn't give up coffee, but he didn't take her there again either. It was the only thing in their life so far she had been better at than him. "Except holding a grudge," Moore said.

Moore never took her anywhere much after they were married. She was no asset, pregnant. Before, they had gone to clubs and races. He liked the horses, but he'd bet on anything running, walking, or flying, any sport, so long as there was action. He'd scratch up the cash to lay down even if he had to pawn something. When he'd win big, he'd spend big. "You've got to live up to your luck," Moore said. He didn't like anything cheap or secondhand.

"Like my car," Rhonda said. "I used up my Fury in the demolition derby, so I've got me a Heavy Chevy now, a Nova with a 355 engine. That's what I race. Moore's dad is helping me keep it tuned." She had only been stock-car racing a year, just since Moore left. She had found a job as a waitress at the VFW, working from two in the afternoon till one at night—"No way to keep my health," she agreed, "but I had bills to pay off." She had got them whittled down to five hundred dollars by hoarding her tips and with what she saved on rent by moving in with Moore's father, in the trailer at the junkyard. "It's easier on the boys, anyway," she said. "They can ride the bus to school, and I know there'll be someone there to meet them when they get home, even if I'm at work.

"What I really wanted to do," Rhonda said, "was drive an over-the-road truck. You know my daddy was a gear-jammer, and I'm still not satisfied with what I know about that story. I'm not even convinced he's dead." She thought he might be out there somewhere, and maybe she could find him, in the truck stops, rest areas, coffee shops. "I'd know him," she said. "Something like that, you know in your heart." In any other city she and Moore had ever traveled to, she had slipped away in cafés, gas stations, or motel lobbies to check the phone directory, furtively flipping through the pages, hoping for news. She wore that questing look on her face, always searching the crowds, every stranger a candidate. Moore didn't understand. He called it flirting. There had more than one fight about it.

"Can you picture it? *Him* jealous of *me*? Maybe I did a little shopping, but I never bought any. I'm no cheat," she said. "All I ever wanted was a man who'd be there for the kids, be a real daddy, not run out on me. And here I am living out my life like history repeating itself.

'So how can I go on the road, full time, with three kids to raise? I can't leave them—don't I know how that feels? They count plenty in my plans, and they know it." Her brother was in prison in Texas.

"Nine to life at Huntsville," she explained. "He's no letter writer." And her mother had dropped out of sight two marriages ago. With no family, and no diploma, she had chosen the best she could, and made the most of her chances. When she read that poster for the demolition derby out at the dirt track, prize purse of one thousand—"That's a one, followed by three zeroes," Rhonda marveled—she had decided to go for it.

Moore said, "I have a bad habit of not taking her seriously, you know? Like night school. She was all fired up over that, too, but she didn't stick with it. I thought racing would be the same way."

Rhonda had dropped out of night school, never getting even close to an equivalency diploma because she was so off and on about attendance. Moore didn't like watching the boys while she was gone, and there was no nursery at the school. The boys made him feel tied down, nervous, even if they slept through.

"I'd give them beer for supper," Rhonda said. The baby would take it right from the bottle and hope for seconds. "They were good babies," Rhonda said. "And they were *his*, but so far as I know, he never once changed a soak-ass diaper or cleaned up any puke but his own." Night school hadn't worked out.

"Nowadays, they let girls go back to high school when they get married. Regular classes, every day. I don't know if I would have, even if I could have. Maybe just gone back once to show my rings." It was Moore's first wife's diamond. "I knew I was number two, and that he had a past, but I thought I was woman enough to handle anything that came up. I don't mean that dirty. . . . Well, maybe. I was pretty cocky back then, before I knew he was keeping score."

She had painted her number—78—on the racer's door. "My first demolition derby was my last. I said to myself, 'Rhonda, why spend your life mostly in reverse, taking cheap shots and being blind-sided? That's too much like everyday life.' I decided right then I was going to race."

"It's just like Rhonda to think she can get ahead by going in circles," Moore said. "And my old man — Christ! — this is his second childhood."

Rhonda said, "Did he tell you that he thinks his daddy and I are a number? He came back from California and found that I was living there at the salvage yard and flung a fit."

"Did Rhonda tell you that she's living with my old man now?" Moore had returned home in a van. He drove it over to the auto salvage to ask his father if he could crash there a couple of days, "Just till I got back on my feet," Moore said. "The van's a home away from home, I just needed a water spigot to hook to and somewhere to plug in my extension cord. There they all were, one big happy family, churning out to see me like peasants around the Pope. Chip had grown. He was as tall as I am, and Corey wasn't sure if he knew me any more. . . ."

Rhonda said, "He didn't have a word for me. He told his daddy, 'I was just going to plug into your outlet, to charge my batteries. God knows you've been doing a little plugging into mine.' He said it right in front of the boys!" Rhonda said, heating up all over again.

Moore's father said, trying to joke them past the awkward moment, but only making it worse, "She's got her pick of dozens of good-looking guys every night at work, why should she settle for a one-armed, gut-busted, short-peckered old-timer with a gap in his beard?" The gap came from a welding accident years before. Moore didn't stick around to listen to his father or Rhonda explain. He backed the van out and headed away, fast, taking the three boys with him.

"I saw those California plates vanishing down Dayton Road and all I could think was: *kidnapping*." She called the state patrol first, "and then every damn number in the world, and threw the book at him," Rhonda explained.

"She hoodooed me," Moore said. "I don't just mean the writ. She visits palm readers. She's put some sort of hex on my love life. I'm telling you, since that afternoon, nothing. As in, zero, *nada*.

It's not just the equipment, it's the want-to. I'm seeing a doc. He says it's in my head, says if I lay off the booze and keep up my jogging program—"

"They got Moore back on the road at the wring-out clinic," Rhonda said. "He's looking one hundred percent better."

"—I'll be good as new in no time. I've just got to take it easy on myself for a while. Avoid challenging and competitive situations. I'm not even working as a rep any more. I'm a plain old nine-to-five jerk clerk for B. Dalton. Just till I get my feet back on the ground. Something's better than nothing. You'd be surprised at what-all you can learn from books. I'm reading more now than I did in all my life before, a book a night. What else do I have to do, you know?"

"He was gone a *year*," Rhonda said, "and he never sent back one penny of child support, one birthday hello, one Merry Christmas. I'm lucky his daddy helped us out, or we'd have been on food stamps from day one." It was Moore's father she had called the night of their battle when Rhonda fired those two shots, the first one burning into the carpet and the second—because Rhonda's attention wandered an instant before she pulled the trigger—breaking the picture window and their lease. His father came right over, asking no questions, taking no sides, with a stapler and a roll of three-mil plastic garden mulch to tack over the empty window frame. By then, Rhonda had thrown all of Moore's stuff out onto the lawn and was praying for rain.

IV

"Moore's dad is so special," Rhonda said. "He loves the kids like they were his own, and they get a kick out of him too. But I quit going over there to see him when Moore was along. We'd go on weekdays instead. Mainly, Moore just hated going, but he didn't like it when we left him home, either. When he's ticked off like that, it's a pain."

Moore liked things better than he found them at the salvage

yard. The junk dealer made jokes about Moore's exalted tastes, saying things like, "You must've hatched from the wrong egg. If we
didn't favor, I'd say the hospital must've pulled a switch on us as
to babies, but they won't take you back now, so I guess we're
stuck." And he'd offer Moore a can of beer.

Moore always brought his own brand, imported. "Green-bot-
tle beer" is what Rhonda called it. He wouldn't drink Old Milwaukee. "A pretty good brew if you ask me," Rhonda said.

Moore used the Old Milwaukee cans for target practice, out
behind the junkyard office. "All they're good for," he said.

"He'd have been a better shot if he'd have worn his glasses,"
Rhonda said, "but heaven forbid anyone seeing him in glasses!"

"Sure I wear a gun," Moore told the therapist he was seeing
about sexual dysfunction. "While I'm breathing I'm toting. It's
legal. I don't go around ventilating people. I just want a little
respect, you know? Who's going to argue with a gun?"

Rhonda had hated it when Moore used to shoot up the beer
cans in the junkyard. The way it sounded when he missed and the
bullet shattered glass in one of the junked cars. The way Moore
laughed. Rhonda wouldn't let the boys play outside when he was
like that. She made them stay in, watching TV. Moore's father sta-
tioned himself at the door, apparently looking at the clouds, talking about the weather like he was a farmer. He had all sorts of
instruments on his roof and kept records — wind speed, humidity,
barometric pressure, records for high and low, precipitation — and
called the television weathermen to correct them when they made
a bad forecast. "It was his hobby," Rhonda said, "till he took up
racing. He'd talk about clouds while Moore shot those cans
through the heart like they were Commies. And the kids would
have the TV going full blast. It was crazy. And his daddy just fretting, saying, 'Looks like a son of mine would have sense enough
to come in out of the rain.'" Moore got as wild as the weather,
sometimes, and he'd stand out in the open, defying the lightning
and the kudzu. Every year the vines and weeds grew nearer, creep-
ing over the acres toward the trailer on the hill, turning the pines

into topiary jungles. On the junkyard's cyclone fence the boys had helped their grandfather spell out H U B C A P S in glittering wheel-covers, and on the pole by the office a weathered flag lifted and drooped in the breezes. This was the flag honoring Moore's brother, who was still listed officially as missing in action. It had, over the years, faded like their hopes.

"Moore and him were jarheads—"

"—leathernecks—"

"*Marines,*" the boys told the counselor.

"His name's on the wall—"

"—in Washington—"

"—D.C."

Moore's father still wore the Remember bracelet. "It's kind of late to start forgetting," he said.

When the boys would beg him to tell about the war, Moore wouldn't say much. He took them to any movie about Vietnam, though.

"We've seen *Rambo* twice, and we're going again," Corey said.

Scott said: "Moore says it's about time—"

"—about *damn* time—" Chip said.

"—we won that war."

Moore's mother had died, not suddenly, and too soon, shortly after Moore and the Marines parted ways. She had, some said, grieved herself into a state. She insisted to the last that she was really ill. She consulted physicians and surgeons in clinic after clinic about the pain. Finally, she found a surgeon who would listen. "Tell us where it hurts and that's where we'll cut," he said.

She lay on the bed and wept, to be understood and taken seriously at last. Her continuing hospitalization and petition finally convinced the Marines to release Moore, on a hardship. He was supposed to be needed at the junkyard. In his fury at how she had manipulated events, Moore hadn't even come home. The junkyard to him was no future. Within two years she had died, her last surgery—elective—being the removal of her navel, after which the pain finally stopped, and so did she. Moore had married by then, and he and his first wife Lana, the stewardess, were on a holiday when the news came of his mother's death. He didn't fly back.

"So far as I know, he's never even been to her grave," Rhonda said. "I ask him, 'You want me to run by there and put some flowers or something?' He never did."

After Moore's mother died, Moore's father sold their house in Paulding and moved into the little trailer on the hilltop at the junkyard. He narrowed his interest in life to the weather and his customers. He paid his bills and filed his taxes. He didn't look for much more out of life. He had pretty well gone to seed when Moore brought Rhonda by for the first time, just married.

Rhonda waded right in. "I'm gonna call you Daddy," she said, "because I never had a real one." She hugged him fiercely, and didn't shy away from his rough beard, his cud of tobacco, or the stump of his left arm. He never would tell her how he lost it. "I'm no hero" is all he'd say. He let her wonder, through all those years—making her silly guesses, calling him in the middle of the night when she thought of some new way it might have happened, driving by in her ratty old car with the boys, teasing, joking, giving him something to look forward to. Gradually he got interested in things again, like a candle that gutters and then steadies and burns tall. She had to remind him not to keep buying the boys bicycles for every birthday, spoiling them, quick to make them happy, generous with his time and his money. He had been so sure his usefulness was over, he took his second chance seriously.

"Second childhood, I'm telling you," Moore said. "A classic case. I thought when Mom cooled that was going to be the end of him. It was a real shock, you know, coming so soon after my brother bought it in Nam. We were in New Mexico when we heard she had died. Or maybe it was Brazil. Anyway, I wired roses. My mom loved roses. She's where I get my romantic side. Not from my old man, that's for damn sure. Hardy peasant stock."

"Moore's daddy stood by me through some rough times, I'll say that much," Rhonda told the counselor. "I never had to wonder if he'd show up. Like that night after Moore left us and went to California —"

"I wasn't having as much fun as she thought," Moore said. "It's dog-eat-dog out there."

"— and Corey had some kind of breathing attack and turned blue. I thought my baby was dead!" When she looked up to see who was coming so fast down the hall, praying it would be Moore —"though that would be a miracle," Rhonda said — that he had somehow got her frantic message and for once come running: it hadn't been Moore. It had been his father instead.

"I was glad to see him, but it wasn't the same, you know? I just bawled."

"Aw, hell, honey," he told her, "He'll be back. If he can't make it to the funeral, he's bound to send an armload of roses."

"Maybe, right then, I could have fallen for him, you know? For being there, and being strong, and laughing at heartache," Rhonda said. "But we didn't screw up a good thing. We're still friends, the way it ought to be. He's always been my friend, the only one I ever had, in my corner every round." And now on her team, as she raced.

"I like winning," she said. "The night I won my first race — not demolition derby, but out on the track, running against the others — maybe that was the best night of my life so far. Except the night Moore and I made Corey. I'll still have to call that one the best. He's the only one where it was love, not lust. I still feel good about him."

V

"They like Moore better than they do me," Rhonda said. "He can give them stuff — trail bikes, waterbeds, tapes. When they're fourteen, they can get him to go to court and ask for a modification in the custody. They can live with him full time. Chip's old enough now."

"The other day," Moore told the counselor, "Corey was dressing on the run, as usual, and as he passed I called him back. 'What's that written on your shirt?' He's always into something. He looked. 'Just my name,' he said, and headed on out the door. . . .

"His *name*," Moore said. "C-o-r-e-y." Moore shook his head. "I thought his name was spelled with a *K*! Can you believe it? He's ten years old, and I didn't even know how to spell his name. That's when it hit me. That's when I started thinking."

VI

"I'm pretty much self-contained," Moore said.

"He doesn't even have a permanent address!" Rhonda said. "He blew in from the West Coast in that van—"

"Listen," Moore said, "we're talking custom conversion here, not telephone-company surplus. I've sunk 23K in this buggy already." He had pictures of it, inside and out, to show to anyone who cared to see. "Take my word for it, the ladies looooove powder-blue shag."

"—with status plates: SEMPRFI—" Rhonda said.

"There are no ex-Marines," Moore said.

"—and a bumper sticker: *If this rig is rockin', don't bother knockin'.*"

Chip said, "Corey thought that meant if the radio was playing too loud!"

"Why do grown-ups act that way?" Corey said.

VII

"You want to know something funny? Rhonda thinks Lana—my first wife—is still around . . . as in, 'not dead.' She thought—all those years—I was divorced."

Lana had died in a plane crash. Not even Moore's father knew much about Lana. She and Moore hadn't been married but a few months. They had been good months, though. They had known each other for about a year, had been flying on Lana's pass —"The airlines give great incentives,"— as husband and wife, and they decided to make it official. They married on one of their trips, and it was on their honeymoon that word came of Moore's mother dying.

"I knew I wasn't a jinx or anything. It's luck, and being home wouldn't have saved my mom. But I really took it hard when Lana died. She begged me to go with her. She didn't want to fly that day. They called her to fill in for another stewardess. She went, of course. Part of the deal. Duty. She was a class act, head to heel. Natural blonde, a lady. She could blush, you know?

"I flipped my lucky quarter— go with her to Orlando or sleep in?— and I still don't know if I won, or lost.

"Don't tell Rhonda what I said about Lana's being dead. She thinks we're divorced. All those years we were married, I told Rhonda I had to pay seventy-five a week alimony. Great little alibi. Kept me in incidentals. I spread it around. I never saved a thing for myself. It all went. I blew Lana's insurance in one week at Vegas. Let me tell you, they're crooked as hell out there, luck doesn't enter into it."

After Lana died, Moore drifted. He didn't see his father again till he married Rhonda and brought her by the junkyard.

"I don't know why I did that," Moore said. "Like I was asking his blessing or something. Maybe I just wanted a witness, this time. Lana was like a dream. None of my family had ever met her. That's why when she died, I just said, 'It's over.' I didn't want any sympathy. I've got a strong mind. I can control my emotions. I'm no quiche-eater, no hugger. . . . I never told anyone, but I put Lana's ashes right there on my mother's grave. I went out there at night, there's no guard, it's just a walk-over. They'd have got along, if anyone could. Lana knew how to treat people. She was Playmate caliber."

After that, Moore didn't think he'd ever feel good again, or want to. "But a man has to get out, meet people, take an interest." Rhonda happened along at the right moment. "Bing-o," Moore

said. "I'm not saying it was a case of something's better than nothing — I had my pick — but I'm not saying I didn't fall for her either.
It was more a case of body than soul. She could be pretty cute.

"Whatever it was, it was no meeting of minds. It was a struggle
all the way, to teach her anything about style. All we had in common at first was the kids. I took her to the museum once. So what
did she ask the guide? *'Where's the clown paintings?'* And she
laughed over Golden Books like she was a second-grader herself.
She never got tired of reading stories to the boys. Said it would
make them smarter."

"In my whole life, nobody ever read me a book," Rhonda said.
"How much time does it take?"

"She saved Green Stamps for a year to get that damn serene picture, big as a coffee table — white horse, red barn, kids on a tire
swing, ducks on a pond, daises, the whole deal. I wish you could
see it! We were married — what, twelve, thirteen years? — "

"Fourteen years," Rhonda said. "We were together fourteen
years."

" — and I couldn't teach her a thing."

VIII

"I learned how to fix appliances," Rhonda said.

She said, "I took remedial English my first course in night
school. After that I picked small-appliance repair and automo-
tive. I didn't tell Moore. I said I was flunking history. History
couldn't teach me how to wind a watch, much less fix one. You
can save a lot of money if you repair things yourself. The library
has what they call trouble-shooter's guides. I'd look it up, order
the parts, get whatever it was going again, and charge Moore
what Sears would've charged me for a service call, thirty-five dollars for driving up in the yard! Not to mention labor. I fixed
Moore's adding machine one time. Those guys make eighty-five
dollars an hour. . . .

"I learned all sorts of little tricks to help out our budget. Moore never suspected half of it. Including me doing his shirts laundry-style. He wanted them just so. But on hangers, not folded. But if he had wanted them folded on cardboard and in those little bags, I'd have figured a way. He never knew the difference. He paid me what the cleaners charge. What I saved like that — including laundry, couponing, repairs, and cigarettes — went into a special fund. He was always running out of cigarettes. He'd give me money and say, 'Rhonda, run to the store and get me some Kents.' I got to thinking. I started buying a pack ahead of time just to save me running to the store, besides which I didn't like him smoking — we'd made a New Year's resolution when I was pregnant with Corey that we'd both quit, and I did, but he didn't. I made him do his smoking outside, not in the house, and yet here I was hiding them for his convenience. What was in it for me? If I think long enough, I'll find an angle. After I wouldn't let him smoke in the house, he kept his cigarettes in the car. I started going out there and taking a pack from his carton, just one pack — and when he ran out, I'd sell it back to him! It all added up. I'm a patient person, generally.

"Anyhow, that's the way I saved enough for the encyclopedia set. I didn't order it right away. I went to the library and asked them which one was best, no doubt about it. It's a good thing I *am* a patient person; they aren't giving those *Britannicas* away. When they finally arrived, I told the boys, 'Anything you ever need to know, begin looking right here.' I told them, 'You won't hurt my feelings any if you wear these out.' They do pretty good about homework, but in the summers, forget it. Scott's the only book-worm I've got. He was reading me about the Appalachian Mountains while I ironed the other day. Did you know, as mountains go, they're *young*?

"I told Moore I won the encyclopedias at a raffle. 'Pearls before swine,' he said. But I could tell he was pleased. He respects knowledge a lot.

"He wanted me to learn. He bought me *The Joy of Cooking*, and that's serious cooking, you know? A page and a half just for pie crust! And what kind of weather is it, and all that hoodoo before you make a meringue. . . . He didn't think much of my cooking but I kept trying."

"If she ever loses the can opener she'll starve to death," Moore said.

"When Moore had clients over, everything had to be per-fect-o. We had honest-to-god butter and cloth napkins. Wine in little mugs on stalks, what-do-you-call-'ems? Goblets, yeah. I told Moore I wasn't going to wheel the food in under pan lids, like at the hospital, but everything else was just what he wanted. The night we got friendly and made Corey, I had cooked Christmas dinner for his crowd. And they didn't show up. Not one of them. Moore thought it was a reflection on him. I said, 'Invite someone else, look at all this food!'

"He said, 'Nobody else rates.' I said, 'How about your dad?' and he finally said okay and went on down to the Quik-Shop to use the pay phone. Ours was disconnected a lot. I had a system on how to pay the bills: rent, electric, water, car payment, Gulf, Visa. Phone was the last on my list, and some months, like when insurance came due, no way I could stretch income to cover outgo. That's why I got so upset at the fancy dress he bought me to wear for entertaining. There I was in that lah-de-dah deal—he wanted me to look high-dollar for his friends: 'No goddamn jeans,' he said—and I could've cried to think what-all he spent on it, and the food too. He went wild when he did the shopping. Anything he wanted, he'd reach for.

"That party dress was something else. I don't know what you call that kind of merchandise; I'm no lady. Light-colored stuff, nothing you'd choose for a funeral or anything. Maybe I could wear it to get married in again. There's just so much you can do in an outfit like that."

IX

"If she gets married again, I won't have to pay alimony, will I? I'm only pulling down minimum wage now," Moore said, "but still I'm saving some. That's better than I've ever done in my whole life. I figured it the other night at Gamblers Anonymous: in the twenty years I've been on my own, since the Marines, I've pissed away half a million dollars. That's conservative.

"Listen, since California, I've tried it all: I've been dried out, shrunk, reformed, recovered, Rolfed, revived, acupunctured, hypnotized, and chiropractically adjusted. I've knocked around some: look at me. And I was no Eagle Scout to begin with. The doctor says it's natural to slow down. . . . I just don't want to chase it much any more. I've got something else on my mind, believe it or not. I'm taking an evening course at the vocational school: blueprint reading. Look at my hands!

"Chip's already saying he's going in the Marines when he's seventeen if I'll sign for him. That'd kill Rhonda. She's been making plans since day one. She's such a piss-ant about money, but I have to hand it to her, she's never been lost a day in her life. She's got this inner map, and she knows which way is *ahead*.

"I was the first-born son, just like Chip, and I can see a lot of myself in him. He wants to be the leader, set the pace, push things right to the edge, and over. At that age, you don't think about death, or even getting old. I want to tell him things, but why should he listen? Did I? I left home on the run when I was seventeen, and never looked back. I guess I thought the clock would stand still if I kept moving.

"I'm not worrying about any of it. One day at a time and all that crap, you know?"

X

"I don't trust him, he's up to something," Rhonda told her Creative Divorce group. She and Moore had been officially divorced—"I've got it in writing," she said—for two months now, and he had completely dropped out of sight, paying child support on time, but not—as he had done before the final decree—driving by the house at all hours, or tailing her as she went to work or shopping, or calling to ask the boys if she was alone or seeing someone else. "He was even hassling my boyfriend," Rhonda said, "the one who drives a dozer." Rhonda liked him a lot.

"Jake don't tell me how to drive or dress," she said. She was back on her feet again, had her own place — having moved out of the junkyard, living now in a rented cottage with Chip and Scott and Corey. "So far, Chip hasn't talked Moore into filing for custody," Rhonda said. "Things are going too smooth," Rhonda said. She didn't see Moore all summer. She raced well, and when she won the Enduro, she got her picture in the local paper. She clipped the article and sent it to Moore in care of his lawyer.

She had cried her eyeliner off. "I looked more like a loser than a winner, but they spelled my name right," she said. She used a red pen and circled the car's number — 78 — and wrote across the picture: BET ON ME!

"I don't know why I did that," Rhonda said.

Then Moore called her at work.

It was her busiest time of night, and she told them to tell him she couldn't leave her post. He called again, in an hour.

"What if I buy a house?" he said.

She said, "You never talked like that when we were married, don't bother now," and hung up. Hard.

Moore called again, in a couple of weeks. "I sold the van," he told her.

"To pay off gambling debts," Rhonda guessed, even though Moore swore he wasn't gambling any more, or drinking either. "He's definitely up to something."

Toward Halloween he drove over to the VFW in an old flatbed Ford.

"Used," Rhonda marveled. "Moore bought a used truck!"

"What if I *build* a house?" Moore said. His credit was still so bad, he couldn't find a bank willing to take a chance. By then, he had completed the blueprint course at Vo-Tech, and had ordered plans from Lowe's.

When she wouldn't talk to him about it, he said, "Just come on out to the parking lot and see . . ."

When she didn't even let him finish asking her, he yelled, "Just walk out to the parking lot, goddammit! I'm not asking you to go to North Carolina. . . ." Heads turned, and Moore sat back down, his face in his hands.

He wouldn't leave. He took a booth and ordered supper and waited. He didn't eat much, Rhonda noticed. The boys told her he had an ulcer. He didn't look much different, only a little more silver-haired. He had a tan like he'd been working outdoors, and he was thin. "Wiry, not thin," she realized. He looked strong enough. She told her boss, as she left on break to go out with Moore to the parking lot to see the truck, "If I'm not back here in five minutes, call the law."

Moore was so proud of that Ford, Rhonda tried to be nice. Conversationally, she pointed out, "I don't get it. It's just an old truck, tilting over under a load of—"

"—cement bags. That's for the footers," Moore said. "I'm doing all the work myself." He had books and books on carpentry. He read late into the night, and dreamed about permits and codes.

"He's building a house," Rhonda told her boss when she went back to work. "Who's the lucky girl?" he asked. Everybody laughed. Rhonda hadn't kept much about her divorce a secret, including Moore's list. Everybody knew why her race car was number 78.

"I talk too much," Rhonda said, for the hundredth time.

"She was vaccinated with a phonograph needle," Moore used to say.

All that fall he worked on the house. His father helped too, in the evenings — not on weekends, when Rhonda needed him at the speedway. The boys were over there every afternoon now. They'd come home and report: "Roof's on." Or, "There's going to be a ceiling fan." Or, "You oughta see the fishing dock!"

Moore called her at work. She kept her phone unplugged at

home, so she could sleep during the days. She had gotten used to nightshift hours, and didn't even mind sleeping in direct sunlight, but she couldn't stand noise. Moore told her, "Chip's getting pretty good with that drywall stuff, you oughta come see. . . ."

"Not now, not ever, not negotiable," Rhonda said.

"It's finished," Moore told her at Christmas.

"You bet," Rhonda said.

There was a party going on at the VFW, and she could hardly hear him on the phone. ". . . you always wanted," Moore was saying, when Rhonda hung up.

She told her boss as she went back to work, "What I always wanted wasn't much."

XI

Rhonda was five days away from marrying Jake — his mother had already taught her to crochet placemats left-handed — when Moore fell through the glass while recaulking the hall skylight. "If he'd just done it right the first time," Rhonda said.

Instead, she spent what would have been her wedding day at Tri-County Hospital, watching Moore breathe. He wasn't very good at it, but better than he had been at first, when they flew him in by Med-Evac, on life support. He lay unconscious in intensive care for three days, and the first thing he said when he woke was, "Don't tell my wife."

Rhonda, hearing that, drew her own conclusions as to what he had been dreaming about while in a coma.

After they moved Moore to a private room, Rhonda went back to work. Moore had a week to go before they could remove the stitches, and he was still in traction. Rhonda told her boss, with some satisfaction, "It'd tear the heart right out of your chest to see him like that."

As she went by the bulletin board after signing in, she ripped the wedding invitation for her and Jake from under its pushpins, and dropped it in the trash. The jukebox was playing "You're a Hard Dog to Keep Under the Porch."

"I hate that tune," Rhonda said. Nobody laughed.

XII

To clean up the glass in Moore's hallway, Rhonda borrowed a pair of heavy leather work gloves from Jake. "Keep 'em," Jake said. It sounded final. Rhonda said, "I'll get back to you," but how could she mean it? She had the boys to see to, and work, and the racing season, just beginning. And there was Moore. . . .

Nothing had been done at Moore's house to clean up after the accident. Rhonda and Moore's father managed to staple plastic over the skylight.

"Reminds me of old times," Rhonda said, thinking of the night she had run Moore off at gunpoint and shot out the picture window in the duplex on Elm Terrace. Her laugh echoed hollow in Moore's empty rooms. Moore hadn't bought furniture yet. When Rhonda turned the key and first looked in — she had not been out to see the house before — she said, "This place looks like 'early marriage.'" She was determined not to be impressed.

There was no way, that many days past its drying, to get all of Moore's blood off the hall floor. She scrubbed at it till her head ached and her hands trembled. Finally she stood up and said, "I've got a scatter rug that'll cover it," and added that to her list.

Rhonda felt funny just being there. Not because of the blood-stains on the floor — one handprint perfectly clear where he had lain broken — but rather on account of the house being built on that very lot where Moore had installed Rosalind in her little lovenest camper.

Rhonda took Moore's last two Tylenol. His medicine chest had only shaving supplies, a bottle of ulcer medication, and cold remedies. She drank from his glass. While she was waiting to feel better, she made his bed and hung up his clothes, checking out his closet as she did — hardly enough stuff to fill a suitcase — and examining the titles of his books — mostly paperbacks, mostly howto's — and prowling shamelessly through the cabinets. She was amazed to see generic labels. Most of the kitchen drawers were empty, sweet-smelling new wood. She dampened a rag and wiped sawdust out of one. When she found his revolver, she spun the cylinder — it wasn't loaded — and put it back. She researched the garbage in the cans outside, marveling: "Even his Pepsi's decaffeinated."

She found not one drop of Southern Comfort, and no green bottles. . . .

It had been the imported beer that finally told Rhonda where to look for Moore's paycheck, in the closing moments of their marriage, when he had countered her arguments about Rosalind by saying, "You're such a piss-ant accountant, you'll find this money in fifteen minutes. . . ." He endorsed and hid his whole paycheck. It was Rhonda's for the keeping if she could find it. He gave her a week, not fifteen minutes. "Seven days," he said.

Rhonda had torn the house apart. Not while Moore was home, watching, but during the days, while he was at work. Sometimes she felt that he could see her, frantic, down on her hands and knees, reaching under the sofa, standing on a chair to look on top of the hutch, probing with her flashlight under the kitchen sink, searching the shoebag, laundry box, flour and sugar canisters. She'd have the house put back together when he came home at night. He'd walk in and head for the refrigerator, stirring through the utensils drawer till he found the can opener, prying the cap off the beer and sighing after the first quenching. He never asked, "Did you find it?" and she never volunteered, "No, dammit," but he knew, by Wednesday, that she still hadn't lucked across it. She had to ask him for money for a loaf of bread and some milk. "For the boys."

"I gave you all I had," he said, with that smile she wanted, always, to slap off his face.

Thursday night he brought three paper hats from the Varsity

Drive-In. "For the boys." They loved those Varsity hot dogs, but Moore didn't bring any home, just the hats. "I had lunch there," he explained. "Hot dogs wouldn't have kept." Corey cried and had to be sent to bed. Moore was mean in little ways like that, when he had been drinking. And it occurred to Rhonda, on Friday, as her week was about up, that Moore might not even have hidden the check. He might have spent it all, and how would she ever know? It made her crazy to think that. She was rubbing lotion on the carpet burns on her knees—the "treasure hunt" had taken its toll on her nerves and flesh—when Moore drove home. She ran to the kitchen, and was washing dishes, when Moore strode by to get his beer. The rule was: Nobody messes with Moore till he gets his beer. "I don't want to be greeted by what broke, who died, or where the dog threw up," Moore always said. Driving the perimeter home left him jumpy. Sometimes he went jogging. This time he didn't. He said, after his first swallow, "The week's up."

Rhonda didn't even turn to look at him. What need? She could see his grinning reflection in the window. Before he tipped back his head to chug the last of the Heineken, he added, so smoothly she knew he had been pleasing himself thinking up the words all the miles home, "Since you haven't spent what I gave you last week, why should I give you any more?"

She said, "How do I know you even hid it?" He had lied before. Hadn't she looked everywhere? Turned the house upside down? With the boys helping, like it was a game? Even behind the pictures on the walls, in the hems of the curtains, in the box of Tide . . .

"You always were a lazy slut," he said, laughing. He drained that bottle and reached for another—sixteen a night; he was just beginning. As he raised it to his lips, Rhonda figured out the hiding place. Just like that.

"That's when I knew," she said later. But she waited till Moore had padded into the living room and shoved his recliner back, staring at the world news through his toes, before she made sure.

She opened the door to the freezer compartment—it always

needed defrosting, it was the job she hated most — and reached for his special beer mug. He had had a pair of them, so one could be in use, and one on ice, at all times. But she had broken one washing it, and after that, Moore said, "Hands off." He never drank from the bottle, always from that mug. "So why had he been pulling on the bottles all week?" Rhonda asked herself, just as she retrieved the answer from the frost. There it was: the endorsed check, dry and negotiable in a baggie. She took it out quick and banked it, with a little shiver, in her bra.

She needed time to think, to make plans. But he noticed, somehow, that the power balance had shifted. Maybe it was the way she unzipped her purse and slipped her car key off the larger ring, and into her pocket. She pretended she was getting a stick of gum. He couldn't have known better, she was so cool. She even turned and offered him a stick, the pack covering the palmed car key. Maybe it was her light-hearted laugh. He looked sharp. Something gave her away. He scrambled to his feet and headed for the kitchen, returning in a moment, incredulous. "You found it."

"You betcha," she said, patting her chest.

"Let me kiss it goodbye, then," he said, reaching for her with both hands.

That's when Rhonda hooked the gun from his armpit holster. Without yelling — the boys were working on homework in the next room — she warned, "Back off."

Moore grabbed her pocketbook and swung it at her, missing, but spilling the wallet and other stuff all over the rug. He snatched up her billfold and dumped it. Pennies rolled under the sofa. She put out her foot and stopped a quarter. By then he had torn her checks into confetti and tossed them at her, and was bending her credit cards into modern art. "Try making it without me," he said. He slapped at the gun. "It's not loaded," he said.

"That lie could cost you," she said, and fired right between his feet.

* * *

"If Chip hadn't opened the bedroom door there's no telling what might've happened next," Rhonda said, to no one in particular. She was sitting on the fishing dock, her feet dangling in the cool lake. She slipped her sneakers back on and started for the house. Moore's father was still on the ladder, stapling weather-stripping around the skylight.

"We'll just make it," she called up to him.

They headed back to town to meet the school bus.

"Do you realize," she said at the outskirts, "he's got nineteen windows needing curtains, plus that weird kitchen door?"

XIII

Of course, this thing led to that. That's how home improvements go. The counselor had warned them, even before they filed formally for divorce, that what can't be argued or bettered, in therapy, is indifference. "No use pretending it's over when it isn't," the counselor said.

"Or it ain't when it is," Rhonda pointed out.

Her lawyer, when she asked him about it, had said, "I've seen clients replaying their vows in candlelit churches the night before heading for divorce court in the morning. And I've seen newly divorced couples get back together before the ink dries on the final decree."

"Then they're fools," Rhonda said.

She said, "Not me, not for Moore."

"Something's different," Moore said, on homecoming, looking around, easing through the doorways on his crutches. Six more weeks in a walking cast, then therapy. "Then back to normal."

"God forbid," Rhonda said, when she heard that.

Those six weeks passed somehow. One Saturday Rhonda looked up on her final lap as she raced by in her Nova: Moore and the boys were in the stands, ketchup and chili on their identical T-shirts, red dust on their identical hats, waving mustardy hands, yelling, "Stand on it!" as she roared by. She didn't take the check-ered flag, though. She finished third. Cooling off in the pits, she didn't even open the long florist's box Moore handed to her. She laid it on the fender, saying, uneagerly, "Roses."

"Did it ever occur to you—" Moore began.

By then, Corey had the ribbon off and was saying, "Look, Mom."

"I could hardly believe my eyes," Rhonda told her boss. "I could've puked."

It was Levolor blinds for that weird kitchen door, custom-made, custom-colored, with an airbrush painting on them of Rhonda's racer, a red Chevy with 78 on the door and a driver looking out, looking very much like Rhonda, giving the thumbs-up sign.

"Happy Mother's Day!" they said. Moore's father had the card. He'd sat on it, and it was pretty well bent, but its wishes were intact.

"At that point, there wasn't a thing I could do to stop it," Rhonda was telling the doctor. "I know it sounds crazy, but he should've started right then building another room on the house. It was just a matter of time." How could she explain it any better than that? Was it her fault? Her resolution had failed in a slow leak, not a dambreak, but still, the reservoir was empty. "Full circle," she said to the nurse, a fan of docudramas, who had no more sense than to ask, "Rape?"

Rhonda said, "The fortune teller swore my next husband's name would start with a J."

"Will it?"

"Yeah," Rhonda said. "Jerk."

When she came fuming back from the doctor's, her worst sus-picion—pregnancy—confirmed, she told Moore, "I should've killed you when I had the chance."

Moore laughed. "You don't mean that," he said.

1987

Bob Shacochis

WHERE PELHAM FELL

*If the great pastime of the South, instead of baseball, were history and lineage, this
story would prompt us to agree with writer Thomas McGuane's assessment of its
author: "Shacochis takes a full swing and gets a lot of wood on the ball." Here, two
ancients, descendants of slave and slave owner, butt heads over some Confederate
bones that turn up in twentieth-century Virginia. Raised in Virginia himself, Bob
Shacochis won the National Book Award for his first book of stories,* Easy in the
Islands, *and has subsequently published two novels and a book of nonfiction.*

L ess than a year after Colonel Taylor Coates had been told
not to drive he was behind the wheel again, smoking
Chesterfields, another habit he had been warned not to pursue,
clear-headed and precise in his own opinion, holding to the patri-
otic speed limit north on Route 29 away from Culpeper in a flow
of armies and horses and artillery across the battlefields of Virginia.
On one flank the landscape pitched toward a fence of blue mountains, on the other it receded through the bogs and level fields of
Tidewater, and as far as Colonel Coates was concerned, there was
no better frame for a gentleman's life. There never had been, there
never would be, which wasn't just a guess, because the Corps of
Engineers had made him world-sore, a forty-year migrant before
they discharged him in the direction of the Piedmont.

The Confederate John Mosby came onto the road at the Rem-
ington turnoff and galloped alongside the car for a mile or two,
spurring his Appaloosa stallion. The Colonel decelerated to keep
in pace. Mosby pointed to a field map clutched in the same hand

that held the reins. His boots were smeared with red clay, the tails of his longcoat flapped, and he held his head erect, his beard divided by the wind. Colonel Coates rolled down the car window and shouted over into the passing lane. *You!* Mosby arched an eyebrow and tapped an ear with his map, leaning to hear the Colonel's voice in the thunder of a diesel truck poised to overtake them. The breeze flipped the Colonel's walking hat into the passenger seat, exposing the white brambles of his hair, blew cigarette ash into his eyes. *That coat you're wearing*, he said, pointing. *Your grandson honored me with a button from the cuff.* The Gray Ghost, as Mosby was known to those who loved or feared him, saluted and rode off onto the shoulder of the pike. The truck rumbled past between them, followed by a long stream of gun caissons pulled by teams of quarter horses showering froth into the air.

Well now, in the presence of consecrated ground even the imaginations of simple men are stirred to hazy visions, and Colonel Coates wasn't simple, only old, recuperating from the shingles and a number of years of puzzling spiritual fatigue, having been given too many years on earth. Brandy Station, two miles south of Elkwood, was where Colonel Coates really headed when he deserted his slumbering wife to replenish the supply of dog food at home, a legitimate errand that he automatically forgot in favor of cruising Fleetwood Hill. The hill was the field of war that engaged him most thoroughly, for there was fought the greatest cavalry battle ever on American soil. The site, virtually unchanged since the mayhem of 1863, had the smell of clover and apple blossoms at this time of year, a nostalgic blend that floated a man's thoughts through the decades of Aprils he'd survived. The Colonel studied accounts of the conflict, knew its opposing strategies, its advances and countercharges, flankings and retreats. He preferred to sit atop a granite outcropping on the knob of the rise and, with an exhilarating rush of details, play out the twelve-hour struggle for himself, the harsh sputtering rake of the enfilades, the agonizing percussion of hooves, swords, musketry. Here the sons of America had devoured one another as if they were Moors and Christians.

Here slaughter within the family was an exquisite legend. History could be scratched by the imagination and made to bleed on a few hundred acres of greensward and farmland fouled magnificently by violence.

Almost a year without independence had made Colonel Coates lust for a prowl at Brandy Station. After the war between North and South, that was all the aristocracy had left, the right to remembrance. Taylor had claimed this right and felt obliged to it; his vigil registered in the bloody heart of the land as if he himself—his existence—were the true outcome of the fray: a florid, half-bald man alone in a rolling pasture, hitching his loose pants up repeatedly to keep them above the horns of his failing hips, stricken by the deep blue plunge of loss for those things he wanted but now knew he would not have; for those things he possessed and loved but whose time was past; for myth and time itself, for what was, for the impossibility of ever being there.

And yet he would return from the battlefield uplifted.

Out on the road, however, the Colonel was distracted by the withdrawal of federal troops back across the Rappahannock, and he bypassed Brandy Station, not realizing his mistake until he spotted the marker post commemorating Pelham on the east side of the highway. Major John Pelham commanded Stuart's Horse Artillery until he fell at the battle of Kelly's Ford, mortally wounded by shrapnel that ribboned his flesh and broke the forelegs of his sorrel mount. The skirmish was between cavalry charging blindly through a terrain of deep woods and dense scrub along the banks of the river, the riders cantering through trackless forest, squads of men blundering into tangled thickets, the legs of their coarse pants cut by lead and briar thorns. Down went Pelham as he inspired his men forward, and the event was memorialized many years later by a roadside marker at a junction on Route 29, erected near Elkwood by the United Daughters of the Confederacy, informing the curious that four miles to the southeast the young major had been martyred to the rebel cause.

Abruptly and without signaling, the Colonel veered to the

shoulder and turned on the country road, grim but unrepentant of the nuisance he made for the traffic behind him. Before the privilege of mobility had been taken from him, he had spent the afternoons in aggravated search for the location of Pelham's slaying. The direction of the marker was vague — four miles to the southeast — and the road that supposedly went there split, forked, crossed, and looped through pine and hayfields without bringing Taylor to the ford of the river. Sixteen miles later he threw up his hands and jogged west, eventually arriving at a surfaced pike that returned him to Route 29.

It was now or never again, the Colonel rationalized. From the diaries of the generals he had learned that an opportunity renewed by destiny could not be prevented. The soldiers themselves often hastened forth under the influence of such patterns through the same geography, wandering here and there until suddenly foes met and clashed. The paths they followed were subject to mortifying change. What was right yesterday might be wrong today. But that was the nature of rebel territory — a free-for-all. The Colonel, in slow reconnaissance, took the road to a T intersection, craning to see the houses at the end of their lanes, under guard of oaks, evergreens, rail fences. Virginia, he thought, was the abattoir of the South, mother of the destruction. These were the estates that sent their young men to war, the houses where the lucky wounded returned to expire, where the enemy plundered, where the secessionist ladies wept through the night as the armies marched by. What did people in the North know of the residue of terror that had settled in the stones and beams of these estates? Where in America were there such noble structures, one after another after another, league after league, each a silent record of strife and defeat? It was not an exaggeration to say that the Colonel adored these houses.

At the intersection the pavement ended and an orangish gravel lane ran left and right. Taylor calculated a southeast direction by examining the sun. The odometer had advanced three miles. He swung left, pleased that the road soon curved, auspiciously by his reckoning, to the south, over swampy ground created, he was sure, by its proximity to the river. For four miles more the road wormed through this low, wet countryside reeking of bog rot, switched its designation twice, and then ascended to higher land, no river in sight, no water crossing, no defunct mill-house, no aura of hostility, nothing but the warm hum of springtime.

By God, I'm missing in action, the Colonel thought, confused as to his whereabouts. And that was how he met President Trass and ended up in possession of the bones.

Cresting a ridge, he sighted the glint of running water a half mile in the distance. The road he was on went off a way from it, but there was a narrower track burrowing through a strand of hardwood that appeared as though it might drop in the right direction. On the opposite fringe of the grove, the Colonel saw he had blundered onto private property—and a trash haven at that. The track wasn't a road at all but a drive dead-ending in ruts around an unpainted frame house, the center of a cluster of shantylike outbuildings and rusted junk. An ancient pink refrigerator stood sentry on a swayback porch, the only color in the monotony of gray and weather-hammered boards. A hound scrambled from under the foundation and barked an alarm. Colonel Coates tried to reverse back through the woods, but he wasn't up to such a maneuver. The rear wheels went off the packed dirt into a spongy muck at the same time the front fender debarked the trunk of a hickory tree. The station wagon lodged across the track, the Colonel demoralized and flustered.

It must be understood that the Colonel was not a man who was unaware, who had no insight into his behavior. He knew full well that he was becoming more spellbound by both the sacred and profane than ever before. Contact with the world at hand was lost or revived on an inscrutable schedule. So distressed was he by this condition, he had devised a plan for its rougher moments: If you get confused, sit down. If you sit down, stay put until the mind brightens.

He remained where he was, smoking Chesterfields with pointless determination, the ashes collecting in his lap. Picket lines formed in the underbrush beneath the skirt of trees. Then the guns played on him, and an ineffective hail of grapeshot bounced across the hood of the wagon. The Colonel withstood the onslaught, battling against the failure of the vision. Then came his capture and subsequent imprisonment at Fort Delaware, the parole, and at last the shameful journey home.

President Trass was a tolerant man but eventually he became annoyed that his bird dog was baying itself hoarse. When Trass came out on the porch of the house he was born into, the Colonel noticed his advance and ducked down onto the car seat, felt immediately foolish in doing so, and rose back into view. He cranked open the window, shouting out with as much vigor as was left in his voice.

"I'm unarmed."

President Trass halted in front of the station wagon, wary of tricks. No telling what was up when a white man blockaded your drive. "Yeah?" he said suspiciously. "That's good news. What y'all want 'round here?"

The Colonel admitted his mission. "I'm looking for Kelly's Ford, where Pelham fell."

"That a fact," President Trass said. He slowly pointed in the direction the Colonel had come from. "You way off. You about two miles east of the crossing."

"Is that so," said the Colonel. "Much obliged." He stepped on the gas. A volley of mud kicked into the air over President Trass's head. The rear wheels spun in place.

Colonel Coates was invited into the house to wait for President Trass's neighbor to bring a tractor over for the car. They sat in the parlor, the Colonel on a threadbare sofa, President Trass in an overstuffed wingback chair. Neatly framed pictures were tacked in a well-sighted line across one wall: four tintypes of nineteenth-century Negroes. A sepia-toned group portrait with a Twenties look, an array of black-and-white snapshots, some of the subjects in the caps and gowns of graduation—presumably President Trass's ancestors and offspring.

To Colonel Coates's eye, President Trass looked like an old sala-mander in bib overalls, a slick, lymphatic edgelessness to the black man's features. President Trass thought that the Colonel, removed of the hat squashed onto his skull like a bottle cap, resembled a newly hatched chicken hawk, hot-skinned, old-ugly, and fierce at birth. They faced each other without exchanging a word. The longer President Trass considered the Colonel's *there*ness in the room, the more he began to believe that it was no coincidence, that something providential had happened, that Jesus had sent him a chicken hawk to relieve the Trass clan of the macabre burden they had accepted as their own for more than a hundred years, the remains of the soldiers President's granddaddy had plowed up on the first piece of land he cleared as a free man, a sharecropper in the year 1867. President Trass licked the dry swell of his lips, looked down at his own cracked hands as if they were a miracle he was beginning to understand.

"What you 'spect to see at ol' Kelly's Ford anyway? Ain't nuthin' there worth even a quick look."

"Eh?" said the Colonel.

"Say there ain't much there."

"That so?"

President Trass kept his head bowed and prayed himself clean: Shared a lot of jokes, Jesus, me and You. First white man I ever *invite* through my door and You lettin' me think he some kinda damn cracker angel. Why's that, Lord? Well, I ain't afraid no more somebody goin' take this all wrong, leastwise this ol' chicken hawk.

"What's worth seein', I got," said President Trass.

The Colonel coughed abruptly and squinted. "I'm not the man who would know," he said.

"You come lookin' for soldiers, you must be the man. They's yo' boys, ain't they?" said President, and he led the Colonel out back to one of the cold sheds and gave him the bones that four genera-tions of Trass family couldn't quite decide what to do with.

So the Colonel had defied Dippy, his wife, sneaked out onto the road ostensibly to buy dog food, and was returning home with two dirty burlap sacks full of what President Trass had described to him as noisy bones. Bones they were, laced with rotted scraps of wool and leather, too sacred for canine bellies and tasteless anyway. But no noise to them the Colonel could detect, other than the dull rattle and chalky shift they made when he and the old black fellow carried them out of the shed and hoisted them into the rear of the station wagon. President Trass had what he and the Colonel agreed was accurately called a nigger notion: The bones talked too much, jabbered like drunk men in an overcrowded rowboat; the men whose flesh had once hung on these disjointed skeletons were still in them, like tone in a tuning fork, refusing the peace of afterlife in favor of their military quarrels. "That's a voodoo I never had use for," the Colonel said. "Men our age find queer ways to pass the time." "I ain't yo' age as yet," President answered back, "and I never said I had trouble fillin' a day like some folks I know."

Colonel Coates wasn't a man to heed mere telling, nor to concede to age what age had not yet earned or taken. "All right," he said to the black man. "With all respect for your habits, I am duty bound to recover the remains of these brave boys."

"That's right. Take 'em," President said. "You might just be gettin' some nigger notions yo'self. Prob'ly do you some good."

"I've been waiting half my life for a younger fellow to set me straight," the Colonel said, "and I don't reckon you're him."

"Well, Colonel," President Trass said with a tight smile, winking at the sacks of bones in the car. "You finally get in with the right crowd to tell you a thing or two."

Since turning eighty, Dippy Barrington Coates slept more during the day, catnaps on the sofa in the den, a quilt pulled over her legs, not because she was tired but because her dreams were more vivid and interesting than they had ever been before, and nothing she witnessed in them frightened her. She hadn't slept so much in daylight since 1942, when she was always tired. Awaking from those naps back then she had been miserable. The extreme loneliness of the dead seemed in her, as if she had been spinning in solitude through the blackness beyond the planets. That ended, though, when she left the house to become a nurse. After the war Taylor came home from Europe. It took some time for him to become her friend again, to settle to his own mind that he wasn't going anywhere without her the rest of his life. The migrations began again, so many places, so many homes she created only to dismantle them a year or two later.

But none of the early years were as hard to endure as the three before the last. Taylor, infirm but alert, first his prostate and then the shingles, which left extensive scars across his shoulders and chest, issuing orders from bed: I want this, I want that. Goddamn the pain, let it off for sixty blasted seconds. You're a nurse, do something. Dippy, have you fed the dogs? Has the *Post* been delivered yet? Did you hire a boy to pick the apples? Dippy, come up here and tell me what's happened to your ability to fix simple egg and toast.

The house and lands were too much for her to manage alone. She had secretly put herself and the Colonel on the waiting list at Vincent Hall up in Fairfax. There were days when she wished to God that He would make Taylor vanish into history, which was what the man had always wanted anyway. Just as she became acclimated to the regimen of his illness and moods, he popped out of bed one day fifteen months ago, announcing he would occupy his last days touring the fields of battle in the area. He recharged the battery in the Ford pickup and motored down the cedar-lined drive on his excursions, to be grounded semivoluntarily three months later after what seemed like, but wasn't, a premeditated string of collisions, mad acts against authority. He plowed into a Prince George County sheriff's patrol car, a state-park maintenance vehicle, a welded pyramid of cannonballs at New Market. None of these accidents injured more than vanity and metal. Each occurred during a low-speed drift, the Colonel mesmerized by the oblique and mystical harmonies played for him by Fredericksburg, by Bull Run, by New Market, where the cadets had fought.

She had made him sell the truck rather than repair it. Taylor sulked and groused for several weeks, the pace of his recuperation slackening to a plateau. He entered a year of book reading, map gazing, talking back to the anchormen on the television news, typing letters to the editors of papers in Washington, Richmond, and Charlottesville, disavowing the new conservatism because its steam was religious jumpabout, lacking in dignity and too hot-blooded for an Episcopalian whose virtue had never faltered to begin with. *Are we cowards?* one letter inquired about a terrorist attack on an embassy. *Many Americans today seem to think so. We are afraid we are but I tell you we are not. What the true citizens and families of this nation have learned is not to abide by courage wasted.*

Writing in his study on the second story of the antebellum brick farmhouse, Taylor could look out across hayfields and orchards to the Blue Ridge. He found the gentility of the view very satisfying. On stormy days the mountains were purple. Dramatic shafts of light would pierce the clouds, and the Colonel was reminded of the colors of the Passion and Golgotha. For his grandchildren he penned accounts of the clan, the Coateses and the Barringtons and Tylers and Holts and Hucksteps, hoping to seduce them into a fascination with their heritage, the precious ancestral silt deposited throughout the land. *My grandpa,* he wrote, *was Major Theodore Coates of the Army of Northern Virginia. He was assigned to General Early's staff and fought valiantly for the Confederate cause until the Battle of Antietam where within an hour's carnage he was struck directly in the ear by a cleaner bullet. The wound itself was not fatal but it destroyed the Major's inner ear, denying him his equilibrium and orientation and causing him to ride in front of his own artillery as they discharged a salvo over the lines. The charge lifted horse and rider far into the air, so witnesses said.*

When one of the grandchildren, a boy at college in New England, wrote back that the rebellion, not to mention the family's participation in it, was too disgraceful and produced in him a guilt by association, Taylor responded, *You might reasonably suppose that your forefathers were on the wrong side in this conflict, but I assure you they were not wrong-minded no more so than the nation itself was.*

White men weren't slaughtering each other because of black men, that was clear from the start. Read about the City of New York during those years. When you go into Boston on your weekends, what is it that you see? Do you really mean to tell me that Northerners died to save the Negro from us?

What do you think of communism? he had asked a married granddaughter last Christmas. It's foo foo, she answered, and afterward the Colonel decided he had communicated enough with the newest generation. Altogether it was a serene year they had passed in each other's company, and neither Dippy nor Taylor had much desire to go beyond their own land. When once a week she took the station wagon into Culpeper to shop, Taylor would occasionally come along, and he did not protest being demoted to the status of a passenger.

She knew last night had been a restless one for him, though. Troubled by a vague insomnia, the Colonel had slipped out of bed three or four times to listen to the radio, stare out the window at the silhouettes of the outbuildings in the Appalachian moonshine. When he urinated he said he felt as though the wrong stuff was streaming out, not liquid waste but vital fluid. Nights such as this he felt were nothing more than waiting to kick off into eternity, to blink and gasp and be a corpse. At breakfast his shingles burned again and his breathing was more constricted. He had difficulty concentrating on the morning paper. He complained that his tongue seemed coated with an aftertaste of medicine that even her coffee couldn't penetrate.

After lunch Dippy snoozed on the couch, the afghan she was knitting bunched on her chest. When she awoke she went right to the kitchen door, knowing he was gone. It was wrong of Taylor to do this to her. Trusting him had never been much of an issue in the course of their marriage except when the children were growing up, and only then because he played too rough with them, wanted them to learn reckless skills, and showed no patience for the slow art of child rearing. He had once knocked out Grover when the boy was twelve years old, demonstrating how to defend yourself.

Throughout his life the Colonel had been a good enough man to admit to his shortcomings, by and by, but now he had survived even his ability to do that.

She walked nervously around the house, emptying the smelly nubs of tobacco he had crammed into ashtrays, thinking about what she might do. Nothing. Phone the sheriff and have the old mule arrested before he banged into someone and hurt them. That would serve him right and placate the annoyance she felt at Taylor's dwindling competence, three-quarters self-indulgence and willful whimsy anyway, she thought, the man trespassing everywhere, scattering his mind over too much ground. It was as though the Colonel had decided to refuse to pay attention. If he hadn't returned within the hour she would call Taylor's nephew in Warrenton for advice. In the meantime she couldn't stay in the house alone, marking his absence.

She put on her black rubber boots, cotton work gloves from out of a kitchen drawer, a blue serge coat over her housedress, wrapped a red chiffon scarf around her tidy hair and knotted it under her chin. On her way out she turned the heat to low beneath the tea kettle. In the yard the dogs ran up to her and she shooed them away, afraid their clumsy affection would knock her down.

Behind the house the pasture was sprayed with wild flowers for the first time she could remember, the result of a Christmas gift called Meadow in a Can from one of the grandchildren. She walked out into it and the air smelled like sun-hot fresh linen. She went as far as the swale, sniffed at its cool stone dampness, and headed back, the dogs leaping in front of her, whirlybirds for tails. She went to the tool shed and found the rake and garden scissors, thinking she'd pull what remained of last autumn's leaves out of the ivy beds, and cut jonquils to take inside. Below the front veranda, where the boxwoods swelled with an aroma that Dippy associated with what was colonial and southern, she tugged at the ivy with the tines of her rake, accomplishing little. Then the Colonel came home.

The station wagon bounced over the cattle bars sunk into the entrance of the drive and lurched ahead, slicing gravel. She looked back toward the road, wondering if Taylor was being chased, but certainly he wasn't. Dippy reached the turnaround as he pulled in, swerving and skidding, making white dust. One of the front fenders was puckered from the headlight to the wheel well. She stamped over and rapped with the handle of the rake on this new damage Taylor dared to bring home.

He remained in the car, veiled behind the glare on the windshield, his hands clawed to the steering wheel, reluctant to drop them shaking onto his lap while he suffered his pride. The dogs barked and hopped into the air outside his door as if they sprang off trampolines. Dippy kept rapping on the fender with the rake, harder and harder, drumming shame. His jaw slackened and his shoulders seemed no longer able to sustain the gravity of the world in its orbit. He prayed for composure, for the muscle of his feckless heart to beat furiously against their damn devilish luck, the fate that had made them two living fossils, clinging to the earth with no more strength than moths in a rising breeze.

The Colonel rolled down his window. "Stop that," he ordered. "You are a hazard, old man."

"Stop that. I won't stand for this Baptist behavior."

"Come out of there."

"Here now, stop that and I will."

Well, Dippy did cease her banging on the fender but she didn't know what to do next to emancipate the sickness that came when she realized Taylor had launched himself back onto the highways where he was likely to murder himself. She jabbed at the fender with the rake once more.

"What was so important you had to sneak off like a hoodlum?"

"Bones," he said too loudly, "bones," followed by a sigh. He had jumped ahead and had to backtrack his explanation.

"Dog food," he corrected himself. She knew better and he had to tell the truth. "I wanted to see where Major Pelham fell, that's all."

She wanted to cry at this irony—an old man's irrepressible desire to see where a young man had died — but she could only shake her head. Taylor coaxed his limbs out of the car and she listened skeptically to him tell the story of what he had been up to. "Noisy bones?" she repeated after him, becoming alarmed. This was not the sort of information she took lightly. He brushed past her to open the tailgate on the wagon. She frowned because inside she felt herself straining to hear the muddled end of an echo ringing across the boundlessness. Was a message being delivered here or not? Her longevity had made her comfortable with the patterns of coincidence and happenstance that life enjoyed stitching, cosmic embroidery on the simple cloth of flesh. She tried to make herself extrareceptive to this peculiar sensation of contrivance, but nothing came through.

"I think you've finally gone cuckoo, Taylor Coates," she said.

"None of that. These are heroes." He patted the sacks. "Gallant boys."

Dippy was bewildered. Goodness, she thought, what sort of intrusion is this? Who's to say how she knew, or what sense was to be made out of it? A bridge formed between somewhere and somewhere else and Dippy understood that the man who had given the Colonel the bones was absolutely right — they were *noisy* bones, not the first she had met either. Oh, you could call those invisible designs by so many names: intuition, spirit and ether, witchery and limbo. Don't think she didn't reflect endlessly about the meaning of each word that could be attached to the force of the unknown. Even as a child her life had been visited by startling moments of clairvoyance and fusion. Each instance felt as if she had just awakened at night to someone calling through a door.

'Look," the Colonel invited, and peeled back the lip of the burlap to reveal the clean dome of a skull.

She had dreamed and redreamed such a thing. There were occasions in Dippy's life, each with its own pitch and resonance, chilling seconds when she attracted information from the atmosphere that translated into impulsive behavior: refusing to allow children out of the house, once persuading Taylor not to buy a horse because she sensed evil in the presence of the animal, sending money to a Buddhist temple she had entered briefly when they lived in Indonesia. She avoided riding in cars with Connecticut license plates if she could. As a nurse at Bethesda Naval Hospital during the war, she watched a sailor die on the operating table after hearing her son's voice say, *He's a goner, Ma.* What about you, she thought. You're dead too, aren't you? and then held her tears while still another dying patient was wheeled in.

There are a few things you don't know about me, she said to the Colonel in February when he saw her mailing a letter to a scientist she had read about in the paper, a man at Duke University who researched these phenomena.

That's not right. After all this time.

Yes it is, she said. Secrets are what crones and children thrive on.

The Colonel pawed through the bones, exhibiting a look of sanctified pleasure. Warriors in a sack, seasoned messengers of glory. Conscripts from the republic of death. Dippy cursed them like any mother or wife. Dog food indeed. Why else were the bones here but to tantalize the Colonel with their chatter.

"I suppose we better call the police."

"The police!" the Colonel said. "Never. I'm going to find where these poor boys belong."

"There's only one place bones belong," she said.

"They'll take their seat in history first," Taylor insisted, shuffling the bones he had pulled out back into their sacks. He straightened up, frail and indignant.

"God wants those souls placed to rest."

"No, He don't, Dippy. Not yet He don't. Not till I find out who they were."

Rally them, Colonel, rally the boys.

As Dippy expected he would, given his interests, the Colonel became obsessed with the bones, the necroscopic opportunities they presented, and she readjusted her daily life to accept the company of both the living and the dead. Because she had forbidden Taylor to bring the two burlap sacks inside the house, he spent his

time in the workshop that adjoined the garage, paying little attention to much else than his mounds of dusty relics. Every two hours
she brought the Colonel his medication. At noon she brought him
lunch and tea, and at 4:00 each afternoon for the full five days he
spent in the workshop, she took him a shot of brandy to tire him
out so he'd come willingly back to the house, complaining of the
heaviness in his arms. Between trips to the workshop she'd fuss
with needless cleaning, cook, or nap, instantly dreaming. She
dreamed of her first daughter's elopement in 1939 with a German
immigrant who later abandoned her. Once she dreamed of the
good-looking doctor who plunged his hand into her drawers
when she worked at Bethesda — she woke up smoothing her skirt,
saying, *Wooh*, that's enough of that. And she dreamed of the two
of her children in their graves, a little girl from influenza, the boy
who died during the liberation of France. They would stay in her
mind all day after she dreamed them. Not so great a distance
seemed to separate them now, and she took comfort in the sensation of a togetherness restored. Even a long life was daunted by its
feeling of brevity and compression.

And Taylor out there in the garage, history's vulture, pecking
through the artifacts. She dreamed him, too, atop a horse, leading
his skeletons toward the fray into which they cheered. They
cheered, and the extent of her sadness awakened her.

"How do we teach our souls to love death?" he asked her in bed
the evening of the second day, the fumes of wintergreen ointment
rising off his skin.

"Who says you have to bother," she said. "Leave those bones
alone."

"They'll be placed with their own," he answered. "I'm working
on it."

What do you remember of your life, the Colonel had asked President Trass in the shed. It ain't over yet, President said. But I
remember everything — the gals, the dances, the weather. What
about white men? the Colonel was eager to know. President
answered, They was around. Then he told the Colonel about his

nigger notion and said take the bones because there wasn't a Trass alive or dead who was willing to put them to rest. Not on Trass property anyway.

The Colonel cleared his worktable of underused tools and spread the contents of the sacks across the length of its gummy surface. He turned on the radio, lit a Chesterfield, and surveyed what he had. He counted twelve pelvic cradles but only ten skulls and nine jawbones. One of the jaws had gold fillings in several of the bare teeth, evidence attesting to the integrity of hate passing through generations of Trass caretakers.

Well, twelve men then, a squad, a lost patrol, eighteen complete though fractured legs between them sharing twenty feet, one still in its boot. The first and second day the Colonel reconstructed what he could of twenty-three hands from two hundred and sixteen finger joints. He divided the ribs up, thirteen to a soldier.

Something curious happened, but he didn't speak of it to Dippy. Metal objects in the workshop began to spark him, fluttering his heart when he touched them, so he put on sheepskin gloves and wore them whenever he was out there. His hands became inept and the pace of his work slowed. He started the third day aligning vertebrae into spines but gave it up by lunch. His interest transferred to those material objects that fell from the sacks: the boot with its rattle of tiny bones, a cartridge box with miniballs intact, a flattened canteen, six belt buckles (five stamped CSA), a coffee can he filled the first day with copper and fragile tin buttons, indeterminate fragments of leather and scraps of delicate gray wool.

On the fourth day he brought to the workshop a wheelbarrowload of books and reprinted documents from his study in the house, prepared to concentrate on the forensic clues that would send the boys home. The weather changed, bringing a frost, and his legs cramped violently. Dippy helped him carry a space heater up from the cellar to supplement the one already glowing in the shop. When she delivered his lunch on the fifth day, she found him on a stool bent over the table, his reading glasses off-balance on his nose, a book opened across his thighs, lost in abstraction as he regarded the buttons arranged in groups of threes. He appeared not to notice when she set down the tray. The radio was louder than usual. Easter was a week away and the announcer preached irritatingly about the sacrifices Christ had made. Dippy turned the sound off. Taylor looked up at her as if she had somehow thwarted his right to sovereignty.

"I'm close, damn it all," he said, scowling, and yet with a fatigued look, the remoteness quickly returning. "These are General Extra Billy Smith's Boys." His voice became unsure. "The Warren Blues, maybe."

"You don't have to tell me how close you are," she said. "I can hear the racket they're making."

The Colonel waved her away and she left. Dippy did not think his devotion to the bones morbid or absurd, only unnecessary, wasted time for a man with nothing more to spend. She could have told Taylor, if he believed in what could not be properly understood, the nature of the noise the bones were making. The bones were preparing to march. She loathed the clamor they made, a frightening, crazed exuberance. She returned to the house and suffered the grief of its emptiness.

That night a thunderstorm moved in from the west, blowing down the eastern slope of the mountains. The Colonel couldn't sleep. He stood at the bedroom window and peered out, seeing atomic sabers strike the land. He slid back under the covers with his wife and felt himself growing backward. His muscles surged, youth and confidence trembling once again in the tissue. Here too was Dippy, ripe in motherhood, squirting milk at his touch. And here were his school chums, the roster of names so familiar, Extra Billy's Boys one and all. *Company D. Company K.* Fellows he grew up with. Well I'll be, he said to himself in wonder. I went to school with them damn bones.

On the sixth day Dippy went to the workshop shortly after Taylor, disturbed by the extreme volume of the radio music coming across the drive. Pushing open the door she was assaulted by a duet from Handel's *Messiah*, the words and music distorted by loudness. The Colonel was on his feet, at attention, singing with abandon although his lyrics were out of sequence with the broadcast of the performance for Holy Week:

O death, where is thy sting? O grave, where is thy victory?

His face turned red and waxy as she watched in anguish. His shirttails flagged out between his sweater and belt, the laces of one shoe were untied. His gloved hands quivered at his side. The Colonel seemed trapped between euphoria and turmoil, singing to his audience of skulls propped along the table. His voice became cracked and tormented as he repeated the lines, faster each time and with increasing passion. Dippy, thinking the Colonel had gone mad, was scared to death. She hurried to the radio and pulled its plug from the wall. Taylor gradually became aware that his wife had joined him. He felt a funny pressure throughout his body, funny because its effect was a joyous feeling of weightlessness — he could levitate if he chose to. He tried to smile lovingly but knew he failed in his expression. Dippy stared back at him, mournful, one hand to her mouth, as if he were insane. Then a calmness came to him.

"Dippy," he bargained feebly. "I don't wish to be buried in my blue suit."

She helped him back to the house, insisted he take a sleeping pill, undressed his dissipating body, and put him to bed. She couldn't raise him for his supper, nor did he stir when she herself retired later in the evening. She woke the following morning startled by the sound of the station wagon leaving the garage. By the time she reached the window there was nothing to see. She telephoned the police to bring him back, covered herself with a house robe, and went to the kitchen to wait.

Two hours later the curator at the Warren Rifles Confederate Museum in Front Royal observed an old man enter the building and perform a stiff-legged inspection of the display cases. Afterward, the same man approached the curator with a request to view the muster rolls of the 49th Regiment. There was nothing unusual about the old man's desire, and the curator agreed. He offered the gentleman a seat while he excused himself and went into the archives, but when he returned to the public area with the lists, the old man had left.

As he waited for the curator the Colonel was overwhelmed by a sense of severe desolation. The room seemed all at once to be crowded beyond capacity. He felt claustrophobic and began to choke. The noise was deafening, unintelligible, and he was stunned to think how Dippy and President Trass could tolerate it.

In the car again he felt better, yet when the road ascended out of the valley to crest the Blue Ridge, suddenly the Colonel couldn't breathe the air for all the souls that thickened it. He died at the wheel, his hands grasping toward his heart, the station wagon sailing off the road into a meadow bright with black-eyed Susans, crashing just enough for Dippy to justify a closed coffin. The undertaker was a childhood friend of Taylor's, loyal to the military caste and the dignity of southern families, understanding of the privacy they required when burying their own. With discretion he gave her the large coffin she asked for, assisted her in carrying the two heavy satchels into the mourning parlor, and then left, closing the doors behind him without so much as a glance over his shoulder to witness her final act as a wife, the act of sealing the Colonel's coffin after she had heaped the bones in there with him.

She was dry-eyed and efficient throughout the service and burial in the Coates's family plot outside Warrenton. Children and grandchildren worried that she was holding up too well, that she had separated from the reality of the event, that when the impact arrived she would die, too. She could have told them not to concern themselves. She could have told them how relieved she was to be the last southern woman, the last of the last to lower the men who had broken from the Union into their graves, how relieved she was to hear the Colonel exhorting the bones, *Keep in ranks, boys, be brave,* until the terrible cheering grew more and more distant and their voices diminished and she was finally alone, free of glory.

1987

Marly Swick

HEART

Every word counts in this story, from the one word title, to the little narrator's nickname, "Sunbeam," which she's called by both of her temporarily out-of-order parents. Its author, Marly Swick, doesn't claim any regional allegiance. Because of her father's job with General Motors, the family moved a lot—the longest stop in her childhood was two years in Atlanta. Maybe it was there that her ear for accent picked up the ones she has so exquisitely recreated here. Marly Swick is the author of two story collections, the most recent of which is The Summer Before the Summer of Love. *She teaches at the University of Nebraska and helps edit the literary journal,* Prairie Schooner.

Mama was smoking a cigarette and talking on Cody's toy telephone when Aunt Lucette and Uncle Bob came for us. We had our suitcases packed. I'd packed Cody's for him because he was too little to know what he'd need. Cody and I sat out on the front stoop while Aunt Lucette and Uncle Bob went inside to see Mama. Cody dug a tunnel in the dirt with an old spoon and I twisted my birthstone ring this way and that to catch the sunlight and make it sparkle. It was an aquamarine and my daddy gave it to me right before he ran off with my teacher, Miss Baker. After a few minutes, Cody got bored and went inside. I could hear them all fighting in there. Uncle Bob was shouting at Mama and then the screen door banged open and he threw Cody's toy phone out into the yard where it landed in the tall grass with a little jingle. Then Aunt Lucette swished out carrying Cody and hurried me into the car. Cody sat in her lap in the front seat and I sat in the backseat with my suitcase. Cody let loose with his tears, like a cloudburst. Aunt Lucette reached over and beeped the horn until Uncle Bob marched out and slid in behind the wheel.

"She's C-R-A-Z-Y," he said. "Breaks my heart."

He mopped the back of his neck with a handkerchief and started up the engine. I traced the letters on the side of my blue suitcase. I felt a little thrill. My daddy'd run off with my teacher and now my mama was crazy. I felt real special.

"She's skunk drunk," Aunt Lucette said. "She'd have to sober up to be crazy."

"We can't just leave her." Uncle Bob crossed his arms over the steering wheel and rested his head on them like he was about to take a nap. "She's liable to burn the place down with one of them fancy cigarillos of hers."

Ever since my daddy'd left, she'd been smoking these cigarettes that came in a flat box like crayons — pink and turquoise and purple. Sometimes she'd light one up and stand in front of the medicine chest mirror, watching herself smoke it down to a stub and then she'd flush it down the toilet.

Uncle Bob shifted the car into reverse. "Maybe we should call a doctor," he said.

"She's heartsick and there's no medicine for that," Aunt Lucette sighed, "except time. We ought to know that."

Uncle Bob nodded and squeezed her hand. "Don't let's start," he said. There were tears shining in his eyes. I figured he was thinking about Little Bob.

As we pulled out of our driveway onto the paved road, I turned around and looked back at our house. Mama was kneeling in the tall grass that hadn't been mowed since Daddy left, clutching Cody's pink plastic phone to her chest. She saw me looking at her and put the receiver to her mouth like she was trying to tell me something.

Once we were onto the highway we stopped for gas at a Sinclair station. I pointed out the green dinosaur to Cody who was only half crying now. Uncle Bob told the man to fill her up, then turned to us and said, "Come on outta there. I wanna buy you kids a root beer."

We climbed out of the car and followed him over to the soda machine. I held Cody while Aunt Lucette went to the ladies' room. Uncle Bob dropped some change into the machine and handed me a root beer.

"You kids," he said, "is going to come live with us. Your mama's sick."

"How long for?" I asked, passing the root beer can to Cody.

"No telling," he shrugged. "Till your mama's her old self again."

"You poor kids." Aunt Lucette reached down and gave Cody and me a bear hug. "It's gonna be all right."

She took a pink Kleenex out of her skirt pocket and dabbed at her eyes. We climbed back in the car and I started whistling "You Are My Sunshine, My Only Sunshine." Daddy showed me how to whistle before he ran off and I'd been practicing up on some of the songs he used to like to whistle. Aunt Lucette swiveled her head around like Mama's old lazy Susan and looked at me like I was something real odd.

"Don't she beat all?" she asked Uncle Bob. "Not one little bitty teardrop. You suppose that's normal?"

"I expect it's the shock," Uncle Bob said.

I was whistling and watching the fields roll by. Some of them smelled real bad. I'd hold my nose and breathe through my mouth. I saw a sign that said WELCOME TO INDIANA.

"You know what, Cody?" I jiggled him on my lap.

"What?" He was half asleep.

"We're in a new state." I pointed over my shoulder. "That back there's Kentucky." I pointed over the front seat. "And that up there's Indiana."

"I wanna go home," Cody whined.

"Look at my ring," I said, holding it eye level so it sparkled right in front of his face. "See how pretty?"

He took his hand out of his mouth and tugged at my ring with his wet fingers.

*   *   *

Cody and I slept in the same bed at their house. At home we slept in the same room but in separate beds. We slept in Little Bob's room. In bed the first night I whispered to Cody about how Little Bob got run over by a bulldozer before Cody was even born. That made him remember his red dump truck my daddy gave him before he ran off, same day he gave me my ring. I'd set it out on the porch to take along, but at the last minute I forgot. Soon as he remembered it, I knew I wasn't going to get any sleep. Cody threw a fit and kept it up even when I lied and said we could go get it first thing in the morning.

The first week we stayed at home. I didn't go to school. Aunt Lucette was always asking me if I felt sad and telling me how it was good to cry.

"Cody cries enough for both of us," I said. "So does my mama. She cried for a solid week when my daddy ran off."

I polished up my ring with the hem of the tablecloth.

"Well, life can be real sad sometimes," Aunt Lucette said, her eyes filling with water. "There's no shame in crying." She looked at me like she was waiting for me to join in, but I just slid off my stool and went out the back door.

I liked sitting in the sun on the old aluminum milk box outside the back door. I'd sit out there with my eyes squeezed shut, pointing my face at the sun, whistling and rocking back and forth on the tin box. Sometimes, if no one bothered me, I could rock myself right into this trance. I felt like I just turned into pure sunlight.

The following Monday Aunt Lucette walked me to the school down the road from their house. She dropped Cody off at the neighbor lady's and we could hear him wailing for most of two blocks. We found the principal's office and I shook the principal's hand and told her my name was Heart Patterson and I was in the fifth grade. Then I sat on a bench and waited in the hall while Aunt Lucette told her all about me.

My new teacher, Mrs. Mitchell, was old and had a jelly belly. While she was writing spelling words on the board, I thought about how if I'd had Mrs. Mitchell back home instead of Miss Baker, my daddy'd still be at home and my mama wouldn't be crazy. He met Miss Baker when my mama was down with the flu and he went to a parents' conference by himself. They brought in a substitute after Miss Baker and Daddy left town, but my mama kept me home from school. She said all the kids would be talking and making fun.

After Daddy left, Mama sat around in her bathrobe all day, not even combing her hair. She cried and watched the TV and drank Daddy's liquor. But one morning she took a bath, set her hair on hot rollers, then put on a fancy dress and painted herself up. She walked out onto the front porch where I was painting my nails. To keep Cody happy, I'd paint the nails on my one hand and let him blow on them. Then I'd do the same with the other hand. I was just starting in on my toenails when Mama sat down on the glider, smelling of perfume.

"Heart," she said. "Do you think I look as pretty as Miss Baker?" She patted at her hair. "I want your honest opinion."

I looked at her for a minute, squinting and tilting my head. "No," I said. "But you smell real nice."

She slammed the screen door and locked herself in the bathroom. When she came back out, she was wearing her old bathrobe and no makeup. She didn't talk to me for two days. She'd say, "Cody, you tell your sister to bring me a beer," or "Cody, you tell that sister of yours she better run on down to the store and buy us some hamburger for dinner." Then Cody'd turn to me real serious and say, "Buy hamburger."

I was the one who found the note my daddy left. My mama was at the hairdresser down the road when I came back home from school and found it under the salt shaker on the kitchen table. He wrote:

Dear Coral,
I won't be home for supper tonight or ever again. I never meant to hurt you or the kids, but I just can't help it. Fourteen years is a long

time for two people like us to be married for. Maybe it's just too long. I don't want that you should be the last to know I'm taking Jean (Miss Baker) with me. She says Heart is a smart girl and she hopes Heart won't hate her now. We both feel sick about this. The money in the bank is yours and I'll send more on a regular basis. I got no intention of letting you starve. It's nothing personal against you, Coral. I never knew I was the type to do something like this.

I sat in the kitchen chair shaking out little ant hills of salt and pushing them around the flowered tablecloth till Mama came home. She set a bag of groceries down on the counter and took off her kerchief.

"Hi, Sunshine, you have a nice day?" She put some Half-and-Half in the refrigerator.

I shrugged.

Mama took some meat out of the bag. "You want pork chops or chicken for dinner?"

"I don't care." I turned my ring backward so that you couldn't see the stone and made a fist around it.

"You feel OK?" Mama studied me and rested her palm against my forehead like a cool rag.

"I'm OK," I said.

"Well, you look like you got a fever." She began stacking some fruit cocktail cans in the cupboard. "How was school?" she asked. "You like my new haircut?"

"Looks real nice," I said. "We had a substitute 'cause Daddy ran off with Miss Baker."

Mama looked at me like she was going to haul off and smack me. I handed her the note and ran outside. I started to skip rope as fast as I could. My feet barely touched the dirt. As I skipped rope, I sang as loud as I could: "'A' my name is Alice, my husband's name is Albert, I come from Alabama, and I sell applejack." Whenever I had to stop to catch my breath, I could hear Mama inside cursing and crying up a storm. Once, when I was on 'Q,' she called me to the porch and asked me had I ever seen my daddy with Miss

Baker. I said no and she went back inside and I picked up where I left off.

Once a week in my new school, Mrs. Mitchell would let me out of class for an hour so I could go talk to the school psychologist. He told me he traveled around from school to school, he was 27, and I should call him Jack. His office was the prettiest room in the school. The walls were bright yellow, there was a hooked rug like Grandma Patterson used to make before she went blind, and there were framed posters on the walls. Jack liked for us, him and me, to sit on big pillows on the floor, but I liked the wood chair. The first time I went to his office we sat on the big pillows and he explained to me that a psychologist was like a special friend. He told me I should feel free to say whatever popped into my mind. He said everything I told him would be a secret. I said OK, but I didn't have anything to say to him really. I'd just sit on the wood chair and look around at the animal posters till it was time to go back to class. Some days Jack would move my chair over by the window where there was this sandbox on legs filled with little toys — tiny plastic adults and babies and animals and furniture and cars. He was always trying to get me to play with the toys and make up stories, but I didn't want to. I thought how my mama would like all those little toys, but I didn't say it out loud. I figured Aunt Lucette and Uncle Bob wanted to find out if I was C-R-A-Z-Y like my mama. That's why I was there. He even had a toy telephone hidden in a box of junk in the corner. There was a tambourine and an Etch-A-Sketch on top, but I spied the receiver dangling down the side of the box.

One night I had a dream our mama was lying in her bed with the house burning down around her. The firemen rescued her and took her to the hospital in an ambulance. When Cody and I visited her there, she was sitting all by herself in her yellow nightgown. The next morning at breakfast I asked Uncle Bob if Mama was in the hospital.

"Now, where'd you go and get an idea like that?" he said. "Your mama's at home like she always was. She's just resting up."

"It's been a month," I said. "We gonna stay here forever?"

"Don't you like it here?" Aunt Lucette slid a pancake onto my plate. She looked like she was about to cry.

"I like it fine," I said. "I just like to know."

"Maybe this Sunday we could call your mama and you and Cody could talk to her. I bet she'd like that," Uncle Bob said.

Cody knocked over his milk and Aunt Lucette sponged it up.

"I don't want to talk to her," I said. I felt cold inside like I'd swallowed an ice cube. I jumped up and ran outside. I sat on my milk box and rocked real fast. I did this whenever I felt like crying and it worked real well. I never cried. I thought about my dream. Jack wanted me to tell him my dreams. Every time he asked me about them I said I couldn't remember. Sometimes I'd tell them to Cody when I woke up in the morning. Cody was always whimpering in his sleep like a dog. I was always shaking him awake. "Bad dream," I'd say. "Wake up." Once he bit me in the shoulder during a bad dream — broke the skin. When I snapped on the light, he looked like one of them werewolves lying there sound asleep with my blood on his baby teeth.

We got two postcards from our daddy in the same week. One had a crocodile and the other was a map of Florida. He said he was missing us and hoping we were taking good care of our mama. He said he would send for us to visit him on holidays just as soon as they found them a permanent place. The postcards arrived in a white envelope with a letter from our mama, but Aunt Lucette wouldn't let me see the letter even though it had Cody's and my name on it. She folded it into squares and slipped it into her brassiere.

"I'll tell Jack if you don't give me that letter." I looked her straight in the eye.

Aunt Lucette flushed and looked all flustered. "Maybe I'll just discuss the matter with him myself," she said. "If he says to give it to you, then I will."

"Hmmmph," I snorted and stormed up to my room. I stared at the ceiling and suddenly hoped that Jack would tell her not to show me the letter. I'd seen this TV show where a crazy person sent a letter that was pasted-up words cut out of the newspaper. The words were all different sizes — some in tiny, thin print and some in fat black print. The envelope my mama sent had her fancy writing on it. Before my daddy ran off, my mama prided herself on her round, curlicued handwriting. I thought maybe my heart would stop beating if I opened up that envelope and saw those paste-up words.

While I was lying on the bed, Aunt Lucette knocked on the door. She put a plate of home-baked gingersnaps and a glass of milk on the bureau.

"I didn't mean to be mean to you, Heart," she said. "I'm just trying to do what's best." Cody was dragging on her skirt and she reached down and brushed his yellow hair out of his eyes. "I know you miss your mama, but that's not your mama talking in that letter."

"Then who is it?" I reached over and took a cookie, still lying down.

Aunt Lucette was halfway out the door. "It's the fury of hell," she said. She put her hands over Cody's ears. "You ever hear that expression 'Hell hath no fury like a woman scorned'?"

"What's 'scorned'?" I was sitting up now. I had the feeling Aunt Lucette was talking to herself and once she remembered I was there, she'd hush up.

"'Scorned' is like when you get tired of something and throw it away," she said. "You understand?"

"You take it to the dump," Cody piped up. Uncle Bob had bought him a new truck like the one we'd left at home.

"I understand," I said. I sort of did.

Aunt Lucette walked over and took the empty plate from the bureau. "You drink your milk up." She started out the door.

"Aunt Lucette?"

She turned around and smiled at me.

"You keep the letter," I said. "I don't want it."

* * *

The next day I was sitting in Jack's office and he put the plastic dogs facing each other in the sand tray. "What do you think the dogs are doing?" he said.

I studied them for a while. "That dog there — the big one — is scorning that little dog," I said.

Jack looked surprised. Usually I didn't answer him when he asked me questions.

"Why's he scorning him?"

"It's not a him — it's a her." I pointed to the small white dog.

"Well, why's he scorning her?"

I shrugged.

"Those dogs remind you of anyone in particular?" He moved his chair closer to mine.

"No," I said.

"Maybe this big dog's sort of like your daddy?" He accidentally bumped his chair against the table and knocked the dogs over in the sand.

"Maybe," I said. I picked up the white dog and set it on its four legs.

"Are you angry with your daddy?"

"No." I moved my chair back a little.

"Then why'd you leave him lying there in the sand?" He pointed to the black dog.

I just looked at him. "My daddy's in Florida," I said. I squeezed up a handful of sand, then let it sift out through my fingers. "In Florida the sand is hotter than this. It's like walking on fire."

"Actually it's not," Jack said. "It's white sand and it stays quite cool."

A bell rang. I could hear the chairs scraping and everyone's loud footsteps racing downstairs to the cafeteria. In a minute it was all quiet again, like a storm had passed us by. Jack patted my hand and smiled at me.

"When I say 'Florida' what's the first word pops into your mind?" he asked.

"Sunglasses," I said. I could see Daddy and Miss Baker driving in a convertible car wearing big sunglasses.

"What are you feeling right now, Heart?" His voice was soft and sneaky.

I looked out the window at the empty playground. One of the students had left his lunch sack by the jungle gym and some brown birds were pecking at it, pecking right through the paper.

"I'm hungry," I said.

After supper, Cody and I were watching TV on the floor in the den when Uncle Bob came in and said, "There's someone on the phone wants to talk with you."

I went into the kitchen and Aunt Lucette kissed me on the cheek as she handed me the receiver. "Hello?" I said.

"Hello, Sunbeam, that you?"

"Daddy?" I put my hand over the receiver and whispered to Cody that it was our daddy.

"You get my postcards? I sent three so far," he said.

"We got them. You still in Florida?"

Cody was yanking on the phone cord. I shooed him away.

"We're in Tallahassee. I just found out this minute you been staying with Uncle Bob. You seen your mama at all?"

"No," I said. "She's crazy."

"That's no way to talk about your mama." He didn't say anything for a minute. "I know your mama. She'll snap out of it. You get your uncle to take you back home for a visit, you hear? Ain't nothing wrong with your mama that seeing you kids won't cure."

Cody was climbing on the kitchen chair trying to grab at the receiver. "Cody wants to talk," I said. "He's talking real grown up now."

"OK. You tell your Uncle Bob I said to take you home," he said. "You kids don't never forget your mama and I love you."

"Here's Cody." I sat Cody down on the chair and handed him the phone. Then I walked out into the living room where Uncle

Bob and Aunt Lucette were talking. They'd turned the volume on the TV down low. Aunt Lucette was twisting her Kleenex.

"Daddy says to tell you to take us home for a visit," I said. Then I turned the volume on the TV back up loud and lay down on my pillow in front of the set.

Saturday morning we woke up early, while it was still dark out, and threw our pajamas and toothbrushes in our suitcases we'd packed the night before. I was making up our bed when Aunt Lucette came in to check on us.

"You got Cody's toothbrush in there?" She walked around to the other side of the bed and helped me with the quilt.

"Yes."

"You excited?" she asked. "You glad we're going?"

"Guess so," I shrugged.

Aunt Lucette reached out and held my chin with her hand so I had to look right at her. "It worries me, honey, the way you act like nothing bothers you. You don't cry, you don't laugh. Dr. Jack says you're just 'repressing' everything—you got all your feelings squashed way down inside you like a jack-in-the-box and if you don't let them out bit by bit like a normal little girl, they're just going to pop out all at once some day."

Uncle Bob walked up behind her, pressing a little wad of bloody Kleenex to his chin where he'd cut himself shaving. "Everybody all set?" he asked, winking at Cody and me. "Don't fill her head up with all that psychiatrist talk," he said to Aunt Lucette. "She got troubles enough already."

Riding in the car I thought about what Aunt Lucette told me Jack told her. Cody and Aunt Lucette were snoozing. Uncle Bob was listening to the ball game on the radio. It was drizzling out and the car windows kept fogging up. I tried to picture my feelings all repressed together inside me—tears and laughs and frowns—trying to come out. I went limp and opened my mouth and closed my eyes and waited. I kept trying to coax them up, calling to them in my mind like you'd call a scared kitty. I pictured them flying up and out like a swarm of mad hornets. Then I pictured them floating up and out, nice and easy, like a row of bubbles. But nothing happened. I didn't feel a thing except a little carsick. I wondered if Dr. Jack had actually said that about me. I figured Aunt Lucette must've got it all wrong.

I bunched my pillow up so I could lean my head against the window. I hadn't thought much about seeing Mama again. Uncle Bob said she was still sick, but he didn't want no one accusing him of keeping our mama from her kids. My birthday was next week. I was going to be eleven. This thought floated into my mind like a bubble that maybe this was my birthday surprise and when we drove up in front of our old house, Mama and Daddy would be standing out on the porch waving to us. Balloons would be tied to the porch railing, fluttering like butterflies in the wind, and inside there'd be a chocolate cake with pink marshmallow icing like I had last year, only with eleven candles instead of ten. Daddy'd be standing there with the camera while Mama lighted each candle with a match, trying not to burn her fingers. He'd be all ready to snap my picture as I blew out the candles and I wouldn't be able to think of anything to wish for.

Everyone was wide awake by the time we turned off the highway into Spottsville. Cody was standing on the seat looking out the window kind of puzzled. I think it was the first time in his life he was old enough to come back to a place he recognized. Aunt Lucette got her comb out of her purse and began yanking it through her hair. Then she handed it to me to do the same. When we turned down our street, we saw Farrah Hodge and Rusty Miller riding their bikes. They stared at us like they seen a ghost. Uncle Bob reached back and gave us two sticks of gum, the kind with sugar that Mama never let us chew. I put mine in my pocket. I didn't want to start off on the wrong foot with Mama.

Even from a distance, I could see there were no balloons. The grass still wasn't mowed and my daddy's red Chevy wasn't parked in the driveway. As we pulled up to the house, Uncle Bob cleared his throat and said, "Remember what I said, now. Your mama's still feeling puny. Don't take anything personal."

"Your mama loves you," Aunt Lucette said. "You just remember that."

We got out of the car and headed up the steps behind Uncle Bob. Cody's dump truck was lying right where I left it on the porch all rusted up.

"It's broke," he said like he was about to throw a fit.

"No it's not," I said. "That's just rust. Looks like a *real* dump truck now."

He brightened up and began playing with his truck. He'd forgot all about Mama and he hadn't even seen her yet.

"Anybody home?" Uncle Bob shouted and knocked on the screen door.

Mama walked out of the bedroom fastening her belt. She had on her good red dress and high heels. She unlatched the screen door and we walked into the living room. Her dress was half unzipped in the back. Aunt Lucette walked over and zipped it up. Mama said hello to everyone and sat down in the rocker. We sat across from her on the sofa. No one said anything for a minute. Then Uncle Bob said, "You're looking good, Coral."

"Am I?" Mama said.

"Real pretty," Aunt Lucette said. "Don't you think so, Heart?" Aunt Lucette jabbed me in the ribs.

"Real pretty," I said. "Prettier than Miss Baker."

Uncle Bob coughed and lit a cigarette. Mama started to cry.

"You seen Frank?" she asked Uncle Bob.

"You know I haven't," he said. "I told you that on the phone."

Mama got up and went to the kitchen. We heard the refrigerator door open. I saw Aunt Lucette looking around the living room. It didn't look like Mama'd done much cleaning since we left. There were piles of dishes and magazines everywhere. I remembered how Mama used to yell at us for leaving a dirty glass or pair of socks in the living room and how she was always wiping this or polishing that, smelling of pine or lemon. She walked back in with a six-pack of beer which she set down on the floor next to her rocker. She peeled off three beers and handed one to each of us. Aunt Lucette reached over and grabbed mine away from me before I had a chance to open it.

"Really, Coral," she said. "Where's your mind at?"

Mama opened her beer and took a long sip. No one said anything. Outside on the porch we could hear Cody yelling, "VVr-rroomm, vroom! VVVrroommm, vrooooomm!"

"It's Heart's birthday next week, Coral," Aunt Lucette said.

Mama didn't say anything. She took another sip of beer and spilled some down the front of her good dress. I got up and walked outside. Cody looked up from his truck.

"Mama's in there," I said.

He steered his truck across the porch to the door. He could just barely reach the door handle now on tiptoe. I reached over and held the door open for him while he vroomm-vvroommed over to Mama's rocker. I saw Mama reach down. I thought she was going to pat his head, but she just moved her beer out of his way. "Don't spill that," she said.

I stood on the porch watching the rain drip off the roof. I heard Mama say, "I saw Frank yesterday. He brought me some candy. He says he's tired of that woman." I heard Uncle Bob say, "You know you didn't see Frank, Coral. You know he's in Florida. You gotta snap yourself out of this. You ain't the only woman whose husband ever run off." I heard Cody making his truck noises. The metal wheels made a real racket on the wood floor. Mama yelled at him to watch where he was going. Then I heard Aunt Lucette say, "You've got to think of your children, Coral. The school psychologist says Heart is too 'withdrawn,' she's like some walking zombie. He says she could end up real warped from all this."

I never heard what Mama said 'cause I went out into the yard. I held my arms straight out in front of me and stared straight ahead like my eyeballs were frozen. I walked back and forth across the yard with my arms and legs stiff as boards like the zombies I'd seen on TV. The tall grass wet my knee socks. I felt my hair frizzing in the rain. From inside I heard Uncle Bob shouting and Cody howling. I got in the car and curled up on the backseat with my head on the pillow. The rain sounded loud beating on the tin roof of the car. I remembered my stick of gum in my pocket and unwrapped it. I had just popped it in my mouth when the car door flew open and Uncle Bob dumped Cody in the backseat. Cody's pants were soaked with beer and he smelled like a brewery, which was what my mama used to tell my daddy when he came home late. Cody was crying and Aunt Lucette was crying but she looked mad, too.

"What happened?" I said, my mouth full of gum.

"She hit me," Cody said.

"Why?" I asked.

"She's crazy," Uncle Bob said and threw the car into reverse.

Uncle Bob backed up so fast we ended up on the lawn and heard a soft crack.

"Hope that wasn't a glass bottle," Aunt Lucette said.

"Jesus." Uncle Bob pounded the steering wheel with his fist. "Don't it never end?"

He got out and looked underneath the car. I noticed how my finger was turning green underneath my ring.

"Look at this." Uncle Bob held Cody's toy telephone up to the window for us to see. It was squashed like a pink pancake. Just as he was about to toss it back into the weeds, I rolled down my window and reached out my arm.

"Give it to me," I said.

Uncle Bob handed it to me. "What you want with that old piece of junk?" He got back in the car.

"I just like it," I said. "It's all repressed."

Uncle Bob shook his head and looked at Aunt Lucette. She reached over with her crumpled Kleenex and touched the little spot of dried blood from this morning still on his chin. Suddenly everyone seemed nice and calm, even Cody. Once we were out onto the paved road, I sat there staring at the telephone in my lap. It reminded me of those dead animals, skunks and squirrels, you see flattened on the highway. I picked up the receiver and tried to dial our home number on the mashed dial. "Hello, Mama?" I said. "This is Heart."

Uncle Bob turned the radio down. It was so quiet I could hear her breathing on the other end.

"I know you're there, Mama," I shouted. "You hear me?"

Cody looked at me like he'd never seen me before in his life. "Don't cry," he said. He reached over and touched me on the arm. "Don't cry."

Aunt Lucette handed me her Kleenex. Cody put his ear up against the receiver and listened, real puzzled, like maybe there was something he didn't understand.

1988

Rick Bass

THE WATCH

If Southern writers, as some scholars claim, are inclined to mythologize what might elsewhere be considered deviant, then Rick Bass's fiction exemplifies the virtue of that inclination. This extraordinary story, the title story of Bass's 1989 collection, features the obsessive dimensions not just of deviance, but also of interdependence and love. Its author is a Texan, by birth and raising. He worked for eight years in Mississippi as a geologist and lives now in Montana. As well known for his nonfiction as for his fiction, his most recent books are The Lost Grizzlies *and* In the Loyal Mountains.

When Hollingsworth's father, Buzbee, was seventy-seven years old, he was worth a thousand dollars, that summer and fall. His name was up in all the restaurants and convenience stores, all along the interstate, and the indistinctions on the dark photocopies taped to doors and walls made him look distinguished, like someone else. The Xerox sheets didn't even say *Reward*, *Lost*, or *Missing*. They just got right to the point: *Mr. Buzbee, $1,000.*

The country Buzbee had disappeared in was piney woods, in the center of the state, away from the towns, the Mississippi — away from everything. There were swamps and ridges, and it was the hottest part of the state, and hardly anyone lived there. If they did, it was on those ridges, not down in the bottoms, and there were sometimes fields that had been cleared by hand, though the soil was poor and red, and could really grow nothing but tall lime-colored grass that bent in the wind like waves in a storm, and was good for horses, and nothing else — no crops, no cattle, nothing worth a damn — and Hollingsworth did not doubt that Buzbee, who had just recently taken to pissing in his pants, was alive, perhaps even just lying down in the deep grass somewhere out there, to be spiteful, like a dog.

Hollingsworth knew the reward he was offering wasn't much. He had a lot more money than that, but he read the papers and he knew that people in Jackson, the big town seventy miles north, offered that much every week, when their dogs ran off, or their cats went away somewhere to have kittens. Hollingsworth had offered only a thousand dollars for his father because nine hundred dollars or some lesser figure would have seemed cheap — and some greater number would have made people think he was sad and missed the old man. It really cracked Hollingsworth up, reading about those lawyers in Jackson who would offer a thousand dollars for their tramp cats. He wondered how they came upon those figures — if they knew what a thing was really worth when they liked it.

It was lonely without Buzbee — it was bad, it was much too quiet, especially in the evenings — and it was the first time in his life that Hollingsworth had ever heard such a silence. Sometimes cyclists would ride past his dried-out barn and country store, and one of them would sometimes stop for a Coke, sweaty, breathing hard, and he was more like some sort of draft animal than a person, so intent was he upon his speed, and he never had time to chat with Hollingsworth, to spin tales. He said his name was Jesse; he would say hello, gulp his Coke, and then this Jesse would be off, hurrying to catch the others, who had not stopped.

Hollingsworth tried to guess the names of the other cyclists. He felt he had a secret over them: giving them names they didn't know they had. He felt as if he owned them: as if he had them on some invisible string and could pull them back in just by muttering their names. He called all the others by French names — François, Pierre, Jacques — as they all rode French bicycles with an unpronounceable name — and he thought they were pansies, delicate, for having been given such soft and fluttering names — but he liked Jesse, and even more, he liked Jesse's bike, which was a black Schwinn, a heavy old bike that Hollingsworth saw made Jesse struggle hard to stay up with the Frenchmen.

Hollingsworth watched them ride, like a pack of animals, up and down the weedy, abandoned roads in the heat, disappearing into the shimmer that came up out of the road and the fields: the cyclists disappeared into the mirages, tracking a straight line, and then, later in the day — sitting on his porch, waiting — Hollingsworth would see them again when they came riding back out of the mirages.

The very first time that Jesse had peeled off from the rest of the pack and stopped by Hollingsworth's ratty-ass grocery for a Coke — the sound the old bottle made, sliding down the chute, Hollingsworth still had the old formula Cokes, as no one — no one — ever came to his old leaning barn of a store, set back on the hill off the deserted road — that first time, Hollingsworth was so excited at having a visitor that he couldn't speak: he just kept swallowing, filling his stomach fuller and fuller with air — and the sound the Coke bottle made, sliding down, made Hollingsworth feel as if he had been struck in the head with it, as if he had been waiting at the bottom of the chute. No one had been out to his place since his father ran away: just the sheriff, once.

The road past Hollingsworth's store was the road of a ghost town. There had once been a good community, a big one — back at the turn of the century — down in the bottom, below his store — across the road, across the wide fields — rich growing grasses there, from the river's flooding — the Bayou Pierre, which emptied into the Mississippi, and down in the tall hardwoods, with trees so thick that three men, holding arms, could not circle them, there had been a colony, a fair-sized town actually, that shipped cotton down the bayou in the fall, when the waters started to rise again.

The town had been called Hollingsworth.

But in 1903 the last survivors had died of yellow fever, as had happened in almost every other town in the state — strangely enough, those lying closest to swamps and bayous, where yellow fever had always been a problem, were the last towns to go under, the most resistant—and then in the years that followed, the new towns that reestablished themselves in the state did not choose to locate near Hollingsworth again. Buzbee's father had been one of the few who left before the town died, though he had contracted it, the yellow fever, and both Buzbee's parents died shortly after Buzbee was born.

Malaria came again in the 1930s, and got Buzbee's wife—Hollingsworth's mother—when Hollingsworth was born, but Buzbee and his new son stayed, dug in, and refused to leave the store. When Hollingsworth was fifteen, they both caught it again, but fought it down, together, as it was the kind that attacked only every other day—a different strain than before—and their days of fever alternated, so that they were able to take care of each other: cleaning up the spitting and the vomiting of black blood, covering each other with blankets when the chills started, and building fires in the fireplace, even in summer. And they tried all the roots in the area, all the plants, and somehow—for they did not keep track of what they ate, they only sampled everything, anything that grew—pine boughs, cattails, wild carrots—they escaped being buried. Cemeteries were scattered throughout the woods and fields; nearly every place that was high and windy had one.

So the fact that no one ever came to their store, that there never had been any business, was nothing for Buzbee and Hollingsworth; everything would always be a secondary calamity, after the two years of yellow fever, and burying everyone, everything. Waking up in the night, with a mosquito biting them, and wondering if it had the fever. There were cans of milk on the shelves in their store that were forty years old; bags of potato chips that were twenty years old, because neither of them liked potato chips.

Hollingsworth would sit on his heels on the steps and tremble whenever Jesse and the others rode past, and on the times when Jesse turned in and came up to the store, so great was

Hollingsworth's hurry to light his cigarette and then talk, slowly, the way it was supposed to be done in the country, the way he had seen it in his imagination, when he thought about how he would like his life to really be — that he spilled two cigarettes, and had barely gotten the third lit and drawn one puff when Jesse finished his Coke and then stood back up, and put the wet empty bottle back in the wire rack, waved, and rode off, the great backs of his calves and hamstrings working up and down in swallowing shapes, like things trapped in a sack, like ominous things, too. So Hollingsworth had to wait again for Jesse to come back, and by the next time, he had decided for certain that Buzbee was just being spiteful.

Before Buzbee had run away, sometimes Hollingsworth and Buzbee had cooked their dinners in the evenings, and other times they had driven into a town and ordered something, and looked around at people, and talked to the waitresses — but now, in the evenings, Hollingsworth stayed around, so as not to miss Jesse should he come by, and he ate briefly, sparingly, from his stocks on the shelves: dusty cans of Vienna sausage, sardines, and rock crackers. Warm beer, brands that had gone out of business a decade earlier, two decades. Holding out against time was difficult, but was also nothing after holding out against death. In cheating death, Hollingsworth and Buzbee had continued to live, had survived, but also, curiously, they had lost an edge of some sort: nothing would ever be quite as intense, nothing would ever really matter, after the biggest struggle.

The old cans of food didn't have any taste, but Hollingsworth didn't mind. He didn't see that it mattered much. Jesse said the other bikers wouldn't stop because they thought the Cokes were bad for them: cut their wind, slowed them down.

Hollingsworth had to fight down the feelings of wildness sometimes, now that his father was gone. Hollingsworth had never married, never had a friend other than his father. He had everything brought to him by the grocery truck, on the rarest of orders, and by the mail. He subscribed to *The Wall Street Journal*. It was eight days late by the time he received it—but he read it—and before Buzbee had run away they used to tell each other stories. They would start at sundown and talk until ten o'clock: Buzbee relating the ancient things, and Hollingsworth telling about everything that was in the paper. Buzbee's stories were always better. They were about things that had happened two, three miles away.

As heirs to the town, Hollingsworth and Buzbee had once owned, back in the thirties, over two thousand acres of land—cypress and water oak, down in the swamp, and great thick bull pines, on the ridges—but they'd sold almost all of it to the timber companies—a forty- or eighty-acre tract every few years—and now they had almost no land left, just the shack in which they lived.

But they had bushels and bushels of money, kept in peach bushel baskets in their closet, stacked high. They didn't miss the land they had sold, but wished they had more, so that the pulp-wood cutters would return: they had enjoyed the sound of the chain saws.

Back when they'd been selling their land, and having it cut, they would sit on their porch in the evenings and listen to it, the far-off cutting, as if it were music, picturing the great trees falling, and feeling satisfied, somehow, each time they heard one hit.

The first thing Jesse did in the mornings when he woke up was to check the sky, and then, stepping out onto the back porch, naked, the wind. If there wasn't any, he would be relaxed and happy with his life. If it was windy—even the faintest stir against his shaved ankles, up and over his round legs—he would scowl, a grimace of concentration, and go in and fix his coffee. There couldn't be any letting up on windy days, and if there was a breeze in the morning, it would build to true and hard wind for sure by afternoon: the heat of the fields rising, cooling, falling back down;

blocks of air as slippery as his biking suit, sliding all up and down the roads, twisting through trees, looking for places to blow, paths of least resistance.

There was so much Hollingsworth wanted to tell someone! Jesse, or even François, Jacques, Pierre! Buzbee was gone! He and Buzbee had told each other all the old stories, again and again. There wasn't anything new, not really, not of worth, and hadn't been for a long time. Hollingsworth had even had to resort to fabricating things, pretending he was reading them in the paper, to match Buzbee during the last few years of storytelling. And now, alone, his imagination was turning in on itself, and growing, like the most uncontrollable kind of cancer, with nowhere to go, and in the evenings he went out on the porch and looked across the empty highway, into the waving fields in the ebbing winds, and beyond, down to the blue line of trees along the bayou, where he knew Buzbee was hiding out, and Hollingsworth would ring the dinner bell, loudly and clearly, with a grim anger, and he would hope, scanning the fields, that Buzbee would stand up and wave, and come back in.

Jesse came by for another Coke in the second week of July. There was such heat. Hollingsworth had called in to Crystal Springs and had the asphalt truck come out and grade and level his gravel, pour hot slick new tar down over it, and smooth it out. It cooled, slowly, and was beautiful, almost iridescent, like a black-snake in the bright green grass: it glowed its way across the yard as if it were made of glass, a path straight to the store, coming in off the road. It beckoned.

"So you got a new driveway," Jesse said, looking down at his feet.

The bottle was already in his hand; he was already taking the first sip.

Nothing lasted; nothing!

Hollingsworth clawed at his chest, his shirt pocket, for cigarettes. He pulled them out and got one and lit it, and then sat down and said, slowly, "Yes." He looked out at the fields and couldn't remember a single damn story.

He groped, and faltered.

"You may have noticed there's a sudden abundance of old coins, especially quarters, say, 1964, 1965, the ones that have still got some silver in them," Hollingsworth said casually, but it wasn't the story in his heart.

"This is nice," Jesse said. "This is like what I race on sometimes." The little tar strip leading in to the Coke machine and Hollingsworth's porch was as black as a snake that had just freshly shed its skin, and was as smooth and new. Hollingsworth had been sweeping it twice a day, to keep twigs off it, and waiting.

It was soft and comfortable to stand on; Jesse was testing it with his foot—pressing down on it, pleasurably, admiring the surface and firmness, yet also the give of it.

"The Russians hoarded them, is my theory, got millions of them from our mints in the sixties, during the cold war," Hollingsworth said quickly. Jesse was halfway through with his Coke. This wasn't the way it was with Buzbee at all. "They've since subjected them to radiation—planted them amongst our populace."

Jesse's calves looked like whales going away; his legs, like things from another world. They were grotesque when they moved and pumped.

"I saw a man who looked like you," Jesse told Hollingsworth in August.

Jesse's legs and deep chest were taking on a hardness and slickness that hadn't been there before. He was drinking only half his Coke, and then slowly pouring the rest of it on the ground, while Hollingsworth watched, crestfallen: the visit already over, cut in half by dieting, and the mania for speed and distance.

"Expect he was real old," Jesse said. "I think he was the man they're looking for." Jesse didn't know Hollingsworth's first or last name; he had never stopped to consider it.

Hollingsworth couldn't speak. The Coke had made a puddle

and was fizzing, popping quietly in the dry grass. The sun was big and orange across the fields, going down behind the blue trees. It was beginning to cool. Doves were flying past, far over their heads, fat from the fields and late-summer grain. Hollingsworth wondered what Buzbee was eating, where he was living, why he had run away.

"He was fixing to cross the road," said Jesse.

He was standing up, balancing carefully, in the little cleat shoes that would skid out from underneath him from time to time when he tried to walk in them. He didn't use a stopwatch the way other cyclists did, but he knew he was getting faster, because just recently he had gotten the quiet, almost silent sensation—just a soft hushing—of falling, the one that athletes, and sometimes other people, get when they push deeper and deeper into their sport, until—like pushing through one final restraining layer of tissue, the last and thinnest, easiest one—they are falling, slowly, and there is nothing left in their life to stop them, no work is necessary, things are just happening, and they suddenly have all the time in the world to perfect their sport, because that's all there is, one day, finally.

"I tried to lay the bike down and get off and chase him," Jesse said. "But my legs cramped up."

He put the Coke bottle in the rack.

The sun was in Hollingsworth's eyes: it was as if he was being struck blind. He could smell only Jesse's heavy body odor, and could feel only the heat still radiating from his legs, like thick andirons taken from a fire: legs like a horse's, standing there, with veins wrapping them, spidery, beneath the thin browned skin.

"He was wearing dirty old overalls and no shirt," said Jesse. "And listen to this. He had a live carp tucked under one arm, and it didn't have a tail left on it. I had the thought that he had been eating on that fish's tail, chewing on it."

Jesse was giving a speech. Hollingsworth felt himself twisting down and inside with pleasure, like he was swooning. Jesse kept talking, nailing home the facts.

"He turned and ran like a deer, back down through the field, down toward the creek, and into those trees, still holding on to the fish." Jesse turned and pointed. "I was thinking that if we could catch him on your tractor, run him down and lasso him, I'd split the reward money with you." Jesse looked down at his legs, the round swell of them so ballooned and great that they hid completely his view of the tiny shoes below him. "I could never catch him by myself, on foot, I don't think," he said, almost apologetically. "For an old fucker, he's fast. There's no telling what he thinks he's running from."

"Hogson, the farmer over on Green Gable Road, has got himself some hounds," Hollingsworth heard himself saying, in a whisper. "He bought them from the penitentiary, when they turned mean, for five hundred dollars. They can track anything. They'll run the old man to Florida if they catch his scent; they won't ever let up."

Hollingsworth was remembering the hounds, black and tan, the colors of late frozen night, and cold honey in the sun, in the morning, and he was picturing the dogs moving through the forest, with Jesse and himself behind them: camping out! The dogs straining on their heavy leashes! Buzbee, slightly ahead of them, on the run, leaping logs, crashing the undergrowth, splashing through the bends and loops in the bayou: savage swamp birds, rafts of them, darkening the air as they rose in their fright, leaping up in entire rookeries . . . cries in the forest, it would be like the jungle. . . . It might take days! Stories around the campfire! He would tear off a greasy leg of chicken, from the grill, reach across to hand it to Jesse, and tell him about anything, everything.

"We should try the tractor first," Jesse said, thinking ahead. It was hard to think about a thing other than bicycling, and he was frowning and felt awkward, exposed, and, also, trapped: cut off from the escape route. "But if he gets down into the woods, we'll probably have to use the dogs."

Hollingsworth was rolling up his pants leg, cigarette still in hand, to show Jesse the scar from the hunting accident when he was twelve: his father had said he thought he was a deer, and had shot him. Buzbee had been twenty-six.

"I'm like you," Hollingsworth said faithfully. "I can't run worth a damn, either." But Jesse had already mounted his bike; he was moving away, down the thin black strip, like a pilot taking a plane down a runway, to lift off, or like a fish running to sea; he entered the dead highway, which had patches of weeds growing up even in its center, and he stood up in the clips and accelerated away, down through the trees, with the wind at his back, going home.

He was gone almost immediately.

Hollingsworth's store had turned dark; the sun was behind the trees. He did not want to go back inside. He sat down on the porch and watched the empty road. His mother had died giving birth to him. She, like his father, had been fourteen. He and his father had always been more like brothers to each other than anything else. Hollingsworth could remember playing a game with his father, perhaps when he was seven or eight, and his father then would have been twenty-one or so — Jessie's age, roughly — and his father would run out into the field and hide, on their old homestead — racing down the hill, arms windmilling, and disappearing suddenly, diving down into the tall grass, while Hollingsworth — Quieter, Quiet — tried to find him. They played that game again and again, more than any other game in the world, and at all times of the year, not just in the summer.

Buzbee had a favorite tree, and he sat up in the low branch of it often and looked back in the direction from which he had come. He saw the bikers every day. There weren't ever cars on the road. The cyclists sometimes picnicked at a little roadside table off of it, oranges and bottles of warm water and candy bars by the dozens — he had snuck out there in the evenings, before, right at dusk, and sorted through their garbage, nibbled some of the orange peelings — and he was nervous, in his tree, whenever they stopped for any reason.

Buzbee had not in the least considered going back to his maddened son. He shifted on the branch and watched the cyclists eat their oranges. His back was slick with sweat, and he was rank, like the worst of animals. He and all the women bathed in the evenings in the bayou, in the shallows, rolling around in the mud. The women wouldn't go out any deeper. Snakes swam in evil S-shapes, back and forth, as if patrolling. He was starting to learn the women well, and many of them were like his son in every regard, in that they always wanted to talk, it seemed — this compulsion to communicate, as if it could be used to keep something else away, something big and threatening. He thought about what the cold weather would be like, November and beyond, himself trapped, as it were, in the abandoned palmetto shack, with all of them around the fireplace, talking, for four months.

He slid down from the tree and started out into the field, toward the cyclists — the women watched him go — and in the heat, in the long walk across the field, he became dizzy, started to fall several times, and for the briefest fragments of time he kept forgetting where he was, imagined that one of the cyclists was his son, that he was coming back in from the game that they used to play, and he stopped, knelt down in the grass and pretended to hide. Eventually, though, the cyclists finished eating, got up and rode away, down the road again. Buzbee watched them go, then stood up and turned and raced back down into the woods, to the women. He had become very frightened, for no reason, out in the field like that.

Buzbee had found the old settlement after wandering around in the woods for a week. There were carp in the bayou, and gar, and catfish, and he wrestled the large ones out of the shallow oxbows that had been cut off from the rest of the water. He caught alligators, too, the small ones.

He kept a small fire going, continuously, to keep the mosquitoes away, and as he caught more and more of the big fish, he hung them from the branches in his clearing, looped vine through their

huge jaws and hung them like villains, all around in his small clearing, like the most ancient of burial grounds. All these vertical fish,
out of the water, mouths gaping in silent death, as if preparing to
ascend — they were all pointing up.

The new pleasure of being alone sometimes stirred Buzbee so
that he ran from errand to errand, as if on a shopping spree or a
game show: he was getting ready for this new life, and with fall
and winter coming on, he felt young.

After a couple of weeks, he had followed the bayou upstream,
toward town, backtracking the water's sluggishness; sleeping
under the large logs that had fallen across it like netting, and he
swatted at the mosquitoes that swarmed him whenever he stopped
moving, in the evenings, and he had kept going, even at night. The
moon came down through the bare limbs of the swamp-rotted
ghost trees, skeleton-white, disease-killed, but as he got higher
above the swamp and closer to the town, near daylight, the water
moved faster, had some circulation, was still alive, and the mosquitoes were not a threat.

He lay under a boxcar on the railroad tracks and looked across
the road at the tired women going in and out of the washateria,
moving so slowly, as if old. They were in their twenties, their thirties, their forties; they carried their baskets of wet clothes in front
of them with a bumping, side-to-side motion, as if they were
going to quit living on the very next step; their forearms sweated,
glistened, and the sandals on their wide feet made flopping
sounds, and he wanted to tell them about his settlement. He
wanted five or six, ten or twenty of them. He wanted them walking around barefooted on the dark earth beneath his trees,
beneath his hanging catfish and alligators, by the water, in the
swamp.

He stole four chickens and a rooster that night, hooded their
eyes, and put them in a burlap sack, put three eggs in each of his
shirt pockets, too, after sucking ten of them dry, greedily, gulping,
in the almost wet brilliance of the moon, behind a chicken farm
back west of town, along the bayou — and then he continued on

down its banks, the burlap sack thrown over his back, the chickens and rooster warm against his damp body, and calm, waiting.

He stopped when he came out of the green and thick woods, over a little ridge, and looked down into the country where the bayous slowed to heavy swamp and where the white and dead trees were and the bad mosquitoes lived — and he sat down and leaned his old back against a tree, and watched the moon and its blue light shining on the swamp, with his chickens. He waited until the sun came up and it got hot, and the mosquitoes had gone away, before starting down toward the last part of his journey, back to his camp.

The rest of the day he gathered seeds and grain from the little raised hummocks and grassy spots in the woods, openings in the forest, to use for feed for the chickens, which moved in small crooked shapes of white, like little ghosts in the woods, all through his camp, but they did not leave it. The rooster flew up into a low tree and stared wildly, golden-eyed, down into the bayou. For weeks Buzbee had been hunting the quinine bushes said to have been planted there during the big epidemic, and on that day he found them, because the chickens went straight to them and began pecking at them as Buzbee had never seen chickens peck: they flew up into the leaves, smothered their bodies against the bushes as if mating with them, so wild were they to get to the berries.

Buzbee's father had planted the bushes, and had received the seeds from South America, on a freighter that he met in New Orleans the third year of the epidemic, and he had returned with them to the settlement, that third year, when everyone went down finally.

The plants had not done well; they kept rotting, and never, in Buzbee's father's time, bore fruit or made berries. Buzbee had listened to his father tell the story about how they rotted — but also how, briefly, they had lived, even flourished, for a week or two, and how the settlement had celebrated and danced, and cooked alligators and cattle, and prayed, and everyone in the settlement had planted quinine seeds, all over the woods, for miles, in every conceivable location . . . and Buzbee knew immediately, when the chickens began to cluck and feed, that it was the quinine berries, which they knew instinctively they must eat, and he went and gathered all the berries, and finally, he knew, he was safe.

The smoke from his fire, down in the low bottom, had spread through the swamp, and from above would have looked as if that portion of the bayou, going into the tangled dead trees, had simply disappeared: a large spill of white, a fuzzy, milky spot—and then, on the other side of the spill, coming out again, bayou once more.

Buzbee was relieved to have the berries, and he let the fire go down; he let it die. He sat against his favorite tree by the water and watched for small alligators. When he saw one, he would leap into the water, splash and swim across to meet it, and wrestle it out of the shallows and into the mud, where he would kill it savagely.

But the days were long, and he did not see that many alligators, and many of the ones he did see were a little too large, sometimes far too large. Still, he had almost enough for winter, as it stood: those hanging from the trees, along with the gaping catfish, spun slowly in the breeze of fall coming, and if he waited and watched, eventually he would see one. He sat against the tree and watched, and ate berries, chewed them slowly, pleasuring in their sour taste.

He imagined that they soured his blood: that they made him taste bad to the mosquitoes, and kept them away. Though he noticed they were still biting him, more even, now that the smoke was gone. But he got used to it.

A chicken had disappeared, probably to a snake, but also possibly to anything, anything.

The berries would keep him safe.

He watched the water. Sometimes there would be the tiniest string of bubbles rising, from where an alligator was stirring in the mud below.

Two of the women from the laundry came out of the woods, tentatively, having left their homes, following the bayou, to see if it was true what they had heard. It was dusk, and their clothes were torn and their faces wild. Buzbee looked up and could see the fear, and he wanted to comfort them. He did not ask what had happened at their homes, what fear could make the woods and the bayou journey seem less frightening. They stayed back in the trees, frozen, and would not come with him, even when he took each by the hand, until he saw what it was that was horrifying them: the grinning reptiles, the dried fish, spinning from the trees — and he explained to them that he had put them there to smoke, for food, for the winter.

"They smell good," said the shorter one, heavier than her friend, her skin a deep black, like some poisonous berry. Her face was shiny.

Her friend slapped at a mosquito.

"Here," said Buzbee, handing them some berries. "Eat these."

But they made faces and spat them out when they tasted the bitterness.

Buzbee frowned. "You'll get sick if you don't eat them," he said. "You won't make it otherwise."

They walked past him, over to the alligators, and reached out to the horned, hard skin, and touched them fearfully, ready to run, making sure the alligators were unable to leave the trees and were truly harmless.

"Don't you ever, you know, get lonely for girls?" Hollingsworth asked, like a child. It was only four days later, but Jesse was back for another half-Coke. The other bikers had ridden past almost an hour earlier, a fast *rip-rip-rip*, and then, much later, Jesse had come up the hill, pedaling hard, but moving slower.

He was trying, but he couldn't stay up with them. He had thrown his bike down angrily, and glowered at Hollingsworth, when he stalked up to the Coke machine, scowled at him as if it was Hollingsworth's fault.

"I got a whore," Jesse said, looking behind him and out across the road. The pasture was green and wet, and fog, like mist, hung over it, steaming from a rain earlier in the day. Jesse was lying; he didn't have anyone, hadn't had anyone in over a year — everybody knew he was slow in his group, and they shunned him for that — and Jesse felt as if he was getting farther and farther away from ever wanting anyone, or anything. He felt like everything was a blur: such was the speed at which he imagined he was trying to travel. Beyond the fog in the pasture were the trees, clear and dark and washed from the rain, and smelling good, even at this distance. Hollingsworth wished he had a whore. He wondered if Jesse would let him use his. He wondered if maybe she would be available if Jesse was to get fast and go off to the Olympics, or something.

"What does she cost?" Hollingsworth asked timidly.

Jesse looked at him in disgust. "I didn't mean it *that* way," he said. He looked tired, as if he was holding back, just a few seconds, from having to go back out on the road. Hollingsworth leaned closer, eagerly, sensing weakness, tasting hesitation. His senses were sharp, from deprivation: he could tell, even before Jesse could, that Jesse was feeling thick, laggard, dulled. He knew Jesse was going to quit. He knew it the way a farmer might see that rain was coming.

"I mean," sighed Jesse, "that I got an old lady. A woman friend. A girl."

"What's her name?" Hollingsworth said quickly. He would make Jesse so tired that he would never ride again. They would sit around on the porch and talk forever, all of the days.

"Jemima."

Hollingsworth wanted her, just for her name.

"That's nice," he said, in a smaller voice.

It seemed to Hollingsworth that Jesse was getting his energy back. But he had felt the tiredness, and maybe, Hollingsworth hoped, it would come back.

"I found out the old man is your father," said Jesse. He was looking out at the road. He still wasn't making any move toward it. Hollingsworth realized, as if he had been tricked, that perhaps Jesse was just waiting for the roads to dry up a little, to finish steaming.

"Yes," said Hollingsworth, "he has run away."

They looked at the fields together.

"He is not right," Hollingsworth said.

"The black women in town, the ones that do everyone's wash at the laundromat, say he is living down in the old yellow-fever community," Jesse said. "They say he means to stay, and that some of them have thought about going down there with him: the ones with bad husbands and too much work. He's been sneaking around the laundry late in the evenings, and promising them he'll cook for them, if any of them want to move down there with him. He says there aren't any snakes. They're scared the fever will come back, but he promises there aren't any snakes, that he killed them all, and a lot of them are considering it." Jesse related all this in a monotone, still watching the road, as if waiting for energy. The sun was burning the steam off. Hollingsworth felt damp, weak, unsteady, as if his mind was sweating with condensation from the knowledge, the way glasses suddenly fog up when you are walking into a humid setting.

"Sounds like he's getting lonely," Jesse said.

The steam was almost gone.

"He'll freeze this winter," Hollingsworth said, hopefully.

Jesse shook his head. "Sounds like he's got a plan. I suspect he'll have those women cutting firewood for him, fanning him with leaves, fishing, running traps, bearing children. Washing clothes."

"We'll catch him," Hollingsworth said, making a fist and smacking it in his palm. "And anyway, those women won't go down into the woods. They're dark, and the yellow fever's still down there. I'll go into town, and tell them it is. I'll tell them Buzbee's spitting up black blood and shivering, and is crazy. Those women won't go down into the woods."

Jesse shook his head. He put the bottle into the rack. The road was dry; it looked clean, scrubbed, by the quick thunderstorm. "A lot of those women have got bruises on their arms, their faces, have got teeth missing, and their lives are too hard and without hope," Jesse said slowly, as if just for the first time seeing it. "Myself, I think they'll go down there in great numbers. I don't think yellow fever means anything compared to what they have, or will have." He turned to Hollingsworth and slipped a leg over his bike, got on, put his feet in the clips, steadied himself against the porch railing. "I bet by June next year you're going to have about twenty half brothers and half sisters."

When Jesse rode off, thickly, as if the simple heat of the air were a thing holding him back, there was no question, Hollingsworth realized, Jesse was exhausted, and fall was coming. Jesse was getting tired. He, Hollingsworth, and Buzbee, and the colored women at the washhouse, and other people would get tired, too. The temperatures would be getting cooler, milder, in a month or so, and the bikers would be riding harder than ever. There would be smoke from fires, hunters down on the river, and at night the stars would be brighter, and people's sleep would be heavier, and deeper. Hollingsworth wondered just how fast those bikers wanted to go. Surely, he thought, they were already going fast enough. He didn't understand them. Surely, he thought, they didn't know what they were doing.

The speeds that the end of June and the beginning of July brought, Jesse had never felt before, and he didn't trust them to last, didn't know if they could; and he tried to stay with the other riders, but didn't know if there was anything he could do to make the little speed he had last, in the curves, and that feeling, pounding up the hills, his heart working thick and smooth, like the wildest, easiest, most volatile thing ever invented. He tried to stay with them.

Hollingsworth, the old faggot, was running out into the road some days, trying to flag him down, for some piece of bullshit, but there wasn't time, and he rode past, not even looking at him, only staring straight ahead.

The doves started to fly. The year was moving along. A newspaper reporter wandered down, to do a short piece on the still-missing Buzbee. It was rumored he was living in an abandoned, rotting shack, deep into the darkest, lowest heart of the swamp. It was said that he had started taking old colored women, maids and such, women from the laundromat, away from town, that they were going back down into the woods with him and living there, and that he had them in a corral, like a herd of wild horses. The reporter's story slipped further from the truth. It was all very mysterious, all rumor, and the reward was increased to twelve hundred dollars by Hollingsworth, as the days grew shorter after the solstice, and lonelier.

Jesse stopped racing. He just didn't go out one day; and when the Frenchmen came by for him, he pretended not to be in.

He slept late and began to eat vast quantities of oatmeal. Sometimes, around noon, he would stop eating and get on his bike and ride slowly up the road to Hollingsworth's — sometimes the other bikers would pass him, moving as ever at great speed, all of them, and they would jeer at him, shout yah-yah, and then they were quickly gone; and he willed them to wreck, shut his eyes and tried to make it happen — picturing the whole pack of them getting tangled up, falling over one another, the way they tended to do, riding so close together — and the pain of those wrecks, the long slide, the drag and skid of flesh on gravel.

The next week he allowed himself a whole Coca-Cola, with Hollingsworth, on the steps of the store's porch. The old man swooned, and had to steady himself against the railing when he saw it was his true love. It was a dry summer. They talked more about Buzbee.

"He's probably averse to being captured," Hollingsworth said. "He probably won't go easy."

Jesse looked at his shoes, watched them, as if thinking about where they were made.

"If you were to help me catch him, I would give you my half of it," Hollingsworth said generously. Jesse watched his shoes.

Hollingsworth got up and went in the store quickly, and came back out with a hank of calf-roping lariat, heavy, gold as a fable, and corded.

"I been practicing," he said. There was a sawhorse standing across the drive, up on two legs, like a man, with a hat on it, and a coat, and Hollingsworth said nothing else, but twirled the lariat over his head and then flung it at the sawhorse, a mean heavy whistle over their heads, and the loop settled over the sawhorse, and Hollingsworth stepped back quickly and tugged, cinched the loop shut. The sawhorse fell over, and Hollingsworth began dragging it across the gravel, reeling it in as fast as he could.

"I could lasso you off that road, if I wanted," Hollingsworth said.

Jesse thought about how the money would be nice. He thought about how it was in a wreck, too, when he wasn't able to get his feet free of the clips and had to stay with the bike, and roll over with it, still wrapped up in it. It was just the way his sport was.

"I've got to be going," he told Hollingsworth. When he stood up, though, he had been still too long, and his blood stayed down in his legs, and he saw spots and almost fell.

"Easy now, hoss," Hollingsworth cautioned, watching him eagerly, eyes narrowed, hoping for an accident and no more riding.

The moonlight that came in through Hollingsworth's window, onto his bed, all night—it was silver. It made things look different: ghostly. He slept on his back, looking up at the ceiling until he fell asleep. He listened to crickets, to hoot owls, and to the silence, too.

We'll get him, he thought. We'll find his ass. But he couldn't sleep, and the sound of his heart, the movement of his blood pulsing, was the roar of an ocean, and it wasn't right. His father did not belong down in those woods. No one did. There was nothing down there that Hollingsworth could see but reptiles, and danger.

The moon was so bright that it washed out all stars. Hollingsworth listened to the old house. There was a blister on the inside of his finger from practicing with the lariat, and he fingered it and looked at the ceiling.

* * *

Jesse went back, again and again. He drank the Coke slowly. He wasn't sweating.

"Let's go hunt that old dog," Hollingsworth said — it was the first thing he said, after Jesse had gotten his bottle out of the machine and opened it — and like a molester, a crooner, Hollingsworth seemed to be drifting toward Jesse without moving his feet: just leaning forward, swaying closer and closer, as if moving in to smell blossoms. His eyes were a believer's blue, and for a moment, still thinking about how slowly he had ridden over and the Coke's coldness and wetness, Jesse had no idea what he was talking about and felt dizzy. He looked into Hollingsworth's eyes, such a pale wash of light, such a pale blue that he knew the eyes had never seen anything factual, nothing of substance — and he laughed, thinking of Hollingsworth trying to catch Buzbee, or anything, on his own. The idea of Hollingsworth being able to do anything other than just take what was thrown at him was ridiculous. He thought of Hollingsworth on a bike, pedaling, and laughed again.

"We can split the reward money," Hollingsworth said again. He was grinning, smiling wildly, trying as hard as he could to show all his teeth and yet keep them close together, uppers and lowers touching. He breathed through the cracks in them in a low, pulsing whistle: in and out. He had never in his life drunk anything but water, and his teeth were startlingly white; they were just whittled down, was all, and puny, from aging and time. He closed his eyes, squeezed them shut slowly, as if trying to remember something simple, like speech, or balance, or even breathing. He was like a turtle sunning on a log.

Jesse couldn't believe he was speaking.

"Give me all of it," he heard himself say.

"All of it," Hollingsworth agreed, his eyes still shut, and then he opened them and handed the money to Jesse slowly, ceremoniously, like a child paying for something at a store counter, for the first time.

Jesse unlaced his shoes, and folded the bills in half and slid them down into the soles, putting bills in both shoes. He unlaced the drawstring to his pants and slid some down into the black dampness of his racing silks: down in the crotch, and padding the buttocks, and in front, high on the flatness of his abdomen, like a girdle, directly below the cinching lace of the drawstring, which he then tied again, tighter than it had been before.

Then he got on the bike and rode home, slowly, not racing anymore, not at all; through the late-day heat that had built up, but with fall in the air, the leaves on the trees hanging differently. There was some stillness everywhere. He rode on.

When he got home he carried the bike inside, as was his custom, and then undressed, peeling his suit off, with the damp bills fluttering slowly to the old rug, like petals and blossoms from a dying flower, unfolding when they landed, and it surprised him at first to see them falling away from him like that, all around him, for he had forgotten that they were down there as he rode.

Buzbee was like a field general. The women were tasting freedom, and seemed to be like circus strongmen, muscled with great strength suddenly, from not being told what to do, from not being beaten or yelled at. They laughed and talked, and were kind to Buzbee. He sat up in the tree, in his old khaki pants, and watched, and whenever it looked like his feeble son and the ex-biker might be coming, he leaped down from the tree, and like monkeys they scattered into the woods: back to another, deeper, temporary camp they had built.

They splashed across the river like wild things, but they were laughing, there was no fear, not like there would have been in animals.

They knew they could get away. They knew that as long as they ran fast, they would make it.

Buzbee grinned, too, panting, his eyes bright, and he watched the women's breasts float and bounce, riding high as they charged across—ankle-deep, knee-deep, waist-deep—hurrying to get away from his mad, lonely son, running fast and shrieking, because they were all afraid of the alligators.

Buzbee had a knife in one hand and a sharpened stick in the other, and he almost wished there would be an attack, so that he could be a hero.

The second camp was about two miles down into the swamp. No one had ever been that far into it, not ever. The mosquitoes were worse, too. There wasn't any dry land, not even a patch, but they sat on the branches, and dangled their feet, and waited. Sometimes they saw black bears splashing after fish, and turtles. There were more snakes, too, deeper back, but the women were still bruised, and some of them fingered their scars as they watched the snakes, and no one went back.

They made up songs, with which they pretended to make the snakes go away.

It wasn't too bad.

They sat through the night listening to the cries of birds, and when the woods began to grow light again, so faintly at first that they doubted it was happening, they would ease down into the water and start back toward their dry camp.

Hollingsworth would be gone, chased away by the mosquitoes, by the emptiness, and they would feel righteous, as if they'd won something: a victory.

None of them had a watch. They never knew what time it was, what day even.

"Gone," said Hollingsworth.

He was out of breath, out of shape. His shoelaces were untied, and there were burrs in his socks. The camp was empty. Just chickens. And the godawful reptiles, twisting from the trees.

"Shit almighty," said Jesse. His legs were cramping, and he was bent over, massaging them: he wasn't used to walking.

Hollingsworth poked around in the little grass-and-wood shacks. He was quivering, and kept saying, alternately, "Gone" and "Damn."

Jesse had to sit down, so bad was the pain in his legs. He put his feet together like a bear in the zoo and held them there, and rocked, trying to stretch them back out. He was frightened of the alligators, and he felt helpless, in his cramps, knowing that Buzbee could come up from behind with a club and rap him on the head, like one of the chickens, and that he, Jesse, wouldn't even be able to get up to stop him, or run.

Buzbee was in control.

"Shit. Damn. Gone," said Hollingsworth. He was running a hand through his thinning hair. He kicked a few halfhearted times at the shacks, but they were kicks of sorrow, not rage yet, and did no damage.

"We could eat the chickens," Jesse suggested, from his sitting position. "We could cook them on his fire and leave the bones all over camp." Jesse still had his appetite from his riding days, and was getting fat fast. He was eating all the time since he had stopped riding.

Hollingsworth turned to him, slightly insulted. "They belong to my father," he said.

Jesse continued to rock, but thought: My God, what a madman.

He rubbed his legs and rocked. The pain was getting worse.

There was a breeze stirring. They could hear the leather and rope creaking, as some of the smaller alligators moved. There was a big alligator hanging from a beech tree, about ten feet off the ground, and as they watched it, the leather cord snapped, from the friction, and the dead weight of the alligator crashed to the ground.

"The mosquitoes are getting bad," said Jesse, rising, hobbled, bent over. "We'd better be going."

But Hollingsworth was already scrambling up through the brush, up toward the brightness of sky above the field. He could see the sky, the space, through the trees, and knew the field was out there. He was frantic to get out of the woods; there was a burning in his chest, in his throat, and he couldn't breathe.

Jesse helped him across the field and got him home; he offered to ride into Crystal Springs, thirty miles, and make a call for an ambulance, but Hollingsworth waved him away

"Just stay with me a little while." he said. "I'll be OK."

But the thought was terrifying to Jesse — of being in the same room with Hollingsworth, contained, and listening to him talk, forever, all day and through the night, doubtless.

"I have to go," he said, and hurried out the door.

He got on his bike and started slowly for home. His knees were bumping against his belly, such was the quickness of his becoming fat, but the relief of being away from Hollingsworth was so great that he didn't mind.

Part of him wanted to be as he had been, briefly: iron, and fast, racing with the fastest people in the world, it seemed — he couldn't remember anything about them, only the blaze and rip of their speed, the *whish-whish* cutting sound they made, as a pack, tucking and sailing down around corners — but also, he was so tired of that, and it felt good to be away from it, for just a little while.

He could always go back.

His legs were still strong. He could start again any time. The sport of it, the road, would have him back. The other bikers would have him back, they would be happy to see him.

He thought all these things as he trundled fatly up the minor hills, the gradual rises, coasting, relievedly, on the down sides.

Shortly before he got to the gravel turnoff, the little tree-lined road that led to his house, the other bikers passed him, coming out of the west, and they screamed and howled at him, passing, and jabbed their thumbs down at him, as if they were trying to unplug a drain or poke a hole in something; they shrieked, and then they were gone, so quickly.

He did not stop blushing for the rest of the day. He wanted to hide somewhere, he was so ashamed of what he had lost, but there was nowhere to hide, for in a way it was still in him: the memory of it.

He dreamed of going down into the woods, of joining Buzbee and starting over, wrestling alligators; but he only dreamed it — and in the morning, when he woke up, he was still heavy and slow, grounded.

He went into the kitchen, and looked in the refrigerator, and began taking things out. Maybe, he thought, Hollingsworth would up the reward money.

Buzbee enjoyed cooking for the women. It was going to be an early fall, and dry; they got to where they hardly noticed the mosquitoes that were always whining around them — a tiny buzzing — and they had stopped wearing clothes long ago. Buzbee pulled down hickory branches and climbed up in trees, often — and he sat hunkered above the women, looking down, just watching them move around in their lives, naked and happy, talking; more had come down the bayou since the first two, and they were shoring up the old shelter; pulling up palmetto plants from the hummocks and dragging logs across the clearing, fixing the largest of the abandoned cabins into a place that was livable, for all of them.

He liked the way they began to look at him, on about the tenth day of their being there, and he did not feel seventy-seven. He slid down out of the tree, walked across the clearing toward the largest woman, the one he had had his eye on, and took her hand, hugged her, felt her broad fat back, the backs of her legs, which were sweaty, and then her behind, while she giggled.

All that week, as the weather changed, they came drifting in, women from town, sometimes carrying lawn chairs, always wild-eyed and tentative when they saw the alligators and catfish, the people moving around naked in camp, brown as the earth itself — but then they would recognize someone, and would move out into the clearing with wonder, and a disbelief at having escaped. A breeze might be stirring, and dry colored hardwood leaves, ash and hickory, and oak and beech, orange and gold, would tumble down into the clearing, spill around their ankles, and the leaves made empty scraping sounds when the women walked through them, shuffling, looking up at the spinning fish.

At night they would sit around the fire and eat the dripping juiciness of the alligators, roasted — fat, from the tails, sweet, glistening on their hands, their faces, running down to their elbows. They smeared it on their backs, their breasts, to keep the mosquitoes away. Nights smelled of wood smoke. They could see the stars above their trees, above the shadows of their catches.

The women had all screamed and run into the woods, in different directions, the first time Buzbee leaped into the water after an alligator; but now they all gathered close and applauded and chanted an alligator-catching song they had made up that had few vowels, whenever he wrestled them. But that first time they thought he had lost his mind: he had rolled around and around in the thick gray-white slick mud, down by the bank, jabbing the young alligator with his pocketknife again and again, perforating it and muttering savage dog noises, until they could no longer tell which was which, except for the jets of blood that spurted out of the alligator's fat belly—but after he had killed the reptile, and rinsed off in the shallows, and come back across the oxbow, wading in knee-deep water, carrying it in his arms, a four-footer, his largest ever, he was smiling, gap-toothed, having lost two in the fight, but he was also erect, proud, and ready for love. It was the first time they had seen that.

The one he had hugged went into the hut after him.

The other women walked around the alligator carefully, and poked sticks at it, but also glanced toward the hut and listened, for the brief and final end of the small thrashings, the little pleasure, that was going on inside, the confirmation, and presently it came: Buzbee's goatish bleats, and the girl's, too, which made them look at one another with surprise, wonder, interest, and speculation.

"It's those berries he's eatin," said one, whose name was Onessimius. Oney.

"They tastes bad," said Tasha.

"They makes your pee turn black," said Oney.

They looked at her with caution.

Jesse didn't have the money for a car, or even for an old tractor. He bought a used lawn-mower engine instead, for fifteen dollars. He found some old plywood in a dry, abandoned barn. He scrounged some wheels, and stole a fan belt from a car rotting in a field, with bright wildflowers growing out from under the hood and mice in the backseat. He made a go-cart, and put a long plastic antenna with an orange flag, a banner, on the back of it that reached high into the sky, so that any motorists coming would see it.

But there was never any traffic. He sputtered and coughed up the hills, going one, two miles an hour: then coasting down, a slight breeze in his face. He didn't wear his biking helmet, and the breeze felt good.

It took him an hour to get to Hollingsworth's sometimes; he carried a sack lunch with him, apples and potato chips, and ate, happily, as he drove.

He started out going over to Hollingsworth's in the midmorning, and always trying to come back in the early afternoon, so that the bikers would not see him: but it got more and more to where he didn't care, and finally, he just came and went as he pleased, waving happily when he saw them; but they never waved back. Sometimes the one who had replaced him, the trailing one, would spit water from his thermos bottle onto the top of Jesse's head as he rushed past; but they were gone quickly, almost as fast as they had appeared, and soon he was no longer thinking about them. They were gone.

Cottonwoods. Rabbits. Fields. It was still summer, it seemed it would always be summer; the smell of hay was good, and dry. All summer, they cut hay in the fields around him.

He was a slow movement of color going up the hills, with everything else in his world motionless; down in the fields, black Angus grazed, and cattle egrets stood behind them and on their backs. Crows sat in the dead limbs of trees, back in the woods, watching him, watching the cows, waiting for fall.

He would reach Hollingsworth's, and the old man would be waiting, like a child wanting his father back. It was a ritual. Hollingsworth would wave tiredly, hiding in his heart the delight at seeing another person.

Jesse would wave back as he drove up into the gravel drive. He would grunt and pull himself up out of the little go-cart, and go over to the Coke machine.

The long slide of the bottle down the chute; the rattle, and *clunk*.

They'd sit on the porch, and Hollingsworth would begin to talk.

"I saw one of those explode in a man's hand," he said, pointing to the bottle Jesse was drinking. "Shot a sliver of glass as long as a knife up into his forearm, all the way. He didn't feel a thing: he just looked at it, and then walked around, pointing to it, showing everybody. . . ."

Hollingsworth remembered everything that had ever happened to him. He told Jesse everything.

Jesse would stir after the second or third story. He couldn't figure it out; he couldn't stand to be too close to Hollingsworth, to listen to him for more than twenty or thirty minutes — he hated it after that point — but always, he went back; every day.

It was as if he got full, almost to the point of vomiting; but then he got hungry again.

He sat on the porch and drank Cokes, and ate cans and cans of whatever Hollingsworth had on the shelf — yams, mushrooms, pickles, deviled ham — and he knew, as if it were an equation on a blackboard, that his life had gone to hell — he could see it in the size of his belly resting between his soft legs — but he didn't know what to do.

There was a thing that was not in him anymore, and he did not know where to go to find it.

Oney was twenty-two, and had had a bad husband. She still had the stitches in her forehead: he had thrown a chair at her, because she had called him a lard-ass, which he was. The stitches in the center of her head looked like a third eyebrow, with the eye missing, and she hadn't heard about the old days of yellow fever and what it could do to one person, or everyone.

That night, even though she slept in Buzbee's arms, she began to shiver wildly, though the night was still and warm. And then two days later, again, she shivered and shook all night, and then two days later, a third time: it was coming every forty-eight hours, which was how it had done when Buzbee and his father had had it.

Onessimius had been pale to begin with, and was turning, as if with the leaves, yellow, right in front of them: a little brighter yellow each day. All of the women began to eat the berries, slowly at first, and then wolfishly, watching Oney as they ate them.

They had built a little palmetto coop for their remaining chickens, which were laying regularly, and they turned them out, three small white magicians moving through the woods in search of bugs, seed, and berries, and the chickens split up and wandered in different directions, and Buzbee and all the women split up, too, and followed them single file, at a distance, waiting for the chickens to find more berries, but somehow two of the chickens got away from them, escaped, and when they came back to camp, with the one remaining white chicken, a large corn snake was in the rooster's cage and was swallowing him, with only his thrashing feet visible: the snake's mouth stretched hideously wide, eyes wide and unblinking, mouth stretched into a laugh, as if he was enjoying the meal. Buzbee killed the snake, but the rooster died shortly after being pulled back out.

Oney screamed and cried, and shook until she was spitting up more black blood, when they told her they were going to take her back into town, and she took Buzbee's pocketknife and pointed it between her breasts and swore she would kill herself if they tried to make her go back to Luscious—because he would kill her for having left, and in a way worse than spitting up black blood and even parts of her stomach—and so they let her stay, but worried, and fed her their dwindling berry supply, and watched the stars, the sunset, and hoped for a hard and cold winter and an early freeze, but the days stayed warm, though the leaves were changing on schedule, and always, they looked for berries, and began experimenting, too, with the things Buzbee and his father had tried so many years ago: cedar berries, mushrooms, hickory nuts, acorns. They smeared grease from the fish and alligators over every inch of their bodies, and kept a fire going again, at all times, but none of the women would go back to town. And none of them other than Oney had started spitting up blood or shivering yet. Ozzie, Buzbee's first woman, had missed her time.

And Buzbee sat up in the trees and looked down on them often, and stopped eating his berries, unbeknownst to them, so that there would be more. The alligators hung from the trees like dead insurgents, traitors to a way of life. They weren't seeing any more in the bayou, and he wasn't catching nearly as many fish. The fall was coming, and winter beyond that. The animals knew it first. Nothing could prevent its coming, or even slow its approach: nothing they could do would matter. Buzbee felt fairly certain that he had caught enough alligators.

Hollingsworth and Jesse made another approach a week later. Hollingsworth had the lariat, and was wearing cowboy boots and a hat. Jesse was licking a Fudgsicle.

Buzbee, in his tree, spotted them and jumped down.

The women grumbled, but they dropped what they were doing and fled, went deeper, to safety.

"Shit," said Hollingsworth when they got to the camp. "He saw us coming again."

"He runs away," said Jesse, nodding. They could see the muddy slide marks where Buzbee and the women had scrambled out on the other side. The dark wall of trees, a wall.

"I've got an idea," said Hollingsworth.

They knew where Buzbee and the women were getting their firewood: there was a tremendous logjam, with driftwood stacked all along the banks, not far from the camp.

Hollingsworth and Jesse went and got shovels, as well as old mattresses from the dump, and came back and dug pits: huge, deep holes, big enough to bury cars, big enough to hold a school bus.

"I saw it on a Tarzan show," said Hollingsworth. His heart was burning; both of the men were dripping with sweat. It was the softest, richest dirt in the world, good and loose and black and easy to move, but they were out of shape and it took them all day. They sang as they dug, to keep Buzbee and the women at bay, hemmed in, back in the trees.

Buzbee and the women sat up on their branches, swatting at mosquitoes, and listened, and wondered what was going on.

"Row, row, row, your boat!" Jesse shouted as he dug, his big belly wet, like a melon. Mopping his brow; his face streaked, with dirt and mud. He remembered the story about the pioneers who went crazy alone, and dug their own graves — standing at the edge, then, and doing it.

"Oh, say — can — you — see," Hollingsworth brayed, "by the dawn's — earl — lee — light?"

Back in the trees, the women looked at Buzbee for an explanation. They knew it was his son.

"He was born too early," he said weakly. "He has never been right."

"He misses you," said Oney. "That boy wants you to come home."

Buzbee scowled and looked down at his toes, hunkered on the branch, and held on fiercely, as if the tree had started to sway.

"That boy don't know *what* he wants," he said.

When Hollingsworth and Jesse had finished the pits, they spread long branches over them, then scattered leaves and twigs over the branches and left.

"We'll catch the whole tribe of them," Hollingsworth cackled.

Jesse nodded. He was faint, and didn't know if he could make it all the way back out or not. He wondered vaguely what Buzbee and the women would be having for supper.

The mosquitoes were vicious; the sun was going down. Owls were beginning to call.

"Come on," said Hollingsworth. "We've got to get out of here."

Jesse wanted to stay. But he felt Hollingsworth pull on his arm; he let himself be led away.

Back in the woods, up in the tree, Oney began to shiver, and closed her eyes, lost consciousness, and fell. Buzbee leaped down and gathered her up, held her tightly, and tried to warm her with his body.

"They gone," said a woman named Vesuvious. The singing had gone away when it got dark, as had the ominous sound of digging.

There was no moon, and it was hard, even though they were familiar with it, to find their way back to camp.

They built fires around Oney, and two days later she was better. But they knew it would come again.

"Look at what that fool boy of yours has done," Tasha said the next day. She had gone to get more wood. A deer had fallen into one of the pits and was leaping about, uninjured, trying to get free.

Buzbee said his favorite curse word, a new one that Oney had told him, "Fuckarama," and they tried to rope the deer, but it was too wild: it would not let them get near.

"We could stone it," Tasha said, but not with much certainty; and they all knew they could not harm the deer, trapped as it was, so helpless.

They felt bad about it, and sat and tried to think of ways to get it out of the pit, but without shovels they were stumped.

They saw Oney's husband one horrible evening, moving through the woods, perilously close to their camp, moving through the gray trees at dusk, stalking their woods with a shotgun, as if squirrel hunting.

They hid in their huts and watched, hoping he would not look down the hill and see their camp, not see the alligators hanging.

"Come on, baby," said Tasha, "find that pit." He was moving in that direction.

They watched, petrified. Oney was whimpering. His dark, slow shape moved cautiously about, but the light was going fast: that darkness of purple, all light being drawn away. He faded; he disappeared; it was dark. Then, into the night, they heard a yell, and a blast, and then the quietest silence they had ever known.

And then, later: owls calling, in the night.

It was a simple matter burying him in the morning. They hadn't thought of letting the deer out that way; they had not thought of filling it in and making it not be there anymore.

"You will get better," they told Oney. She believed them. On the days in which she did not have the fever, she believed them. There was still, though, the memory of it.

It was escapable. Some people lived through it and survived. It didn't get everyone. They didn't all just lie down and die, those who got it.

She loved old Buzbee, on her good days. She laughed, and slept with him, rolled with him, and put into the back of her mind what had happened before, and what would be happening again.

Her teeth, when she was laughing, pressing against him, clutching him, shutting her eyes. She would fight to keep it in the back of her mind, and to keep it behind her.

Jesse rode out to Hollingsworth's in the go-cart. He took a back road, a different route. The air was cooler, it seemed that summer could be ending, after all, and he felt like just getting out and seeing the country again. It was a road he had always liked to ride on, with or without the pack, back when he had been racing, and he had forgotten how fresh it had been, how it had tasted, just to look at it. He drove through a tunnel of trees; a pasture, on the other side of the trees, a stretch of pastel green, a smear of green, with charcoal cattle standing in it, and white egrets at their sides, pressed an image into the sides of his slow-moving vision. It was almost cold down in the creek bottom, going through the shade, so slowly.

He smiled and gave a small whoop, and waved a fist in the air. The light on the other side of the trees, coming down onto the field, was the color of gold smoke.

He had a sack of groceries with him, behind the engine, and he reached back and got a sandwich and a canned drink. The go-cart rumbled along, carrying him; threatening to stop on the hill, but struggling on.

* * *

They went to check the traps, the pits, flushing Buzbee's troops back into the swamp, as ever.

"I'd hoped we could have caught them all," said Hollingsworth. His eyes were pale, mad, and he wanted to dig more holes.

"Look," he said. "They buried my mattress." He bent down on the fresh mound and began digging at it with his hands; but he gave up shortly, and looked around blankly, as if forgetting why he had been digging in the first place.

Buzbee and the women were getting angry at being chased so often, so regularly. They sat in the trees and waited. Some of the women said nothing, but hoped, to themselves, that Hollingsworth and Jesse would forget where some of the pits lay, and would stumble in.

Jesse and Hollingsworth sat on Hollingsworth's porch.

"You don't talk much," Hollingsworth said, as if noticing for the first time.

Jesse said nothing. It was getting near the twenty-minute mark. He had had two Cokes and a package of Twinkies. He was thinking about how it had been, when he had been in shape, and riding with the others, the pack: how his old iron bike had been a traitor some days, and his legs had laid down and died, and he had run out of wind — but how he had kept going, anyway, and how eventually — though only for a little while — it had gotten better.

The bikers rode past. They were moving so fast. Hills were nothing to them. They had light bikes, expensive ones, and the climbs were only excuses to use the great strength of their legs. The wind in their faces, and pressing back against their chests, was but a reason and a direction, for a feeling: it was something to rail against, and defeat, or be defeated by — but it was tangible. Compared to some things, the wind was actually tangible.

They shouted encouragement to one another as they jockeyed back and forth, sharing turns, breaking the wind for each other.

* * *

"I'm ready," Hollingsworth told Jesse on his next visit, a few days later.

He was jumping up and down like a child.

"I'm ready, I'm ready," Hollingsworth sang. "Ready for anything."

He had a new plan. All he had been doing was thinking: trying to figure out a way to get something back.

Jesse rode his bike to town, to get the supplies they would need: an extra lariat, and rope for trussing him up with; they figured he would be senile, and wild. Muzzles for the dogs. Jesse rode hard, for a fat man.

The wind was coming up. It was the first week in September. The hay was baled, stood in tall rolls, and the fields looked tame, civilized, smoothed — flattened.

They muzzled the dogs and put heavy leashes on their collars, and started out across the field. Owls were beginning to call again, it was the falling of dusk, and Jesse and Hollingsworth carried with them a kerosene lantern and some food and water.

When they had crossed the field — half running, half being dragged, by the big dogs' eagerness — and came to the edge of the woods, and started down into them, toward the swamp, they were halted by the mosquitoes, which rose up in a noisy dark cloud and fell upon them like soft fingers. The dogs turned back, whining in their muzzles, yelping, instinct warning them of the danger of these particular mosquitoes, and they kept backing away, back into the field, and would not go down into the swamp.

So Hollingsworth and Jesse camped back in the wind of the pasture, in the cool grass, and waited for daylight.

They could smell the smoke from Buzbee's camp, but could see nothing, the woods were so dark. There was a quarter-moon, and it came up so close to them, over the trees, that they could see the craters. Hollingsworth talked.

He talked about the space program. He asked Jesse if this wasn't better than riding his old bike. They shared a can of Vienna sausage. Hollingsworth talked all night. Chuck-will's-widows called, and bullbats thumped around in the grass, not far from their small fire: flinging themselves into the grass and flopping around as if mourning, rising again, flying past, and then twisting and slamming hard and awkwardly down, without a cry, as if pulled there by a sudden force, hidden — as if their time was up. All around them, the bullbats flew like this, twisting and then diving into the ground, until it seemed to Jesse that without a doubt they were trying to send a message: Go back, go back.

And he imagined, as he tried not to listen to Hollingsworth babblings, that the bikers he had ridden with, the Frenchmen, were asleep, or making love to soft women, or eating ice-cream cones.

A light drizzle woke Hollingsworth and Jesse and the dogs in the morning, and they stood up and stretched, and then moved on the camp. Crickets were chirping quietly in the soft rain, and the field was steaming. There wasn't any more smoke from the fire. The dogs had been smelling Buzbee and his camp all night, and were nearly crazed: their chests swelled and strained like barrels of apples, like hearts of anger, and they jumped and twisted and tugged against their leashes, pulling Hollingsworth and Jesse behind them in a stumbling run through the wet grasses.

Froth came from their muzzles, their rubbery lips. Their eyes were wild. They were too hard to hold. They pulled free of their leashes, and raced, silently, like the fastest thing in the world, accelerating across the field and into the woods, straight for the camp, the straightest thing that ever was.

Jesse bought a bike with the reward money: a French bicycle, a racer, with tires that were thinner than a person's finger held sideways. It could fly. It was light blue, like an old man's eyes.

Hollingsworth had chained Buzbee to the porch: had padlocked the clasp around his ankle, with thirty feet of chain. It disgusted Jesse, but even more disgusted was he by his own part in the capture, and by the size of his stomach, his loss of muscularity.

Date _Feb 10,_ 19_98_

TO

TERMS

IN ACCOUNT WITH

		Best of the South			
		by			
		Anne Tyler			15. 95
			Tax		92
					16. 87

He began to ride again, not with the pack but by himself.

He got fast again, as he had thought he could. He got faster than he had been before, faster than he had ever imagined, and bought a stopwatch and raced against himself, timing himself, riding up and down the same roads over and over again.

Sometimes, riding, he would look up and see Buzbee out on the porch, standing, with Hollingsworth sitting behind him, talking. Hollingsworth would wave, wildly.

One night, when Jesse got in from his ride, the wind had shifted out of the warm west and was from the north, and serious, and in it, after Jesse had bathed and gotten in bed, was the thing, not for the first time, but the most insistent that year, that made Jesse get back out of bed, where he was reading, and go outside and sit on the steps beneath his porch light. He tried to read.

Moths fell down off the porch light's bulb, brushed his shoulders, landed on the pages of his book, spun, and flew off, leaving traces of magic. And the wind began to stir harder. Stars were all above him, and they glittered and flashed in the wind. They seemed to be challenging him: daring him to see what was true.

Two miles away, up on the hill, back in the trees, the A.M.E. church was singing. He couldn't see their lights, but for the first time that year he could hear them singing, the way he could in the winter, when there were no leaves on the trees and when the air was colder, more brittle, and sounds carried. He could never hear the words, just the sad moaning that sometimes, finally, fell away into pleasure.

He stood up on the porch and walked out into the yard, the cool grass, and tried some sit-ups. When he was through, he lay back, sweating slightly, breathing harder, and he watched the stars, but they weren't as bright, it seemed, and he felt as if he had somehow failed them, had not done the thing expected or, rather, the thing demanded.

When he woke up in the morning, turned on his side in the yard, sleeping, lying out in the grass like an animal, the breeze was still blowing and the light of the day was gold, coming out of the pines on the east edge of his field.

He sat up, stiffly, and for a moment forgot who he was, what he did, where he was — it was the breeze moving across him, so much cooler suddenly — and then he remembered, it was so simple, that he was supposed to ride.

It was early November. There was a heaviness to all movements, to all sights. It was impossible to look at the sky, at the trees, at the cattle in the fields even, and not know that it was November. The clasp around Buzbee's ankle was cold; his legs were getting stronger from pulling the chain around with him. He stood out on the porch, and the air, when he breathed deeply, went all the way down into his chest: he felt good. He felt like wrestling an alligator.

He had knocked Hollingsworth to the ground, tried to get him to tell him where the key was. But Hollingsworth, giggling, with his arm twisted behind his back — the older man riding him, breathing hard but steadily, pushing his son's face into the floor — had told Buzbee that he had thrown the key away. And Buzbee, knowing his son, his poisoned loneliness, knew that it was so.

The chain was too big to break or smash.

Sometimes Buzbee cried, looking at it. He felt as if he could not breathe; it was as if he were being smothered. It was like a thing was about to come to a stop.

He watched the field all the time. Jesse raced by, out on the road, checking his watch, looking at it, holding it in one hand, pedaling hard; flying, it seemed.

Buzbee heard Hollingsworth moving behind him; coming out to gab. It was like being in a cell.

Buzbee could see the trees, the watery blur of them, on the other side of the field.

"Pop," said Hollingsworth, ready with a story.

Pop, my ass, thought Buzbee bitterly. He wanted to strangle his own son.

He had so wanted to make a getaway—to have an escape, clean and free.

He looked out at the field, remembering what it had been like with the women, and the alligators, and he thought how he would be breaking free again, shortly, for good.

This time, he knew, he would get completely away.

The blue line of trees, where he had been with the women, wavered and flowed, in watercolor blotches, and there was a dizziness high in his forehead. He closed his eyes and listened to his mad son babble, and he prepared, and made his plans.

When he opened his eyes, the road was empty in front of him. Jesse was gone—a streak, a flash—already gone.

It was as if he had never even been there.

Buzbee narrowed his eyes and gripped the porch railing, squinted at the trees, scowled, and plotted, and tried to figure another way out.

Madison Smartt Bell

CUSTOMS OF THE COUNTRY

Madison Smartt Bell, born and raised in Tennessee, is one of the most prolific writers of his generation, having published eleven books of fiction in the last twelve years. In this story of a mother's remorse, his technical brilliance is reflected in the emotional tension of the first-person narration. And, for sheer reader satisfaction, it would be hard to beat this story's climax. Bell, who won the Lillian Smith Award for Southern fiction in 1989, is writer-in-residence at Goucher College in Baltimore, Maryland. His most recently published book is the 1995 novel, All Souls' Rising.

I don't remember much about that place anymore. It was nothing but somewhere I came to put in some pretty bad time, though that was not what I had planned on when I went there. I had it in mind to improve things, but I don't think you could fairly claim that's what I did. So that's one reason I might just as soon forget about it. And I didn't stay there all that long, not more than about nine months or so, about the same time, come to think, that the child I was there to try to get back had lived inside my body.

It was a cluster-housing thing a little ways north out of town from Roanoke, on a two-lane road that crossed the railroad cut and went about a mile further up through the woods. The buildings looked something like a motel, a little raw still, though they weren't new. My apartment was no more than a place that would barely look all right and yet cost me little enough so I had something left over to give the lawyer. There was fresh paint on the walls and the trim in the kitchen and bathroom was in fair shape.

And it was real quiet mostly, except that the man next door used to beat up his wife a couple of times a week. The place was sound-proof enough I couldn't usually hear talk but I could hear yelling plain as day and when he got going good he would slam her bang into our common wall. If she hit in just the right spot it would send my pots and pans flying off the pegboard where I'd hung them above the stove.

Not that it mattered to me that the pots fell down, except for the noise and the time it took to pick them up again. Living alone like I was, I didn't have the heart to do much cooking and if I did fix myself something I mostly used an old iron skillet that hung there on the same wall. All the others I only had out for show. The whole apartment was done about the same way, made into something I kept spotless and didn't much care to use. I wore my hands out scrubbing everything clean and then saw to it that it stayed that way. I sewed slipcovers for that threadbare batch of Goodwill furniture I'd put in the place, and I hung curtains and found some sunshiny posters to tack on the walls, and I never cared a damn about any of it. It was an act, and I wasn't putting it on for me or for Davey, but for all the other people I expected to come to see it and judge it. And however good I could get it looking, it never felt quite right.

I felt even less at home there than I did at my job, which was waitressing three snake-bends of the counter at the Truckstops of America out at the I-81 interchange. The supervisor was a man named Tim that used to know my husband Patrick from before we had the trouble. He was nice about letting me take my phone calls there and giving me time off to see the lawyer, and in most other ways he was a decent man to work for, except that now and then he would have a tantrum over something or other and try to scream the walls down. Still, it never went beyond yelling, and he always acted sorry once he got through. The other waitress on my shift was an older lady named Prissy, and I liked her all right in spite of the name.

We were both on a swing shift that rolled over every ten days, which was the main thing I didn't like about that job. The six-to-two I hated the worst because it would have me getting back to my apartment building around three in the morning, not the time it looked its best. It was the kind of place where at that time of night I could expect to find the deputies out there looking for somebody, or else some other kind of trouble. I never got to know the neighbors any too well, but a lot of them were pretty sorry—small-time criminals, dope-dealers, and thieves, none of them much good at whatever it was they did. There was one check forger that I knew of, and a man who would break into the other apartments looking for whiskey. One thing and another, along that line.

The man next door, the one that beat up his wife, didn't do crimes or work either that I ever heard. He just seemed to lay around the place, maybe drawing some kind of welfare. There wasn't a whole lot of him, he was just a stringy little man, hair and mustache a dishwater brown, cheap green tattoos running up his arms. Maybe he was stronger than he looked, but I did wonder how come his wife would take it from him, since she was about a head taller and must have outweighed him an easy ten pounds. I might have thought she was whipping on him—stranger things have been known to go on—but she was the one that seemed like she might break out crying if you looked at her crooked. She was a big fine-looking girl with a lovely shape, and long brown hair real smooth and straight and shiny. I guess she was too hammered down most of the time to pay much attention to how she dressed, but still she had pretty brown eyes, big and long-lashed and soft sort of like a cow's eyes, except I never saw a cow that looked that miserable.

At first I thought maybe I might make a friend of her, she was about the only one around there I felt like I might want to. Our paths crossed pretty frequent, either around the apartment building or in the Kwik Sack back toward town, where I'd find her running the register some days. But she was shy of me, shy of anybody, I suppose. She would flinch if you did so much as say hello.

So after a while I quit trying. She'd get hers about twice a week, maybe other times I wasn't around to hear it happen. It's a wonder all the things you can learn to ignore, and after a month or so I was that accustomed I barely noticed when they would start in. I would just wait till I thought they were good and through, and then get up and hang those pans back on the wall where they were supposed to go. And all the while I would just be thinking about some other thing, like what might be going on with my Davey.

The place where he had been fostered out was not all that far away, just about ten or twelve miles up the road, out there in the farm country. The people were named Baker. I never got to first names with them, just called them Mr. and Mrs. They were older than me, both just into their forties, and they didn't have any children of their own. The place was only a small farm but Mr. Baker grew tobacco on the most of it and I'm told he made it a paying thing. Mrs. Baker kept a milk cow or two and she grew a garden and canned in the old-time way. Thrifty people. They were real sweet to Davey and he seemed to like being with them pretty well. He had been staying there almost the whole two years, which was lucky too, since most children usually got moved around a whole lot more than that.

And that was the trouble, like the lawyer explained to me, it was just too good. Davey was doing too well out there. He'd made out better in the first grade than anybody would have thought. So nobody really felt like he needed to be moved. The worst of it was the Bakers had got to like him well enough they were saying they wanted to adopt him if they could. Well, it would have been hard enough for me without that coming into it.

Even though he was so close, I didn't go out to see Davey near as much as I would have liked to. The lawyer kept telling me it wasn't a good idea to look like I was pressing too hard. Better take it easy till all the evaluations came in and we had our court date and all. Still, I would call and go on out there maybe a little more than once a month, most usually on the weekends, since that seemed to suit the Bakers better. They never acted like it was

any trouble, and they were always pleasant to me, or polite might
be a better word yet. The way it sometimes seemed they didn't
trust me did bother me a little. I would have liked to take him
out to the movies a time or two, but I could see plain enough the
Bakers wouldn't have been easy about me having him off their
place.

But I can't remember us having a bad time, any of those times I
went. He was always happy to see me, though he'd be quiet when
we were in the house, with Mrs. Baker hovering. So I would get
us outside quick as ever I could, and once we were out, we would
just play like both of us were children. There was an open pasture,
a creek with a patch of woods, a hay barn where we would play
hide-and-go-seek. I don't know what all else we did, silly things
mostly. That was how I could get near him the easiest, he didn't
get a whole lot of playing in, way out there. The Bakers weren't
what you would call playful and there weren't any other children
living near. So that was the thing I could give him that was all mine
to give. When the weather was good we would stay outside
together most all the day and he would just wear me out. But over
the winter those visits seemed to get shorter and shorter, like the
days.

Davey called me Momma still, but I suppose he had come to
think your mother was something more like a big sister or just
some kind of a friend. Mrs. Baker was the one doing for him all
the time. I don't know just what he remembered from before, or
if he remembered any of the bad part. He would always mind me
but he never acted scared around me, and if anybody says he did
they lie. But I never really did get to know what he had going on
in the back of his mind about the past. At first I worried the Bakers might have been talking against me, but after I had seen a little more of them I knew they wouldn't have done anything like
that, wouldn't have thought it right. So I expect whatever Davey
knew about that other time he remembered on his own. He never
mentioned Patrick hardly and I think he really had forgotten about
him. Thinking back I guess he never saw that much of Patrick even

when we were all living together. But Davey had Patrick's mark all over him, the same eyes and the same red hair.

Patrick had thick wavy hair the shade of an Irish setter's, and a big rolling mustache the same color. Maybe that was his best feature, but he was a good-looking man altogether, still is I suppose, though the prison haircut don't suit him. If he ever had much of a thought in his head I suspect he had knocked it clean out with dope, yet he was always fun to be around. I wasn't but seventeen when I married him and I didn't have any better sense myself. Right to the end I never thought anything much was the matter, all his vices looked so small to me. He was good-tempered almost all the time, and good with Davey when he did notice him. Never once did he raise his hand to either one of us. In little ways he was unreliable, late, not showing up at all, gone out of the house for days sometimes. Hindsight shows me he ran with other women, but I managed not to know anything about that at the time. He had not quite finished high school and the best job he could hold was being an orderly down at the hospital, but he made a good deal of extra money stealing pills out of there and selling them on the street.

That was something else I didn't allow myself to think on much back then. Patrick never told me a lot about it anyhow, always acted real mysterious about whatever he was up to in that line. He would disappear on one of his trips and come back with a whole mess of money, and I would spend up my share and be glad I had it too. I never thought much about where it was coming from, the money or the pills either one. He used to keep all manner of pills around the house, Valium and ludes and a lot of different kinds of speed, and we both took what we felt like whenever we felt in the mood. But what Patrick made the most on was Dilaudid. I used to take it without ever knowing what it really was, but once everything fell in on us I found out it was a bad thing, bad as heroin they said, and not much different, and it was what they gave Patrick most of his time for.

I truly was surprised to find out that it was the strongest dope we had, because I never really even felt like it made you all that high. You would just take one and kick back on a long slow stroke and whatever trouble you might have, it would not be able to find you. It came on like nothing but it was the hardest habit to lose, and I was a long time shaking it. I might be thinking about it yet if I would let myself, and there were times, all through the winter I spent in that apartment, I'd catch myself remembering the feeling.

You couldn't call it a real bad winter, there wasn't much snow or anything, but I was cold just about all the time, except when I was at work. All I had in the apartment was some electric baseboard heaters, and they cost too much for me to leave them running very long at a stretch. I'd keep it just warm enough so I couldn't see my breath, and spend my time in a hot bathtub or under a big pile of blankets on the bed. Or else I would just be cold.

There was some kind of strange quietness about that place all during the cold weather. If the phone rang it would make me jump. Didn't seem like there was any TV or radio ever playing next door. The only sound coming out of there was Susan getting beat up once in a while. That was her name, a sweet name, I think. I found it out from hearing him say it, which he used to do almost every time before he started on her. "Susan," he'd call out, loud enough I could hear him through the wall. He'd do it a time or two, he might have been calling her to him, and I suppose she went. After that would come a bad silence that reminded you of a snake being somewhere around. Then a few minutes' worth of hitting sounds and then the big slam as she hit the wall, and the clatter of my pots falling on the floor. He'd throw her at the wall maybe once or twice, usually when he was about to get through. By the time the pots had quit spinning on the floor it would be real quiet over there again, and the next time I saw Susan she'd be walking in that ginger way people have when they're hiding a hurt, and if I said hello to her she'd give a little jump and look away.

After a while I quit paying it much mind, it didn't feel any dif-

ferent to me than hearing the news on the radio. All their carrying on was not any more to me than a bump in the rut I had
worked myself into, going back and forth from the job, cleaning
that apartment till it hurt, calling up the lawyer about once a week
to find out what was happening, which never was much. He was
forever trying to get our case before some particular doctor or
social worker or judge who'd be more apt to help us than another,
so he said. I would call him up from the TOA, all eager to hear
what news he had and every time it was another delay. In the
beginning I used to talk it all over with Tim or Prissy after I hung
up, but after a while I got out of the mood to discuss it. I kept
ahead making those calls but every one of them just wore out my
hope a little more, like a drip of water wearing down a stone. And
little by little I got in the habit of thinking that nothing really was
going to change.

Somehow or other that winter passed by, with me going from
one phone call to the next, going out to wait on that TOA counter,
coming home to shiver and hold hands with myself and lie awake
all through the night, or the day, depending what shift I was on.
It was springtime, well into warm weather, before anything really
happened at all. That was when the lawyer called *me*, for a change,
and told me he had some people lined up to see me at last.

Well, I was all ready for them to come visit, come see how I'd
fixed up my house and all the rest of my business to get set for having Davey back with me again. But as it turned out, nobody
seemed to feel like they were called on to make that trip. "I don't
think that will be necessary" was what one of them said, I don't
recall which. They both talked about the same, in voices that
sounded like filling out forms.

So all I had to do was drive downtown a couple of times and see
them in their offices. That child psychologist was the first and I
doubt he kept me more than half an hour. I couldn't tell the point
of most of the questions he asked. My second trip I saw the social
worker, who turned out to be a black lady once I got down there,
though I never could have told it over the phone. Her voice

sounded like it was coming out of the TV. She looked me in the eye while she was asking her questions, but I couldn't tell a thing about what she thought. It wasn't till I was back in the apartment that I understood she must have already had her mind made up.

That came to me in a sort of a flash, while I was standing in the kitchen washing out a cup. Soon as I walked back in the door I saw my coffee mug left over from breakfast, and I kicked myself for letting it sit out. I was giving it a hard scrub with a scouring pad when I realized it didn't matter anymore. I might just as well have dropped it on the floor and got what kick I could out of watching it smash, because it wasn't going to make any difference to anybody now. But all the same I rinsed it and set it in the drainer, careful as if it was an eggshell. Then I stepped backward out of the kitchen and took a long look around that cold shabby place and thought it might be for the best that nobody was coming. How could I have expected it to fool anybody else when it wasn't even good enough to fool me? A lonesomeness came over me, I felt like I was floating all alone in the middle of cold air, and then I began to remember some things I would just as soon as have not.

No, I never did like to think about this part, but I have had to think about it time and again, with never a break for a long, long time, because I needed to get to understand it at least well enough to believe it never would ever happen anymore. And I had come to believe that, in the end. If I hadn't, I never would have come back at all. I had found a way to trust myself again, though it took me a full two years to do it, and though of course it still didn't mean that anybody else would trust me.

What had happened was that Patrick went off on one of his mystery trips and stayed gone a deal longer than usual. Two nights away, I was used to that, but on the third I did start to wonder. He normally would have called at least, if he was going to be gone that long of a stretch. But I didn't hear a peep until about halfway through the fourth day. And it wasn't Patrick himself that called, but one of those public-assistance lawyers from downtown.

Seemed like the night before Patrick had got himself stopped on the interstate loop down there. The troopers said he was driving like a blind man, and he was so messed up on whiskey and ludes I suppose he must have been pretty near blind at that. Well, maybe he would have just lost his license or something like that, only that the backseat of the car was loaded up with all he had lately stole out of the hospital.

So it was bad. It was so bad my mind just could not contain it, and every hour it seemed to be getting worse. I spent the next couple of days running back and forth between the jail and that lawyer, and I had to haul Davey along with me wherever I went. He was too little for school and I couldn't find anybody to take him right then, though all that running around made him awful cranky. Patrick was just grim, he would barely speak. He already knew pretty well for sure that he'd be going to prison. The lawyer had told him there wasn't no use in getting a bondsman, he might just as well stay on in there and start pulling his time. I don't know how much he really saved himself that way, though, since what they ended up giving him was twenty-five years.

That was when all my troubles found me, quick. Two days after Patrick got arrested, I came down real sick with something. I thought at first it was a bad cold or the flu. My nose kept running and I felt so wore out I couldn't hardly get up off the bed and yet at the same time I felt real restless, like all my nerves had been scraped bare. Well, I didn't really connect it up to the fact that I'd popped the last pill in the house a couple of days before. What was really the matter was me coming off that Dilaudid, but I didn't have any notion of that at the time.

I was laying there in bed not able to get up and about ready to jump right out of my skin at the same time when Davey got the drawer underneath the stove open. Of course he was getting restless himself with all that had been going on, and me not able to pay him much mind. All our pots and pans were down in that drawer then, and he began to take them out one at a time and throw them on the floor. It made a hell of a racket, and the shape I was in, I felt like he must be doing it on purpose to devil me. I

called out to him and asked him to quit. Nice at first: "You stop
that, now, Davey, Momma don't feel good." But he kept right
ahead. All he wanted was to have my attention, I know, but my
mind wasn't working right just then. I knew I should get up and
just go lead him away from there, but I couldn't seem to get myself
to move. I had a picture of myself doing the right thing, but I just
wasn't doing it. I was still lying there calling to him to quit and he
was still banging those pots around and before long I was screaming at him outright, and starting to cry at the same time. But he
never stopped a minute. I guess I had scared him some already and
he was just locked into doing it, or maybe he wanted to drown me
out. Every time he flung a pot it felt like I was getting shot at. And
the next thing I knew I got myself in the kitchen someway and I
was snatching him up off the floor.

To this day I don't remember doing it, though I have tried and
tried. I thought if I could call it back then maybe I could root it
out of myself and be shed of it for good and all. But all I ever knew
was one minute I was grabbing ahold of him and the next he was
laying on the far side of the room with his right leg folded up
funny where it was broke, not even crying, just looking surprised.
And I knew that it had to be me that threw him over there because
as sure as hell is real there was nobody else around that could have
done it.

I drove him to the hospital myself. I laid him straight on the
front seat beside me and drove with one hand all the way so I
could hold on to him with the other. He was real quiet and real
brave the whole time, never cried the least bit, just kept a tight
hold on my hand with his. Well, after a while, we got there and
they ran him off somewhere to get his leg set and pretty soon the
doctor came back out and asked me how it had happened.

It was the same hospital where Patrick had worked and I even
knew that doctor a little bit. Not that being connected to Patrick
would have done me a whole lot of good around there at that
time. Still, I have often thought since then that things might have
come out better for me and Davey both if I just could have lied to

that man, but I was not up to telling a lie that anybody would be apt to believe. All I could do was start to scream and jabber like a crazy person, and it ended up I stayed in that hospital quite a few days myself. They took me for a junkie and I guess I really was one too, though I hadn't known it till that very day. And I never saw Davey again for a whole two years, not till the first time they let me go out to the Bakers'.

Sometimes you don't get but one mistake, if the one you pick is bad enough. Do as much as step in the road one time without looking, and your life could be over with then and there. But during those two years I taught myself to believe that this mistake of mine could be wiped out, that if I struggled hard enough with myself and the world I could make it like it never had been.

Three weeks went by after I went to see that social worker, and I didn't have any idea what was happening, or if anything was. Didn't call anybody, I expect I was afraid to. Then one day the phone rang for me out there at the TOA. It was the lawyer and I could tell right off from the sound of his voice I wasn't going to care for his news. Well, he told me all the evaluations had come in now, sure enough, and they weren't running in our favor. They weren't against *me*, he made sure to say that, it was more like they were *for* the Bakers. And his judgment was it wouldn't pay me anything if we went on to court. It looked like the Bakers would get Davey for good anyhow, and they were likely to be easier about visitation if there wasn't any big tussle. But if I drug them into court, then we would have to start going back over that whole case history—

That was the word he used, *case history*, and it was around about there that I hung up. I went walking stiff-legged back across to the counter and just let myself sort of drop on a stool. Prissy had been covering my station while I was on the phone and she came right over to me then.

"What is it?" she said. I guess she could tell it was something by the look on my face.

"I lost him," I said.

"Oh, hon', you know I'm so sorry," she said. She reached out for my hand but I snatched it back. I know she meant it well but I just was not in the mood to be touched.

"There's no forgiveness," I said. I felt bitter about it. It had been a hard road for me to come as near forgiving myself as I ever could. And Davey forgave me, I really knew that, I could tell it in the way he acted when we were together. And if us two could do it, I didn't feel like it ought to be anybody else's business but ours. Tim walked up then and Prissy whispered something to him, and then he took a step nearer to me.

"I'm sorry," he told me.

"Not like I am," I said. "You don't know the meaning of the word."

"Go ahead and take off the rest of your shift if you feel like it," he said. "I'll wait on these tables myself, need be."

"I don't know it would make any difference," I said.

"Better take it easy on yourself," he said. "No use in taking it so hard. You're just going to have to get used to it."

"Is that a fact?" I said. And I lit myself a cigarette and turned my face away. We had been pretty busy, it was lunchtime, and the people were getting restless seeing all of us standing around there not doing a whole lot about bringing them their food. Somebody called out something to Tim, I didn't hear just what it was, but it set off one of his temper fits.

"Go on and get out of here if that's how you feel," he said. He was getting red in the face and waving his arms around to include everybody there in what he was saying. "Go on and clear out of here, every last one of you, and we don't care if you never come back. There's not one of you couldn't stand to miss a meal anyhow. Take a look at yourselves, you're all fat as hogs. . . ."

It seemed like he might be going to keep it up a good while, and he had already said I could leave, so I hung up my apron and got my purse and I left. It was the first time he ever blew up at the customers that way, it had always been me or Prissy or one of the cooks. I never did find out what came of it all because I never went back to that place again.

I drove home in such a poison mood I barely knew I was driving a car or that there were any others on the road. I was ripe to get killed or kill somebody, and I wouldn't have cared much either way. I kept thinking about what Tim had said about having to get used to it. It came to me that I was used to it already, I really hadn't been all that surprised. That's what I'd been doing all those months, just gradually getting used to losing my child forever.

When I got back to the apartment I just fell in a chair and sat there staring across at the kitchen wall. It was in my mind to pack my traps and leave that place, but I hadn't yet figured out where I could go. I sat there a good while, I guess. The door was ajar from me not paying attention, but it wasn't cold enough out to make any difference. If I turned my head that way I could see a slice of the parking lot. I saw Susan drive up and park and come limping toward the building with an armload of groceries. Because of the angle I couldn't see her go into their apartment but I heard the door open and shut and after that it was quiet as a tomb. I kept on sitting there thinking about how used to everything I had got. There must have been generous numbers of other people too, I thought, who had got themselves accustomed to all kinds of things. Some were used to taking the pain and the rest were used to serving it up. About half of the world was screaming in misery, and it wasn't anything but a habit.

When I started to hear the hitting sounds come toward me through the wall, a smile came on my face like it was cut there with a knife. I'd been expecting it, you see, and the mood I was in I felt satisfied to see what I had expected was going to happen. So I listened a little more carefully than I'd been inclined to do before. It was *hit hit hit* going along together with a groan and a hiss of the wind being knocked out of her. I had to strain pretty hard to hear that breathing part, and I could hear him grunt too, when he got in a good one. There was about three minutes of that with some little breaks, and then a longer pause. When she hit the wall it was the hardest she had yet, I think. It brought down every last one of my pots at one time, including that big iron skillet that was the only one I ever used.

It was the first time they'd managed to knock that skillet down, and I was so impressed that I went over and stood looking down at it like I needed to make sure it was a real thing. I stared at the skillet so long it went out of focus and started looking more like a big black hole in the floor. That's when it dawned on me that this was one thing I didn't really have to keep on being used to.

It took three or four knocks before he came to the door, but that didn't worry me at all. I had faith, I knew he was going to come. I meant to stay right there till he did. When he came, he opened the door wide and stood there with his arms folded and his face all stiff with his secrets. It was fairly dark behind him, they had all the curtains drawn. I had that skillet held out in front of me in both my hands, like maybe I had come over to borrow a little hot grease or something. It was so heavy it kept wanting to dip down toward the floor like a water witch's rod. When I saw he wasn't expecting anything, I twisted the skillet back over my shoulder like baseball players do their bats, and I hit him bang across the face as hard as I knew how. He went down and out at the same time and fetched up on his back clear in the middle of the room.

Then I went in after him, with the skillet cocked and ready in case he made to get up. But he didn't look like there was a whole lot of fight left in him right then. He was awake, at least partly awake, but his nose was just spouting blood and it seemed like I'd knocked out a few of his teeth. I wish I could tell you I was sorry or glad, but I didn't feel much of anything really, just that high lonesome whistle in the blood I used to get when I took all that Dilaudid. Susan was sitting on the floor against the wall, leaning down on her knees and sniveling. Her eyes were red but she didn't have any bruises where they showed. He never did hit her on the face, that was the kind he was. There was a big crack coming down the wall behind her and I remember thinking it probably wouldn't be too much longer before it worked through to my side.

"I'm going to pack and drive over to Norfolk," I told her. I hadn't thought of it before but once it came out my mouth I knew it was what I would do. "You can ride along with me if you want to. With your looks you could make enough money serving drinks to the sailors to buy that Kwik Sack and blow it up."

She didn't say anything, just raised her head up and stared at me kind of bug-eyed. And after a minute I turned around and went out. It didn't take me any time at all to get ready. All I had was a suitcase and a couple of boxes of other stuff. The sheets and blankets I just pulled off the bed and stuffed in the trunk all in one big wad. I didn't care a damn about that furniture, I would have lit it on fire on a dare.

When I was done I stuck my head back into the other apartment. The door was still open like I had left it. What was she doing but kneeling down over that son of a bitch and trying to clean off his face with a washrag. I noticed he was making a funny sound when he breathed, and his nose was still bleeding pretty quick, so I thought maybe I had broke it. Well, I can't say that worried me much.

"Come on now if you're coming, girl," I said. She looked up at me, not telling me one word, just giving me a stare out of those big cow eyes of hers like I was the one had been beating on her that whole winter through. And I saw then that they were both of them stuck in their groove and that she would not be the one to step out of it. So I pulled back out of the doorway and went on down the steps to my car.

I was speeding on the road to Norfolk, doing seventy, seventy-five. I'd have liked to gone faster if the car had been up to it. I can't say I felt sorry for busting that guy, though I didn't enjoy the thought of it either. I just didn't know what difference it had made, and chances were it had made none at all. Kind of a funny thing, when you thought about it that way. It was the second time in my life I'd hurt somebody bad, and the other time I hadn't meant to do it at all. This time I'd known what I was doing for sure, but I still didn't know what I'd done.

Frank Manley

THE RAIN OF TERROR

This story corroborates for all time the reason so many Southern writers credit their gift for fiction to the South's rich tradition of oral storytelling. Frank Manley uses the telling of one chilling story to bring the reader another that's even more chilling. Inside a mobile home, a husband and wife join in an eerie duet to create the portrait of a weirdly and profoundly symbiotic marriage. A Renaissance scholar, Frank Manley has published several books in his field as well as a collection of stories entitled Within the Ribbons. *He lives in his hometown, Atlanta, Georgia, and teaches creative writing and Renaissance literature at Emory University.*

M y name is Oletta Crews."
It sounded like a public announcement.

"This is James Terry Crews, my husband." She indicated the old man on the sofa beside her. He was dressed in khaki trousers and six-inch work boots. The woman had on a print dress, a bold floral pattern like slashes. She wore no shoes.

James Terry Crews gestured silently, acknowledging himself.

"Don't act like an idiot," Oletta Crews said, and the man dropped his hand.

"Just sit there." She turned away from him.

"This is James Terry Crews, my husband." She spoke in a powerful voice, lifted like a singer's from her diaphragm. "He's retired. We're both retired," she added significantly. "Him from work and me from housework. I got a bad heart, and I'm stout besides. You can see that. Doctor says I'm hundreds of pounds overweight, shortening my life with every bite of food I take. But what if I didn't. You think that'd help?"

She leaned forward and spoke confidentially. "There's more dies of hunger than does of the other."

She leaned back and gestured toward her husband again. "He helps me," she said. "He does what he needs to."

James Terry Crews sat beside her and stared straight ahead. He looked afraid.

"Listen to me," Oletta Crews said.

James Terry Crews started to get up, but she held out a hand and restrained him.

"Sit there," she ordered.

"Listen," she said. "I live here alone all by myself, a poor old woman, except for him. He lives here, too. Both together."

There were one or two aluminum windows, an aluminum door, a dinette set, strings of laundry overhead, a scattering of shoes and other debris on the floor, aluminum cans, some in plastic sacks, some loose, piled in the corner. The feeling was that of a cave or a nest—the secret bestial place.

"This is a trailer, you notice that?"

James Terry Crews corrected her. "Mobile home."

"Same damn thing." She was suddenly angry. "I told you that. Pay attention."

James Terry Crews ignored her. "Trailer's something you trail after you," he explained. "That's what it means, trailer. You hitch it on the back of a car and hit the trail."

"And mobile home's mobile," Oletta Crews shouted. "That means it moves."

It seemed like an argument they had had before, the lines already memorized, the positions taken not only well known but entrenched and fortified.

"Tell them about the rain of terror."

"The rain of terror," Oletta Crews said, repeating the words, savoring them. She turned to James Terry Crews. "They don't want to hear about mobile homes. They want to hear about the rain of terror." She bugged her eyes as she said *the rain of terror*. The effect was not comic. Her eyes were filled with something other than fear.

"It was at night."

"Two nights ago." James Terry Crews sounded incredulous.

"It was two nights ago," Oletta Crews said. "And it was dark. James Terry was already home soaking wet from the weeds where he'd been and changed his clothes already to dry them. He was picking aluminum cans. I'm too stout to get out and help or else I'd be there driving the truck, but I can't even drive no more. It's bad on my heart, and the pedals are too close anyway. They're all underfoot. It's hell to be old." She leaned forward. "If I was you, I'd die before I got there." She laughed silently, baring her gums.

"I used to be a house painter," James Terry Crews announced suddenly. "Twenty-eight years and every day sober on the job."

"That don't matter," Oletta Crews shouted. "They don't want to hear about that. You're retired. He sells aluminum cans," she explained. "That's what he does now. They got a yard in town buys them. Beer cans and such as that."

"I didn't always do it," James Terry Crews said. "I used to paint with the best of them."

"That was then. This is now. I'm telling this," Oletta Crews said, picking up where she had left off. "He came in sopping wet from the rain of terror where he been out in the weeds all day looking for beer cans, and I told him what I saw on TV so he don't fall too far behind. And he was changing his socks. I can close my eyes and still see him sitting right there." She pointed across the room at an overstuffed chair that matched the sofa. The arms were shiny and greasy with wear. The seat was piled high with clothes, the upper layers of which had toppled over onto the floor. "Sitting in that chair right there changing his socks, when I heard this knocking at the door."

"What did you think?"

"I thought, Who's that?"

"Me, too," James Terry Crews said. "I thought, Who's that?"

"I thought, Who's that knocking on the door in the dark? I knew it wasn't nobody I knew. His children are gone, and I don't have none, and all my kinfolks are dead before me."

"Tell them about the news."

"I don't generally watch the news if I can help it," Oletta Crews said. "But this night was special. The good Lord led me to it this night. It's like I almost heard this voice said, 'Don't touch the TV. I got something on the news.' I was too tired to get up, and it said, 'Don't do it then. I got something better for you to do than get up and change the channel. I got something to show you right here on this one you're watching.' It's like I almost heard this voice beside the still waters, leading me on in the valley of the shadow of death where I fear no evil for thou art with me. Thy rod and staff they comfort me."

"And you were afraid."

"Of course I was afraid after hearing what I heard and knowing it was some kind of message delivered on TV special for me. Of course I was afraid. Who wouldn't be? I knew he'd protect me like he done. That's why I'm alive and the other one's dead because I could walk through the valley of the shadow of death and fear no evil. So the answer is no. No, I wasn't afraid. But I *was* interested. When I heard how he escaped from the work camp and killed two men, and it wasn't more than five miles down the road and was coming this way, I wasn't afraid, but I *was* interested."

"She heard the knock," James Terry Crews explained.

"I heard the knock and wondered, Who is it? But I already knew. I said, 'It's him.' "

"And I said, 'Who?' "

"Let me tell it," Oletta Crews shouted. "You weren't even there when it happened. I'm telling it. Listen," she said. "This is how it happened. I heard the knock, and I said, 'It's him,' and James Terry looked up from his sock and said, 'Who you mean?' and I said, 'The one on TV when you wasn't here escaped from the work camp and killed two men. It's him at the door,' and he put on his sock," indicating her husband, "and said, 'What you want to do?' And I said, 'Go get it. He might have some money hid.' "

"And I said, 'Money? What you mean money?' "

"Where he hid it after he stole it," Oletta Crews said. "I thought he might have some, and I said, 'Let him in. He might have some money hid.' And James Terry went to the door, one shoe on and one in his hand, and it was him. I was sitting right here where I always sit on this side of the sofa, and I saw him standing in the door soaking wet where it was raining outside in the dark as far as the eye could see. Looked like silver knives. And he said, 'Can I come in? I'm awful wet.' And I yelled, 'I can see you are, honey. Let him in, James Terry. Let him in to get dry.' And he came in, and I said, 'Get him a towel.' And James Terry got him a towel and sat down and put on his shoe. And I said to him, 'I know who you are.' "

"She knew who he was."

"I told him I saw his picture on TV, and I knew who he was, thanks to God, and what he was there for."

"What was that?' " James Terry Crews asked.

"You were there. Don't ask things you already know. He was there to rob us. He came there to rob us."

"Your life was in danger."

"My life was in danger. As soon as I saw him, I knew I might not live."

She paused, staring at something in the distance.

"Go on."

"I told him his name. I said, 'You're Q. B. Farris, escaped from the work camp.' And he said, 'Yes, ma'am. I can't fool you, I can see that.' And I said, 'That's right. There's many a one better than you tried all my life, and they didn't do it so why should you?' And he laughed. He was good-hearted. I can say that for him. He might have been mean, but he was good-hearted. He didn't care."

"I liked him," James Terry Crews said.

"Then he said, 'You know who I am? You know what I done?' And I said, 'Some. I know the most recent.' And I told him he killed two men. And he said that was exaggerated. And I said, 'It's on TV.' And he said he didn't care. It was exaggerated. And I said, 'Don't kill me. I'm just a poor old woman. It won't help to kill me. I don't know where your money's hid.' And I saw him looking at James Terry where he just finished putting on his shoe, and I knew what he was thinking. I said, 'Don't kill him either. He got to help me. I'm retired.' And he laughed like he done and said, 'What you retired from, momma?' And I said, 'Don't call me momma. I ain't your momma. I ain't nobody's momma.' And he said, 'You look like you ought to be. You got a kind face and a big bosom.' And I thought then, He's going to rape me. Been in prison with men too long."

"His name was Duke," James Terry Crews explained.

"Q. B. Farris. He said his name was Duke. He said, 'Call me Duke. I don't know who Q. B. is.'"

"And I said, 'What's the Q. B. stand for?'" James Terry Crews said. "And you know what he said? He said, 'Queer Bastard.' I didn't know what to make of that."

"Except he wasn't queer," Oletta Crews said. "Else he wouldn't have wanted to rape me."

"Unless he was both."

"I'm telling this," Oletta Crews shouted. "We already agreed on that." She looked straight ahead. "That's the kind of person he was, full of useless jokes like that. He didn't care. You know what he said when I said don't kill me? He said, 'I wouldn't kill you or him either, momma. I got a momma of my own.'"

"What did you think about that?"

"I thought, Well where is she? I said, 'You say you got a momma, where is she?' I figured she might have the money. And he said, 'Oconee, Tennessee — in the graveyard,' and looked at me and laughed. And I said, 'You laughing because she's dead or you laughing because you broke her heart?' That straightened him out. He quit laughing and said, 'Neither one. I loved my momma. She's the only one I trust.' And I said, 'I reckon. I'd trust her too, state she's in now.' That's when he hit me."

"He hit you?" James Terry Crews glanced at her, then turned away.

"He tried to," Oletta Crews said. "Then he looked at me and said, 'She died when I was still in prison. I never got to go to the funeral because it was out of state.' Said if it'd been in the state, they'd have let him, but she was buried in Tennessee, and that's a whole other system. And I thought, So what? She wouldn't know if you were there or not—chained like a wild dog at a funeral. 'They all die. That's a common fact,' I told him. 'She'd have died if you were in jail or not.' And he said it wasn't the dying he minded. It was they wouldn't let him out to be there. That's what he hated. And that's when he told me about the nine years. He said, 'I ain't been my own man in nine years and nine more to go.' And I thought, Whose fault is that? Don't come crying on my shoulder. You should have thought about that when you decided what you wanted to be."

"What do you mean?"

"What do I mean? I mean a robber—steals money and hides it somewhere. And I said, 'Your momma's house still standing? That where you going?' And he said no, he liked it here. And I said, 'I don't got no money. You might want to go and get yours.' And he said, 'Mine?' like he didn't know what I was talking about. He said, 'I don't got no money. What are you talking about?' And I said, 'That money you got hid you come out of jail to get?' And he said, 'I don't got no money hid. I come out because I couldn't stand to stay in,' and laughed like he done so I knew he was lying. I said, 'Where's your home at in Oconee? You from town?' I figured that's where he hid the money. And he said, 'Oconee? I ain't from Oconee. I'm from right here.' He was born and raised in this county. Reason his momma died in Oconee, she was living with her sister, and they buried her there. That's when I knew he had it on him. All the money he stole and buried, it was right there beside me. Only difference was he had it, not me, and he was fixing to leave if he could."

"I didn't know what that meant," James Terry Crews explained, "but she said it was stolen already and buried nine years, and besides they're all dead anyway. . . ."

"I said I'd tell it," Oletta Crews said, each word heavy with its own weight.

James Terry Crews did not look at her. He did not answer.

"And that's when he said, 'How about some supper?' He was looking at me. And I said, 'You talking to me?' And he said, 'I was. I ain't now,' and laughed like it was some kind of joke. He said, 'You look like you might be hungry. How about you and me eating something?' And I said, 'I ain't hungry.' And he said, 'Well then why don't you rustle up something for me?' And I said, 'I don't cook. I'm retired.' And he said, 'Retired? What are you retired from?' And I said, 'The human race.' That took him back. And he said, 'Lord God, I thought you had to be dead for that.' And I said, 'Some do. Your momma maybe.' And he said, 'Don't talk about my momma. She's some kind of saint in heaven when you rot in hell.' And I said, 'I don't believe in saints.' And he said he didn't care, he knew her, I didn't, and he started doing these things on his head like he was beating up on himself. And I said, 'What's that?'"

She turned to her husband. "Show how he done."

James Terry Crews looked surprised. He took off his glasses and slapped at his forehead, then at his ears. First with one hand, then with the other.

"I saw Duke do that," Oletta Crews said. "I said, 'What you do that for?' And he said it was something he learned in prison. Means you're sorry for what you done. And I said, 'What for?' And he said, 'Whatever. It works for all.'"

"I thought he was crazy," James Terry Crews said.

"Me too. I figured he was going to kill us both or else stay there and keep us for ransom."

"What she means is hostages."

"That's right. Stay with us here till he was safe and then kill us as soon as he walked out that door going to California."

"She wants to die in California," James Terry Crews explained.

"That's right. I'm a poor old woman. That's my only hope, to see California and die happy there. That's all I want."

"That's all she wants."

"They got the Pacific Ocean out there. I got a picture in the bathroom from *National Geographic*. You ever see that one on California? That picture I got's the best one in it. I see that picture, I get all smooth inside. The jitters fall off like leaves off a tree. Shows the ocean and the sun going down, smooth and calm as far as the eye can see. Another thing—it don't ever rain. There ain't no rain of terror out there. Nature is mild. They got orange trees, bloom all year, and you want an orange, you pick it yourself."

"They got retirement," James Terry Crews said.

Oletta Crews turned and stared at him. James Terry Crews fell silent.

"What he was saying is they take care of you out there even if you don't got no children."

"I got a daughter."

"There ain't no minimum social security," Oletta Crews said. "No matter how much you made, they fix it up so you live like a prince. It ain't like here. They care about you in California. All it takes is getting out there. You got a bus ticket to California, you got a ticket to the Garden of Eden. It's like what they call your Heart's Desire. 'Lay up for yourselves treasure in heaven, where neither moth nor rust doth corrupt, and where thieves do not break through nor steal. For where your treasure is, there will be your heart also.'"

"They know all that," James Terry Crews said. "Tell them what happened."

"That's what I'm trying to do. He was going to California, and we stopped him, that's all." Oletta Crews stopped suddenly as though slamming a door. "We already told the police."

"That was yesterday. This is today," her husband explained.

"What do I care? I'm old." She paused. "I said, 'Fix your own supper. I'm too old.'"

"I fixed it for him."

"He fixed it."

"I told him I'd fix it. I said, 'I generally fix the meals around here.'"

"And he said, 'You know how to cook?'" Oletta Crews turned to her husband. "I'm telling this."

James Terry Crews stared straight ahead as in an old photo-graph. He gave no sign of having heard. He looked as though he might have been dead the last twenty or thirty years.

"All right," Oletta Crews said, leaning forward. "Listen to this. Duke said, 'You know how to cook?' like he was surprised at a man cooking. And I said, 'How you think you ate in prison?' And he said 'With my hands.' And I said, 'What?' And he said, 'I ate with my hands. Haw haw.' And I said, 'I thought you might have used a spoon.' That straightened him up. And then I said, 'He learned in the army,'" meaning James Terry Crews. "He was in the Second World War and cooked for generals when he wasn't killing folks."

"I cooked for General Eisenhower." The memory seemed to stir the ashes in James Terry Crews. "I cooked steaks and eggs for breakfast, and he drank whiskey. He didn't touch a drop of coffee. He said, 'I'll have whiskey, Cookie. You got some bourbon?' And I said, 'Damn right. I'll make it myself.' I didn't even know what I was talking about. He was the most famous man in the world. This was overseas in France."

"They don't want to hear about that," Oletta Crews shouted. "That's too long ago, and he's dead anyway. They want to hear about Q. B. Farris."

"He's dead, too."

"He died more recent."

James Terry Crews turned away.

"Now, where was I?" Oletta Crews asked.

"Cooking supper," James Terry Crews replied.

"You were out cooking supper. I was entertaining him. I asked what he robbed to get in the work camp for eighteen years. I figured it must have been a bank. And he said, 'Robbed? Who told you that?' And I said, 'I don't need nobody to tell me nothing. I can figure it out by myself.' And he said, 'Then in that case you tell me.' And I said, 'A bank. I figure you for robbing a bank.' And he looked up quick under his hair. Had this hair over his eyes. And that's when it came to me. If he robbed a bank, there must have been a lot of money. Where was the suitcase? I said, 'You got a car?' And he said, 'Not yet. I'm fixing to.' And I said, 'How'd you get here then?' And he said, 'Through the woods. I walked.' And that's when I knew he had it on him, thousands of dollars wrapped up in plastic inside his pocket. And I said, 'You going to California?' And he said, 'Not if I can stay with you, momma. I love you too much to go off and leave you.'"

"Then we ate supper," James Terry Crews said, "and I told him about the army. He said it sounded a lot like prison, and I told him he was wrong about that. 'There's a world of difference between them,' I said."

"They just talked about this and that," Oletta Crews said. "Most of it him and the other one. I didn't listen. I was thinking about what comes next. And then I asked him, 'Are we prisoners?' And he said, 'Not any more than I am.' And I said, 'What's that supposed to mean?'"

"That was what you might call a threat," James Terry Crews explained.

"A threat?"

"Meaning we were hostages."

"That's right," Oletta Crews said. "We were hostages. It was a threat."

"Then we finished supper."

"We finished supper," Oletta Crews said. "And he said, 'Here, let me help you.' And I said, 'Help what?' And he said, 'Clean up. Don't you clean up the dishes? You let them stay dirty or you got dogs?' And I said, 'Dogs? What dogs got to do with it?' And he said, 'A joke.' He was joking. He was a jokey fellow, he said. That's one thing I got to get used to. And I said, 'What for?' And he said, 'What for? To understand what I'm saying. That's what for. To get the good out of me.' And I said, 'I don't see nothing funny about dogs.' And he said he meant lick the dishes. Clean them that way. And I said, 'James Terry does the dishes. And besides that I never had a dog in my life. Dogs unclean. It says in the Bible.' Then I told him, 'They don't have dogs in California.' And he looked surprised at that and said, 'California? You ever been out to California?' And I said, 'Not yet. I'm fixing to.'"

"As soon as she can sell this place," James Terry Crews explained. "She's been talking about it ever since she retired. 'Going to California,' I told him. 'That's where she wants to go and die happy.'"

"And he laughed at that," Oletta Crews shouted. "I said, 'What are you laughing at? That some kind of joke like dogs?' And he said, 'No ma'am. I was thinking about dying happy.' That struck him funny. He said, 'I can't figure that one out.' And I didn't even look at him. I told my husband, I said, 'You better clean up the dishes before he calls in some dogs to do it.' And he laughed and made like he was going to hug me, but I flung him off. And he said, 'That's why I like you, momma. You're so fast and full of jokes.'"

"Then we went and washed the dishes," James Terry Crews said. "He called me dad."

"Same way he called me momma," Oletta Crews shouted. "He didn't mean it. I told him, 'I ain't your momma. Your momma's dead. I wouldn't have a son in the work camp.' And he said, 'It'd break your heart. It'd break your heart, wouldn't it, momma?' And I told him it'd kill me for sure if I had a child and he ended up in the work camp for eighteen years. And he said, 'Nine'— like he was setting me straight. He laughed and said, 'I stayed for nine. I ain't fixing to stay for the rest. That way I'm ahead.' He didn't care."

"Tell them about the dictionary."

Oletta Crews reached under the sofa and pulled out a book. The covers were torn off, the pages dirty and dog-eared. She held it up for inspection.

"This is the dictionary," Oletta Crews announced. It was like an exhibit, a piece of evidence. "I was reading it."

"Reads it all day, that and the Bible, when she ain't watching television," James Terry Crews explained. "That's what she does. She does that to pass the time."

"It's all in there, everything you need to know," Oletta Crews said. "One's the head and the other's the heart. I got something to figure out, I read the dictionary till I find what it is."

"The Bible's the heart," James Terry Crews explained. "She reads it to ease her heart."

"When it gets too full," Oletta Crews said. "When I get to suffering too much. It puts my weary heart to rest. But I couldn't find it. It was there, but I couldn't find it."

"Find what?"

Oletta Crews looked at her husband as though she could not believe he was stupid enough to have asked such a question.

"What comes next," she said. "And then it came to me. I was in the bathroom, and I heard them washing dishes and talking like bees in the wall, and I was looking out at the ocean, that picture I told you about of the water. And that's when it came to me."

"That's when she decided," James Terry Crews explained.

"I didn't decide. Something told me."

"Something told her."

"Like a voice in California. I got up and flushed the toilet and went back and sat down and turned it over in my mind."

Oletta Crews held up her hand. "Listen to me," she said. "This is the main part. I knew what he was fixing to do, and he knew I knew. He already killed two men to get here. I heard that where God led me this far on TV, and now he was telling me what to do next."

"God," James Terry Crews explained. It was like nailing a pelt on a wall. "The voice she heard. It was God."

Oletta Crews looked at him with contempt. "They know that. Who else got a voice? Of course it was God. Speaks in your heart just like he led me on TV to know who it was came to the door in the rain of terror. And he opened it," indicating her husband, "and I looked out and knew who it was like in a mirror he looked so familiar."

"You were afraid."

"Yes."

"You killed him because you were afraid."

"Yes." And then, "I didn't kill him."

"I killed him."

"Don't listen to him," Oletta Crews shouted. "Listen to me. He don't know nothing."

"I don't know nothing."

"He just did it. I heard the voice."

"She heard the voice. I'm the one murdered him."

"It wasn't a murder. Police say that. Police say, 'You shoot whoever you want to, lady, breaks in your house and keeps you hostage.'"

"Damn right, wouldn't you? She was afraid he might kill her."

"And I was afraid he might kill him, too," Oletta Crews said, indicating her husband. "I need him to help me. Besides I heard the voice. It spoke in my heart." She stopped as though reflecting. "'You can't serve two masters.' That's what it said. 'No man can serve two masters: for either he will hate the one, and love the other; or else he will hold to the one and despise the other.'"

"That's right. Then what?"

"I thought how to do it."

"How to kill him."

"I thought of ways of how to do it. Like roach tablets. Putting them in his grits at breakfast. And then I thought, What if they don't work? What if they just work on roaches? Then I thought of rat poison. But what if he tastes it? Drano. That's too strong. Lysol and Clorox. He might have to drink a gallon. Poison is out."

"I told her about the nail."

"That was later, when he went to bed."

"You were still thinking about it."

"Not that way I wasn't."

"In the ear . . ." James Terry Crews began.

"Let me tell it," Oletta Crews shouted. "I'm telling this. It was all over by then. I already figured it out. He said, 'What about a nail?' And I said, 'A nail?' And he said, 'I read about it in the paper.'"

"No, I didn't. It was in the *Police Gazette*. In the Charlotte, North Carolina, bus station. I was there waiting, and I went to the newsstand and picked up the magazines like you do, looking for pictures. . . ."

"They got pictures of half-naked women where they been raped in the *Police Gazette*," Oletta Crews said. "That's what he was looking at."

"No I wasn't. I was just looking, waiting for the time to pass till I got my bus, and I picked up the *Police Gazette*, and the first thing I turned to, that was it. Nail Murder. All about how this farmer in Kansas and this girlfriend he got killed her husband by driving a thirty-penny nail in his ear." James Terry Crews glared about him in triumph. "They killed him by driving a nail in his ear." He leaned forward. "You know why they did that?"

"So it wouldn't be a wound," Oletta Crews shouted. "They know that. The nail went in, and they wiped up the blood and burned the rag and called the doctor and said, 'He rose up in the bed and shouted and fell over dead.' And the doctor didn't even look in the ear. Said, 'Must have been a heart attack.' And they almost got away with it except for the farmer. He went crazy and confessed it all. Otherwise, they'd have joined the farms, his and the one she got from the murder, and made a million dollars by now selling it off for shopping centers."

"You ever hear anything like that?" James Terry Crews said proudly. "That's what you call a perfect crime except he went crazy."

"That's where he went wrong," Oletta Crews said. "That's why it ain't perfect. So I told him the nail was out." She lowered her voice. "I even thought of cutting his throat. Waiting till he was asleep and then creep in the light at the end of the hall shining in so we could see the vein in his neck beating and then pull the razor across it. But what if it's too deep? What if the gristle is too hard to cut through? I ain't that strong, and I knew he couldn't do it," indicating her husband. "He can talk about nails all he wants to, but I knew he couldn't even hold it still. He's too soft. He might look at him and feel sorry for him. I couldn't chance it. I didn't want Duke getting up, throat flapping open from ear to ear where I cut at it and him not dead. Ain't no telling what he might do bleeding like that, bubbling and shouting. He'd kill me for sure. That's when I knew James Terry would have to shoot him."

"I had to. You heard her."

"Hold on," Oletta Crews shouted. "Don't rush ahead. They ain't finished the dishes yet. I got out of the bathroom, and they came in and sat down, and James Terry said, 'Duke's been telling me about all the good times they had in the work camp. He liked it there.' And I said, 'If he liked it so much, why didn't he stay? Why come around here bothering us?' And then Duke says, 'What's on TV?' And I say, 'Nothing.' And he says, 'They got Monday Night Football.' And I say, 'I don't watch it. I don't know the rules.' And he says, 'What about you, old dad?' speaking to my husband, James Terry Crews."

"'I don't watch it either,' I said. And he said, 'Why not? You don't know the rules?' And I said, 'I know them. I just don't watch it.'" He glanced at his wife. "It's too rough."

"That's right," Oletta Crews said. "I told him that game's all right for the work camp. I said, 'Rough men done worse than that to each other every day of their lives, but it ain't all right for women and children. It's too rough. Besides which,' I told him, 'it ain't Monday night.' And he said, 'Not Monday?' And I said, 'That's right. Yesterday was Monday. This is Tuesday.' And he laughed and said, 'Lord God,' and grinned like he just ate something he shouldn't."

"He had this kind of shit-eating grin," James Terry Crews explained.

"It was attractive, I don't mean that," Oletta Crews said, "but it's like he been eating something he shouldn't. And he said, 'I can keep up with it in the work camp. It's when I get out, that's when I lose track.' And I said, 'How many times you get out?' And he said every chance he got. That and Monday Night Football's his only pleasure, he said. That and beating up on folks to get in the work camp in the first place. 'And grinning,' I said. 'You left out grinning.' And he laughed and said, 'That's right, momma. That's the only pleasure I got, that and being here with you. What about going to bed?' And I thought, This is when the raping commences. And I said, 'Not me. I don't go to bed and get raped.' And you know what he did? He laughed. He fell on the floor like he couldn't stand up and kicked his feet in the air pretending. Looked like the devil come up through the floor from hell. And he said, 'Momma, you ever think you going to get raped, you know what I'd do?' But I didn't answer. I was too ashamed. And he laughed and said he'd stay up instead. 'I'd stay up all night before I'd go to bed and get raped,' and so on like that. But I didn't look at him. I heard him scrabbling around down there, but I didn't dare cast my eyes on him to see what nasty thing he was doing."

"He was getting up," James Terry Crews explained.

"I didn't want to see what it was for fear it might be something I didn't want to see. That's how he was. He didn't care. Then I felt him lean over me, grinning and mocking, and say what he meant was for me to go to one bed and him to another and sleep this time if that was all right with me. And that's when I knew there wasn't no way. Even if I could have saved him before, I knew I couldn't after that. I was a prisoner in my own house."

"He trusted us," James Terry Crews explained. "He said, 'I sleep light, but I trust you anyway, old dad. I know you don't want me to go back to the work camp for nine more years.' And he said to Mrs. Crews, 'Wake me for breakfast, you hear me, momma? Don't let me oversleep my welcome. I'm just going to rest a minute. Then I'm going to have to leave you, much as you hate to see me go.'"

"And I thought, To California. He's going to California without me," Oletta Crews shouted, "and leave me alone and take all the money. And that's when I told James Terry to kill him. I said, 'Go get your gun.'"

"I got this single-barrel shotgun," James Terry Crews said. "First gun I ever owned."

"They don't want to hear about that."

But James Terry Crews turned on her. "Let me talk," he said. "This is interesting. I got that gun in Fayetteville when I was a boy.

Walked in and slapped down seven dollars and said, 'I'll take that Stevens single-barrel,' and Mr. Robert reached up and got it out of the cradle. Had this cradle made out of deer hoofs, and he said, 'This squirrel gun?' And I said, 'Squirrel gun? I could bring you down with it if I had some buckshot.' That's the way I was then. I didn't take no smart talk from nobody. I said, 'This gun cost too much to waste on squirrels.' And he said, 'What you fixing to shoot with it, if you don't shoot me?' And I said, 'I don't know,' like I was still thinking about it. I said, 'I ain't made up my mind yet.' And then I said, 'Give me some buckshot' and looked right at him. That got his attention. Buckshot'll blow a hole in a man big as a melon. I was a man when I was fourteen, when I first went to work for the sawmill. I worked there till I hurt myself and moved to Atlanta and got married and went to painting. But I kept that gun. I had others, but it was my favorite. It reminded me."

"That's beside the point," Oletta Crews said. "The point is I could say, 'Go in there and do it,' and James Terry would go in there, and I'd feel it shake where he shot at him—once, twice, three times maybe—in the head or in the back, wherever it hit him. But what then? He was laying in my bed, and he'd bleed on it and ruin the mattress."

"Not to mention the shot," James Terry Crews said. "She didn't even think about that. I had to tell her. I said, 'Blood ain't nothing. Blood washes off. But buckshot—buckshot'll blow a hole in a man as big as a melon right through him and the mattress both. Might even blow a hole in the floor.'" His face lit up. "I ever tell you about the time we were moving, and there was a copperhead in the house, and I had the gun, but the shells were packed up somewhere in boxes?"

"Don't be an idiot."

"I shot a hole in the floor," James Terry Crews shouted, hurrying to finish while he still had the chance. "I found the shells and shot the floor clean out. Snake with it." He looked at his wife. "Ever see buckshot hit a melon?"

"Hush up," Oletta Crews said. "You're talking too much."

James Terry Crews said, "It explodes. You can't even find the pieces. It just lifts and disappears. Same way with heads."

"I knew I'd smell it," Oletta Crews said. "Whenever I put my face to it, I knew I'd smell it in my sleep no matter how good I washed it. The police would come and take off the body, but they'd leave all the blood in the mattress and on the sheets and on the rug across the floor where it runs out when they carry him off, and I'd have to clean it up. He can't clean," indicating her husband. "All he can do is paint."

"I say paint it. If it's dirty enough to wash it, it's dirty enough to paint it, I say."

"Only trouble is you can't paint sheets and mattresses where all the blood ran out." She leaned forward and spoke confidentially. "If it wasn't drinking, it was talking. All his life. He'd get to painting a house and talk himself right off the job. Couldn't even climb the ladder or mix the paint, he talked so much. Folks don't like that. They run him off. And it wasn't even drinking sometimes. It's what he calls high spirits."

James Terry Crews looked at her balefully. "High spirits," he said.

"Besides which I thought of something else," Oletta Crews said, rocking forward again. "What about Q. B. Farris?" She bugged her eyes as someone else might simulate fright. "Where was his gun? And then I thought about the money. What if he had it in his pocket and James Terry shot it all full of holes? Would they still take it? What do they do with money like that?"

"They don't do nothing," James Terry Crews replied. "Because it blows away just like a melon. If he had that money in his pocket, you couldn't even find the pieces."

"That what I thought. Besides which he can't even see in the daytime let alone in the dark at night. He might point it at his head and hit the wrong place, where the money is, and just wound him, and he'd come crawling out at me."

"That's why I picked up two other loads," James Terry Crews explained. "In case I missed. I ain't never shot a man before."

"He said he might miss the first but not the second. But I told him, 'No. It's too dangerous. There's some other way.' And he said, 'I can't think of it.' And I said, 'I know. I wasn't expecting you to. Give me a minute.'" She paused and then spoke in an altered voice. "'Even though I walk through the valley of the shadow of death, I fear no evil, for thou art with me.' And then it said, 'It ain't your death. That's why it's a shadow. If it was your death, it'd be real. But killing him's only a shadow.' And as soon as I heard that, I knew who it was, and all my fear fell off me like sweat, and I dried up, it's like I was reborn. I knew what was promised. And I said to James Terry, 'Let it go. Don't shoot him now. Wait till later.' And he said, 'When?' And I said, 'When he's fixing to kill us.'"

"And I said, 'What if it's too late? What if he beats me to it?' And she said, 'Then you don't have to worry. You'll already be dead by then.' That don't make no sense to me."

"And I said, 'It won't come to that. Just get it loaded. I'll give you a sign—like this.'" She winked her eye and waved her hand.

"And I said, 'What if I'm tying my shoe and don't see you do it?'" James Terry Crews said. "What if I get up and go to the bathroom?'"

"We heard him rattling around in there," Oletta Crews said. "And I said, 'Get ready. He's fixing to kill us.' And James Terry said, 'What do I do?' And I said, 'Sit here.'" She patted the cushion beside her. "'Sit down here and hide the gun under the sofa where you can get at it.'"

"And I said, 'That's too slow. He'll shoot us both before I get to it.' And she said, 'That's good. In that case you don't got nothing to worry about.'"

"And my fear dried up like sweat."

"And I cocked it and put it under the sofa. There ain't no safety on a single-barrel Stevens," James Terry Crews started to say, but his wife interrupted him.

"They don't want to hear about that. We were sitting on the sofa waiting."

"Not me. I was thinking about what if he kills me. That worried me. I knew what she said, but it still worried me."

"And always will," Oletta Crews said. "That's what's wrong with you." She paused suddenly. "We heard him stirring and singing, and then he came in tucking James Terry's shirt in his pants where he hid the gun and stopped and fell back all of a sudden like he was surprised and said, 'I didn't see you sitting there. You almost scared me to death sitting there side by side. You know what you look like?' But I ignored him. And he said, 'Two cats. You look like two cats lined up waiting for dinner. Ever see that?'— grinning and laughing to show he was lying. He tried to hug me, but I pushed him off. And then he said, 'I got to go, much as I hate to leave you, momma.'"

"And I said, 'Why don't you stay then? What's your hurry?'" James Terry Crews said. "I didn't mind him so much. He wasn't too bad except he might kill us. He had a good heart. Then I saw her look at me, and I felt my bowels tighten up. They were feeling loose. . . ."

Oletta Crews ignored him. "And then Duke said, 'I'd sure like to stay, old dad. It feels just like home.' And I said, 'Home? It ain't your home. I don't want children. I never had them.' And he laughed at that and said, 'I know. I'd have guessed it at how you kept your figure even if you hadn't told me about it. You sure look good for a woman your age'— laughing and grinning so I didn't know if he meant it or not. And I tried to hit him. I said, 'Go on. Don't talk like that, my husband sitting right here beside me.'"

"And I said, 'Don't mind me. I think she's pretty good-looking myself.'"

"And then he said, 'They'll be along directly looking for me. Don't tell them I been here. I'd rather be dead than go back to the work camp the rest of my life. How would you like it?' And I said, 'I wouldn't. But I wouldn't deserve to.' That straightened him up. And he said, 'Well, I got to go. Much obliged for the company. It ain't often I get to have such high old times.'"

"And I said, 'Me neither,'" James Terry Crews said. " 'I enjoyed it,' I said. 'Come back. You ever get where they ain't looking for you, come back. You know where it's at. Come back and stay. We'd like to have you. You're good company.'"

"I didn't say nothing," Oletta Crews said. "And he said, 'How about you? You want me to come back too, momma?' And I said, 'I won't be here. I'm fixing to go to California.' Then he got serious all of a sudden. His face fell, and he looked old. He said, 'I sure do wish you luck,' reaching over to shake James Terry by the hand. And he said to me, 'I know how you feel wanting to go someplace like that, even if it's only to go there and die. That's one thing I learned in the work camp.'"

"Then he slapped me on the shoulder," James Terry Crews said, "and hugged me like that and backed off and said, 'I might buy this place myself if I had the time.'"

"That's how I knew he had the money," Oletta Crews said. "He wasn't lying."

"He'd have done it if he had the time."

"And the money," Oletta Crews said. "That's when I told him I might see him out there. And he said, 'Where?' And I said, 'California.' And he grinned and said, 'You might do it?' Then he looked at me. He looked me right in the eye and said, 'I'll see you in California, momma.' And I knew then I was right. He's fixing to walk right out that door and shut it behind him and stomp his feet down the steps like he's going somewhere and then creep back when we're sitting here side by side on the sofa thinking he's gone now, the danger is over, our lives are safe in our own hands again, praising God and weeping for joy we ain't dead, he didn't kill us, when all of a sudden the door flings open, and there he is standing there grinning and laughing like a devil from hell because it's a joke, don't you see, pretending to leave and then coming back and shooting us both right on the sofa side by side, one after the other — bang, bang, bang — till it wasn't even a sofa no more, just a hole in the floor and us in it, bits and pieces mixed with the stuffing."

"That's a shotgun," James Terry Crews explained. "You're talking about a twelve-gauge shotgun."

"That was his plan," Oletta Crews said. "I saw it as clear as I'm seeing you, and I knew I was right. It's just like him, I thought to myself — kill us like we were some kind of joke. You ain't got no will if you're a hostage. It's like you get tired. You can't even move. You got to sit there and wait."

"Unless you kill him first. That's right, ain't it, Letta?"

"It's like you can't move. You ain't got no will of your own."

"That's what I mean. That's why I killed him. No matter how good a heart he had, he was conceited."

"Listen to this," Oletta Crews shouted. She held up her hand again. "I said, 'Ain't you scared?' And he said, 'What for?' I didn't know if he was joking or not. I said, 'There's a posse of police out there waiting.' And he said, 'What for?' like he didn't know what I was talking about and went to the door and stuck his head out like he was trying to see who was out there. And I said, 'Because you don't care. You joke too much. You ain't serious.'"

"He was conceited. I could see that."

"I made the sign. And James Terry reached under and got the shotgun, and Duke turned around and looked at James Terry, and James Terry looked at Duke, and then his head lifted off. If it weren't for the roaring in my ears and the light and the smoke and the shaking on the sofa beside me where James Terry shot it off, I'd have thought it busted or something, like a balloon. One minute it was Duke Farris, the next minute it was gone like it went out the door. It was still raining, and I thought to myself, It ain't there. It ain't out there. You can look all you want to, but there ain't even bits and pieces. It lifted clean off. That head exploded."

She paused. "I was glad the door was open. That way it went right out. It didn't blow a hole in the wall, and there wasn't nothing left to clean up. I said, 'Here. Help me up.' But he didn't move. I got up and went over there, and you know what he had in his pockets? A ring snap off an aluminum can. He didn't even have a wallet. If he was hit by a car on the highway and killed on the spot, you wouldn't have even known who he was. I searched everywhere, and I told my husband, I said, 'James Terry, I can't find the money?' I couldn't believe it. And he said, 'What money?' He didn't even know what I was talking about. And I said, 'That money he's going to California with. The money he hid and come out to dig up.' And James Terry said, 'Where is it?' And I said, 'I don't know. You shot him too soon.'"

"He didn't even have a gun," James Terry Crews explained.

"He didn't have nothing except a ring snap off an aluminum can," Oletta Crews said. "But how was I to know that? The police said, 'Don't worry. You shot him on your own property.' And I said, 'My own property? I shot him in my own house. How was I to know?' And they said, 'No way. He might have had a gun to kill you.'"

"That's probably even my ring snap off an aluminum can," James Terry Crews said. "He had on my trousers. There wasn't nothing in his at all."

"Police said it was self-defense," Oletta Crews continued. "Said, 'You killed him to save yourself. That's only natural.'"

"Ain't a jury in the land convict you of that."

"I couldn't move it," Oletta Crews said. "I sat down on the floor beside it and tried to push it out with my feet. I wanted to close the door. It was still raining. I said to James Terry, 'I can't move it by myself. Get up and help.' And he got up. Then I saw him lift an arm and start to drag him out. A leg slid by me and then a foot, and then I was free. The door was open, and I looked out and saw the rain. The floodlight was still on. It went out in the yard like a room and lit up the rain. I could see it coming down like knives. It was all silver, and in the tree, it was all silver like ice — like the whole world turned to ice. And James Terry started to come in, and I said, 'Get the light.' And he got the light, and it was dark. It was dark out there as far as the eye could see, and I could still hear it raining. It was like it was moving, like a great wind lifting and heaving. And I said to James Terry, 'Close the door. Close the door on it.' And he closed the door."

"He wasn't so bad," James Terry Crews said as though in eulogy. "I don't care what they say he done. He had a good heart. Lots of folks rob banks got better hearts than the people that own them. He was what you might call a godsend. I thought that. I thought to myself, Q. B. Farris — Duke, you're what you might call some kind of godsend."

"We were hostages," Oletta Crews shouted. "He took our will."

"I mean before that."

"There wasn't no before that. As soon as he came and knocked at that door, he took our will."

"I mean when we were doing the dishes. I thought to myself, He's some kind of a godsend. I wouldn't be here laughing and talking and cutting the fool if he wasn't here. I'm grateful to him. I'm grateful he's here. He reminded me of when I was working." He paused. "Robbing banks. . . . Robbing banks ain't so bad. I might have done that myself if I hadn't got hurt and moved to Atlanta and got married. It's a whole other way of doing — a whole other kind of life."

"Listen to me," Oletta Crews shouted. "I know about godsend. As soon as I heard that knock on the door, I felt it knocking in my heart, and I said to myself, It's God knocking at the door of my heart, asking me to open up and let him come in and change me, change my whole life." She paused. "There's a better place than this, and I thought I was going. But I know better now, even if he don't," indicating James Terry Crews. She lowered her voice, increasing its intensity. It sounded like someone else speaking inside her: "'For even Satan disguises himself as an angel of light. His end shall be according to his deeds.' And his shows that," Oletta Crews said, "when James Terry shot him and there wasn't no money."

"And no gun."

"And nothing to show except mockery. All my hopes mocked and bleeding half in and half out the door where I couldn't even shut it myself, and he dragged it out where it'd been killed, I felt like something inside me was dead."

"Me, too. It felt like something inside me was dead too. I didn't know what it was."

"I did. I sat on the floor where I'd been looking for money and thought to myself, 'You can't serve two masters.' Satan appeared as an angel of light and killed all my hopes, took my will and killed all my hopes. But I'm still alive. I ain't dead, and I ain't changed. I'm just like I was."

1989

Lewis Nordan

A HANK OF HAIR,
A PIECE OF BONE

In this story, a bored ten-year-old boy digs under his house and unearths "a dead woman, beautiful, with auburn hair and fair skin . . . On one finger . . . a gold ring in the shape of a bent spoon." Mississippian Nordan's funny, sad, fascinating fiction has been variously defined as a cross between Thurber's and Faulkner's and between the songs sung by Elvis Presley and Bessie Smith. It's fiction that's hard to pin down and impossible to put down . . . or to forget. Lewis Nordan's most recent novel is The Sharpshooter Blues. *A new edition of fifteen of his early stories,* Sugar Among the Freaks, *is just published.*

The summer I turned ten years old, I had a secret — it was a small collapsible military shovel, an entrenching tool, it was called.

I saw it in a junk store in Arrow-Catcher, my little hometown in Mississippi, and something about the fold-up-and-tuck-away nature of the implement made it attractive to me. At the same time I almost bought a metal canteen with a canvas cover — the metal dented and scratched, the canvas sun-faded and water-stained, ripe with authenticity. I envisioned filling it with Coca-Cola and, at night, secretly removing the cap and drinking lustily and privately in the dark. But when I unscrewed the lid and smelled inside, there was a hint of something that may have been urine, and so I passed on the canteen and paid my dollar for what was the real treasure anyway, the secret shovel.

There was no reason to hide the shovel; no one would have cared that I had it. And yet it was an instrument that begged to be hidden.

My bedroom was in the upstairs of my parents' home. It was small and interesting, with drawers and bookcases built into the walls to conserve space. In one wall there was also a desk, with pigeonholes and an inkwell, that could be revealed by unhooking a metal hook and dropping the desktop into place. There was a nice privacy in the hidden quality of the furniture in the walls.

And as long as I'm describing the room, I might as well tell that on the ceiling above my bed my mother had pasted luminous decals of stars and a moon and the planets — Saturn was prominent with its rings — and a comet with a tail. For a while after I turned off the lights at night, the little lunar system above me glowed with whatever sweet magic there is in such novelties. Outside my window the vastness of the Delta sky and its bright million stars and peach-basket-sized moon could not compete with the galaxies inside my tiny bedroom and all its hidden geographies.

What I'm really getting at, though, is that in the back of my clothes closet — behind the hangers with trousers and shirts, behind the winter coats in plastic bags — there was a panel that could be removed to allow entrance into an even more secret spot, a crawl space in the rafters.

On the day I bought the shovel, I removed the panel in the back of the closet and slipped inside the crawl space to sit.

I had a stash of kitchen matches, from which I chose one and struck it and lighted a stub of a candle and then, careful not to set a fire, extinguished the match and spit on the tip. I sat cross-legged and sweaty in my hideout, inhaling the bad air of insulation and candle smoke, and thrilled at the invisibility of things.

And that was how I lived with my shovel for a while, I'm not sure how long, a couple of weeks I think.

Every day, when there was time, I crept into the crawl space and found the wooden matches and lighted the candle stub and extended the collapsed handle of the shovel and heard the extension snap into place. And then, in the broiling Mississippi afternoon, or mornings if I woke early enough, or sometimes at night when I should have been in my bed beneath the fake stars, my life was filled with the joy of secret things in secret places.

Soldier, miner, escaping prisoner—these were the games I played with the entrenching tool.

I had not yet used the shovel out-of-doors.

The summer inched through its humid hours. The figs on the trees along the chicken-yard fence swelled up ("swole up," we said) and ripened and turned purple and fat. I played barefoot and barebacked in the shade of the broad fig leaves and sometimes picked the fruit from the limbs and watched the ooze of fig milk from the stem as it covered my fingers. The figs were like soft wood on my tongue, and a sweet residue of poison hung in the Delta air, where the ditches had been sprayed for mosquitoes.

Some days my father brought home a watermelon, green-striped and big as a washtub, and the three of us, mother, father, and myself, cut it beneath the walnut tree and ate big seedy red wedges of melon in the metal lawn chairs.

Evenings my father fed the chickens—the Plymouth Rocks, the Rhode Island Reds, slow and fat and powdered with dust—and my mother made fig preserves and sealed the syrupy fruit in Mason jars with hot paraffin lids.

It is tempting to look back at this time and to remember only those images of ripeness and joy.

Many evenings my father was drinking whiskey. He never drank before he was bathed and clean at the end of a day's work—he smelled of Lifebuoy soap and Fitch's shampoo and Wildroot Cream Oil, and of course of the Four Roses bourbon, masculine and sweet as wooden barrels.

Sometimes my parents fought their strange fight. The day I am remembering was a Friday.

The three of us were in the kitchen. My mother said to my father, "I wish you wouldn't do that, Gilbert."

I was standing in front of the refrigerator with the door open, looking for nothing in particular.

My father was at the sink with the water running. He held a tall water glass beneath the spigot and allowed it to fill up, and then he poured the glass of water into the sink. He filled the glass again, and then poured it into the sink again. And as the water ran from the tap, he filled the glass and poured out its contents, over and over, glass after glass, maybe twenty times without speaking.

My mother could only say, "I wish you wouldn't do that, Gilbert," as she watched him, silent and withdrawn, filling and pouring, filling and pouring at the sink.

I closed the refrigerator door and watched my father pour out one final glass of water. Then he stopped. This was a thing he did every day, and it gave my mother distress. When he was finished, he did as always — he placed the glass on the sink and stood for a while longer and watched the water run from the pipe into the drain. Then slowly, deliberately, he turned the handle and shut off the flow.

That was the end of it. After the water-pouring episode, my father went to his room and closed the door and my mother went into her own room — she called it a guest bedroom, but it was her own, with her underwear in the drawers, her bobby pins on the dresser — and lay across her bed and cried.

I could hear her from the kitchen, and I could hear music from my father's phonograph, and I knew that he was drinking from a bottle hidden in his chest of drawers and that he would not come out until morning.

I wanted to comfort my mother, but there was nothing to say. I stood by the kitchen sink and looked at the glass my father had been filling and emptying, and I believed for the one millionth time that if I looked at it long enough, tried hard enough, I could understand what my parents' strange fighting meant.

Tonight I went to my father's room, a thing I ordinarily never did after they fought, or after he closed the door and started to drink in earnest.

I knocked at his door and waited. I knew he would not answer and he did not. I knocked again and said, "Daddy," and waited again.

I heard movement inside his room, his chair, I supposed — a green-painted metal lawn chair, which he used as an easy chair — scraping against the hardwood floor. The chair sat on a rounded frame, which allowed it to rock back and forth.

After a silence the door opened and I could tell that my father was already very drunk. He looked at me and finally moved aside to let me in. He sat in his strange lawn chair and his record kept playing softly on the phonograph, a slow ballad sung by Elvis. The whiskey bottle was not in sight.

He said, "What is it, Sugar?"

My father was not a tall man, no more than five feet six inches, and his childlike shoes, with crepe soles and shiny uppers, were covered with tiny speckles of paint. His feet did not reach the floor except as the chair rocked forward. He was wearing Big Smith khakis and an open-necked shirt, and I noticed that the face of his watch was flecked with paint.

I said, "I bought a shovel." I had not known I was going to say this.

My father let a few seconds pass and then he said, "Is that right."

I said, "I've got it in my room."

He said, "Do you want a peppermint puff?" My father reached across the top of the phonograph to a cellophane bag filled with peppermint candy and brought out a small handful and put one piece of candy into his mouth. I held out my hand and received a piece.

I said, "I haven't dug anything with it yet." I put the candy in my mouth, the peppermint puff, and it was light and airy as magic. It seemed almost to float instead of melt inside my mouth.

And then, as unexpectedly as I had announced the existence of the shovel, my father said, "The Delta is filled up with death."

Now that I look back on this moment I think that he meant nothing at all by this remark. Probably the mention of a shovel made him think of graves and that made him think of death, which was his favorite drunken subject anyway. Self-pity, self-dramatization — the boring death-haunted thoughts of an alcoholic, nothing more.

And yet at the time the words that he spoke seemed directly

related to my accidental, unintentional mention of the shovel, the way advice is related to a problem that needs to be solved.

I said, "It is?"

He said, "Yep. To the brim."

The conversation was over. I stayed a little longer, but already my father was growing irritable and restless, and I knew he wished I would leave so that he could drink from the bottle in the chest of drawers.

The Delta was filled with death. The information came like a summons, a moral imperative to search.

And so that day, and for many days afterwards, I took the shovel outside and started to dig. In the front yard the shovel blade cut through the grass and scarred the lawn. I replaced the squares of sod before my mother could see the damage, but already I knew I was doing the right thing. Earthworms retreated to cooler, safer depths. Roly-polies curled up into little balls. The blade of the shovel shone at the edges, the dirt was fragrant and cool to my touch.

My first serious digging was a trench alongside the back of the chicken yard, near the fence. The earth there was loamy and soft and worm-rich and easy to dig. I threw spadefuls of loose dirt at the busy old hens and watched them scatter and puff out their feathers as large as beach balls.

What was I digging for? Indians had lived on this land, Chickasaws and Choctaws. Slaves had died here. There might be bones. A well-digger once dug up a Confederate mortar shell near the dog pen, and it was still on display in the Plantation Museum in Leflore. Sometimes a kid would find an arrowhead or spearpoint. My father was right—the remains of other civilizations did still occasionally poke through into our own.

So there was a sense in which I was only following my father's advice—I was digging for evidence of other worlds. And for a while the hard work of digging, and the work of hiding its consequences, were enough.

The trench by the fence was a mistake. A neighborhood dog crawled under and killed my father's blue Andalusian rooster, and I had to fill the trench and get the dog out before anyone could figure out that I was responsible. I threw the dead rooster into some tall weeds near the trailer where the midgets lived, and so my father thought it had flown the coop and been killed as a result of its own restlessness and vanity. So that was good.

I kept on digging. All the holes I dug were in some way unsatisfactory.

Beneath the walnut tree the earth was rock hard and root congested and I was afraid of breaking the shovel handle.

The last of several holes I dug on the lake bank, which was softer ground, finally yielded a few bones, but they were in a plastic garbage bag and, though it took me a while, I finally understood that they were the skeleton of a big tomcat that belonged to a neighbor-woman, Mavis Mitchum. The cat had been hit by a car last winter.

Along the ditch at the back of the house I dug up a nest of ground-hornets and was stung seven times. I dug each day and found a good deal of unpleasantness but little death in the Delta. I have to ask the question again: What was I digging for? — skeletons? — Indians? Not really, not at first, though I thought of those things in a general way. I think I was only playing, only digging for fun. I was a child, and I enjoyed child's play, as I had enjoyed the games behind my closet, in the crawl space.

And yet the more I dug — the greater number of holes I emptied and refilled, the more often I heard the shovel blade cut the soil and breathed the mold-and-mulch-rich fragrance of overturned earth and felt its heft in my hands, and watched the retreat of the earthworms and the vivid attack of the hornets and the other evidences of life beneath the surface of the earth — mole tunnels and rabbit holes — the more I feared and was driven to discover evidence of death.

And so by some process I became not the soldier or prisoner I had pretended to be in the crawl space, not a child with a game, but a person driven by some need born of my father's pain, my mother's despair.

My occupation became not only more necessary but more real, more dark in character. I was no longer pretending to be a soldier or prisoner, but now, without the protection of fantasy at all, I was a real-life grave digger, possessed and compulsive — and not merely a grave digger but a hopeful grave robber, a sad, innocent little ghoul spading my way through the Delta looking for God knows what, some signal or symbol, I don't know, whatever a child in need and fear is capable of looking for after talking to his drunken father about a shovel.

I don't blame my father. What would be the point? There is a sense in which I blame the geography itself, though that, of course, is useless as well.

The more I dug in the Delta earth, the more it seemed to call me to dig, the more certain I became that it would finally yield up some evil treasure.

I turned over spadeful after spadeful. I dug all over our small property — backyard and front yard and chicken yard. I dug out by Roebuck Lake, and even in Mavis Mitchum's yard, the neighbor-woman. Some of the holes were deep, some were long shallow trenches. I looked in each spadeful of earth for some sign — a toe, a tooth, some small thing, a knuckle. There was nothing.

I moved underneath the house — (Delta houses have no basements) — and here beneath the floorboards and water pipes, in the slick, sun-untouched hard-packed earth, my digging took new meaning. No longer frantic, no longer directionless, my entire body slowed down, the way a body is slowed down by age. I was a strong child — thin but sturdy — and I had the will to dig, the iron will of a child's burden of his parents' unhappiness. I would dig to China if necessary. I was digging a hole beneath my house, and I knew I would find whatever I had been looking for.

The underside of the house was a different world to me. Suddenly plumbing made sense — pipes going in and coming out. The light was filtered and cool. The dirt was slick and ungrassed for half a century. The outside world, glimpses of it, was allowed into my vision only through chinks in the brick foundation. Above me were the boards of the floor where my parents walked. Refuse had been thrown under here, a slick tire, a bald baby-doll, a wood case of Coke bottles. The house was an old structure, sixty or seventy years old, and other families had lived here before my own. Even in the refuse—the broken glass, a dog food can, two cane poles— there was a sense that lives had been lived here, that death had defeated them.

I kept on digging. I could not stand up to dig—the floor was directly above me—so I lay on my side. I stabbed the blade into the earth and, with the strength of my arms, lifted out the dirt. The work was slow and laborious. Spadeful after spadeful, I dragged dirt out of the hole and piled it away from me in a mound.

Each day I was tired and filthy, the muscles of my arms were hot with strain. I worried that my mother would stop me from what I was doing.

She did not. She only knew that I was playing under the house. She warned me about broken bottles, she grouched at me about the dirt in my jeans. But our lives went on. I continued to dig.

There were happy days, with watermelon, and sad days of whiskey. The hole beneath the house grew deeper and wider, and the mound beside the hole grew taller. My father continued to pour glasses of water down the sink, my mother begged him not to. "I wish you wouldn't do that, Gilbert." I had a sense of doing something worthwhile, or at least necessary in the face of the many things I could not otherwise control.

I kept on, possessed I would say, and sometimes fear of what I was looking for would overtake me. I would sit beside the hole and cry—*weep* is a better word, since there was as much drama in this as there was sadness—and often I would wish that I had never heard of this hole, that I had never bought this shovel, that I had bought the wicked canteen instead.

I was afraid that whatever I found—joint, knuckle, or tooth—

would be too personal to endure. Suddenly, or rather gradually, this became no abstraction I was searching for, not merely *death*. I believed now that whatever bone I found—and I had no doubt I would find something, however small—was not without a human history, that a single bone was a person, someone whose life was as filled with madness and loss as the lives of my father and mother.

I believed I could not endure knowing more about such sadness than I already suspected. My throat ached. I imagined that whatever relic I found would contain within it the power to reconstruct an entire self, a finger joint becoming a hand, the hand re-creating an arm, the arm a torso, with chest hair and a head and knees. Dry bones becoming meat and, immediately, the meat reclaiming the right and capacity to rot and fall away, the bones to be scattered and lost.

So I continued to dig underneath the house. I dug long past the time when I enjoyed it. It was a job to me, this digging, it was medicine necessary in some way to my continued life, neither joyful nor joyless, a thing to be done, a hole to be dug.

The underside of my house became as familiar to me as the crawl space behind my closet. I stopped digging sometimes and lay on my back beneath the house, beside the hole, which now was deep—two feet deep and two feet wide, and then wider and deeper. I dug down to three feet, and the hole was squared off, like the grave of a child. I kept on digging. I lay in exhaustion, down in the hole, and looked up at the floorboards of the house. I heard my mother's footsteps above me in the kitchen. I heard the boards make their small complaint. Water ran through the pipes around me—surging up through pipes into the house and into the sink, or going the other way, out of the house through the larger pipes, down into the earth and away.

I lay in the dirt and looked at the floorboards, as sweat drained out of me, my back and arms, and soaked down into the same earth. I imagined that my sweat flowed under the earth like a salty river, that it entered the water table and into a seepage of sand grains and clay and, from there, into Roebuck Lake, its dark still waters. Around me sunlight broke through the cracks in the foundation in points as brilliant as diamonds, and underneath my house was always twilight, never day and never dark.

One day in my digging—who can remember which day, a Thursday, a Saturday?—all the summer days were the same—my shovel struck something and my heart stopped, seemed to stop, tried to stop. I had found whatever I had been destined to find. Directed to find: by the man at the junk store, by the canteen, which had whispered *take the shovel not me*, by my father at the sink. My shovel struck something—hard, solid, long, like a sheet of heavy glass, a tabletop—and my heart, stopped dead by fear and awe, cried out for this to be some innocent thing, a pirate's chest, a sewer line.

I took only one look, and never looked again, and so what I tell you is only what I saw, not what I know to have been there. I was lying in the hole I had dug, this grave, its dark dirt walls on four sides of me. I was comfortable with my entrenching tool. I touched the earth again with the shovel, and again heard the noise of its blade against a sheet of heavy glass.

I thought, in that moment before I brushed away the dirt and took one brief look through a glass window into the past, or into my own troubled heart, whichever it really was, of a nursery rhyme my mother had said to me many times at night, beneath the fake stars.

It was the tale of a woman who goes to the fair and falls asleep beneath a tree and, while she sleeps, has the hem of her petticoat cut off and stolen by a thief. Without her petticoat she doesn't recognize herself when she wakes up, and she wonders who this strange woman with no petticoat can be. Even when she gets home and looks in the mirror, she is unfamiliar to herself. She says, "Dearie dearie me, is it really I?"

I could not believe that I was the person with this shovel, on this brink.

I brushed the dirt off the sheet of glass and allowed my eyes their one second of looking. Beneath the glass was a dead woman, beautiful, with auburn hair and fair skin. Her head was resting on a blanket of striped ticking.

One second, less than a second, and I never looked again. I averted my eyes and put down the shovel and crawled up out of the hole. Without looking down into the hole again, I filled the hole with the dirt I had taken out. I pushed it with my hands until it spilled over the sides of the grave and covered the shovel and whatever else was there or not there.

The dress she was wearing was red velvet, down to her ankles. Her shoes were tiny, with pointed toes. The slipper was leather and the boot was of some fabric, silk I thought. On one finger was a gold ring in the shape of a bent spoon.

It is impossible that I saw all this in one glance — her whole length, her tiny feet and fingers. It is impossible that I brushed away a bit of dirt and saw her entirely, her fingers, her hair, an exposed calf that showed the fabric of her boot.

And yet I know that I did see this, and that one second later I covered it up and did not look again.

I sat there in the dirt, beneath the floorboards of my parents' home, and I saw another thing, a gaggle of white geese being chased by a fox, but I knew even then that these were not real geese but only the erratic beating of my heart made visible. The woman in the glass coffin? — still I am not sure what was real and what my mind invented.

The sound of my parents' footsteps was above me, where I sat in the twilight of this cloistered world. In the dead woman's face I had seen my mother's beauty, the warm blood of her passion, as my father had once known her and had forgotten. I heard water running in the sink above me and imagined, whether it was true or not, that it was my father filling and emptying tumblers of water, and all around me I heard this poured-out water gurgling down through pipes, headed for sewers, the water table, the gills of gars in Roebuck Lake. Through the floorboards I could hear voices, the sound not the words, and I believed it was my mother's voice begging my father not to pour his life down this sad drain, glass after glass, day after day, until she too was empty of life and hope.

I kept sitting there, thinking of the dead woman, and I imagined her in a church pew with a songbook on her lap. I imagined her on a riverboat (if she was real she might have died a hundred years before and been buried here, pickled, perfectly preserved in alcohol or some other fluid, mightn't she? — could she not have died on one of the riverboats that once floated from the Yazoo into the Roebuck harbor?), on the deck of a boat and holding a yellow parasol. I imagined her in a green backyard, hanging out sheets on a line. I saw her eat cantaloupe and spit out the seeds, secret and pretty, into a bed of bright flowers. I saw her leading a horse by a blue bridle from an unpainted barn.

I named her pretty names. Kate and Molly and Celia, even Leda, and I called her none of these names for fear of changing something too fragile ever to be named, the same reason I did not look at her longer, for fear she could not exist in the strength of more than a second's looking. In my mind, as I named her, my father's name kept ringing, over and over, with a sound like wooden ducks in a carnival shooting gallery when they are knocked over, the ding and ding and ding, and the slap of their collapse.

I left the underside of the house and never went back.

I went inside and surprised my mother by bathing and washing my hair with Fitch's shampoo in the middle of the afternoon, and without being told. I put my dirty clothes into the washer and set the dial, and while the machine made them clean, I dressed in fresh blue jeans and a button-up shirt and dug the dirt out from under my fingernails and cleaned the mud off my shoes.

In my mind I gave the woman gifts. I gave her a candle stub. I gave her a box of wooden kitchen matches. I gave her a cake of Lifebuoy soap. I gave her a ceilingful of glow-in-the-dark planets. I gave her a bald baby-doll. I gave her a ripe fig, sweet as new wood, and a milkdrop from its stem. I gave her a peppermint puff.

I gave her a bouquet of four roses. I gave her fat earthworms for her grave. I gave her a fish from Roebuck Lake, a vial of my sweat for it to swim in.

I combed my hair with Wildroot Cream Oil and ate an entire package of my father's peppermint candy and puked in the toilet.

My mother said, "Sugar, are you all right?"

I said, "You bet," and walked boldly into my father's room and stole two rubbers from a box of Trojans in the drawer of his bed-side table, and as long as I had the drawer open, took out his pistol and spun the cylinder and aimed it at the green lawn rocker and cocked the hammer with my thumb and then eased it back down. I stole two bullets from a box of cartridges in the drawer.

Later I walked beside Roebuck Lake and threw away the rubbers and the bullets and hated my father and myself.

The summer was long and its days were all the same. The poison in the ditches was sweet, the mosquitoes were as loud as violins, as large as owls. The cotton fields smelled of defoliant, and the cotton stalks were skeletons in white dresses. As summer deepened, the rain stopped, and so the irrigation pumps ran night and day in the rice paddies. My father took my mother dancing at the American Legion hut, and I went with them and put a handful of nickles in the slot machine near the bar and won enough money to keep on playing for hours.

The black man behind the bar — his name was Al, and he drove an Oldsmobile — took me to the piano and showed me an eight-beat measure with his left hand and said it was the boogie-woogie beat and that if I listened right I could hear it behind every song ever written, every song that for a lifetime would ever make my toes feel like tap-tap-tapping.

That night it was true, and I still listen for it. I could hear it, this under-music, like a heartbeat, in the tunes my parents were dancing to. I could hear it in the irrigation pumps in the rice paddies. I could hear it in the voice of the preacher at the Baptist church, and in the voices of the pigeons in the church rafters. I heard it in the voice of a carny who barked at the freak show. I heard it in the stories my mother told me at night. I heard it in the tractors in the fields and in the remembered music of my shovel, my entrenching tool, its blade cutting into the earth, and in the swarm of hornets, and in the bray of mules, and in the silence of earthworms.

I watched my father and mother dance in the dim light of the dance floor, the only two dancers that night, and I fell in love with both of them, their despair and their fear and also their strange destructive love for each other and for some music I was growing old enough to hear, that I heard every day in the memory of the woman in her private grave. My father was Fred Astaire, he was so graceful, and my mother — though before this night I had seen her only as a creature in a frayed bathrobe standing in the unholy light of my father's drinking — she was an angel on the dance floor. The simple cotton dress that she wore was flowing silk — or was it red velvet? — and her sensible shoes were pointy-toed leather slippers with a silk boot. I understood why the two of them had been attracted to each other. I understood, seeing them, why they continued in their mutual misery. Who can say it was not true love, no matter how terrible?

In this dim barnlike room — the felt-covered poker tables, the dark bright wood of the dance floor, the upright piano, a lighted Miller sign turning slowly on the ceiling, a nickle slot by the bar — here I loved my parents and the Mississippi Delta, its poisoned air and rich fields, its sloughs and loblollies and coonhounds and soybeans. In everything, especially in the *whisk-whisk-whisk* of my parents' feet on the sawdusty dance floor, I heard the sound of the boogie-woogie beat, eight notes — five up the scale and three down — I heard it in the clash and clatter of the great machines in the compress, where loose cotton, light as air, was smashed into heavy bales and wrapped in burlap and tied with steel bands. I held on to my secret, the dead woman under our house, and wished that I could have known these things about my parents and our geography and its music without first having looked into the dead woman's face and held inside me her terrible secret.

My father and mother danced and danced, they twirled, their bodies swayed to the music, their eyes for each other were bright. My father sang to my mother an old tune, sentimental and frightening, crooning his strange love to her, *oh honeycomb won't you be my baby oh honeycomb be my own,* he sang, this small man enormous in his grace, *a hank of hair and a piece of bone my honeycomb.* My mother placed her head on his shoulder as they danced, and when she lifted her face he kissed her lips and they did not stop dancing.

There is one more thing to tell.

Late in the summer, deep in August, when the swamps were steam baths, and beavers as big as collies could be seen swimming in Roebuck Lake from a canebreak to a willow shade, I passed my tenth birthday.

I still had told no one about the corpse, if it was a corpse and not something equally terrifying, a vision or hallucination born of heartbreak and loss, beneath our house. The shovel was a forgotten toy.

My mother made me a birthday cake in the shape of a rabbit — she had a cake pan molded in that shape — and she decorated it with chocolate icing and stuck on carrot slices for the eyes. It was a difficult cake to make stand up straight, but with various props it would balance on its hind legs on the plate, so that when I came into the room it looked almost real standing there, its little front feet tucked up to its chest.

At the sight of the rabbit I started to cry. My mother was startled by my tears. She had been standing in the doorway between the kitchen and the dining room. The table was set with a white tablecloth and linen napkins, three settings for my birthday dinner.

I could not stop crying, looking at that rabbit cake. I knew that my mother loved me, I knew something of her grief — something in the desperate innocence of the rabbit, its little yellow carrot eyes. I thought of the hopelessness of all love, and that is why I was crying I think.

My mother came to me and held me to her and I felt her

warmth and smelled her woman-smell. I wanted to dance with her at the Legion Hut. I wanted to give her a gift of earthworms.

I kept crying.

My mother said, "Oh, Sugar-man . . ."

I kept on crying, sobbing, trying to talk between the sobs. I said, "There's a woman under the house."

She said, "I know, Sugar-man, I know, hush now . . ."

I said, "I don't want to listen to the boogie-woogie beat."

She said, "I know, darling, I know . . ."

She kept on holding me, rocking me where we stood.

I said, "It's a dead woman. Under our house."

She said, "I know, Sugar-man, I know . . ."

I said, "In a grave."

She said, "I know, darling, you hush now . . ."

I said, "I don't want my toes to go tap-tap-tapping."

1990

Richard Bausch

LETTER TO THE LADY
OF THE HOUSE

A reviewer once commented that Richard Bausch's fiction combines the best of women's writing with the best of men's writing, an intriguing insight that comes to mind in reading this story. The letter that this husband of almost fifty years writes to his wife represents exactly what a woman wants to hear from a man. Bausch, born in Georgia and raised in Washington, D.C., is the author of six novels and three collections of stories. His forthcoming novel, Good Evening Mr. & Mrs. America, and All the Ships at Sea, *is due in Fall 1996.*

It's exactly twenty minutes to midnight, on this the eve of my seventieth birthday, and I've decided to address you, for a change, in writing—odd as that might seem. I'm perfectly aware of how many years we've been together, even if I haven't been very good about remembering to commemorate certain dates, certain days of the year. I'm also perfectly aware of how you're going to take the fact that I'm doing this at all, so late at night, with everybody due to arrive tomorrow, and the house still unready. I haven't spent almost five decades with you without learning a few things about you that I can predict and describe with some accuracy, though I admit that, as you put it, lately we've been more like strangers than husband and wife. Well, so if we are like strangers, perhaps there are some things I can tell you that you won't have already figured out about the way I feel.

Tonight, we had another one of those long, silent evenings after an argument (remember?) over pepper. We had been bickering all day, really, but at dinner I put pepper on my potatoes and you said

198

that about how I shouldn't have pepper because it always upsets my stomach. I bothered to remark that I used to eat chili peppers for breakfast and if I wanted to put plain old ordinary black pepper on my potatoes, as I had been doing for more than sixty years, that was my privilege. Writing this now, it sounds far more testy than I meant it, but that isn't really the point.

In any case, you chose to overlook my tone. You simply said, "John, you were up all night the last time you had pepper with your dinner."

I said, "I was up all night because I ate green peppers. Not black pepper but green peppers."

"A pepper is a pepper, isn't it?" you said.

And then I started in on you. I got, as you call it, legal with you — pointing out that green peppers are not black pepper — and from there we moved on to an evening of mutual disregard for each other that ended with your decision to go to bed early. The grandchildren will make you tired, and there's still the house to do; you had every reason to want to get some rest, and yet I felt that you were also making a point of getting yourself out of proximity with me, leaving me to my displeasure, with another ridiculous argument settling between us like a fog.

So, after you went to bed, I got out the whiskey and started pouring drinks, and I had every intention of putting myself into a stupor. It was almost my birthday, after all, and — forgive this, it's the way I felt at the time — you had nagged me into an argument and then gone off to bed; the day had ended as so many of our days end now, and I felt, well, entitled. I had a few drinks, without any appreciable effect (though you might well see this letter as firm evidence to the contrary), and then I decided to do something to shake you up. I would leave. I'd make a lot of noise going out the door; I'd take a walk around the neighborhood and make you wonder where I could be. Perhaps I'd go check into a motel for the night. The thought even crossed my mind that I might leave you altogether. I admit that I entertained the thought, Marie. I saw our life together now as the day-to-day round of petty quarrelling and tension that it's mostly been over the past couple of years or so, and I wanted out as sincerely as I ever wanted anything.

My God, I wanted an end to it, and I got up from my seat in front of the television and walked back down the hall to the entrance of our room to look at you. I suppose I hoped you'd still be awake, so I could tell you of this momentous decision I felt I'd reached. And maybe you were awake: one of our oldest areas of contention being the feather-thin membrane of your sleep that I am always disturbing with my restlessness in the nights. All right. Assuming you were asleep, and don't know that I stood in the doorway of our room, I will say that I stood there for perhaps five minutes, just looking at you in the half-dark, the shape of your body under the blanket—you really did look like one of the girls when they were little and I used to stand in the doorway of their rooms; your illness last year made you so small again—and, as I said, I thought I had decided to leave you, for your peace as well as mine. I know you have gone to sleep crying, Marie. I know you've felt sorry about things, and wished we could find some way to stop irritating each other so much.

Well, of course, I didn't go anywhere. I came back to this room and drank more of the whiskey and watched television. It was like all the other nights. The shows came on and ended, and the whiskey began to wear off. There was a little rain shower. I had a moment of the shock of knowing I was seventy. After the rain ended, I did go outside for a few minutes. I stood on the sidewalk and looked at the house. The kids, with their kids, were on the road somewhere between their homes and here. I walked up to the end of the block and back, and a pleasant breeze blew and shook the drops out of the trees. My stomach was bothering me some, and maybe it was the pepper I'd put on my potatoes. It could just as well have been the whiskey. Anyway, as I came back to the house, I began to have the eerie feeling that I had reached the last night of my life. There was this small discomfort in my stomach, and no other physical pang or pain, and I am used to the small ills and side effects of my way of eating and drinking; yet I felt the sense of the end of things more strongly than I can describe. When I stood in the entrance of our room and looked at you again, wondering if I would make it through to the morning, I suddenly found myself trying to think what I would say to you if indeed this *was* the last time I would ever be able to speak to you. And I began to know I would write you this letter.

At least words in a letter aren't blurred by tone of voice, by the old aggravating sound of me talking to you. I began with this, and with the idea that, after months of thinking about it, I would at last try to say something to you that wasn't colored by our disaffections. What I have to tell you must be explained in a rather roundabout way.

I've been thinking about my cousin Louise and her husband. When he died, and she stayed with us last summer, something brought back to me what is really only the memory of a moment; yet it reached me, that moment, across more than fifty years. As you know, Louise is nine years older than I, and more like an older sister than a cousin. I must have told you at one time or another that I spent some weeks with her, back in 1933, when she was first married. The memory I'm talking about comes from that time, and what I have decided I have to tell you comes from that memory.

Father had been dead four years. We were all used to the fact that times were hard and that there was no man in the house, though I suppose I filled that role in some titular way. In any case, when Mother became ill there was the problem of us, her children. Though I was the oldest, I wasn't old enough to stay in the house alone, or to nurse her, either. My grandfather came up with the solution—and everybody went along with it—that I would go to Louise's for a time, and the two girls would go to stay with Grandfather. You'll remember that people did pretty much what that old man wanted them to do.

So we closed up the house, and I got on a train to Virginia. I was a few weeks shy of fourteen years old. I remember that I was not able to believe that anything truly bad would come of Mother's pleurisy, and was consequently glad of the opportunity it afforded me to travel the hundred miles south to Charlottesville, where Cousin Louise had moved with her new husband only a month earlier, after her wedding. Because *we* travelled so much at the beginning, you never got to really know Charles when he was young; in 1933, he was a very tall, imposing fellow, with bright-red hair and a graceful way of moving that always made me think of athletics, contests of skill. He had worked at the Navy yard in Washington, and had been laid off in the first months of Roosevelt's New Deal. Louise was teaching in a day school in Charlottesville, so they could make ends meet, and Charles was spending most of his time looking for work and fixing up the house. I had only met Charles once or twice before the wedding, but already I admired him, and wanted to emulate him. The prospect of spending time in his house, of perhaps going fishing with him in the small streams of central Virginia, was all I thought about on the way down. And I remember that we did go fishing one weekend, that I wound up spending a lot of time with Charles, helping to paint the house, and to run water lines under it for indoor plumbing. Oh, I had time with Louise, too — listening to her read from the books she wanted me to be interested in, walking with her around Charlottesville in the evenings and looking at the city as it was then. Or sitting on her small porch and talking about the family, Mother's stubborn illness, the children Louise saw every day at school. But what I want to tell you has to do with the very first day I was there.

I know you think I use far too much energy thinking about and pining away for the past, and I therefore know that I'm taking a risk by talking about this ancient history, and by trying to make you see it. But this all has to do with you and me, my dear, and our late inability to find ourselves in the same room together without bitterness and pain.

That summer, 1933, was unusually warm in Virginia, and the heat, along with my impatience to arrive, made the train almost unbearable. I think it was just past noon when it pulled into the station at Charlottesville, with me hanging out one of the windows, looking for Louise or Charles. It was Charles who had come to meet me. He stood in a crisp-looking seersucker suit, with a straw boater cocked at just the angle you'd expect a young, newly married man to wear a straw boater, even in the middle of economic disaster. I waved at him and he waved back, and I might've jumped out the window if the train had slowed even a little more than it had before it stopped in the shade of the platform. I made my way out, carrying the cloth bag my grandfather had given me for the trip — Mother had said through her rheum that I looked like a carpetbagger — and when I stepped down to shake hands with Charles I noticed that what I thought was a new suit was tattered at the ends of the sleeves.

"Well," he said. "Young John."

I smiled at him. I was perceptive enough to see that his cheerfulness was not entirely effortless. He was a man out of work, after all, and so in spite of himself there was worry in his face, the slightest shadow in an otherwise glad and proud countenance. We walked through the station to the street, and on up the steep hill to the house, which was a small clapboard structure, a cottage, really, with a porch at the end of a short sidewalk lined with flowers — they were marigolds, I think — and here was Louise, coming out of the house, her arms already stretched wide to embrace me. "Lord," she said. "I swear you've grown since the wedding, John." Charles took my bag and went inside.

"Let me look at you, young man," Louise said.

I stood for inspection. And as she looked me over I saw that her hair was pulled back, that a few strands of it had come loose, that it was brilliantly auburn in the sun. I suppose I was a little in love with her. She was grown, and married now. She was a part of what seemed a great mystery to me, even as I was about to enter it, and of course you remember how that feels, Marie, when one is on the verge of things — nearly adult, nearly old enough to fall in love. I looked at Louise's happy, flushed face, and felt a deep ache as she ushered me into her house. I wanted so to be older.

Inside, Charles had poured lemonade for us, and was sitting in the easy chair by the fireplace, already sipping his. Louise wanted to show me the house, and the backyard — which she had tilled and turned into a small vegetable garden — but she must've sensed how thirsty I was, and so she asked me to sit down and have a cool drink before she showed me the upstairs. Now, of course, looking back on it, I remember that those rooms she was so anxious to show me were meager indeed. They were not much bigger than closets, really, and the paint was faded and dull; the furniture she'd arranged so artfully was coming apart; the pictures she'd put on the walls were prints she'd cut out — magazine covers, mostly — and the curtains over the windows were the same ones that had hung in her childhood bedroom for twenty years. ("Recognize these?" she said with a deprecating smile.) Of course, the quality of her pride had nothing to do with the fineness — or lack of it — in these things but in the fact that they belonged to her, and that she was a married lady in her own house.

On this day in July, 1933, she and Charles were waiting for the delivery of a fan they had scrounged enough money to buy from Sears, through the catalogue. There were things they would rather have been doing, especially in this heat, and especially with me there. Monticello wasn't far away, the university was within walking distance, and without too much expense one could ride a taxi to one of the lakes nearby. They had hoped that the fan would arrive before I did, but since it hadn't, and since neither Louise nor Charles was willing to leave the other alone that day while traipsing off with me, there wasn't anything to do but wait around for it. Louise had opened the windows and drawn the shades, and we sat in her small living room and drank the lemonade, fanning ourselves with folded parts of Charles's newspaper. From time to time an anemic breath of air would move the shades slightly, but then everything grew still again. Louise sat on the arm of Charles's chair, and I sat on the sofa. We talked about pleurisy, and, I think, about the fact that Thomas Jefferson had invented the dumbwaiter, and how the plumbing at Monticello was at least a century ahead of its time. Charles remarked that it was the spirit of invention that would make a man's career in these days. "That's what I'm aiming for — to be inventive in a job. No matter what it winds up being."

When the lemonade ran out, Louise got up and went into the kitchen to make some more. Charles and I talked about taking a weekend to go fishing. He leaned back in his chair and put his hands behind his head, looking satisfied. In the kitchen, Louise was chipping ice for our glasses, and she began singing something low, for her own pleasure, a barely audible lilting, and Charles and I sat listening. It occurred to me that I was very happy. I had the sense that soon I would be embarked on my own life, as Charles was on his, and that an attractive woman like Louise would be there with me. Charles said, "God, listen to that. Doesn't Louise have the loveliest voice?"

And that's all I have from that day. I don't even know if the fan arrived later, and I have no clear memory of how we spent the rest of the afternoon and evening. I remember Louise singing a song, her husband leaning back in his chair, folding his hands behind his head, expressing his pleasure in his young wife's voice. I remember that I felt quite extraordinarily content just then. And that's all I remember.

But there are, of course, the things we both know: we know they moved to Colorado to be near Charles's parents; we know they never had any children; we know that Charles fell down a shaft at a construction site in the fall of 1957 and was hurt so badly that he never walked again. And I know that when she came to stay with us last summer she told me she'd learned to hate him, and not for what she'd had to help him do all those years. No, it started earlier and was deeper than that. She hadn't minded the care of him — the washing and feeding and all the numberless small tasks she had to perform each and every day, all day — she hadn't minded this. In fact, she thought there was something in her makeup that liked being needed so completely. The trouble was simply that whatever she had once loved in him she had stopped loving, and for many, many years before he died she'd felt only suffocation when he was near enough to touch her, only irritation and anxiety when he spoke. She said all this, and then looked at me, her cousin, who had been fortunate enough to have children, and to be in love over time, and said, "John, how have you and Marie managed it?"

And what I wanted to tell you has to do with this fact — that while you and I had had one of our whispering arguments only moments before, I felt quite certain of the simple truth of the matter, which is that, whatever our complications, we *have* managed to be in love over time.

"Louise," I said.

"People start out with such high hopes," she said, as if I wasn't there. She looked at me. "Don't they?"

"Yes," I said.

She seemed to consider this a moment. Then she said, "I wonder how it happens."

I said, "You ought to get some rest." Or something equally pointless and admonitory.

As she moved away from me, I had an image of Charles standing on the station platform in Charlottesville that summer, the straw boater set at its cocky angle. It was an image I would see most of the rest of that night, and on many another night since.

I can almost hear your voice as you point out that once again I've managed to dwell too long on the memory of something that's past and gone. The difference is that I'm not grieving over the past now. I'm merely reporting a memory, so that you might understand what I'm about to say to you.

The fact is, we aren't the people we were even then, just a year ago. I know that. As I know things have been slowly eroding between us for a very long time; we are a little tired of each other, and there are annoyances and old scars that won't be obliterated with a letter — even a long one written in the middle of the night

in desperate sincerity, under the influence, admittedly, of a considerable portion of bourbon whiskey, but nevertheless with the
best intention and hope: that you may know how, over the course
of this night, I came to the end of needing an explanation for our
difficulty. We have reached this—place. Everything we say seems
rather aggravatingly mindless and automatic, like something one
stranger might say to another in any of the thousand circumstances
where strangers are thrown together for a time and the silence
begins to grow heavy on their minds and someone has to say
something. Darling, we go so long these days without having anything at all to do with each other, and the children are arriving
tomorrow, and once more we'll be in the position of making all
the gestures that give them back their parents as they think their
parents are, and what I wanted to say to you, what came to me as
I thought about Louise and Charles on that day so long ago, when
they were young and so obviously glad of each other, and I looked
at them and knew it and was happy—what came to me was that
even the harsh things that happened to them, even the years of
anger and silence, even the disappointment and the bitterness and
the wanting not to be in the same room anymore, even all that
must have been worth it for such loveliness. At least I am here, at
seventy years old, hoping so. Tonight, I went back to our room
again and stood gazing at you asleep, dreaming whatever you were
dreaming, and I had a moment of thinking how we were always
friends, too. And what I wanted finally to say was that I remember well our own sweet times, our own old loveliness. I would like
to think that even if at the very beginning of our lives together I
had somehow been shown that we would end up here, with this
longing to be away from each other, this feeling of being trapped
together, of being tied to each other in a way that makes us wish
for other times, some other place, I would have known enough to
accept it all freely for the chance at that love. And if I could, I
would do it all again, Marie. All of it, even the sorrow. My sweet,
my dear adversary. For everything that I remember.

1990

Reginald McKnight

THE KIND OF LIGHT THAT SHINES ON TEXAS

This story, the title story in Reginald McKnight's acclaimed 1992 collection, points as much at intra-racial relations as it does at racism, but its ultimate message unfolds slowly and subtley. As Carolyn See said of the author in her Newsday *review of the collection, "[his] stories are like an acupuncturist's needles. They don't hurt going in, but man, when they come out!" McKnight, whose father was in the Air Force, was born in Furstenfeldbruck, Germany. Even so, he spent part of his childhood in his father's home state (Texas) and in his mother's (Alabama). He teaches at the University of Maryland.*

I never liked Marvin Pruitt. Never liked him, never knew him, even though there were only three of us in the class. Three black kids. In our school there were fourteen classrooms of thirty-odd white kids (in '66, they considered Chicanos provisionally white) and three or four black kids. Primary school in primary colors. Neat division. Alphabetized. They didn't stick us in the back, or arrange us by degrees of hue, apartheidlike. This was real integration, a ten-to-one ratio as tidy as upper-class landscaping. If it all worked, you could have ten white kids all to yourself. They could talk to you, get the feel of you, scrutinize you bone deep if they wanted to. They seldom wanted to, and that was fine with me for two reasons. The first was that their scrutiny was irritating. How do you comb your hair — why do you comb your hair — may I please touch your hair — were the kinds of questions they asked. This is no way to feel at home. The second reason was Marvin. He embarrassed me. He smelled bad, was at least two grades behind, was hostile, dark-skinned, homely, close-mouthed. I feared him for his size, pitied him for his dress, watched him all the time. Marveled at him, mystified, astonished, uneasy.

He had the habit of spitting on his right arm, juicing it down till it would glisten. He would start in immediately after taking his seat when we'd finished with the Pledge of Allegiance, "The Yellow Rose of Texas," "The Eyes of Texas Are upon You," and "Mistress Shady." Marvin would rub his spit-flecked arm with his left hand, rub and roll as if polishing an ebony pool cue. Then he would rest his head in the crook of his arm, sniffing, huffing deep like blackjacket boys huff bagsful of acrylics. After ten minutes or so, his eyes would close, heavy. He would sleep till recess. Mrs. Wickham would let him.

There was one other black kid in our class, a girl they called Ah-so. I never learned what she did to earn this name. There was nothing Asian about this big-shouldered girl. She was the tallest, heaviest kid in school. She was quiet, but I don't think any one of us was subtle or sophisticated enough to nickname our classmates according to any but physical attributes. Fat kids were called Porky or Butterball; skinny ones were called Stick or Ichabod. Ah-so was big, thick, and African. She would impassively sit, sullen, silent as Marvin. She wore the same dark blue pleated skirt every day, the same ruffled white blouse every day. Her skin always shone as if worked by Marvin's palms and fingers. I never spoke one word to her, nor she to me.

Of the three of us, Mrs. Wickham called only on Ah-so and me. Ah-so never answered one question, correctly or incorrectly, so far as I can recall. She wasn't stupid. When asked to read aloud she read well, seldom stumbling over long words, reading with humor and expression. But when Wickham asked her about Farmer Brown and how many cows, or the capital of Vermont, or the date of this war or that, Ah-so never spoke. Not one word. But you always felt she could have answered those questions if she'd wanted to. I sensed no tension, embarrassment, or anger in Ah-so's reticence. She simply refused to speak. There was something unshakable about her, some core so impenetrably solid, you got the feeling that if you stood too close to her she could eat your thoughts like a black star eats light. I didn't despise Ah-so as I despised Marvin. There was nothing malevolent about her. She sat like a great icon in the back of the classroom, tranquil, guarded, sealed up, watchful. She was close to sixteen, and it was my guess she'd given up on school. Perhaps she was just obliging the wishes of her family, sticking it out till the law could no longer reach her.

There were at least half a dozen older kids in our class. Besides Marvin and Ah-so there was Oakley, who sat behind me, whispering threats into my ear; Varna Willard with the large breasts; Eddie Limon, who played bass for a high school rock band; and Lawrence Ridderbeck, who everyone said had a kid and a wife. You couldn't expect me to know anything about Texan educational practices of the 1960s, so I never knew why there were so many older kids in my sixth-grade class. After all, I was just a boy and had transferred into the school around midyear. My father, an air force sergeant, had been sent to Viet Nam. The air force sent my mother, my sister Claire, and me to Connolly Air Force Base, which during the war housed "unaccompanied wives." I'd been to so many different schools in my short life that I ceased wondering about their differences. All I knew about the Texas schools is that they weren't afraid to flunk you.

Yet though I was only twelve then, I had a good idea why Wickham never once called on Marvin, why she let him snooze in the crook of his polished arm. I knew why she would press her lips together, and narrow her eyes at me whenever I correctly answered a question, rare as that was. I knew why she badgered Ah-so with questions everyone knew Ah-so would never even consider answering. Wickham didn't like us. She wasn't gross about it, but it was clear she didn't want us around. She would prove her dislike day after day with little stories and jokes. "I just want to share with you all," she would say, "a little riddle my daughter told me at the supper table th'other day. Now, where do you go when you injure your knee?" Then one, two, or all three of her pets would say for the rest of us, "We don't know, Miz Wickham," in that skin-

chilling way suckasses speak, "where?" "Why, to Africa," Wickham
would say, "where the knee grows."

The thirty-odd white kids would laugh, and I would look across
the room at Marvin. He'd be asleep. I would glance back at Ah-so.
She'd be sitting still as a projected image, staring down at her desk.
I, myself, would smile at Wickham's stupid jokes, sometimes fake
a laugh. I tried to show her that at least one of us was alive and alert,
even though her jokes hurt. I sucked ass, too, I suppose. But I
wanted her to understand more than anything that I was not like
her other nigra children, that I was worthy of more than the nonat-
tention and the negative attention she paid Marvin and Ah-so. I
hated her, but never showed it. No one could safely contradict that
woman. She knew all kinds of tricks to demean, control, and pun-
ish you. And she could swing her two-foot paddle as fluidly as a
big-league slugger swings a bat. You didn't speak in Wickham's class
unless she spoke to you first. You didn't chew gum, or wear "hood"
hair. You didn't drag your feet, curse, pass notes, hold hands with
the opposite sex. Most especially, you didn't say anything bad about
the Aggies, Governor Connolly, LBJ, Sam Houston, or Waco. You
did the forbidden and she would get you. It was that simple.

She never got me, though. Never gave her reason to. But she
could have invented reasons. She did a lot of that. I can't be sure,
but I used to think she pitied me because my father was in Viet
Nam and my uncle A.J. had recently died there. Whenever she
would tell one of her racist jokes, she would always glance at me,
preface the joke with, "Now don't you nigra children take offense.
This is all in fun, you know. I just want to share with you all something Coach Gilchrest told me th'other day." She would tell her
joke, and glance at me again. I'd giggle, feeling a little queasy. "I'm
half Irish," she would chuckle, "and you should hear some of those
Irish jokes." She never told any, and I never really expected her to.
I just did my Tom-thing. I kept my shoes shined, my desk neat,
answered her questions as best I could, never brought gum to
school, never cursed, never slept in class. I wanted to show her we
were not all the same.

I tried to show them all, all thirty-odd, that I was different. It worked to some degree, but not very well. When some article was stolen from someone's locker or desk, Marvin, not I, was the first accused. I'd be second. Neither Marvin nor Ah-so nor I were ever chosen for certain classroom honors—"Pledge leader," "flag holder," "noise monitor," "paper passer outer"— but Mrs. Wickham once let me be "eraser duster." I was proud. I didn't even care about the cracks my fellow students made about my finally having turned the right color. I had done something that Marvin, in the deeps of his never-ending sleep, couldn't even dream of doing. Jack Preston, a kid who sat in front of me, asked me one day at recess whether I was embarrassed about Marvin. "Can you believe that guy?" I said. "He's like a pig or something. Makes me sick."

"Does it make you ashamed to be colored?"

"No," I said, but I meant yes. Yes, if you insist on thinking us all the same. Yes, if his faults are mine, his weaknesses inherent in me.

"I'd be," said Jack.

I made no reply. I was ashamed. Ashamed for not defending Marvin and ashamed that Marvin even existed. But if it had occurred to me, I would have asked Jack whether he was ashamed of being white because of Oakley. Oakley, "Oak Tree," Kelvin "Oak Tree" Oakley. He was sixteen and proud of it. He made it clear to everyone, including Wickham, that his life's ambition was to stay in school one more year, till he'd be old enough to enlist in the army. "Them slopes got my brother," he would say. "I'mna sign up and git me a few slopes. Gonna kill them bastards deader'n shit." Oakley, so far as anyone knew, was and always had been the oldest kid in his family. But no one contradicted him. He would, as anyone would tell you, "snap yer neck jest as soon as look at you." Not a boy in class, excepting Marvin and myself, had been able to avoid Oakley's pink bellies, Texas titty twisters, Moon Pie punches, or worse. He didn't bother Marvin, I suppose, because Marvin was closer to his size and age, and because Marvin spent five-sixths of the school day asleep. Marvin probably never crossed Oakley's mind. And to say that Oakley hadn't bothered me is not to say he had no intention of ever doing so. In fact, this haphazard sketch of hairy fingers, slash of eyebrow, explosion of acne, elbows, and crooked teeth, swore almost daily that he'd like to kill me.

Naturally, I feared him. Though we were about the same height, he outweighed me by no less than forty pounds. He talked, stood, smoked, and swore like a man. No one, except for Mrs. Wickham, the principal, and the coach, ever laid a finger on him. And even Wickham knew that the hot lines she laid on him merely amused him. He would smile out at the classroom, goofy and bashful, as she laid down the two, five, or maximum ten strokes on him. Often he would wink, or surreptitiously flash us the thumb as Wickham worked on him. When she was finished, Oakley would walk so cool back to his seat you'd think he was on wheels. He'd slide into his chair, sniff the air, and say, "Somethin's burnin. Do y'all smell smoke? I swanee, I smell smoke and fahr back here." If he had made these cracks and never threatened me, I might have grown to admire Oakley, even liked him a little. But he hated me, and took every opportunity during the six-hour school day to make me aware of this. "Some Sambo's gittin his ass broke open one of these days," he'd mumble. "I wanna fight somebody. Need to keep in shape till I git to Nam."

I never said anything to him for the longest time. I pretended not to hear him, pretended not to notice his sour breath on my neck and ear. "Yep," he'd whisper. "Coonies keep ya in good shape for slope killin." Day in, day out, that's the kind of thing I'd pretend not to hear. But one day when the rain dropped down like lead balls, and the cold air made your skin look plucked, Oakley whispered to me, "My brother tells me it rains like this in Nam. Maybe I oughta go out at recess and break your ass open today. Nice and cool so you don't sweat. Nice and wet to clean up the blood." I said nothing for at least half a minute, then I turned half right and said, "Thought you said your brother was dead." Oakley, silent himself, for a time, poked me in the back with his pencil and hissed, "*Yer* dead." Wickham cut her eyes our way, and it was over.

It was hardest avoiding him in gym class. Especially when we played murderball. Oakley always aimed his throws at me. He threw with unblinking intensity, his teeth gritting, his neck veining, his face flushing, his black hair sweeping over one eye. He could throw hard, but the balls were squishy and harmless. In fact, I found his misses more intimidating than his hits. The balls would whizz by, thunder against the folded bleachers. They rattled as though a locomotive were passing through them. I would duck, dodge, leap as if he were throwing grenades. But he always hit me, sooner or later. And after a while I noticed that the other boys would avoid throwing at me, as if I belonged to Oakley.

One day, however, I was surprised to see that Oakley was throwing at everyone else but me. He was uncommonly accurate, too; kids were falling like tin cans. Since no one was throwing at me, I spent most of the game watching Oakley cut this one and that one down. Finally, he and I were the only ones left on the court. Try as he would, he couldn't hit me, nor I him. Coach Gilchrest blew his whistle and told Oakley and me to bring the red rubber balls to the equipment locker. I was relieved I'd escaped Oakley's stinging throws for once. I was feeling triumphant, full of myself. As Oakley and I approached Gilchrest, I thought about saying something friendly to Oakley: Good game, Oak Tree, I would say. Before I could speak, though, Gilchrest said, "All right, boys, there's five minutes left in the period. Y'all are so good, looks like, you're gonna have to play like men. No boundaries, no catch outs, and you gotta hit your opponent three times in order to win. Got me?"

We nodded.

"And you're gonna use these," said Gilchrest, pointing to three volleyballs at his feet. "And you better believe they're pumped full. Oates, you start at the end of the court. Oak Tree, you're at th'other end. Just like usual, I'll set the balls at mid-court, and when I blow my whistle I want y'all to haul your cheeks to the middle and th'ow for all you're worth. Got me?" Gilchrest nodded at our nods, then added, "Remember, no boundaries, right?"

I at my end, Oakley at his, Gilchrest blew his whistle. I was faster than Oakley and scooped up a ball before he'd covered three quarters of his side. I aimed, threw, and popped him right on the knee. "One-zip!" I heard Gilchrest shout. The ball bounced off his knee and shot right back into my hands. I hurried my throw and missed. Oakley bent down, clutched the two remaining balls. I remember being amazed that he could palm each ball, run full out, and throw left-handed or right-handed without a shade of awkwardness. I spun, ran, but one of Oakley's throws glanced off the back of my head. "One-one!" hollered Gilchrest. I fell and spun on my ass as the other ball came sailing at me. I caught it. "He's out!" I yelled. Gilchrest's voice boomed, "No catch outs. Three hits. Three hits." I leapt to my feet as Oakley scrambled across the floor for another ball. I chased him down, leapt, and heaved the ball hard as he drew himself erect. The ball hit him dead in the face, and he went down flat. He rolled around, cupping his hands over his nose. Gilchrest sped to his side, helped him to his feet, asked him whether he was OK. Blood flowed from Oakley's nose, dripped in startlingly bright spots on the floor, his shoes, Gilchrest's shirt. The coach removed Oakley's T-shirt and pressed it against the big kid's nose to stanch the bleeding. As they walked past me toward the office I mumbled an apology to Oakley but couldn't catch his reply. "You watch your filthy mouth, boy," said Gilchrest to Oakley.

The locker room was unnaturally quiet as I stepped into its steamy atmosphere. Eyes clicked in my direction, looked away. After I was out of my shorts, had my towel wrapped around me, my shower kit in hand, Jack Preston and Brian Nailor approached me. Preston's hair was combed slick and plastic looking. Nailor's stood up like frozen flames. Nailor smiled at me with his big teeth and pale eyes. He poked my arm with a finger. "You fucked up," he said.

"I tried to apologize."

"Won't do you no good," said Preston.

"I swanee," said Nailor.

"It's part of the game," I said. "It was an accident. Wasn't my idea to use volleyballs."

"Don't matter," Preston said. "He's jest lookin for an excuse to fight you."

"I never done nothing to him."

"Don't matter," said Nailor. "He don't like you."

"Brian's right, Clint. He'd jest as soon kill you as look at you."

"I never done nothing to him."

"Look," said Preston, "I know him pretty good. And jest between you and me, it's cause you're a city boy—"

"Whadda you mean? I've never—"

"He don't like your clothes—"

"And he don't like the fancy way you talk in class."

"What fancy—"

"I'm tellin him, if you don't mind, Brian."

"Tell him then."

"He don't like the way you say 'tennis shoes' instead of sneakers. He don't like coloreds. A whole bunch a things, really."

"I never done nothing to him. He's got no reason—"

"*And*," said Nailor, grinning, "*and*, he says you're a stuck-up rich kid." Nailor's eyes had crow's-feet, bags beneath them. They were a man's eyes.

"My dad's a sergeant," I said.

"You chicken to fight him?" said Nailor.

"Yeah, Clint, don't be chicken. Jest go on and git it over with. He's whupped pert near ever'body else in the class. It ain't so bad."

"Might as well, Oates."

"Yeah, yer pretty skinny, but yer jest about his height. Jest git im in a headlock and don't let go."

"Goddamn," I said, "he's got no reason to—"

Their eyes shot right and I looked over my shoulder. Oakley stood at his locker, turning its tumblers. From where I stood I could see that a piece of cotton was wedged up one of his nostrils, and he already had the makings of a good shiner. His acne burned red like a fresh abrasion. He snapped the locker open and kicked his shoes off without sitting. Then he pulled off his shorts, revealing two paddle stripes on his ass. They were fresh red bars speckled with white, the white speckles being the reverse impression of the paddle's suction holes. He must not have watched his filthy mouth while in Gilchrest's presence. Behind me, I heard Preston and Nailor pad to their lockers.

Oakley spoke without turning around. "Somebody's gonna git his skinny black ass kicked, right today, right after school." He said it softly. He slipped his jock off, turned around. I looked away. Out the corner of my eye I saw him stride off, his hairy nakedness a weapon clearing the younger boys from his path. Just before he rounded the corner of the shower stalls, I threw my toilet kit to the floor and stammered, "I — I never did nothing to you, Oakley." He stopped, turned, stepped closer to me, wrapping his towel around himself. Sweat streamed down my rib cage. It felt like ice water. "You wanna go at it right now, boy?"

"I never did nothing to you." I felt tears in my eyes. I couldn't stop them even though I was blinking like mad. "Never."

He laughed. "You busted my nose, asshole."

"What about before? What'd I ever do to you?"

"See you after school, Coonie." Then he turned away, flashing his acne-spotted back like a semaphore. "Why?" I shouted. "Why you wanna fight me?" Oakley stopped and turned, folded his arms, leaned against a toilet stall. "Why you wanna fight *me*, Oakley?" I stepped over the bench. "What'd I do? Why me?" And then unconsciously, as if scratching, as if breathing, I walked toward Marvin, who stood a few feet from Oakley, combing his hair at the mirror. "Why not him?" I said. "How come you're after *me* and not *him*?" The room froze. Froze for a moment that was both evanescent and eternal, somewhere between an eye blink and a week in hell. No one moved, nothing happened; there was no sound at all. And then it was as if all of us at the same moment looked at Marvin. He just stood there, combing away, the only body in motion, I think. He combed his hair and combed it, as if seeing only his image, hearing only his comb scraping his scalp. I knew he'd heard me. There's no way he could not have heard me. But all he did was slide the comb into his pocket and walk out the door.

"I got no quarrel with Marvin," I heard Oakley say. I turned toward his voice, but he was already in the shower.

I was able to avoid Oakley at the end of the school day. I made my escape by asking Mrs. Wickham if I could go to the restroom.

"'Restroom,'" Oakley mumbled. "It's a damn toilet, sissy."

"Clinton," said Mrs. Wickham. "Can you *not* wait till the bell rings? It's almost three o'clock."

"No, ma'am," I said. "I won't make it."

"Well, I should make you wait just to teach you to be more mindful about . . . hygiene . . . uh things." She sucked in her cheeks, squinted. "But I'm feeling charitable today. You may go." I immediately left the building, and got on the bus. "Ain't you a little early?" said the bus driver, swinging the door shut. "Just left the office," I said. The driver nodded, apparently not giving me a second thought. I had no idea why I'd told her I'd come from the office, or why she found it a satisfactory answer. Two minutes later the bus filled, rolled, and shook its way to Connolly Air Base.

When I got home, my mother was sitting in the living room, smoking her Slims, watching her soap opera. She absently asked me how my day had gone and I told her fine. "Hear from Dad?" I said.

"No, but I'm sure he's fine." She always said that when we hadn't heard from him in a while. I suppose she thought I was worried about him, or that I felt vulnerable without him. It was neither. I just wanted to discuss something with my mother that we both cared about. If I spoke with her about things that happened at school, or on my weekends, she'd listen with half an ear, say something like, "Is that so?" or "You don't say?" I couldn't stand that sort of thing. But when I mentioned my father, she treated me a bit more like an adult, or at least someone who was worth listening to. I didn't want to feel like a boy that afternoon. As I turned from my mother and walked down the hall I thought about the day my father left for Viet Nam. Sharp in his uniform, sure behind his aviator specs, he slipped a cigar from his pocket and stuck it in mine. "Not till I get back," he said. "We'll have us one when we go fishing. Just you and me, out on the lake all day, smoking and casting and sitting. Don't let Mamma see it. Put it in y' back pocket." He hugged me, shook my hand, and told me I was the man of the house now. He told me he was depending on me to take good care of my mother and sister. "Don't you let me down, now, hear?" And he tapped his thick finger on my chest. "You almost as big as me. Boy, you something else." I believed him when he told me those things. My heart swelled big enough to swallow my father, my mother, Claire. I loved, feared, and respected myself, my manhood. That day I could have put all of Waco, Texas, in my heart. And it wasn't till about three months later that I discovered I really wasn't the man of the house, that my mother and sister, as they always had, were taking care of me.

For a brief moment I considered telling my mother about what had happened at school that day, but for one thing, she was deep down in the halls of "General Hospital," and never paid you much mind till it was over. For another thing, I just wasn't the kind of person—I'm still not, really—to discuss my problems with anyone. Like my father I kept things to myself, talked about my problems only in retrospect. Since my father wasn't around, I consciously wanted to be like him, doubly like him, I could say. I wanted to be the man of the house in some respect, even if it had to be in an inward way. I went to my room, changed my clothes, and laid out my homework. I couldn't focus on it. I thought about Marvin, what I'd said about him or done to him—I couldn't tell which. I'd done something to him, said something about him; said something about and done something to myself. *How come you're after me and not him?* I kept trying to tell myself I hadn't meant it that way. *That* way. I thought about approaching Marvin, telling him what I really meant was that he was more Oakley's age and weight than I. I would tell him I meant I was no match for Oakley. *See Marvin, what I meant was that he wants to fight a colored guy, but is afraid to fight you cause you could beat him*. But try as I did, I couldn't for a moment convince myself that Marvin would believe me. I meant it *that* way and no other. Everybody heard. Everybody knew. That afternoon I forced myself to confront the notion that tomorrow I would probably have to fight both Oakley and Marvin. I'd have to be two men.

I rose from my desk and walked to the window. The light made my skin look orange, and I started thinking about what Wickham had told us once about light. She said that oranges and apples, leaves and flowers, the whole multicolored world, was not what it appeared to be. The colors we see, she said, look like they do only because of the light or ray that shines on them. "The color of the thing isn't what you see, but the light that's reflected off it." Then she shut out the lights and shone a white light lamp on a prism. We watched the pale splay of colors on the projector screen; some people ooohed and aaahed. Suddenly, she switched on a black light and the color of everything changed. The prism colors vanished, Wickham's arms were purple, the buttons of her dress were as orange as hot coals, rather than the blue they had been only seconds before. We were all very quiet. "Nothing," she said after a while, "is really what it appears to be." I didn't really understand then. But as I stood at the window, gazing at my orange skin, I wondered what kind of light I could shine on Marvin, Oakley, and me that would reveal us as the same.

I sat down and stared at my arms. They were dark brown again. I worked up a bit of saliva under my tongue and spat on my left arm. I spat again, then rubbed the spittle into it, polishing, working till my arm grew warm. As I spat, and rubbed, I wondered why Marvin did this weird, nasty thing to himself, day after day. Was he trying to rub away the black, or deepen it, doll it up? And if he did this weird, nasty thing for a hundred years, would he spit-shine himself invisible, rolling away the eggplant skin, revealing the scarlet muscle, blue vein, pink and yellow tendon, white bone? Then disappear? Seen through, all colors, no colors. Spitting and rubbing. Is this the way you do it? I leaned forward, sniffed the arm. It smelled vaguely of mayonnaise. After an hour or so, I fell asleep.

I saw Oakley the second I stepped off the bus the next morning. He stood outside the gym in his usual black penny loafers, white socks, high-water jeans, T-shirt, and black jacket. Nailor stood with him, his big teeth spread across his bottom lip like playing cards. If there was anyone I felt like fighting, that day, it was Nailor. But I wanted to put off fighting for as long as I could. I stepped toward the gymnasium, thinking that I shouldn't run, but if I hurried I could beat Oakley to the door and secure myself near Gilchrest's office. But the moment I stepped into the gym, I felt Oakley's broad palm clap down on my shoulder. "Might as well stay out here, Coonie," he said. "I need me a little target practice." I turned to face him and he slapped me, one-two, with the back, then the palm of his hand, as I'd seen Bogart do to Peter Lorre in *The Maltese Falcon*. My heart went wild. I could scarcely breathe. I couldn't swallow.

"Call me a nigger," I said. I have no idea what made me say this. All I know is that it kept me from crying. "Call me a nigger, Oakley."

"Fuck you, ya black ass slope." He slapped me again, scratching my eye. "I don't do what coonies tell me."

"Call me a nigger."

"Outside, Coonie."

"Call me one. Go ahead."

He lifted his hand to slap me again, but before his arm could swing my way, Marvin Pruitt came from behind me and calmly pushed me aside. "Git out my way, boy," he said. And he slugged Oakley on the side of his head. Oakley stumbled back, stiff-legged. His eyes were big. Marvin hit him twice more, once again to the side of the head, once to the nose. Oakley went down and stayed down. Though blood was drawn, whistles blowing, fingers pointing, kids hollering, Marvin just stood there, staring at me with cool eyes. He spat on the ground, licked his lips, and just stared at me, till Coach Gilchrest and Mr. Calderon tackled him and violently carried him away. He never struggled, never took his eyes off me.

Nailor and Mrs. Wickham helped Oakley to his feet. His already fattened nose bled and swelled so that I had to look away. He looked around, bemused, wall-eyed, maybe scared. It was apparent he had no idea how bad he was hurt. He didn't even touch his nose. He didn't look like he knew much of anything. He looked at me, looked me dead in the eye in fact, but didn't seem to recognize me.

That morning, like all other mornings, we said the Pledge of Allegiance, sang "The Yellow Rose of Texas," "The Eyes of Texas Are upon You," and "Mistress Shady." The room stood strangely empty without Oakley, and without Marvin, but at the same time you could feel their presence more intensely somehow. I felt like I did when I'd walk into my mother's room and could smell my father's cigars, or cologne. He was more palpable, in certain respects, than when there in actual flesh. For some reason, I turned to look at Ah-so, and just this once I let my eyes linger on her face. She had a very gentle-looking face, really. That surprised me. She must have felt my eyes on her because she glanced up at me for a second and smiled, white teeth, downcast eyes. Such a pretty smile. That surprised me too. She held it for a few seconds, then let it fade. She looked down at her desk, and sat still as a photograph.

1991

Nanci Kincaid

THIS IS NOT THE PICTURE SHOW

Was the phrase "picture show" ever used anywhere else but the American South? Who cares? What's to care about is the way the phrase is used in this delicious story of self-recognition. No story has ever pegged junior high school romance, the sixties, or small town society more precisely than Nanci Kincaid's does here. Claiming as home states both Florida and Alabama, Kincaid is the author of two novels, Crossing Blood *and* Balls. *She now lives in Charlotte, North Carolina, where she teaches at the University of North Carolina at Charlotte.*

M e and Pat Lee go to town every Saturday. It is a social responsibility. Only the country kids don't go because they have to feed chickens and stuff, which we think is the saddest of circumstances.

When we get to town we buy five-cent bags of boiled peanuts first thing from crazy old men who sit on the sidewalk, some with their legs cut off and their pants all folded and pinned in strange arrangements, some blind who take all day making change, feeling each coin, counting out loud, and some who are okay on the outside, but crazy in the head the way they sing songs without words, or make a bunch of kissing noises when they see me and Pat Lee walking up.

"Shut up, you stupid old men," Pat Lee mumbles.

Mother says these crazy old men are left over from the war or else let out of Chattahoochee Mental Hospital. She drops us off at the park right where they sit and says, "It's pitiful. You two be nice to those pitiful men." And every Saturday of our lives we pay one of them our nickel and get ourselves little warm, wet bags of juicy boiled peanuts.

Then we roam through all the stores in downtown Tallahassee looking at merchandise. Actually we are looking for other junior-high people who are also roaming. When there are seven or eight of us, maybe more, we go from place to place, trying out 45 records in the listening booths at the Sammy Seminole Music Store. Sometimes we connect the dots on the acoustical tiles to see what they come out to be. (Once we fit thirteen people in one listening booth, just for the heck of it, and played Chubby Checker records on 78 speed, which is the funniest thing you ever heard.) Then we eat French fries at the Rexall and write messages on the tabletops without getting caught. Me and Pat Lee make up initials, like T.B. + V.D., and paint them on in fingernail polish, knowing other people will come along and try to figure out who it is. The waitress has never mentioned a thing about it.

After that everybody rides the elevator at Mendelson's Department Store. We hold the buttons down and just keep going up and down — not stopping to let any other people on. We do that ten or fifteen times and then we go to the cosmetics counter and spray each other with sample cologne. Until, finally, it is time for the picture show and we all walk down the street to the State Theater.

Now the State Theater does a good business. They could show black-and-white slides of "How to Care for Houseplants" and we would line up to see it. It is fifty-five cents to get in and for another nickel you can get an all-day Sugar Daddy on a stick, which we always do. If you are ever going to have any experience with boys this is the place to get started with it, which makes me nervous, although I manage to be as suave as the next girl about it. I have to be. Because of Pat Lee and all.

It comes natural to her, driving boys crazy. She does it by acting rotten to them. She does it by being mad at them all the time, or bored to death or aggravated with them for some reason they never can figure out. I've seen boys get in a fistfight outside the State Theater over who was going to sit by Pat Lee, only to have her get mad and refuse to sit by either one of them. I've seen her sit by Bobby Castle all the way through an Elvis Presley movie with her arms crossed, pouting, not saying a word to him. But he still bought her buttered popcorn, an Orange Crush, and a box of Milk Duds. And when the movie was over he asked her if he could sit by her again the next Saturday, tried to make her promise, and she walked right out of the theater without even looking at him. That night he called and asked her to go steady. It's like that all the time.

Pat Lee says the reason the boys don't like me as much is because I'm too nice to them. She says I make her sick going around smiling and being thoughtful. She says no boy will ever take me seriously until I stop it. I try to tell her that I don't mean to smile this much, it's just that my face seems to automatically go into a smile, even when it's in a resting state. Pat Lee says it's disgusting and is trying to get me to start saying "shit" and "tits" and "screw" and a bunch of other words that will wipe this smile off my face. She gives up on me all the time. She says deep down boys cannot stand a nice girl. "You're prettier than me," she says, "but I'm a whole lot more popular than you. So I guess it balances out." I can only hope she's right.

Pat Lee's popularity got started in the sixth grade when she was the fastest runner in the school—and nobody could beat her and almost every boy in the class tried. She did not throw like a girl either, which made boys go crazy over her. They would line up at P.E. just to watch Pat Lee pitch a baseball. And she could hit home runs and shoot baskets from midcourt and do a backward flip off the high dive in her red bathing suit. Everything boys respect. Then all that admiration just mushroomed into this other thing. And Pat Lee is the most popular girl at Augusta Raa Junior High School. She gets elected to everything she tries out for. And I kind of like it because I get the spillover from her popularity. If a boy can't sit by Pat Lee, then he wants to sit by me, since I'm her best friend. I don't have to go to much trouble over it. I even let Proctor James sit by me, despite the fact he never washes his hair. He sat by Pat Lee first, but she got up and moved, making all the rest of the boys laugh at him. The next thing I know I felt so sorry for Proctor I was smiling at him.

"You're hopeless," Pat Lee said to me. "I swear to God, you're hopeless."

"He's sort of nice," I lied.

The only boy Pat Lee thinks is nice is Tony Kelly, and that's only because Tony is almost as mean as she is. And he is a country boy too — not like the rest of the boys at the picture show on Saturday in their penny loafers. His brother lets him out in front of the State Theater in a souped-up green truck — which anybody else would be embarrassed over — and Tony neither speaks nor looks at a single person in the picture show line. And he wears boots, which are not in style at all. And sometimes lights up a cigarette like he has a perfect right to do it. He does not fit in in any way, and doesn't even try to, and so people can't help but stare at him and wonder just what he thinks he's doing. I stare at him myself.

The first Saturday he showed up at the State Theater all the regular junior-high people got quiet and looked at him. He didn't care. And before you know it Pat Lee walked over to Tony — the whole civilized junior-high population gawking — and said, "Hey, Tony. You here by yourself?"

"You see anybody with me?" he answered.

"Do you want to sit with me and Connie Jean?" (I was hoping he'd say no. Pat Lee had already promised to sit with Bobby Castle.)

"It depends," Tony said.

"On what?" Pat Lee said, not smiling exactly, but sort of playing with her hair.

"I don't like a bunch of talking when I go to the picture show," Tony said. "I'm not paying my money to listen to girls talk."

Pat Lee didn't get mad, and she sat beside him that Saturday and every Saturday since. Nobody can understand it. She has let Tony kiss her three times. Once at *Beach Blanket Bingo*, once at *Pillow Talk*, and once at *Fort Apache*. I was sitting right next to her every time. When they start that, it makes my hands sweat. And worse than that, it gives the town boys the same idea. They think Pat Lee is practically a goddess now that they know she will kiss in front of everybody.

And Tony, even though his hair is too long, he doesn't peg his blue jeans, and just wears white T-shirts all the time, nobody makes fun of him. If he walks into the State Theater late and Pat Lee is sitting with Bobby Castle because she thinks Tony is not coming, all Tony does is walk down the aisle with his hands in his pockets, not even looking for Pat Lee, just maybe chewing a toothpick, and he goes and sits by himself and waits. And when Pat Lee sees him she hurries over there, saying, "I'm sorry. I didn't know you were coming." And Tony says, "Shhhhh, I'm trying to watch the show."

At school Tony will not speak to Pat Lee. He's in the dumb classes for one thing, the vocational boys, woodshop and all, and so he just minds his business at school. If you ask me he's failed a grade or two. It wouldn't surprise me if he'd been to reform school. Pat Lee laughs and says I'm crazy when I tell her that. "You're jealous," she says.

"I don't have anything against boys from reform school," I say.

"You don't have anything against anybody," she says. "That's what's wrong with you."

Pat Lee tried to save Tony a seat at lunch once, but he said, "No," and took his tray and sat at a table all by himself.

She got so mad she stormed over there saying, "I don't see what gives you the right to go around acting like you're better than everybody."

"Go sit with your friends," he said.

I thought for a minute Pat Lee was going to cry. But she said, "Are you coming to the show Saturday?"

"Maybe," he said.

Me and Pat Lee usually get to the State Theater early but we are probably the only two people in junior high who don't always get to see the show. Our mothers worry about appropriateness.

On this occasion, when *Gypsy* was the Saturday show, our mothers said, "I can't think of a reason in this world why two young girls need to see a movie about a stripper!" So we had to just stand outside the State Theater and watch everybody else go in. We could just see all the junior-high people sitting in the first rows, and it made us miserable to think we wouldn't be sitting there too. It made Pat Lee even more miserable than me, for fear Tony would come and she would miss seeing him, or worse, that some other girl might try to sit next to him and he might let her do it.

We stood on the sidewalk sucking soft-boiled peanut hulls, then spitting them on the ground. We stood there until every single person had filed inside and there was no one left but the two of us.

"I guess he's not coming," Pat Lee said.

"Who?"

"Who do you think?" Pat Lee said, shoving me down the street. "Let's go to Woolworth's."

Woolworth's is two doors down from the State Theater and they have this banana-split special. They have a bunch of balloons taped to the wall above the counter. The customer picks out one and the waitress pops it and gets a piece of paper out of it with the price of the banana split on it. Sometimes a person gets a banana split for a penny, but most of them are thirty-nine cents.

We sat in the booth up by the window, chose our balloons and sat waiting for our thirty-nine-cent banana splits. We have never paid less for a banana split and don't know anybody else who has, but we believe in the game and remain hopeful.

Pat Lee is one of the few people I can talk to in a serious way. We've been best friends since third grade, and over the years we developed a radar. For example, I knew, without Pat Lee saying so, that she was watching every vehicle that went down Monroe Street, hoping to see that souped-up green truck.

"You still looking for Tony?" I said.

"Nope."

"You know why he makes you so miserable?" I said. "It's because he's as mean as you are."

"At least I don't hold hands with Proctor James."

"I DID NOT HOLD HANDS."

"You sat by him."

"ONCE."

"You are so nice you make me sick," Pat Lee said. "I bet you grow up and marry one of those boiled-peanut men."

"Shut up," I said.

"This is the real world out here," she said. "This is not the picture shows."

The waitress brought our banana splits just then, two beauties with beehives of whipped cream on top and red cherries sliding, leaving pink trails. She set them down carefully, trickles of chocolate dripping down the sides of the glass boats. As soon as the waitress left, Pat Lee said, "Yours is bigger than mine."

"Good," I said.

"But your banana has a rotten spot on it," she said, scooping a mound of vanilla ice cream into her mouth, "so it balances out."

Pat Lee is my best friend. But she can make me hate myself sometimes. It's because she's honest, I think, which Mother says never has been in style and never will be. Mother says that honest is another word for rude. Like if somebody is fat Pat Lee'd say, "Lord, that girl wears her groceries, don't she?" When Beth was too flat-chested to undress in P.E., Pat Lee said, "Listen, Beth, get you a bra and stick some toilet paper in it. That's what Caroline does." Caroline was mad at Pat Lee for a long time, but Pat Lee didn't care. You'd think her mother had never mentioned the first word about good manners.

I don't hold this against Pat Lee, though, because she is Catholic and I feel like that has something to do with it. My mother says that Catholics just do what the Pope says and they don't have to think for themselves, so I always keep that in mind.

We paid the waitress and began wandering up and down the dime-store aisles. We know the store by heart, same as we know every store in Tallahassee.

Neither one of us really felt like hanging around uptown by ourselves, knowing the rest of the world was in the dark theater watching some grown woman undress to music.

"Today's been a bomb," Pat Lee said. I was surprised at Pat Lee sounding ready to go home. She usually loves to stay in town more than anybody. "Let's walk over to Penney's," she said. "I'll call Mother to come get us."

JCPenney's is between Woolworth's and the State Theater. It is the official place where people call their mothers. I gave Pat Lee a dime to call with, since it was her mother coming to get us. Things are always confused at her house. They have eight kids. It usually takes a lot of time just to get the right person to the phone and then her mother has to remember where everybody is or should be. It is mass confusion, which is why Pat Lee doesn't like to be home much and doesn't like people to come over to her house and see what a mess it always is. One of her brothers has drawn a Sears truck on the living room wall with an orange crayon. Now they have to paint the whole room. There is a lot of crying going on over there and screen doors slamming. That's why Pat Lee prefers to come to my house. It's quiet. My mother spends her life cleaning everything up. After saying "okay" about ten times, Pat Lee hangs up.

"Mother said she has to take Missy to tumbling class at the armory and then she'll come get us. She said to meet her in front of Penney's because her hair is rolled up and no way is she going to trek through the Penney's store looking for us with her hair rolled up."

"Okay," I said. "Let's go upstairs and look at the clothes a few minutes."

They had a whole rack of new bathing suits set up. We both headed straight for it. "Are you getting a two-piece this year?" I asked Pat Lee.

"Probably. If you don't, boys think there is something the matter with your body." She held up a little butterfly bikini. "Shoot, I bet seeing me in this could straighten Tony Kelly out. Bet this could turn the boy nice."

Pat Lee was greatly exaggerating her powers—believe me—and besides, her mother would never in a million years let her buy a bathing suit like that.

"Good gosh," she said, pulling out a second bathing suit and waving it around in my face, "they must have chased a nigger down for this one."

"Shhhhh," I said on instinct. I looked around us, afraid some colored person would hear her. Afraid some colored person would get mad and give us that quiet look I hate more than anything. There were a couple of salesladies at the counter deep in whispered conversation, and some girl older than us carrying a dress into the fitting room. "Be quiet," I said.

"This bathing suit is even too tacky for a nigger," Pat Lee said.

And then I saw her—an old lady, who came walking from between some racks of raincoats. Pat Lee was analyzing bathing suits a mile a minute by this time.

"Hey," she said, "get a load of this."

But I was watching the old lady. She moved slow, like she was dragging something, watching her feet every step she took. On her head was a black straw hat—the kind old ladies wear—and she carried a big tourist pocketbook with gaudy flowers all over it and the word FLORIDA stitched in red straw across it. She stood at a counter of madras shorts and as slow as Christmas picked up one thing, put it down, picked up another thing, put it down.

She had on a pair of old Hush Puppies—somebody probably gave them to her—and dark stockings with a run in both legs, showing streaks of skin. And her dress, it probably used to fit somebody just right, some other woman a long time ago. There was a hole in the elbow of her sweater, which it was too hot to be wearing anyway. But it wasn't her clothes that got my attention, it was her face and the fact that I couldn't see it. She was stooped over and her eyes stayed down. Just that black hat on her head shining out like a blank face with the eyes, nose, and mouth erased off of it.

I guess she'd picked up and put down every item on that table.

Her back was to me now. And with unnatural stillness she moved her arms at such a slant, like she was reaching for something, and that pocketbook of hers came open. Then quick — so quick I wasn't sure I saw it — she stuffed a handful of shorts into her pocketbook, and it was closed again.

I got hot all over. There I was watching her and the old lady stole something. My heart was beating away, like it was me doing it, stealing. I couldn't move my eyes away from her.

"What's with you?" Pat Lee was hollering. "Hey, what are you staring at?"

"Shhhhhh," I said.

Pat Lee turned to see what I was looking at. When she did, the old lady was sticking some more clothes in her pocketbook and Pat Lee saw her too.

By this time I knew it was the real thing. But Pat Lee felt that same shock like I had. "Good gosh," she whispered. "Look at that. She's stealing. Would you look?"

I couldn't quit looking.

The old lady should have felt us staring at her. Our eyes should have seemed like little bullets going into her back.

"We've got to tell somebody," Pat Lee said. "Come on. Let's tell somebody. She can't come in here and clean the place out. Shoot, a granny like that."

"Wait a minute," I said, grabbing Pat Lee's arm so she couldn't go. "She's old."

"Have you gone crazy?"

"Look at that pitiful dress," I said. "It's so pitiful." It crossed my mind that this old woman might be a sister to some of those old men that sat in the park selling peanuts. She might be crazy like some of them and have spent her whole life at the Chattahoochee Mental Hospital and just got released into Tallahassee without having any idea how to act in the regular world.

"What's right is right," Pat Lee said. "You know that."

But I didn't. There is nothing in this world that I am sure of. "What do you think they'll do to her if we tell?" I said.

The old lady didn't look anything like my two grandmothers. Both of them are fat. I knew for a fact it had never crossed either of their minds to steal anything.

"It's our duty to turn in people when they start robbing the place blind," Pat Lee said, her eyes contracting into slits. "You wait here if you're chicken. Just keep your eye on her. Don't let her get away."

I tried to act regular watching the old lady shuffling around the counters. Maybe it was a terrible thing — shoplifting. It probably was, since they send people to jail over it. What if everybody did like me and watched old ladies steal shorts from the junior-teen department? JCPenney's would have to close down in no time.

If she could be a colored woman stealing, I thought, well, then it would make sense and I wouldn't be so worried about it, because everybody knows colored people have certain reasons for what they do. But everybody also knows there is no good reason for any decent white woman to be stealing. My mother has explained it to me, that any wrong thing a colored person does, it is because we make them do it. Us. White people. But I don't know where she gets that. Because I can honestly say that I, myself, have never made a colored person do anything.

I stared at the old woman like she was stark naked, scooting around in nothing but those Hush Puppies. It was not my fault she was poor, was it? It was not my fault she had that wrinkled face and wore that pitiful dress and had got caught stealing like any other thief in the world. Why did it seem like my fault?

I thought about running up and telling her to empty that tacky pocketbook before the police came. I thought about screaming for her to run like heck. I could have warned her. But then I bet Pat Lee would say it was her duty to turn ME in as an accomplice. I would have to go to court, which would break my daddy's heart and make him divorce Mother for the crazy ideas she put in my head. I would be sent off to reform school, where I would turn into one of those vocational girls who takes cosmetology classes, dyes her hair, and wears bras as pointy as two sharp arrows. They would probably kill me at reform school because I am so nice. They would tie me up in ropes and leave me on a cold cement floor, or else beat me with slats of lumber until I go unconscious. And they would scream, "You are too nice. This is what you get for being so nice!"

The old woman floated like a small gray ghost around the store. I am afraid of any person who will not let you see her face. It seemed forever before Pat Lee came back. Some man wearing a name tag came with her. And it was done.

"Let's get out of here," Pat Lee said. "We've done our part. Besides, Mother's probably waiting out front."

The man with the name tag walked over to the old lady, taking hold of her arm. "You'll have to come with me," he said.

A great puff of air seemed to go out of the woman, shriveling her the last bit, but she was obedient and allowed herself to be led away, shuffling along beside the stern, closed-faced JCPenney's man, clutching her Florida bag with its cheerful straw flowers. "I need to call my grandson," she said.

"Yes, ma'am," the man said with strange politeness. Maybe, like me, he believes this is all somehow his fault.

"Hurry," Pat Lee said. "Mother will kill us if she has to get out of the car with her hair rolled up."

The man slowly escorted the little bent-over robber downstairs to call the police. They passed in front of Pat Lee and me, the old lady watching her step, staring at those hand-me-down Hush Puppies.

We passed a full-length mirror in the men's department before we reached the front door. Pat Lee stopped a minute and looked at herself, pushing her hair up with her fingers, puffing it.

"Do you think I ought to start ratting my hair more?" she said. "I bet it would make me look older. I bet Tony would like it."

"You're too nice to Tony," I said. "Every other boy you treat hateful and they all like you because of it, but Tony you're nice to and he hardly pays you any attention at all. You make a fool of yourself acting so nice."

"You don't understand," Pat Lee said, fluffing her hair again, twirling around, holding her arms out at her side. "It's love," she said, grinning. "It balances things out."

Pat Lee's mother was late. We stood on the sidewalk for twenty minutes, waiting, before Pat Lee finally went back into Penney's and called her mother again. "She forgot us," Pat Lee said, coming back out of the store, "but Missy says she's on her way now."

Just as Pat Lee finished speaking, like the timing in a movie, that green pickup truck Pat Lee had hoped to see all day came lurching to a halt in front of JCPenney's. Tony sprang out of the front seat, leaving the door hanging open, and hurried toward us. His brother sat in the driver's seat and kept the motor running. He was smoking a cigarette and had a tattoo on his arm. He looked like one of those men my mother sees and says, "The army would be the best thing in the world for him." He did not look like Tony, who has not got so sour yet, and who walked past us full of intent, his boots clicking across the sidewalk.

"Hey, Tony," Pat Lee said, but he seemed unable to hear her or see her, either one. He seemed only able to see what was directly in front of him and he walked straight ahead toward it, whatever it was, right past us, and through JCPenney's swinging doors.

"He didn't even speak," Pat Lee said.

"He didn't see you," I told her.

Just then Pat Lee's mother pulled up in her station wagon and began blowing the horn, as if we were likely to miss seeing her otherwise. She had brush rollers with pink spikes stabbed through them all over her head and a scarf tied uselessly over them. She was happy because she and Pat Lee's daddy had been invited to dinner at Tallahassee Country Club that very night. They were not members but socialized with lots of people who were. Her fingernails were painted red and she had the radio going, playing Glenn Miller's "Little Brown Jug." Three of Pat Lee's younger sisters were huddled in the very back of the station wagon with a scattered set of paper dolls to keep them busy. One of her brothers sat in the front seat with his arm hanging out the window. "Hurry up," he

said. Me and Pat Lee got in the back seat after scooting over some
bags of groceries that were piled in our way.

"You won't believe what we saw," Pat Lee said to her mother.
"There was this really old woman in Penney's teen department . . ."

As Pat Lee was speaking, the old woman appeared, walking out
of Penney's, shuffling slowly, looking down. She was holding on
to her grandson, who walked patiently beside her, extending his
crooked arm so that she could brace herself walking.

"Isn't she pitiful," Pat Lee's mother said, noticing the old woman
and craning her neck to look harder. "So pitiful."

The pair moved across the sidewalk to the waiting green truck
and its open door, she in her Hush Puppies and he in his pointed
cowboy boots and white T-shirt.

Tony gently helped his grandmother into the truck. It didn't
seem to matter to him whether she was crazy, or a criminal, or
wearing raggedy mismatched clothes. It didn't seem to matter to
him that she had just got caught stealing, and it would probably
say so in the *Tallahassee Democrat* the next day. It wouldn't matter
to him if she was just released from Chattahoochee yesterday or
due to check in tomorrow. He spoke softly to her and when she
was seated in the truck cab he slid in beside her and slammed the
door closed.

The green truck jerked out into traffic right in front of us, and
when it did Tony caught sight of Pat Lee, her face watching him
from the backseat of the station wagon. His elbow was jutted out
the window, and keeping his arm still he lifted his hand in recog-
nition as he passed, raising a couple of stiff fingers and nodding
slightly.

Pat Lee fell back against the seat, silently. And I understood it.
Why Tony makes her smile like that. Why she loves him more than
any other boy in Tallahassee. For a minute there, I loved him
myself.

Mark Richard

THE BIRDS FOR CHRISTMAS

In this story about Christmas on a hospital ward for poor crippled children some-where in the poor crippled South, Mark Richard's profane Michael Christian suc-cessfully murders any lingering echo of Dickensian sentimentality. When the Head Nurse suggests watching the Rudolph or Frosty special on the night before Christ-mas Eve, Michael says, "Fuck Frosty . . . I seen that a hunrett times." Richard, who spent some of his own childhood on a children's ward, was born in Lake Charles, Louisiana, and grew up in Texas, Virginia, and North Carolina. He has published one collection of stories, and a novel, Fishboy, *and lives now in California.*

We wanted "The Birds" for Christmas. We had seen the commercials for it on the television donated thirdhand by the Merchant Seamen's and Sailors' Rest Home, a big black-and-white Zenith of cracked plastic and no knobs, a dime stuck in the channel selector. You could adjust the picture and have no sound, or hi-fi sound and no picture. We just wanted the picture. We wanted to see "The Birds."

The Old Head Nurse said not to get our hopes up. It was a "Late Show" after Lights Out the night before Christmas Eve. She said it would wake the babies and scare the Little Boys down on the far end of the ward. Besides, she said, she didn't think it was the type of movie we should be seeing Christmas week. She said she was certain there would be Rudolph and Frosty on. That would be more appropriate for us to watch on the night before Christmas Eve.

"*Fuck* Frosty," Michael Christian said to me. "I seen that a *hun-rett* times. I want to see 'The Birds,' man. I want to see those birds get all up *in* them people's hair. That's some real Christmas TV to me."

Michael Christian and I were some of the last Big Boys to be claimed for Christmas. We were certain *someone* would eventually come for us. We were not frightened yet. There were still some other Big Boys around — the Big Boy who ran away to a gas station every other night, the Human Skeleton who would bite you, and the guy locked away on the sun porch who the Young Doctors were taking apart an arm and a leg at a time.

The Young Doctors told Michael Christian that their Christmas gift to him would be that one day he would be able to do a split onstage like his idol, James Brown. There never seemed to be any doubt in Michael Christian's mind about that. For now, he just wanted to see "The Birds" while he pretended to be James Brown in the Hospital.

Pretending to be James Brown in the Hospital was not without its hazards for Michael Christian; he had to remember to keep his head lifted from his pillow so as not to *bedhead* his budding Afro. Once, when he was practicing his singing, the nurses rushed to his bed asking him where it hurt.

"I'm warming up 'I Feel Good,' stupid bitches," said Michael Christian. Then his bed was jerked from the wall and wheeled with great speed, pushed and pulled along by hissing nurses, jarring other bedsteads, Michael Christian's wrists hanging over the safety bedrails like jailhouse-window hands; he was on his way to spend a couple of solitary hours out in the long, dark, and empty hall, him rolling his eyes at me as he sped past, saying, "Aw, man, now I feel BAD!"

Bed wheeling into the hall was one of the few alternatives to corporal punishment the nurses had, most of them being reluctant to spank a child in traction for spitting an orange pip at his neighbor, or to beat a completely burned child for cursing. Bed wheeling into the hall was especially effective at Christmastime, when it carried the possibility of missing Christmas programs. A veteran of several Christmases in the hospital and well acquainted with the

grim Christmas programs, Michael Christian scoffed at the trea-
sures handed out by the church and state charities — the aging
fruit, the surplus ballpoint pens, the occasional batches of recycled
toys that didn't work, the games and puzzles with missing pieces.
Michael Christian's Christmas Wish was as specific as mine. I
wanted a miniature train set with batteries so I could lay out the
track to run around on my bed over the covers. Not the big Lionel
size or the HO size. I wanted the set you could see in magazines,
where they show you the actual size of the railroad engine as being
no larger than a walnut.

"You never get that, man," Michael Christian said, and he was
right.

James Brown in the Hospital's Christmas Wish was for "The
Birds" for Christmas. And, as Michael Christian's friend, I became
an accomplice in his desire. In that way, "birds" became a code, the
way words can among boys.

"Gimme some BIRDS!" Michael Christian would squawk when
the society ladies on their annual Christmas visit asked us what we
wanted.

"How about a nice hairbrush?" a society lady said, laying one
for white people at the foot of Michael Christian's bed.

"I want a pick," Michael Christian told her.

"A pick? A shovel and pick? To dig with?" asked the society lady.

"I think he wants a comb for his hair," I said. "For his Afro."

"That's right: a pick," said Michael Christian. "Tell this stupid
white bitch something. *Squawk, squawk*," he said, flapping his
elbows like wings, as the nurses wheeled him out into the hall.
"Gimme some BIRDS!" he shouted, and when they asked me, I
said to give me some birds, too.

Michael Christian's boldness over the Christmas programs
increased when Ben, the night porter, broke the television. Looking back, it may not be fair to say that Ben, the night porter,
actually broke the television, but one evening it was soundlessly
playing some kiddie Christmas show and Ben was standing near
it mopping up a spilt urinal can when the screen and the hope of

Michael Christian's getting his Christmas Wish blackened simultaneously. Apologetic at first, knowing what even a soundless television meant to children who had rarely seen any television at all, Ben then offered to "burn up your butt, Michael Christian, legs braces and all" when Michael Christian hissed "stupid nigger" at Ben, beneath the night nurse's hearing. It was a sombre Lights Out.

The next night, a priest and some students from the seminary came by. Practice Preachers, Michael Christian said. While one of the students read the Christmas story from the Bible, Michael Christian pretended to peck his own eyes out with pinched fingers. When the story was finished, Michael Christian said, "Now, you say the sheepherding guys was so afraid, right?"

"*Sore* afraid," said the Practice Preacher. "The shepherds had never seen angels before, and they were *sore* afraid."

"Naw," said Michael Christian. "I'll tell you what—they saw these big white things flapping down and they was big *birds*, man. I know *birds*, man, I know when you got bird *problems*, man!"

"They were *angels*," said the young seminary student.

"Naw," said Michael Christian. "They was big white birds, and the sheepherding guys were *so* afraid the big white birds was swooping down and getting all up in they *hair* and stuff! *Squawk, squawk!*" he said, flapping around in his bed.

"*Squawk, squawk!*" I answered, and two of the Practice Preachers assisted the nurses in wheeling Michael Christian into the hall and me into the linen cupboard.

One night in the week before Christmas, a man named Sammy came to visit. He had been a patient as a child, and his botched cleft-palate and harelip repairs were barely concealed by a weird line of blond mustache. Sammy owned a hauling company now, and he showed up blistering drunk, wearing a ratty Santa suit, and began handing out black-strapped Timex junior wristwatches. I still have mine, somewhere.

One by one we told Sammy what we wanted for Christmas, even though we were not sure, because of his speech defect, that that was what he was asking. Me, the walnut train; Michael Christian, "The Birds." We answered without enthusiasm, without hope: it was all by rote. By the end of the visit, Sammy was a blubbering sentimental mess, reeking of alcohol and promises. Ben, the night porter, put him out.

It was Christmas Eve week. The boy who kept running away finally ran away for good. Before he left, he snatched the dime from the channel selector on our broken TV. We all saw him do it and we didn't care. We didn't even yell out to the night nurse, so he could get a better head start than usual.

It was Christmas Eve week, and Michael Christian lay listless in his bed. We watched the Big Boy ward empty. Somebody even came for one of the moaners, and the guy out on the sun porch was sent upstairs for a final visit to the Young Doctors so they could finish taking him apart.

On the night before Christmas Eve, Michael Christian and I heard street shoes clicking down the long corridor that led to where we lay. It was after Lights Out. We watched and waited and waited. It was just Sammy the Santa, except this time he was wearing a pale-blue leisure suit, his hair was oiled back, and his hands, holding a red-wrapped box, were clean.

What we did not want for Christmas were wristwatches. What we did not want for Christmas were bars of soap. We did not want any more candy canes, bookmarks, ballpoint pens, or somebody else's last year's broken toy. For Christmas we did not want plastic crosses, dot books, or fruit baskets. No more handshakes, head pats, or storybook times. It was the night before Christmas Eve, and Michael Christian had not mentioned "The Birds" in days, and I had given up on the walnut train. We did not want any more Christmas Wishes.

Sammy spoke with the night nurse, we heard him plead that it was Christmas, and she said all right, and by her flashlight she brought him to us. In the yellow spread of her weak batteries, we watched Michael Christian unwrap a portable television.

There was nothing to be done except plug the television into the wall. It was Christmas, Sammy coaxed the reluctant night nurse. They put the little TV on a chair, and we watched the end of an Andy Williams Christmas Special. We watched the eleven-o'clock news. Then the movie began: "The Birds." It was Christmas, Sammy convinced the night nurse.

The night nurse wheeled her chair away from the chart table and rolled it to the television set. The volume was low, so as not to disturb the damaged babies at the Little Boy end of the ward— babies largely uncollected until after the holidays, if at all. Sammy sat on an empty bed. He patted it. Michael Christian and I watched "The Birds."

During the commercials, the night nurse checked the hall for the supervisor. Sammy helped her turn any infant that cried out. The night nurse let Sammy have some extra pillows. Michael Christian spoke to me only once during the entire movie: quietly, during a commercial when we were alone, he said, "Those birds messing them people *up*."

When the movie was over, it was the first hours of Christmas Eve. The night nurse woke Sammy and let him out through the sun porch. She told us to go to sleep, and rolled her chair back to her chart table. In the emptiness you could hear the metal charts click and scratch, her folds of white starch rustle. Through a hole in the pony blanket I had pulled over my head I could see Michael Christian's bed. His precious Afro head was buried deep beneath his pillow.

At the dark end of the ward a baby cried in its sleep and then was still.

It was Christmas Eve, and we were sore afraid.

1991

Lee Smith

INTENSIVE CARE

Cherry Oxendine's long, drawn-out dying is the topic of conversation at the Beauty Nook in Lee Smith's gorgeously gossipy story. But the author's topic of concern is Cherry Oxendine's full-fledged—if foreshortened—living. By the time she dies, Cherry has shared all she knew of that art with her first several husbands and her children. It is what her last husband, Harold Stikes, learns from her (including the value of UFOs) that this story immortalizes. Lee Smith, born and raised in Grundy, Virginia, is the author of nine novels and two books of stories. She lives in Chapel Hill, North Carolina.

Cherry Oxendine is dying now, and everybody knows it. Everybody in town except maybe her new husband, Harold Stikes, although Lord knows he ought to, it's as plain as the nose on your face. And it's not like he hasn't been *told* either, by both Dr. Thacker and Dr. Pinckney and also that hotshot young Jew doctor from Memphis, Dr. Shapiro, who comes over here once a week. "Harold just can't take it in" is what the head nurse in Intensive Care, Lois Hickey, said in the Beauty Nook last week. Lois ought to know. She's been right there during the past six weeks while Cherry Oxendine has been in Intensive Care, writing down Cherry's blood pressure every hour on the hour, changing bags on the IV, checking the stomach tube, moving the bed up and down to prevent bedsores, monitoring the respirator—and calling in Rodney Broadbent, the respiratory therapist, more and more frequently. "Her blood gases is not but twenty-eight," Lois said in the Beauty Nook. "If we was to unhook that respirator, she'd die in a day."

"I would go on and do it then, if I was Harold," said Mrs. Hooker, the Presbyterian minister's wife, who was getting a permanent. "It is the Christian thing."

"You wouldn't either," Lois said, "because she *still knows him*. That's the awful part. She still knows him. In fact she peps right up ever time he comes in, like they are going on a date or something. It's the saddest thing. And ever time we open the doors, here comes Harold, regular as clockwork. Eight o'clock, one o'clock, six o'clock, eight o'clock, why shoot, he'd stay in there all day and all night if we'd let him. Well, she opens her mouth and says *Hi honey*, you can tell what she's saying even if she can't make a sound. And her eyes get real bright and her face looks pretty good too, that's because of the Lasix, only Harold don't know that. He just can't take it all in," Lois said.

"Oh, I feel so sorry for him," said Mrs. Hooker. Her face is as round and flat as a dime.

"Well, I don't." Dot Mains, owner of the Beauty Nook, started cutting Lois Hickey's hair. Lois wears it too short, in Dot's opinion. "I certainly don't feel sorry for Harold Stikes, after what he did." Dot snipped decisively at Lois Hickey's frosted hair. Mrs. Hooker made a sad little sound, half sigh, half words, as Janice stuck her under the dryer, while Miss Berry, the old-maid home demonstration agent waiting for her appointment, snapped the pages of *Cosmopolitan* magazine one by one, blindly, filled with somewhat gratuitous rage against the behavior of Harold Stikes. Miss Berry is Harold Stikes's ex-wife's cousin. So she does not pity him, not one bit. He got what's coming to him, that's all, in Miss Berry's opinion. Most people don't. It's a pleasure to see it, but Miss Berry would never say this out loud since Cherry Oxendine is of course dying. Cherry Oxendine! Like it was yesterday, Miss Berry remembers how Cherry Oxendine acted in high school, wearing her skirts too tight, popping her gum.

"The doctors can't do a thing," said Lois Hickey.

Silence settled like fog then on the Beauty Nook, on Miss Berry and her magazine, on Dot Mains cutting Lois Hickey's hair, on little Janice thinking about her boyfriend Bruce, and on Mrs. Hooker crying gently under the dryer. Suddenly, Dot remembered something her old granny used to say about such moments of sudden absolute quiet: "An angel is passing over."

After a while, Mrs. Hooker said, "It's all in the hands of God, then." She spread out her fingers one by one on the tray, for Janice to give her a manicure.

And as for Harold Stikes, he's not even considering God. Oh, he doesn't interfere when Mr. Hooker comes by the hospital once a day to check on him — Harold was a Presbyterian in his former life — or even when the Baptist preacher from Cherry's mama's church shows up and insists that everybody in the whole waiting room join hands and bow heads in prayer while he raises his big red face and curly gray head straight up to heaven and prays in a loud voice that God will heal these loved ones who walk through the Valley of Death, and comfort these others who watch, through their hour of need. This includes Mrs. Eunice Sprayberry, whose mother has had a stroke, John and Paula Ripman, whose infant son is dying of encephalitis, and different others who drift in and out of Intensive Care following surgery or wrecks. Harold is losing track. He closes his eyes and bows his head, figuring it can't hurt, like taking out insurance. But deep down inside, he knows that if God is worth His salt, He is not impressed by the prayer of Harold Stikes, who knowingly gave up all hope of peace on earth and heaven hereafter for the love of Cherry Oxendine.

Not to mention his family.

He gave them up too.

But this morning when he leaves the hospital after his eight-o'clock visit to Cherry, Harold finds himself turning left out of the lot instead of right toward Food Lion, his store. Harold finds himself taking 15-501 just south of town and then driving through those ornate marble gates that mark the entrance to Camelot Hills, his old neighborhood. Some lucky instinct makes him pull into the little park and stop there, beside the pond. Here comes his ex-wife,

Joan, driving the Honda Accord he paid for last year. Joan looks straight ahead. She's still wearing her shiny blond hair in the pageboy she's worn ever since Harold met her at Mercer College so many years ago. Harold is sure she's wearing low heels and a shirt-waist dress. He knows her briefcase is in the backseat, containing lesson plans for today, yogurt, and a banana. Potassium is important. Harold has heard this a million times. Behind her, the beds are all made, the breakfast dishes stacked in the sink. As a home ec teacher, Joan believes that breakfast is the most important meal of the day. The two younger children, Brenda and Harold Jr., are already on the bus to the Academy. James rides to the high school with his mother, hair wet, face blank, staring straight ahead. They don't see Harold. Joan brakes at the stop sign before entering 15-501. She always comes to a complete stop, even if nothing's coming. Always. She looks both ways. Then she's gone.

Harold drives past well-kept lawn after well-kept lawn and lovely house after lovely house, many of them houses where Harold has attended Cub Scout meetings, eaten barbecue, watched bowl games. Now these houses have a blank, closed look to them, like mean faces. Harold turns left on Oxford, then right on Shrewsbury. He comes to a stop beside the curb at 1105 Cambridge and just sits there with the motor running, looking at the house. His house. The Queen Anne house he and Joan planned so carefully, down to the last detail, the fish-scale siding. The house he is still paying for and will be until his dying day, if Joan has her way about it.

Which she will, of course. Everybody is on her side: *desertion*. Harold Stikes deserted his lovely wife and three children for a red-headed waitress. For a fallen woman with a checkered past. Harold can hear her now. "I fail to see why I and the children should lower our standards of living, Harold, and go to the dogs just because you have chosen to become insane in mid-life." Joan's voice is slow and amiable. It has a down-to-earth quality which used to appeal to Harold but now drives him wild. Harold sits at the curb with the motor running and looks at his house good. It looks fine. It looks just like it did when they picked it out of the pages of *Southern Living* and wrote off for the plans. The only difference is, that house was in Stone Mountain, Georgia, and this house is in Greenwood, Mississippi. Big deal.

Joan's response to Harold's desertion has been a surprise to him. He expected tears, recriminations, fireworks. He did not expect her calm, reasonable manner, treating Harold the way she treats the Mormon missionaries who come to the door in their black suits, for instance, that very calm sweet careful voice. Joan acts like Harold's desertion is nothing much. And nothing much appears to have changed for her except the loss of Harold's actual presence, and this cannot be a very big deal since everything else has remained exactly the same.

What the hell. After a while Harold turns off the motor and walks up the flagstone walk to the front door. His key still fits. All the furniture is arranged exactly the way it was arranged four years ago. The only thing that ever changes here is the display of magazines on the glass coffee table before the fireplace, Joan keeps them up to date. *Newsweek, National Geographic, Good Housekeeping, Gourmet*. It's a mostly educational grouping, unlike what Cherry reads—*Parade, Coronet, National Enquirer*. Now these magazines litter the floor at the side of the bed like little souvenirs of Cherry. Harold can't stand to pick them up.

He sits down heavily on the white sofa and stares at the coffee table. He remembers the quiz and the day he found it, four years ago now, although it feels like only yesterday, funny thing though that he can't remember which magazine it was in. Maybe *Reader's Digest*. The quiz was titled "How Good Is Your Marriage?" and Harold noticed that Joan had filled it in carefully. This did not surprise him. Joan was so law-abiding, such a *good girl*, that she always filled in such quizzes when she came across them, as if she *had to*, before she could go ahead and finish the magazine. Usually Harold didn't pay much attention.

This time, he picked the magazine up and started reading. One of the questions said: "What is your idea of the perfect vacation?

(a) a romantic getaway for you and your spouse alone; (b) a family trip to the beach; (c) a business convention; (d) an organized tour of a foreign land." Joan had wavered on this one. She had marked and then erased "an organized tour of a foreign land." Finally she had settled on "a family trip to the beach." Harold skimmed along. The final question was: "When you think of the love between yourself and your spouse, do you think of (a) a great passion; (b) a warm, meaningful companionship; (c) an average love; (d) an unsatisfying habit." Joan had marked "(c) an average love." Harold stared at these words, knowing they were true. An average love, nothing great, an average marriage between an average man and woman. Suddenly, strangely, Harold was filled with rage.

"It is not enough!" He thought he actually said these words out loud. Perhaps he *did* say them out loud, into the clean hushed air-conditioned air of his average home. Harold's rage was followed by a brief period, maybe five minutes, of unbearable longing, after which he simply closed the magazine and put it back on the table and got up and poured himself a stiff shot of bourbon. He stood for a while before the picture window in the living room, looking out at his even green grass, his clipped hedge, and the impatiens blooming in their bed, the clematis climbing the mailbox. The colors of the world fairly leaped at him — the sky so blue, the grass so green. A passing jogger's shorts glowed unbearably red. He felt that he had never seen any of these things before. Yet in another way it all seemed so familiar as to be an actual part of his body — his throat, his heart, his breath. Harold took another drink. Then he went out and played nine holes of golf at the country club with Bubba Fields, something he did every Wednesday afternoon. He shot 82.

By the time he came home for dinner he was okay again. He was very tired and a little lightheaded, all his muscles tingling. His face was hot. Yet Harold felt vaguely pleased with himself, as if he had been through something and come out the other side of it, as if he had done a creditable job on a difficult assignment. But right then, during dinner, Harold could not have told you exactly what had happened to him that day, or why he felt this way. Because the mind will forget what it can't stand to remember, and anyway the Stikeses had beef Stroganoff that night, a new recipe that Joan was testing for the Junior League cookbook, and Harold Jr. had written them a funny letter from camp, and for once Brenda did not whine. James, who was twelve that year, actually condescended to talk to his father, with some degree of interest, about baseball, and after supper was over he and Harold went out and pitched to each other until it grew dark and lightning bugs emerged. This is how it's supposed to be, Harold thought, father and son playing catch in the twilight.

Then he went upstairs and joined Joan in bed to watch TV, after which they turned out the light and made love. But Joan had greased herself all over with Oil of Olay, earlier, and right in the middle of doing it, Harold got a crazy terrified feeling that he was losing her, that Joan was slipping, slipping away.

But time passed, as it does, and Harold forgot that whole weird day, forgot it until *right now*, in fact, as he sits on the white sofa in his old house again and stares at the magazines on the coffee table, those magazines so familiar except for the date, which is four years later. Now Harold wonders: If he hadn't picked up that quiz and read it, would he have even *noticed* when Cherry Oxendine spooned out that potato salad for him six months later, in his own Food Lion deli? Would the sight of redheaded Cherry Oxendine, the Food Lion smock mostly obscuring her dynamite figure, have hit him like a bolt out of the blue the way it did?

Cherry herself does not believe there is any such thing as coincidence. Cherry thinks there is a master plan for the universe, and what is *meant* to happen will. She thinks it's all set in the stars. For the first time, Harold thinks maybe she's right. He sees part of a pattern in the works, but dimly, as if he is looking at a constellation hidden by clouds. Mainly, he sees her face.

Harold gets up from the sofa and goes into the kitchen, suddenly aware that he isn't supposed to be here. He could be arrested, probably! He looks back at the living room but there's not a trace of him left, not even an imprint on the soft white cushions of the sofa. Absentmindedly, Harold opens and shuts the refrigerator door. There's no beer, he notices. He can't have a Coke. On the kitchen calendar, he reads:

Harold Jr. to dentist, 3:30 P.M. Tues
Change furnace filter 2/18/88 (James)

So James is changing the furnace filters now, James is the man of the house. Why not? It's good for him. He's been given too much, kids these days grow up so fast, no responsibilities, they get on drugs, you read about it all the time. But deep down inside, Harold knows that James is not on drugs and he feels something awful, feels the way he felt growing up, that sick little flutter in his stomach that took years to go away.

Harold's dad died of walking pneumonia when he was only three, so his mother raised him alone. She called him her "little man." This made Harold feel proud but also wild, like a boy growing up in a cage. Does James feel this way now? Harold suddenly decides to get James a car for his birthday, and take him hunting.

Hunting is something Harold never did as a boy, but it means a lot to him now. In fact Harold never owned a gun until he was thirty-one, when he bought a shotgun in order to accept the invitation of his regional manager, "Little Jimmy" Fletcher, to go quail hunting in Georgia. He had a great time. Now he's invited back every year, and Little Jimmy is in charge of the company's whole eastern division. Harold has a great future with Food Lion too. He owns three stores, one in downtown Greenwood, one out at the mall, and one over in Indianola. He owned two of them when his mother died, and he's pleased to think that she died proud — proud of the good little boy he'd always been, and the good man he'd become.

Of course she'd wanted him to make a preacher, but Harold never got the call, and she gave that up finally when he was twenty.

Harold was not going to pretend to get the call if he never got it, and he held strong to this principle. He *wanted* to see a burning bush, but if this was not vouchsafed to him, he wasn't going to lie about it. He would just major in math instead, which he was good at anyway. Majoring in math at Mercer College, the small Baptist school his mother had chosen for him, Harold came upon Joan Berry, a home ec major from his own hometown who set out single-mindedly to marry him, which wasn't hard. After graduation, Harold got a job as management trainee in the Food Lion store where he had started as a bagboy at fourteen. Joan produced their three children, spaced three years apart, and got her tubes tied. Harold got one promotion, then another. Joan and Harold prospered. They built this house.

Harold looks around and now this house, his house, strikes him as creepy, a wax museum. He lets himself out the back door and walks quickly, almost runs, to his car. It's real cold out, a gray day in February, but Harold's sweating. He starts his car and roars off toward the hospital, driving — as Cherry would say — like a bat out of hell.

They're letting Harold stay with her longer now. He knows it, they know it, but nobody says a word. Lois Hickey just looks the other way when the announcement "Visiting hours are over" crackles across the PA. Is this a good sign or a bad sign? Harold can't tell. He feels slow and confused, like a man underwater. "I think she looks better, don't you?" he said last night to Cherry's son Stan, the TV weatherman, who had driven down from Memphis for the day. Eyes slick and bright with tears, Stan went over to Harold and hugged him tight. This scared Harold to death, he has practically never touched his own sons, and he doesn't even *know* Stan, who's been grown and gone for years. Harold is not used to hugging anybody, especially men. Harold breathed in Stan's strong go-get-'em cologne, he buried his face in Stan's long, curly hair. He thinks it is possible that Stan has a permanent. They'll do anything up in Memphis. Then Stan stepped back and put one hand on each of Harold's shoulders, holding him out at arm's length. Stan has his mother's wide, mobile mouth. The bright white light of Intensive Care glinted off the gold chain and the crystal that he wore around his neck. "I'm afraid we're going to lose her, Pop," he said.

But Harold doesn't think so. Today he thinks Cherry looks the best she's looked in weeks, with a bright spot of color in each cheek to match her flaming hair. She's moving around a lot too, she keeps kicking the sheet off.

"She's getting back some of that old energy now," he tells Cherry's daughter, Tammy Lynn Palladino, when she comes by after school. Tammy Lynn and Harold's son James are both members of the senior class, but they aren't friends. Tammy Lynn says James is a "stuck-up jock," a "preppie," and a "country-clubber." Harold can't say a word to defend his own son against these charges, he doesn't even *know* James anymore. It might be true, anyway. Tammy Lynn is real smart, a teenage egghead. She's got a full scholarship to Millsaps College for next year. She applied for it all by herself. As Cherry used to say, Tammy Lynn came into this world with a full deck of cards and an ace or two up her sleeve. Also she looks out for Number One.

In this regard Tammy Lynn is as different from her mama as night from day, because Cherry would give you the shirt off her back and frequently has. That's gotten her into lots of trouble. With Ed Palladino, for instance, her second husband and Tammy Lynn's dad. Just about everybody in this town got took by Ed Palladino, who came in here wearing a seersucker suit and talking big about putting in an outlet mall across the river. A lot of people got burned on that outlet mall deal. But Ed Palladino had a way about him that made you want to cast your lot with his, it is true. You wanted to give Ed Palladino your savings, your time-sharing condo, your cousin, your ticket to the Super Bowl. Cherry gave it all.

She married him and turned over what little inheritance she had from her daddy's death — and that's the only time in her life she ever had *any* money, mind you — and then she just shrugged and smiled her big crooked smile when he left town under cover of night. "*C'est la vie*," Cherry said. She donated the rest of his clothes to the Salvation Army. "*Que será, será*," Cherry said, quoting a song that was popular when she was in junior high.

Tammy Lynn sits by her mama's bed and holds Cherry's thin dry hand. "I brought you a Chick-Fil-A," she says to Harold. "It's over there in that bag." She points to the shelf by the door. Harold nods. Tammy Lynn works at Chick-Fil-A. Cherry's eyes are wide and blue and full of meaning as she stares at her daughter. Her mouth moves, both Harold and Tammy Lynn lean forward, but then her mouth falls slack and her eyelids flutter shut. Tammy sits back.

"I think she looks some better today, don't you?" Harold asks.

"No," Tammy Lynn says. She has a flat little redneck voice. She sounds just the way she did last summer when she told Cherry that what she saw in the field was a cotton picker working at night, and not a UFO after all. "I wish I did but I don't, Harold. I'm going to go on home now and heat up some Beanee Weenee for Mamaw. You come on as soon as you can."

"Well," Harold says. He feels like things have gotten all turned around here some way, he feels like he's the kid and Tammy Lynn has turned into a freaky little grown-up. He says, "I'll be along directly."

But they both know he won't leave until Lois Hickey throws him out. And speaking of Lois, as soon as Tammy Lynn takes off, here she comes again, checking something on the respirator, making a little clucking sound with her mouth, then whirling to leave. When Lois walks, her panty girdle goes *swish*, *swish*, *swish* at the top of her legs. She comes right back with the young black man named Rodney Broadbent, Respiratory Therapist. It says so on his badge. Rodney wheels a complicated-looking cart ahead of himself. He's all built up, like a weightlifter.

"How you doing tonight, Mr. Stipe?" Rodney says.

"I think she's some better," Harold says.

Lois Hickey and Rodney look at him.

"Well, lessee here," Rodney says. He unhooks the respirator tube at Cherry's throat, sticks the tube from his own machine down the opening, and switches on the machine. It makes a whirring sound. It looks like an electric ice-cream mixer. Rodney Broadbent looks at Lois Hickey in a significant way as she turns to leave the room.

They don't have to tell him, Harold knows. Cherry is worse, not better. Harold gets the Chick-Fil-A, unwraps it, eats it, and then goes over to stand by the window. It's already getting dark. The big mercury arc light glows in the hospital parking lot. A little wind blows some trash around on the concrete. He has had Cherry for three years, that's all. One trip to Disney World, two vacations at Gulf Shores, Alabama, hundreds of nights in the old metal bed out at the farm with Cherry sleeping naked beside him, her arm thrown over his stomach. They had a million laughs.

"Alrightee," Rodney Broadbent nearly sings, unhooking his machine. Harold turns to look at him. Rodney Broadbent certainly looks more like a middle linebacker than a respiratory therapist. But Harold likes him.

"Well, Rodney?" Harold says.

Rodney starts shadow-boxing in the middle of the room. "Tough times," he says finally. "These is tough times, Mr. Stipe." Harold stares at him. Rodney is light on his feet as can be.

Harold sits down in the chair by the respirator. "What do you mean?" he asks.

"I mean she is drowning, Mr. Stipe," Rodney says. He throws a punch which lands real close to Harold's left ear. "What I'm doing here, see, is suctioning. I'm pulling all the fluid up out of her lungs. But now looka here, Mr. Stipe, they is just too damn much of it. See this little doohickey here I'm measuring it with? This here is the danger zone, man. Now Mrs. Stipe, she has been in the danger zone for some time. They is just too much damn fluid in there. What she got, anyway? Cancer and pneumonia both, am I right? What can I tell you, man? She is *drowning*." Rodney gives Harold a short affectionate punch in the ribs, then wheels his cart away.

From the door, apparently struck by some misgivings, he says, "Well, man, if it was me, I'd want to know what the story is, you follow me, man? If it was me, what I'm saying." Harold can't see Rodney anymore, only hear his voice from the open door.

"Thank you, Rodney," Harold says. He sits in the chair. In a way he has known this already, for quite some time. In a way, Rodney's news is no news, to Harold. He just hopes he will be man enough to bear it, to do what will have to be done. Harold has always been scared that he is not man enough for Cherry Oxendine, anyway. This is his worst secret fear. He looks around the little Intensive Care room, searching for a sign, some sign, anything, that he will be man enough. Nothing happens. Cherry lies strapped to the bed, flanked by so many machines that it looks like she's in the cockpit of a jet. Her eyes are closed, eyelids fluttering, red spots on her freckled cheeks. Her chest rises and falls as the respirator pushes air in and out through the tube in her neck. He doesn't see how she can sleep in the bright white light of Intensive Care, where it is always noon. And does she dream? Cherry used to tell him her dreams, which were wild, long Technicolor dreams, like movies. Cherry played different parts in them. If you dream in color, it means you're intelligent, Cherry said. She used to tease him all the time. She thought Harold's own dreams were a stitch, dreams more boring than his life, dreams in which he'd drive to Jackson, say, or be washing his car.

"Harold?" It's Ray Muncey, manager of the Food Lion at the mall.

"Why, what are you doing over here, Ray?" Harold asks, and then in a flash he *knows*, Lois Hickey must have called him, to make Harold go on home.

"I was just driving by and I thought, Hey, maybe Harold and me might run by the Holiday Inn, get a bite to eat." Ray shifts from foot to foot in the doorway. He doesn't come inside, he's not supposed to, nobody but immediate family is allowed in Intensive Care, and Harold's glad — Cherry would just die if people she barely knows, like Ray Muncey, got to see her looking so bad.

"No, Ray, you go on and eat," Harold says. "I already ate. I'm leaving right now, anyway."

"Well, how's the missus doing?" Ray is a big man, afflicted with big, heavy manners.

"She's drowning," Harold says abruptly. Suddenly he remembers Cherry in a water ballet at the town pool, it must have been the summer of junior year, Fourth of July, Cherry and the other girls floating in a circle on their backs to form a giant flower — legs high, toes pointed. Harold doesn't know it when Ray Muncey leaves. Out the window, the parking lot light glows like a big full moon. Lois Hickey comes in. "You've got to go home now, Harold," she says. "I'll call if there's any change." He remembers Cherry at Glass Lake, on the senior class picnic. Cherry's getting real agitated now, she tosses her head back and forth, moves her arms. She'd pull out the tubes if she could. She kicks off the sheet. Her legs are still good, great legs in fact, the legs of a beautiful young woman.

Harold at seventeen was tall and skinny, brown hair in a soft flat crew cut, glasses with heavy black frames. His jeans were too short. He carried a pen-and-pencil set in a clear plastic case in his breast pocket. Harold and his best friend, Ben Hill, looked so much alike that people had trouble telling them apart. They did everything together. They built model rockets, they read every science-fiction book they could get their hands on, they collected Lionel train parts and Marvel comics. They loved superheroes with special powers, enormous beings who leaped across rivers and oceans. Harold's friendship with Ben Hill kept the awful loneliness of the only child at bay, and it also kept him from having to talk to girls. You couldn't talk to those two, not seriously. They were giggling and bumping into each other all the time. They were immature.

So it was in Ben's company that Harold experienced the most private, the most *personal* memory he has of Cherry Oxendine in high school. Oh, he also has those other memories you'd expect, the big public memories of Cherry being crowned Miss Greenwood High (for her talent, she surprised everybody by reciting "Abou Ben Adhem" in such a stirring way that there wasn't a dry eye in the whole auditorium when she got through), or running out onto the field ahead of the team with the other cheerleaders, red curls flying, green-and-white skirt whirling out around her hips like a beach umbrella when she turned a cartwheel. Harold noticed her then, of course. He noticed her when she moved through the crowded halls of the high school with her walk that was almost a prance, she put a little something extra into it, all right. Harold noticed Cherry Oxendine then in the way that he noticed Sandra Dee on the cover of a magazine, or Annette Funicello on "American Bandstand."

But such girls were not for the likes of Harold, and Harold knew it. Girls like Cherry always had boyfriends like Lamar Peebles, who was hers — a doctor's son with a baby-blue convertible and plenty of money. They used to drive around town in his car, smoking cigarettes. Harold saw them, as he carried out grocery bags. He did not envy Lamar Peebles, or wish he had a girl like Cherry Oxendine. Only something about them made him stand where he was in the Food Lion lot, watching, until they had passed from sight.

So Harold's close-up encounter with Cherry was unexpected. It took place at the senior class picnic, where Harold and Ben had been drinking beer all afternoon. No alcohol was allowed at the senior class picnic, but some of the more enterprising boys had brought out kegs the night before and hidden them in the woods. Anybody could go back there and pay some money and get some beer. The chaperones didn't know, or appeared not to know. In any case, the chaperones all left at six o'clock, when the picnic was officially over. Some of the class members left then too. Then some of them came back with more beer, more blankets. It was a free lake. Nobody could *make* you go home. Normally, Harold and Ben would have been among the first to leave, but because they had had four beers apiece, and because this was the first time they had ever had *any* beer ever, at all, they were still down by the water, skipping rocks and waiting to sober up so that they would not wreck Harold's mother's green Gremlin on the way home. All the cool kids were on the other side of the lake, listening to transistor radios. The sun went down. Bullfrogs started up. A mist came out all around the sides of the lake. It was a cloudy, humid day anyway, not a great day for a picnic.

"If God is really God, how come He let Himself get crucified, is what I want to know," Ben said. Ben's daddy was a Holiness preacher, out in the county.

But Harold heard something. "Hush, Ben," he said.

"If I was God I would go around and really kick some ass," Ben said.

Harold heard it again. It was almost too dark to see.

"Damn." It was a girl's voice, followed by a splash.

All of a sudden, Harold felt sober. "Who's there?" he asked. He stepped forward, right up to the water's edge. Somebody was in the water. Harold was wearing his swim trunks under his jeans, but he had not gone in the water himself. He couldn't stand to show himself in front of people. He thought he was too skinny.

"Well, *do something.*" It was the voice of Cherry Oxendine, almost wailing. She stumbled up the bank. Harold reached out and grabbed her arm. Close up, she was a mess, wet and muddy, with her hair all over her head. But the thing that got Harold, of course, was that she didn't have any top on. She didn't even try to cover them up either, just stomped her little foot on the bank and said, "I am going to *kill* Lamar Peebles when I get ahold of him." Harold had never even imagined so much skin.

"What's going on?" asked Ben, from up the bank.

Harold took off his own shirt as fast as he could and handed it over to Cherry Oxendine. "Cover yourself," he said.

"Why, thank you." Cherry didn't bat an eye. She took his shirt and put it on, tying it stylishly at the waist. Harold couldn't believe it. Close up, Cherry was a lot smaller than she looked on the stage or the football field. She looked up at Harold through her dripping hair and gave him her crooked grin.

"Thanks, hey?" she said.

And then she was gone, vanished into the mist and trees before Harold could say another word. He opened his mouth and closed it. Mist obscured his view. From the other side of the lake he could hear "Ramblin' Rose" playing on somebody's radio. He heard a girl's high-pitched giggle, a boy's whooping laugh.

"What's going on?" asked Ben.

"Nothing," Harold said. It was the first time he had ever lied to Ben. Harold never told anybody what had happened that night, not ever. He felt that it was up to him to protect Cherry Oxendine's honor. Later, much later, when he and Cherry were lovers, he was astonished to learn that she couldn't remember any of this, not who she was with or what had happened or what she was doing in the lake like that with her top off, or Harold giving her his shirt. "I think that was sweet, though," Cherry told him.

When Harold and Ben finally got home that night at nine or ten o'clock, Harold's mother was frantic. "You've been drinking," she shrilled at him under the hanging porch light. "And where's your shirt?" It was a new madras shirt which Harold had gotten for graduation. Now Harold's mother is out at Hillandale Cemetery. Ben died in Vietnam, and Cherry is drowning. This time, and Harold knows it now, he can't help her.

Oh, Cherry! Would she have been so wild if she hadn't been so cute? And what if her parents had been younger when she was born—normal-age parents—couldn't they have controlled her better? As it was, the Oxendines were sober, solid people living in a farmhouse out near the county line, and Cherry lit up their lives like a rocket. Her dad, Martin "Buddy" Oxendine, went to sleep in his chair every night right after supper, woke back up for the eleven-o'clock news, and then went to bed for good. Buddy was an elder in the Baptist church. Cherry's mom, Gladys Oxendine, made drapes for people. She assumed she would never have children at all because of her spastic colitis. Gladys and Buddy had started raising cockapoos when they gave up on children. Imagine

Gladys's surprise, then, to find herself pregnant at thirty-eight, when she was already old! They say she didn't even know it when she went to the doctor. She thought she had a tumor.

But then she got so excited, that old farm woman, when Dr. Grimwood told her what was what, and she wouldn't even consider an abortion when he mentioned the chances of a mongoloid. People didn't use to have babies so old then as they do now, so Gladys Oxendine's pregnancy was the talk of the county. Neighbors crocheted little jackets and made receiving blankets. Buddy built a baby room onto the house and made a cradle by hand. During the last two months of the pregnancy, when Gladys had to stay in bed because of toxemia, people brought over casseroles and boiled custard, everything good. Gladys's pregnancy was the only time in her whole life that she was ever pretty, and she loved it, and she loved the attention, neighbors in and out of the house. When the baby was finally born on November 1, 1944, no parents were ever more ready than Gladys and Buddy Oxendine. And the baby was everything they hoped for too, which is not usually the case — the prettiest baby in the world, a baby like a little flower.

They named her Doris Christine, which is who she was until eighth grade, when she made junior varsity cheerleader and announced that she was changing her name to Cherry. Cherry! Even her parents had to admit it suited her better than Doris Christine. As a little girl, Doris Christine was redheaded, bouncy, and busy — she was always into something, usually something you'd never thought to tell her not to do. She started talking early and never shut up. Her old dad, old Buddy Oxendine, was so crazy about Doris Christine that he took her everywhere with him in his red pickup truck. You got used to seeing the two of them, Buddy and his curly-headed little daughter, riding the country roads together, going to the seed-and-feed together, sharing a shake at the Dairy Queen. Gladys made all of Doris Christine's clothes, the most beautiful little dresses in the world, with hand-smocking and French seams. They gave Doris Christine everything they could think of — what she asked for, what she didn't. "That child is going to get spoiled," people started to say. And of course she did get spoiled, she couldn't have helped *that*, but she was never spoiled rotten as so many are. She stayed sweet in spite of it all.

Then along about ninth grade, soon after she changed her name to Cherry and got interested in boys, things changed between Cherry and the old Oxendines. Stuff happened. Instead of being the light of their lives, Cherry became the bane of their existence, the curse of their old age. She wanted to wear makeup, she wanted to have car dates. You can't blame her — she was old enough, sixteen. Everybody else did it. But you can't blame Gladys and Buddy either — they were old people by then, all worn out. They were not up to such a daughter. Cherry sneaked out. She wrecked a car. She ran away to Pensacola with a soldier. Finally, Gladys and Buddy just gave up. When Cherry eloped with the disc jockey, Don Westall, right after graduation, they threw up their hands. They did not do a thing about it. They had done the best they could, and everybody knew it. They went back to raising cockapoos.

Cherry, living up in Nashville, Tennessee, had a baby, Stan, the one that's in his twenties now. Cherry sent baby pictures back to Gladys and Buddy, and wrote that she was going to be a singer. Six years later, she came home. She said nothing against Don Westall, who was still a disc jockey on WKIX, Nashville. You could hear him on the radio every night after 10:00 P.M. Cherry said the breakup was all her fault. She said she had made some mistakes, but she didn't say what they were. She was thin and noble. Her kid was cute. She did not go back out to the farm then. She rented an apartment over the hardware store, down by the river, and got a job downtown working in Ginger's Boutique. After a year or so, she started acting more like herself again, although not *quite* like herself, she had grown up somehow in Nashville, and quit being spoiled. She put Stan, her kid, first. And if she did run around a little bit, or if she was the life of the party sometimes out at the country club, so what? Stan didn't want for a thing. By then the Oxendines were failing and she had to take care of them too, she had to drive her daddy up to Grenada for dialysis twice a week. It was not an easy life for Cherry, but if it ever got her down, you couldn't tell it. She was still cute. When her daddy finally died and left her a little money, everybody was real glad. Oh *now*, they said, Cherry Oxendine can quit working so hard and put her mama in a home or something and have a decent life. She can go on a cruise. But then along came Ed Palladino, and the rest is history.

Cherry Oxendine was left with no husband, no money, a little girl, and a mean old mama to take care of. At least by this time Stan was in the Navy. Cherry never complained, though. She moved back out to the farm. When Ginger retired from business and closed her boutique, Cherry got another job, as a receptionist at Wallace, Wallace, and Peebles. This was her undoing. Because Lamar Peebles had just moved back to town with his family, to join his father's firm. Lamar had two little girls. He had been married to a tobacco heiress since college. All this time he had run around on her. He was not on the up-and-up. And when he encountered redheaded Cherry Oxendine again after the passage of so many years, all those old fireworks went off again. They got to be a scandal, then a disgrace. Lamar said he was going to marry her, and Cherry believed him. After six months of it, Mrs. Lamar Peebles checked herself into a mental hospital in Silver Hill, Connecticut. First, she called her lawyers.

And then it was all over, not even a year after it began. Mr. and Mrs. Lamar Peebles were reconciled and moved to Winston-Salem, North Carolina, her hometown. Cherry Oxendine lost her job at Wallace, Wallace, and Peebles, and was reduced to working in the deli at Food Lion. Why did she do it? Why did she lose all the goodwill she'd built up in this community over so many years? It is because she doesn't know how to look out for Number One. Her own daughter, Tammy Lynn Palladino, is aware of this.

"You have got a fatal flaw, Mama," Tammy said after learning about fatal flaws in English class. "You believe everything everybody tells you."

Still, Tammy loves her mother. Sometimes she writes her mother's whole name, Cherry Oxendine Westall Palladino Stikes, over and over in her Blue Horse notebook. Tammy Lynn will never be half the woman her mother is, and she's so smart she knows it. She gets a kick out of her mother's wild ideas.

"When you get too old to be cute, honey, you get to be eccentric," Cherry told Tammy one time. It's the truest thing she ever said.

It seems to Tammy that the main thing about her mother is, Cherry always has to have *something* going on. If it isn't a man it's something else, such as having her palm read by that woman over in French Camp, or astrology, or the grapefruit diet. Cherry believes in the Bermuda Triangle, Bigfoot, Atlantis, and ghosts. It kills her that she's not psychic. The UFO Club was just the latest in a long string of interests, although it has lasted the longest, starting back before Cherry's marriage to Harold Stikes. And then Cherry got cancer, and she kind of forgot about it. But Tammy still remembers the night her mama first got so turned on to UFOs.

Rhonda Ramey, Cherry's best friend, joined the UFO Club first. Rhonda and Cherry are a lot alike, although it's hard to see this at first. While Cherry is short and peppy, Rhonda is tall, thin, and listless. She looks like Cher. Rhonda doesn't have any children. She's crazy about her husband, Bill, but he's a workaholic who runs a string of video rental stores all over northern Mississippi, so he's gone a lot, and Rhonda gets bored. She works out at the spa, but it isn't enough. Maybe this is why she got so interested when the UFO landed at a farm outside her mother's hometown of Como. It was first spotted by sixteen-year-old Donnie Johnson just at sunset, as he was finishing his chores on his parents' farm. He heard a loud rumbling sound "in the direction of the hog house," it said in the paper. Looking up, he suddenly saw a "brilliantly lit mushroom-shaped object" hovering about two feet above the ground, with a shaft of white light below and glowing all over with an intensely bright multicolored light, "like the light of a welder's arc."

Donnie said it sounded like a jet. He was temporarily blinded and paralyzed. He fell down on the ground. When he came back to his senses again, it was gone. Donnie staggered into the kitchen where his parents, Durel, fifty-four, and Erma, forty-nine, were eating supper, and told them what had happened. They all ran back outside to the field, where they found four large imprints and four small imprints in the muddy ground, and a nearby clump of sage grass on fire. The hogs were acting funny, bunching up, looking dazed. Immediately, Durel jumped in his truck and went to get the sheriff, who came right back with two deputies. All in all, six people viewed the site while the bush continued to burn, and who knows how many people — half of Como — saw the imprints the next day. Rhonda saw them too. She drove out to the Johnson farm with her mother, as soon as she heard about it.

It was a close encounter of the second kind, according to Civil Air Patrol head Glenn Raines, who appeared on TV to discuss it, because the UFO "interacted with its surroundings in a significant way." A close encounter of the first kind is simply a close-range sighting, while a close encounter of the third kind is something like the most famous example, of Betty and Barney Hill of Exeter, New Hampshire, who were actually kidnapped by a UFO while they were driving along on a trip. Betty and Barney Hill were taken aboard the alien ship and given physical exams by intelligent humanoid beings. Two hours and thirty-five minutes were missing from their trip, and afterward, Betty had to be treated for acute anxiety. Glenn Raines, wearing his brown Civil Air Patrol uniform, said all this on TV.

His appearance, plus what had happened at the Johnson farm, sparked a rash of sightings all across Mississippi, Louisiana, and Texas for the next two years. Metal disklike objects were seen, and luminous objects appearing as lights at night. In Levelland, Texas, fifteen people called the police to report an egg-shaped UFO appearing over State Road 1173. Overall, the UFOs seemed to show a preference for soybean fields and teenage girl viewers. But a pretty good photograph of a UFO flying over the Gulf was taken by a retired man from Pascagoula, so you can't generalize. Clubs sprang up all over the place. The one that Rhonda and Cherry went to had seventeen members and met once a month at the junior high school.

Tammy recalls exactly how her mama and Rhonda acted the night they came home from Cherry's first meeting. Cherry's eyes sparkled in her face like Brenda Starr's eyes in the comics. She started right in telling Tammy all about it, beginning with the Johnsons from Como and Betty and Barney Hill.

Tammy was not impressed. "I don't believe it," she said. She was president of the Science Club at the junior high school.

"You are the most irritating child!" Cherry said. "*What* don't you believe?"

"Well, any of it," Tammy said then. "All of it." And this has remained her attitude ever since.

"Listen, honey, *Jimmy Carter* saw one," Cherry said triumphantly. "In nineteen seventy-one, at the Executive Mansion in Georgia. He turned in an official report on it."

"How come nobody knows about it, then?" Tammy asked. She was a tough customer.

"Because the government covered it up!" said Rhonda, just dying to tell this part. "People see UFOs all the time, it's common knowledge, they are trying to make contact with us right now, honey, but the government doesn't want the average citizen to know about it. There's a big cover-up going on."

"It's just like Watergate." Cherry opened a beer and handed it over to Rhonda.

"That's right," Rhonda said, "and every time there's a major incident, you know what happens? These men from the government show up at your front door dressed all in black. After they get through with you, you'll wish you never heard the word 'saucer.' You turn pale and get real sick. You can't get anything to stay on your stomach."

Tammy cracked up. But Rhonda and Cherry went on and on. They had official-looking gray notebooks to log their sightings in. At their meetings, they reported these sightings to each other, and studied up on the subject in general. Somebody in the club was responsible for the educational part of each meeting, and somebody else brought the refreshments.

Tammy Lynn learned to keep her mouth shut. It was less embarrassing than belly dancing; she had a friend whose mother took belly dancing at the YMCA. Tammy did not tell her mama about all the rational explanations for UFOs that she found in the school library. They included: (1) hoaxes; (2) natural phenomena, such as fungus causing the so-called fairy rings sometimes found after a landing; (3) real airplanes flying off course; and Tammy's favorite, (4) the Fata Morgana, described as a "rare and beautiful type of mirage, constantly changing, the result of unstable layers of warm and cold air. The Fata Morgana takes its name from fairy lore and is said to evoke in the viewer a profound sense of longing," the book went on to say. Tammy's biology teacher, Mr. Owens, said he thought that the weather patterns in Mississippi might be especially conducive to this phenomenon. But Tammy kept her mouth shut. And after a while, when nobody in the UFO Club saw anything, its membership declined sharply. Then her mama met Harold Stikes, then Harold Stikes left his wife and children and moved out to the farm with them, and sometimes Cherry forgot to attend the meetings, she was so happy with Harold Stikes.

Tammy couldn't see *why*, initially. In her opinion, Harold Stikes was about as interesting as a telephone pole. "But he's so *nice*!" Cherry tried to explain it to Tammy Lynn. Finally Tammy decided that there is nothing in the world that makes somebody as attractive as if they really love you. And Harold Stikes really did love her mama, there was no question. That old man—what a crazy old Romeo! Why, he proposed to Cherry when she was still in the hospital after she had her breast removed (this was back when they thought that was *it*, that the doctors had gotten it all).

"Listen, Cherry," he said solemnly, gripping a dozen red roses. I want you to marry me."

"What?" Cherry said. She was still groggy.

"I want you to marry me," Harold said. He knelt down heavily beside her bed.

"Harold! Get up from there!" Cherry said. "Somebody will see you."

"Say yes," said Harold.

"I just had my breast removed."

"Say yes," he said again.

"*Yes, yes, yes!*" Cherry said.

And as soon as she got out of the hospital, they were married out in the orchard, on a beautiful April day, by Lew Uggams, a JP from out of town. They couldn't find a local preacher to do it. The sky was bright blue, not a cloud in sight. Nobody was invited except Stan, Tammy, Rhonda and Bill, and Cherry's mother, who wore her dress inside out. Cherry wore a new pink lace dress, the color of cherry blossoms. Tough little Tammy cried and cried. It's the most beautiful wedding she's ever seen, and now she's completely devoted to Harold Stikes.

So Tammy leaves the lights on for Harold when she finally goes to bed that night. She tried to wait up for him, but she has to go to school in the morning, she's got a chemistry test. Her mamaw is sound asleep in the little added-on baby room that Buddy Oxendine built for Cherry. Gladys acts like a baby now, a spoiled baby at that. The only thing she'll drink is Sprite out of a can. She talks mean. She doesn't like anything in the world except George and Tammy, the two remaining cockapoos.

They bark up a storm when Harold finally gets back out to the farm, at one-thirty. The cockapoos are barking, Cherry's mom is snoring like a chain saw. Harold doesn't see how Tammy Lynn can sleep through all of this, but she always does. Teenagers can sleep through anything. Harold himself has started waking up several times a night, his heart pounding. He wonders if he's going to have a heart attack. He almost mentioned his symptoms to Lois Hickey last week, in fact, but then thought, What the hell. His heart is broken. Of course it's going to act up some. And everything, not only his heart, is out of whack. Sometimes he'll break into a sweat for no reason. Often he forgets really crucial things,

such as filing his estimated income tax on January 15. Harold is not
the kind to forget something this important. He has strange aches
that float from joint to joint. He has headaches. He's lost twelve
pounds. Sometimes he has no appetite at all. Other times, like
right now, he's just starving.

Harold goes in the kitchen and finds a flat rectangular casserole,
carefully wrapped in tinfoil, on the counter, along with a Tupper-
ware cake carrier. He lifts off the top of the cake carrier and finds
a piña colada cake, his favorite. Then he pulls back the tinfoil on
the casserole. Lasagna! Plenty is left over. Harold sticks it in the
microwave. He knows that the cake and the lasagna were left here
by his ex-wife. Ever since Cherry has been in Intensive Care, Joan
has been bringing food out to the farm. She comes when Harold's
at work or at the hospital, and leaves it with Gladys or Tammy. She
probably figures that Harold would refuse it, if she caught him at
home, which he would. She's a great cook, though. Harold takes
the lasagna out of the microwave, opens a beer, and sits down at
the kitchen table. He loves Joan's lasagna. Cherry's idea of a terrific
meal is one she doesn't have to cook. Harold remembers eating in
bed with Cherry, tacos from Taco Bell, sour-cream-and-onion
chips, beer. He gets some more lasagna and a big wedge of piña
colada cake.

Now it's two-thirty, but for some reason Harold is not a bit
sleepy. His mind whirls with thoughts of Cherry. He snaps off
all the lights and stands in the darkened house. His heart is racing. Moonlight comes in the windows, it falls on the old patterned rug. Outside, it's as bright as day. He puts his coat on,
goes out, with the cockapoos scampering along beside him. They
are not even surprised. They think it's a fine time for a walk.
Harold goes past the mailbox, down the dirt road between the
fields. Out here in the country, the sky is both bigger and closer
than it is in town. Harold feels like he's in a huge bowl turned
upside down, with tiny little pinpoints of light shining through.
And everything is silvered by the moonlight—the old fenceposts,
the corn stubble in the flat long fields, a distant barn, the high-

way at the end of the dirt road, his own strange hand when he holds it out to look at it.

He remembers when she waited on him in the Food Lion deli, three years ago. He had asked for a roast beef sandwich, which come prepackaged. Cherry put it on his plate. Then she paused, and cocked her hip, and looked at him. "Can I give you some potato salad to go with that?" she asked. "Some slaw?"

Harold looked at her. Some red curls had escaped the required net. "Nothing else," he said.

But Cherry spooned a generous helping of potato salad onto his plate. "Thank you so much," he said. They looked at each other.

"I know I know you," Cherry said.

It came to him then. "Cherry Oxendine," said Harold. "I remember you from high school."

"Lord, you've got a great memory, then!" Cherry had an easy laugh. "That was a hundred years ago."

"Doesn't seem like it." Harold knew he was holding up the line.

"Depends on who you're talking to," Cherry said.

Later that day, Harold found an excuse to go back over to the deli for coffee and apple pie, then he found an excuse to look through the personnel files. He started eating lunch at the deli every day, without making any conscious decision to do so. In the afternoons, when he went back for coffee, Cherry would take her break and sit at a table with him.

Harold and Cherry talked and talked. They talked about their families, their kids, high school. Cherry told him everything that had happened to her. She was tough and funny, not bitter or self-pitying. They talked and talked. In his whole life, Harold had never had so much to say. During this period, which lasted for several weeks, his whole life took on a heightened aspect. Everything that happened to him seemed significant, a little incident to tell Cherry about. Every song he liked on the radio he remembered, so he could ask Cherry if she liked it too. Then there came the day when they were having coffee and she mentioned she'd left her car at Al's Garage that morning to get a new clutch.

"I'll give you a ride over there to pick it up," said Harold instantly. In his mind he immediately canceled the sales meeting he had scheduled for four o'clock.

"Oh, that's too much trouble," Cherry said.

"But I insist." In his conversations with Cherry, Harold had developed a brand-new gallant manner he had never had before.

"Well, if you're sure it's not any trouble . . ." Cherry grinned at him like she knew he really wanted to do it, and that afternoon when he grabbed her hand suddenly before letting her out at Al's Garage, she did not pull it away.

The next weekend Harold took her up to Memphis and they stayed at the Peabody Hotel, where Cherry got the biggest kick out of the ducks in the lobby, and ordering from room service.

"You're a fool," Harold's friends told him later, when the shit hit the fan.

But Harold didn't think so. He doesn't think so now, walking the old dirt road on the Oxendine farm in the moonlight. He loves his wife. He feels that he has been ennobled and enlarged by knowing Cherry Oxendine. He feels like he has been specially selected among men, to receive a precious gift. He stepped out of his average life for her, he gave up being a good man, but the rewards have been extraordinary. He's glad he did it. He'd do it all over again.

Still walking, Harold suddenly knows that something is going to happen. But he doesn't stop walking. Only, the whole world around him seems to waver a bit, and intensify. The moonlight shines whiter than ever. A little wind whips up out of nowhere. The stars are twinkling so brightly that they seem to dance, actually dance, in the sky. And then, while Harold watches, one of them detaches itself from the rest of the sky and grows larger, moves closer, until it's clear that it is actually moving across the sky, at an angle to the earth. A falling star, perhaps? A comet?

Harold stops walking. The star moves faster and faster, with an erratic pattern. It's getting real close now. It's no star. Harold hears a high whining noise, like a blender. The cockapoos huddle against his ankles. They don't bark. Now he can see the blinking red lights on the top of it, and the beam of white light shooting out the bottom. His coat is blown straight out behind him by the wind. He feels like he's going blind. He shields his eyes. At first it's as big as a barn, then a tobacco warehouse. It covers the field. Although Harold can't say exactly how it communicates to him or even if it does, suddenly his soul is filled to bursting. The ineffable occurs. And then, more quickly than it came, it's gone, off toward Carrollton, rising into the night, leaving the field, the farm, the road. Harold turns back.

It will take Cherry Oxendine two more weeks to die. She's tough. And even when there's nothing left of her but heart, she will fight all the way. She will go out furious, squeezing Harold's hand at the very moment of death, clinging fast to every minute of this bright, hard life. And although at first he won't want to, Harold will go on living. He will buy another store. Gladys will die. Tammy Lynn will make Phi Beta Kappa. Harold will start attending the Presbyterian church again. Eventually Harold may even go back to his family, but he will love Cherry Oxendine until the day he dies, and he will never, ever, tell anybody what he saw.

1992

Patricia Lear

AFTER MEMPHIS

The narrator of this story about a family uprooted by a father's ambitions, is the little sister who spends a summer wandering around loose, depressed, floating, and, above all, free in a way her brother would never be simply because of what was expected of boys. The New York Times Book Review *called this story, included in Patricia Lear's 1992 collection,* Stardust, 7-Eleven, Route 57, A&W, and So Forth, *"surely one of the finest American stories ever written." The author, born and raised in Memphis, Tennessee, now lives in Evanston, Illinois.*

My big brother was the one who had lashed the Confederate flag to the antenna, and so there we were, the four of us under the blaze of our banner, my brother and I two small heads sticking up proud in the backseat sucking on Popsicles — assuming we were ever noticed at all, which probably we weren't but maybe we were, by a gas-station attendant or something — and with our dad's big company-president Cadillac tires rubbering us relentlessly north, and with us inside with the car windows up, and with the car doors locked so that when we fought and roughhoused we would not accidentally hit the door handle and fling ourselves out, there was always around us a protective haze from our parents' cigarette smoke Spanish-mossing into drapey shapes in the corners.

In the night, after night fell, our parents were mostly just little red dots darting through the stillness of that hurtling tunnel of time that was all of us grinding on along on the old highways, our parents writing circles and S's and slashes with their cigarette ends that my brother and I could, you know, eye-blinkingly, see from the back in the dark when we opened our eyes — but also, and mostly in their murmurings to each other, our parents were the only things standing between us and the stories they told each other about, us saying, "What, what, what?" when we couldn't hear a part, and which stories were to us, of course, what life was about with a capital *L*.

Our mom had stayed on with us to finish the school year, as is often done, and she did the usual things that go with the waiting for the school year to be out — she took us to the pediatrician for our shots and kept being assistant leader for my Camp Fire girls and took us to the swimming pool and put the house up for sale and went to exciting places like to the beauty parlor while we were in school, our dad already having gone on ahead of us across the Mason-Dixon line and taken out bank loans and all, spending a year getting things going such as starting his company and finding us a house, and then coming back to chip us with a chisel out of the South, haul us with a crane out of the country club swimming pool — which is how he said it was for him from the way we were acting.

And with us packed by his own hands into the backseat with the line taped down the middle in red tape, also by him, so that we would not fight or start the next Civil War by touching each other, our dad made a beeline straight through downtown Memphis to get it over with, to speed us as fast as possible across that bridge over the Mississippi River, since my brother and I were suddenly swamped emotionally with a great southern pride-flowering that had started us singing and yelling "Dixie," and me hanging out the windows, screaming.

I had just gotten old enough to care about the South, which was really just as everybody was packing up around me for the move. My brother cared first, of course, and then me. In the car my brother was occasionally shrieking out, "Why, why, why?" between "Dixie" verses, so our mom had to say to us that if we were happy people, we could be happy people anywhere, and our dad, who was landing us in West Memphis, Arkansas, down in the industrial section of town (after a jillion stoplights and direction-readings from our mom, and after the usual gas-station phone calls to the place we were trying to get to) down at the visitor parking lot of the Razorback Ice Cream Company, our dad said it was up to us in this life as far as he knew and not the other way around.

And this was the exact day in West Memphis, Arkansas, right after we left the Razorback Ice Cream Company, that was the last time we ever were as kids to have our born-and-bred Memphian accents, and it was the first time we ever knew we even had Memphian accents in the first place. It was from that day on in West Memphis, Arkansas, from where our dad had threaded our way out of the industrial section of town, it was from lunch of that exact first day in West Memphis, Arkansas, that I think our accents started eroding. I believe it began while we were ordering our Rebel Dogs from the Yankee-looking waitress and while, waiting to eat, we were taking in the speech of everybody sitting around us.

It was just business that we all ate ice cream—Peanut Buster Dairy Queens, little Dixie cups, regular ice-cream sandwiches, Creamsicles, Bomb Pops, Drumsticks. You name it, we probably sampled some of it, as our father went zigzagging us from ice-cream store to ice-cream factory (the Razorback only the first) through Tennessee, Arkansas, and Missouri to teach himself everything he could about the processing end of it and the business end of the ice-cream business and to sit around swapping ideas with the other novelty-ice-cream-company presidents and take us all on long, lengthy tours of manufacturing and production areas, storage and freezer space, shipping dock and on-site lunchroom and convenience vending machines, even snaking us single file through the front office to meet management and to chat with the secretarial and clerk-typist pool. We would drink bottles of pop, and listen to the men talking about sugar prices and overruns, milk solids and packaging, as our mom chatted with one of the employee ladies and drank from a paper cone of coffee that was fitted into a little plastic-handled holder.

At night, though, we mixed business with pleasure by staying only in motels with swimming pools, where water bugs frog-legged around in the water with us. Back on the road, we discussed the Civil War and how they had it all wrong in the history books, especially with regard to what we were up to and what they *really* were up to. They did not care about our slaves and our slaves' freedom and their welfare and all. They were just jealous of how good we were doing. They just wanted our raw materials, is what it was. Us plantation owners were left with nothing, no help to keep our crops and cotton going without our slaves, which we loved and cared for.

And the slaves, hell, they even had it worse free than with us!

I was feeling a deep personal unfairness done to me and was get-ting madder and madder about wanting our slaves back, as well as the life that went along with us having them, and it was then that my brother brought up with great suspicion, "Hey, how soon is it anyway, or how late is it exactly, that the state of Missouri, where we are moving to, joined in with the Confederacy, and how is it that Kansas never joined in, though it wavered for about a minute, but in the end, what's the deal with Kansas going blue, not gray?"

"Don't know, don't care," our father said, driving us up through the Ozark Mountains at this point and impressing the hillbillies with our company-president Cadillac flying the Confederate flag. "Anyway, all that is over," he said, pointing out a big truck passing us going the opposite way on the highway with his own name emblazoned across its big side. "Anyway, all that is over," our dad said. "Especially the old moldy Civil War." Then he asked our mom to hand us over into the backseat some rolled-up floor plans and a sketch of what our new house could look like once it was finished — although they had yet to decide exactly which front to put on it from the choices available: ranch, French Provincial, or antebellum.

It was the floor plans and house-front choices my brother and I spread out across us in the backseat that got me to remember-ing my giant drawing book I carried with me everywhere to draw in, and after fixing the elasticized shoulders on my peasant blouse that had snapped up, I was soon busying myself with my art-work—I was drawing plantation houses with pillars standing across the front, and drawing also cotton fields with slaves. On other pages, tucked away, I have to admit, there were pages and pages of penises, like on my brother and on our dog we used to have, and then on other pages there were also a few very, very styl-ized vaginas as seen from the front—as in the mirror, and though I did these items in a very, very stylized way, that is what they *were*. So I was humming "Dixie" and drawing and was thinking about all the old times that I would not forget that we were leav-ing back in Tennessee—such as the *lap, lap, lap* of the country club swimming pool electrically underlit after dark by a splintery light and top-lit by that magical Memphis moon and floated with a drizzle of fallen cottonwood blossoms (not ten thousand water bugs). Such as Elvis, barbecue pork sandwiches from the Pig 'N Whistle, polo ponies we could ride out in Germantown, the Christmas Cotillion where some day I would be a debutante sort of like Scarlett O'Hara because of not one thing I myself would ever have to have done.

But it was on the road that wends through Springfield, Mis-souri—the home of the Ozark Big Wheel Ice Cream Delight sand-wich—and on up through the Ozark Mountains and around the many finger lakes of the Lake of the Ozarks, which I remember clearly, because it was about there as we were suddenly coming up over a big surprise hill in the road that lifted us up into the air and my brother said, "Is this us? The South rising again?" that the truth of this move-we-did-not-want-to-make began seeping out sideways. I was sitting next to my brother, at first peacefully drawing more of what I said I was drawing in the backseat as the family talked on without me, more about the Civil War that I did not understand or care to learn about just then—since unlike my brother I did have a limit to my caring about the teensiest details, and my brother was droning away with his head stuck up between our parents in the front seat droning names and battles and summits and dates — my brother knew everything, every little detail, his caring knew no limits, so it was about then our dad cut it short finally and began telling us the usual stories about his Uncle Winn (so what) we had all heard all our lives anyway, and about "the farm" (so what) where this Uncle Winn lived. Our mom said, "Oh, Winn . . . ," trailing off, but our dad talked on about this Uncle Winn and this farm where we were in fact going to be living until our house was finished being built, our dad telling us story after story, as he hurtled us evermore deeper and farther into the North, the upchuck of all which was that it was because of this Uncle Winn was the reason we were all riding along so comfy in this Cadillac in the first place (so what), because it was from this Uncle Winn that our dad had learned the meaning of the word "work."

Our dad spoke about Uncle Winn in the same tones, I noticed, as my brother did when he was talking about Robert E. Lee or Jefferson Davis. He spoke about how Uncle Winn was the only one of anyone in our whole family to last through the Depression — no one else did, that is for sure, no one else did. "But how he had a temper!" our dad said. "And when he lost it, watch out! You all remember I told you about the time when the stubborn mule refused to plow and Winn did the darndest thing."

"Mule rocked the wrong boat there," our mom said, smiling back at me.

"It was the darndest thing," our dad said.

Oh hell and so what. We had heard that mule story a million times, and I still never liked it. I was the kind of kid that could be made hysterical by such a story. I thought it was mean to the mule.

But just awestruck was our dad in the presence of this story, I could tell from his eyes glittering up in some approaching headlights, intent as he was with keeping that Cadillac hood ornament plowing a straight furrow north back to where he was going to dip back in to the same "good character" pond for some more of whatever it was that he had gotten back then for us all. And there was to be no way out, what with our mom who I could see in plane-lit profile nodding along with him, her eyes turning velvety and soft, her fingers working up his shoulder to his neck, and whose stories were mostly aimed at me, and were mostly about how not wanting anything was the only way to get anything, while our dad's were mostly aimed at my brother, and were about how you just had to go out there and *get* anything, if you were ever going to *have* anything.

Our dad said, "It was the darndest thing."

I was sad all over again about the mule because I very much wanted a horse and a mule was closer to being a horse than what I then had. I would have wanted to ride that mule. I would have taken good care of that mule, and he would have been pretty decrepit by now and old.

The first thing I remember from when we turned into the driveway of the farm and parked ourselves over by the barn was the rising of the sausage-commercial sun to the crowing of the sausage-commercial cocks, our dad having decided to push on and just get there, even though our mom said she could not sit anymore and had to go to the bathroom so bad she could "pop."

The second thing I remember is my brother in front of the barn, looming through the dawn from a place high up on a ladder, nails bristling from his teeth. I could see a big Confederate flag caped up over his shoulders and his hair ruffling along with the wheat crop in an early morning breeze.

The third thing I remember is that there was an old barn turned dance studio right across the highway from the farm that had a spotlit dancer in a top hat and cane stuck up on the roof.

Uncle Winn was watching us all swarming in on him, watching us advancing up the yard from his rented hospital bed set up in the front parlor, us to him probably like the *Night of the Living Dead* with our suitcases and leftover Popsicle wrappers and comic books and fistfuls of trip garbage we were made to clean out from the floor of the car, and me also with my blanket and pillow from the backseat.

Our dad was soon sitting in the pulled-up BarcaLounger, and

those two!—our dad telling Winn—what was it?—something—
it was something about butter-brickle ice cream back then our dad
was all fired up about, just having cut a deal with Heath Bar to
supply the butter-brickle part.

"Wait until you try it," our dad was saying to Winn. "It was the
best thing you will ever eat," as Winn was saying, "What in the
Sam Hill is that?" since he was staring out the picture window at
my brother up on the ladder above the hayloft nailing in the last
nail of our Confederate flag.

Winn sure would not be doing to any more mules what he had
done to his own mule, I could see that from when I was made to
go over and give him a kiss. The local Missouri mule population
was safe.

Next morning it was "Up and at 'em, you-all!" from our dad
who was dressed in his flight suit from the war when he bombed
all the Germans, our dad who sang, "Off we go into the wild blue
yonder," like my brother and I sang "Dixie," who never slept much,
though he would of if he could of, and who never found it in himself to do the thing, to do the sleep method that our mom always
said worked for her where you bore yourself to sleep is basically
what you do. You lie in bed, and you get yourself and your arms
and legs all settled how they feel best—you might want to try out
a couple of positions first before choosing because here is the hard
part—you *stay* in that same position. *No matter what*. Especially
when the urge comes, *and it will*, to move or roll over, you by force
of WILL *stay* in that same position. If you do this long enough,
you are guaranteed by our mom of going to sleep. Our mom does
this sleep method and says it works for her even on the night
before Christmas. And the proof is in the pudding because whenever I would go in to check on our mom in bed, such as if I was
up going to the bathroom, there she would be, so calm and so
asleep. Barely breathing.

Saying, "Work time!" our dad was coming up the stairs to our
room and then picking my brother's bed up on its right side legs

so it crashed down on the wood floor with my brother trying to stay asleep, no matter what, my brother was going to cling to sleep next to me no matter what was done to him, me, of course watching all this through flittery eyelashes and listening to my brother's breath breathing out Whys and I don't believe thises as our dad was by this time finished with this part of his morning and was tromping on back downstairs to help Winn get going for the day, our dad doing what I know he did all that summer — lifting Winn gently up in his hospital bed, then leading Winn by the elbow over to the Porta Potti he had rolled in from the dining room, and then waiting in the kitchen for him, maybe making toast or reading some of the newspaper business section while he was waiting, or maybe staying in the parlor with Winn but politely messing around with his back turned, spreading the covers over Winn's bed for him, all this while he was waiting, all while my brother would be stomping around my bed pulling all the chains on the antiquey lamps that we had in there and then going into the bathroom, door left wide open, where he would sound like the mule must have sounded to Winn when the mule was going on some solid ground and Winn was stuck behind him, waiting, hanging on to the plow.

My brother would suit up in his work coveralls — his T-shirt underneath peeping the Confederate flag through some unsnapped snaps — and he would sing "Dixie" like he thought if he could wake me up that would mean something, which it in no way meant anything as our mom was in charge of me, so him flinging his arms around and throwing his Eagle Scout slingshot to an end-on-end clatter across the wood floor before slamming out the door was just what I had to live with to get rid of him in those summer mornings.

The men would be packing themselves into the Cadillac; I could hear their voices and see them from the upstairs window as I dragged my bones out of bed to get up and go flush the toilet. I could see out there in the driveway my brother sinking back down into the backseat and settling his boots up flat against one of the rear windows, hear the engine starting, hear, I think, "Mack the Knife" playing on the radio, and it was like this that the men left the farm in the mornings all that summer before our house was built, while our house was just a hole in the ground. They left spewing loose gravel from underneath the Cadillac tires, probably scaring frogs out of the drainpipe sections along where the driveway met the highway where they would take a hard left to get out on the highway, passing along the row of Burma-Shave signs in the Cadillac, passing them by, flying the Confederate banner, like starting flags.

After crossing the bridge over into K.C., they would thump a bumper dragging left down on the old road down by the river flats where, whirling dust, our dad would be driving along and lifting his hand up off the steering wheel or tapping his horn at the drivers going the other way, drivers driving trucks of all sizes with his name stenciled on the sides, our dad all the while running organizational plans and ways to secure debt and flavor combination ideas by Winn, and Winn, his whole body pitched about by the car ride, Winn, not my brother, would be listening as our dad drove the three of them deep into the industrial section of town to where his ice-cream plant was tucked behind the Empire Cold Storage Company.

Once, hay mower in the distance, sun a bright butter curl on the silver butter plate of the midday midwestern sky, two men from the plant arrived out at the farm with Winn—he was old and he got tired—and also bringing along with them an institutional-sized and industrial-quality top-opening freezer case with three double lift-up black rubber lids to plug in on the kitchen porch. They were carrying it up the yard toward the porch, the very porch where I would usually be lying on the old tasseled sofa that was moved there from where Winn's hospital bed now was, our dad having changed the furniture around for Winn's special needs—rented the hospital bed, hired on some help, bought the Barca-Lounger, moved the tasseled sofa out to where I would lie in a loose Hawaiian shirt I found in the cedar closet left over from the story about when our dad made Winn go on that Hawaiian cruise, forced him to leave the state of Missouri and fly all the way to Honolulu and get on a cruise boat. I wore that shirt all that summer for its comfort, switching off from my Memphis peasant blouse. I even sometimes slept in it at night, and in the hot afternoons after the freezer arrived, me in the Hawaiian shirt lying on the tasseled sofa, I could reach over my hand to the institutional freezer for, say, another ice-cream sandwich as I was reading my comic books or drawing, and being lulled even more into our new life here in the North by the sleepy ironing-board creak of "our help," Roberta, the fine churchwoman who was coming to Winn for a few hours each day, who hummed whiney church songs as she ironed Winn's shirts, her ironing board set up in the afternoons between the BarcaLounger and the picture window while Winn would lie in his hospital bed moving his lips along to whatever Roberta was singing.

From time to time, dropping a foot on the floor and elevating my old bones upright to a standing position to see better what kinds of novelty items there were in our new freezer, I would go on into the kitchen and drop down at the kitchen table next to our mom who would be sitting there having a cigarette and some iced Constant Comment tea everybody had started drinking in Memphis, her pockets wadded with Kleenexes and soothing herself with doing her bad habit she never could break; she would be fidgeting and peeling at her fingernails until they peeled off in layers.

So we sat, while the dishwasher chugged and threw the dishes around inside, her with her fingernails and sipping her tea and smoking her cigarette, and me eating a Cho Cho cup with a little wooden spoon, and together we would stare into the parlor at Roberta ironing, watch to find out when it was that Roberta made those iron-shaped scorch marks on Winn's shirts. It was when the carpools came and caused a big honking ruckus in the dancing-school parking lot across the highway.

* * *

Even my hostile brother and, most especially, our grinning ener-getic dad would smell good and manly whenever they came home to call it a day, to seek out some plain old R and R, their clothes and hair and skin dusted over with powdered milk and cane sugar and chocolate mix powder, plus dirt and sweat, and bringing along cartons of new ice-cream items that they had thrown in the back of the Cadillac and brought home packed on dry ice. They were ready to eat chicken-fried steak, pot roast, or chicken, chicken, chicken — that is, if they were home any time close to a dinner hour since our dad worked everything; he worked production alongside his crews, all the shifts our dad worked in the course of a week since they kept the plant running around the clock in the summers for the obvious reasons. And also he did figures and answered phones in the front office right along with the clerical ladies, his fingers virtuoso on the keys of the adding machine processing orders and tallying inventory and doing the payroll. He might slip into one of the quilted freezer-room jackets that were kept hang-ing on pegs and two-handed pull open the bank vault of a freezer door and disappear into the thick spill of arctic air before the door slammed shut behind him.

And then he might be coming around the back to the loading dock, to load up the trucks, then he was not beyond jumping into the cab of a truck, making the deliveries himself, even driving those great big trailer jobbies, the ones with sixteen gears and a copilot, driving them down to Chillicothe. He was always going to places like Chillicothe back then.

It was the things that did not sell that he brought home to stock our freezer with as much as the good stuff. He would bring home eggnog ice cream in half-gallon cartons and Coconut Xmas Snow-balls with the real little wax candles sticking up out of the middle of a holly-berry bunch toothpicked in the top. He'd bring pump-kin-flavored turkeys and green dye #11 Christmas trees. At the plant, there were bags of green dye #11. Roberta would serve more bowls of eggnog ice cream than any other flavor to Winn and my mom and me at noontime with our cold-cut sandwiches. We never saw from her hand an Eskimo Pie or a Drumstick. The vanilla and pumpkin-flavored turkeys she would serve occasionally. The strawberry Valentine hearts once in a while — but it was something about the eggnog ice cream that had Roberta in a thrall.

There were times in the evenings that summer when I would have to go the long way around to get from my room to the kitchen to where my mom would be starting our dinner, maybe grating carrots for our little salads or peeling potatoes, it being too early for her to start on me about my job — pouring the milks for dinner. I would have to go through the dark dining room, slip past the set of sliding oak doors of the parlor where I could hear our dad and my brother in there, with Winn asleep or watching the action in his hospital bed, our dad always sitting in the BarcaLounger and my brother always sitting in the needlepointed armchair with the arm doilies. Basically what it was was our dad loving my brother so much he could not let him alone, so afraid was he for my brother concerning life, and wanting everything for him to be so proud and good and strong, for him to be strong and good, and my brother just wanting to be left alone to have some one or two of his own experiences just for himself all by himself, to be proud and good and strong and good just all by himself without our dad acting as brilliant, genius interpreter to every little thing, every little time he brushed his teeth, and Winn sometimes even sleeping, who knows how, through those two saying, "Why do you think why?" to each other, or, "Just what do you mean by that?"

Or, "Is that what you think life is?" It could be either one of them saying that.

"What do you think life is? Tell me right now, please, your theories on what life is."

My brother would finally somehow get himself excused, and then he would head outside past the floured chicken parts frying up in the iron skillet and the others waiting their turn on a waxed-paper sheet, past the finished pieces draining on paper towels on the countertop, past the Jell-O mold quivering in our mom's hands as she was maybe walking it over to the refrigerator, past me and the institutional freezer with the black rubber lift-up tops. He would maybe yell something at me, seeing me reading a comic book on the tasseled sofa, "Taylor, you lazy imbecile, go get the dandelion digger," and then he would go on out into the downy evening light to pull out the old rusty push mower from the shed. I would watch him from where I would climb up on the freezer to watch, and I saw him more than once that summer drop down on his knees in some grass beside the push mower to examine something on the mower blades or wheels, some little thing, a mud clot or something dried up and stuck up there in the mower, and my brother would just get down there close next to it and poke it with a stick.

Our dad would stand beside me and watch. "What in the Sam Hill?" he would breathe while he watched my brother doodle around with the stick, then our dad would follow out, not really being able to stay away from my brother, and he would go off across the yard the opposite way from my brother, like he could not watch anymore, but still, so my brother could see him, like maybe he was going on back to work, he would back his Cadillac out of the barn, back it right underneath my brother's Confederate flag, then at this point, our mom would run out in the yard and our dad would hit the brakes and pretty soon he would cut the engine and come on back in the house, going back past me again, me with my bare foot rummaging around in one of the pull-up top openings of the freezer, and he would go on in to sit with Winn where they would together look at the TV evening news or do figures or just wait for the chicken to finally get itself fried.

Then one night, early on, all of us lying out in the sweet-smelling, just-mown grass my brother was made-to-mow-by-our-dad, we all were lying out after supper having our dessert ice-cream bars in some ratty lawn chairs I found stuck up in the rafters of the barn I had been crawling around in that day, trying to hang out of the hayloft and fix the corner of our Confederate flag where it had come loose. We all were much interested in Creamsicles at that time — vanilla ice cream on a stick covered over with an orange sherbet — something our dad was giving a try that hit BIG, and still is BIG, as you probably know if you frequent the freezer case at the 7-Eleven, but what you would not know was it was my dad that made it that way. We were eating the first Creamsicles on the planet earth and looking around us like you do, and we could see Winn watching TV and eating a Creamsicle, too, lit up in the picture window in his hospital bed. We could see him perfectly, like it looks when you are in the dark outside and somebody is on the inside with all the lights flipped on and funny just because they *are* so totally unaware. The TV noise was blaring far louder out there in the crystalline country air than it would have seemed to be if we were, say, back in the city of Memphis and standing in front of the Peabody Hotel waiting for our car to be brought around front and this same TV noise was blaring out from one of the upstairs hotel windows.

And with us each shifting our bones around in our wooden lawn chairs, we could see the back of a billboard the Motel 6 motel chain, headquartered around there somewhere, had up there, with electric lights haloing out from around the dark oblong of its backside, since it was set forward for the oncoming traffic to see, not our way. The Burma-Shave signs we could not see, but there was the perky spotlit dancer on top of the dance studio across the highway outfitted with her top hat and cane, and actually it was she and Winn that outshone by far even the Motel 6 or the Confederate flag that was nailed up on the barn and lit up ghostlike from all the night neon, and from our pride — my brother's and mine — though that was a shame; the Confederate flag was by far the more beautiful and really meant something important, too. It meant the human spirit and causes.

Our family conversations were mostly round-and-rounds where one person would get on some topic dear to his heart, and then one other person, or persons, would have to get him off that topic

ASAP because it was becoming a threat to one or more of the other family members' equilibrium. And then another party would launch off with a topic that soon could not be tolerated by one or more of the others. And around and around it went like that with conversations in our family.

Our mom would say (I know this since this is what she said all that summer), "Houses are never done on time," and our dad would let her run on for a while to get that off her chest, then he would change the subject because what could he do about the house anyway, build it himself? He would change the topic to something like "work"— his work in particular or just "work" in general— and my brother would pretty soon launch into the Civil War and start talking about a battle or a summit even more obscure than the one he talked about the night before since that is what he was talking about all that summer. He might as well have been in the Civil War for all he knew about it. Or he was also saying every other sentence, such as when our mom was going on about the house never being ready, "Let's go back, let's don't do this," and our dad would get us off that topic lickety-split by launching into something like what he said the night I am remembering.

He said, "Oh, family, this place has a history. Oh this place right here and that old man up there in that picture window really have a history. It scares me to think if it weren't for this place and that man."

And how could we not, even my brother, how could we not look up at that picture window and see Winn who, at this point, was holding his popsicle stick in his mouth and drooping it down like I saw the French apache dancers do with their cigarettes on TV, and my brother then said, "What is that he is wearing? Is he wearing my T-shirt? Is that my T-shirt?" and I remember I jumped to my feet to get a better look at Winn.

Our dad then could have said, for example, to get us off that topic, I don't remember exactly but this is close, "Taylor-tater-tot? Do you know how to snap the head off a snake? Winn in there does," which is probably the thing that started my mom down the road I am going to tell about now, because our mom did say one of those drive-in-movie-perfecto nights, one of those early nights while we were probably all still trip rattled, which is maybe why this thing she told had such a BIG impact on me, why I sucked it up like a damp sponge being wiped across an old kitchen counter, our mom said, "You-all? Oh, I heard this story. Oh, I just heard the most horrible story from home in a letter. Something so sad. Something so terrible."

"Don't tell us," I yelled out at her, attuned as I was to her different tones of storytelling voices, as I was getting myself back in my lawn chair from trying, but not succeeding, in seeing Winn's shirt front. "Don't tell us," I yelled out, wanting but not wanting, I didn't really think, to know her story—all this I had decided just from her tone.

"Snakes reminded me," our mom said.

"Oh boy. Hold your horses right there just a minute," our dad said, working at getting himself up out of his low rickety lawn chair, getting up and then going in the back kitchen door where we could see him stick his head in the electrified parlor where Winn was, then disappear, then come back and toss something in Winn's lap. Then our dad came back out and threw us underhanded, one after the other, a round of spoons and each our own Coconut Xmas Snowball.

"Here's yours, here's yours, here's yours," he said. "Come on. We got to eat these up before they get freezer burn."

"Well, okay," our mom said, as flakes of coconut were drifting down into her lap from the split she had made in the cellophane wrapper with her teeth. I got our dad's Zippo and went around lighting the little candles on everybody's Snowball, staving off the story since I did not need a new story. I had plenty of other stories stored up to get hysterical about. I did not need any more right then. There was the move-story that we were living, so it was not yet really a story; it was our life. There were the kitten drownings. There were penises. I had not yet reconciled myself to penises. There was the mule.

"Well, okay. Here I go," our mom said, gazing into her tiny dancing candle flame. "You know Pete and Jenny Rogers and their little girl from the cotillion, don't you, honey?" she said to our dad. "And it was the Cylinders, the Richard Cylinders, not his brother Benjamin, not the one that you know. John Cylinder married to Linelle, and Patience, her niece, was on the swim team with you, Taylor, at the country club. Peter was a year behind you in Scouts. They were the ones that lent them their cabin over by Pittick Place, down on the Hamlin's road by South Tar Creek. Not Arkansas and not Mississippi."

"What in the Sam Hill are you talking about?" our dad said, just barely ever was he able to tolerate the way our mom went about telling a story, but not daring to shift us off the topic altogether by bringing up the further adventures of Winn or something, as she had her rights, such as to tell an occasional story.

I was working hard on my granite-hard Snowball, also letting the candle drip wax on my fingers as I chipped off little bites.

My brother was staring over at our mom, interested in spite of however she was going to get the story out.

"Okay," our mom said, inhaling a deep breath of honeysuckled air and clearing the decks by setting her Snowball down to melt in the grass by her lawn chair. "I'll try again. There were young newlyweds, the young Pearson couple you all remember from Memphis that were getting married even before we left? Mary Rogers. Mary Rogers Pearson. You saw her picture, Taylor, in the society section a few weeks back. Remember? I showed you? Well they were lent a brand-new cabin for their honeymoon up in the Smokies — and it was the first night right after their wedding party and you know, they were very tired, so they got in bed —"

Here my ears pricked up like the mule's must have done when he saw Uncle Winn walk over to the wood pile and reach his bare arm down.

"On the bed I hear there was one of those chenille bedspreads with the peacock," our mom said, lighting up a cigarette just then, finally relaxing a little into her story, finally having gotten a couple of sentences out unimpeded by the rest of us. The smoke hazed over my way where I smoked it in through my nose.

Now this story our mom was about to tell, I have repeated many times. Over the course of my girlhood, I have told this story, I think, whenever I have spent the night with any one of my many girlfriends, also boyfriends, men, and husbands later, now that I am grown. But this version I am writing here is the most permanent record there has ever been of this story.

Well, the honeymoon couple, Mary Rogers Pearson and her husband, got in bed (sex, penis), and they soon heard things moving around on the floor — slithering noises (snake) — and the husband (penis) said to his beloved, Mary Rogers Pearson, he said that he "must take a small break, my darling, so stay just like that in the bed for just a moment," so he could go and see what was causing those noises (snakes slithering, plus rattles being dragged across the floor) before he continued on with what tender, gentle bliss (penis) he was bringing to his bride for the first time in all her life, and as he hit the floor with his feet and began to feel along the wall for a light switch, he was right then stepping on top of rattlesnake on top of rattlesnake on top of rattlesnake. It was a whole nest of them he was stepping on! Some damn idiot fool had had the stupidity to build that cabin right over the site of the biggest nest of diamondbacks in the whole state of Tennessee!! And those snakes were tangled up everywhere! And the noise level! But the young husband was a Southern boy and thought only of his bride, Mary Rogers Pearson — which it would behoove me to be like her, however she was, so I could find someone to think of *me* like that, so our mom's look said to me, our mom with her cigarette smoke ribboning into the natural plus neon-lit sky — and though the young husband never made it to the light switch in that dolt's cabin (there was a lawsuit), what with those rattlesnakes striking and striking at him as they would of course do, them being wild animals, and him stomping all over them barefooted like a grape stomper, he screamed out to Mary Rogers Pearson, "Oh! My darling! For God's sakes! My love!

Stay-in-the-bed! Oh my darling!" as he was, by that time, simply sacrificing himself for her because he could have instead, if you think about it, screamed for her to go and get him some help. But he didn't. He said to her, "My love. Don't move a muscle! Don't move! Don't even breathe! Just-stay-in-bed! Just-please-for-Christ-sake-stay-still in the bed!"

And then he was quiet. And the rattlesnakes even began calming down.

And Mary Rogers Pearson, beautiful, luminous, huddled up on the bed, her bare shoulders marbled in the wedding-night moonlight that was streaming down across those Smoky Mountains and on in through the cabin window, Mary Rogers Pearson, who was armed only with her honeymoon nightgown of Italian lace that was bought for her in Memphis at the Helen Shop, Mary held on.

Now our mom's cigarette tip brightened considerably as she took a deep drag, and we all sat quietly for a while, each alone with our own thoughts.

"She bowed at the Christmas Cotillion," our mom said.

"And they had their wedding reception at the country club," she said.

"The minute we left Memphis, this all happened. The minute we left, or the day after," our mom said.

Oh!

Oh!

Hearing the sounds she had to have heard! Knowing what she must have known, maybe even seen, because probably she could see shapes and shadows and even more. I mean *really* SEE.

Oh!

I could not imagine that much — being big enough for that much TERROR. And in the morning — as our mom was telling it to us, us glommed on to her every word by now, us at her complete mercy — there was the poor dead husband with too many rattlesnake bites to even count, his WHOLE body a mass of bites, the rattlesnakes by now all gone back down to their nests underneath the floorboards of that cabin like they had never even been there at all. No one really saw them come and no one saw them leave except for what Mary Rogers Pearson said she could see.

"Did that really happen?" I said, wanting my drawing book, my fingers itching to get around a pencil. "Did that happen? Who told you that? When did that happen?" I said struggling underneath the crushing weight of this story.

Now the mule and mule-type stories that were so rampant back then — plus there were others I haven't even mentioned (such as the kitten drownings and the "wild" dog shootings — dogs people did not want anymore, dogs people brought out from Kansas City and let go out on the road by the farm) — maybe, maybe, maybe I could just barely tolerate life knowing those stories happened in the same world I did, and that living things had felt what I had the unique genius to imagine in minute detail that they felt from what I was being told had happened to them, and maybe the violence of us being Rebels forced to live here in the North with the Yankees, that too I could make a semblance of peace with if given a little time, but this story with the honeymoon and the snakes coming up in the dark from underneath and no way out but by getting in with the snakes, and Mary Rogers Pearson in her lace nightgown from the Helen Shop — that story pushed me over the edge, because I was never one who could make peace with things by saying what seemed to take care of everything for everybody else, which was, oh well, that's just the way it goes. That's life for you. *C'est la vie.*

"It happened," our mom said, glancing down at her fingernails. "You see, listen to me, Taylor!" she said as I was busy balling up my Coconut Xmas Snowball wrapper and struggling out of my chair.

"Taylor-tot!" our dad said, meaning he knew I was sealing over and they were not done with me yet.

"The bride," our mom said, "Mary Rogers Pearson, she stayed right there in the bed and she kept still. She did not allow herself to lose control. She kept *still*. And that was smart. That was her only way out of this mess. And well, how she did it, Taylor, if you are wondering just how she did it — well how she did it was how anybody does anything. She *had* to do it. She *had* to, that's how she did it," our mom said, facing me with eyes as glittery with purpose and adamation as our dad's were when he was driving us up here from our happy home down in the South.

"I saw Winn do a rattlesnake," our dad said. "Winn just grabbed him up by its rattler and cracked it like a whip. Head popped off. Then Winn kept cracking until he had cracked him off into nice little wiener-sized sections for the buzzards."

We all gazed up at Winn's picture window and there was Winn sitting straight up in his hospital bed peering back out the window at us. And he *was* wearing my brother's Confederate flag T-shirt.

"She's okay," our mom said. "Mary Rogers Pearson is doing pretty good now. Went to a Fourth of July brunch at the country club."

Now. I could see no path from that night and those snakes to being anything like "pretty good." None whatsoever. The only path I could make out was the path where I would start screaming my head off and all the snakes would charge up and jump all over me — or maybe, maybe I could make it through the night by accident, by being frozen by fear or something, or by some survival mechanism just built into the species that I did not even know I had, but that would be only to be carted off to the insane asylum the next morning where I would spend all the rest of my life reliving the snake-night honeymoon from the picture screen buried deep in my head.

In the late afternoons at a certain time, I would go and lie down on the wood floor under my brother's bed to wait for him to come back from his day of work at the ice-cream factory. If I had the time right, my brother would stumble in and flop down in his big rubber work boots on top of where I was stowed, and I could hear him up there talking conversations to himself about things he would be thinking about and remembering and trying hard to figure out. He would lie still on the bed and sigh loud enough so

I could hear his breath swoosh out. He had not yet really begun to unpack his heart from his over-and-done-with life he used to have back in Memphis where he would do things like take the bus crosstown with his friends and go to the movies.

I was younger and my heart maybe unpacked quicker.

My brother would get up off the bed and kick his boots off and go into the bathroom and get himself a glass of water, then he would come back and lie down and breathe and sigh some more. Sometimes he would get off the bed and ramble down to the kitchen to get a loaf of Wonder Bread, his afternoon food of choice, and sometimes he would trap me by coming back in our room at the wrong time, such as when I was half in and half out from under his bed.

Lots of times when I was lying under his bed, I would find down there beside me a loaf or two of older, forgotten Wonder Bread. I would lie down there, and like he did, pull the crust off slices, then ball up the soft middle part to make bread dough, and I found I liked eating it that way as much as he was liking it up above me. For the most part, I was sympathetic and together with my brother in most ways, but he never knew it. Back then, I would even have been him if I could have.

Like our dad, I had quit sleeping. Like our dad, I found our mom's sleep method was too hard for me. I could not bear the idea of boring myself any more than I already was bored by not being able to sleep.

During the day, I found boards nailed to an oak tree I could climb up in and take my drawing book. I began drawing, along with the usuals you already know about, I drew that cabin in the Smokies and Mary Rogers Pearson in bed with her young husband, I drew the rattlesnakes snarled and snaked around under the floorboards. I drew one of the snakes peeping up through a little knothole in the floor. Then I would look through the tree leaves and draw the silhouette of the dancer in a top hat and cane on the top of the dance studio across the highway. I drew our good old

Confederate flag nailed up on the barn, the billboards and Burma-Shave signs, the waving fields of grain and the puffy clouds, the cars that shot by out on the highway. I drew where the mule used to be, where the kittens were drowned as fast as they could get themselves born — and I would draw these things as my brother was pushing the mower around in the grass below me — learning more about the meaning of the word "work."

When I climbed higher in the oak tree, I could see farther out to where the subdivision was with our new house going in, to where the municipal airport was, to where there were turnpikes and interstates all crimped together with tollbooths — the "I-this" and the "I-that," the "I," I suppose, that had brought us here from the South.

I started taking walks. For something to do, I'd lumber down the old cracking highway that went by in front of the farm, and I would go toward the future, toward our subdivision with the special fancy entrance gate, and brand-new sod, and the new flagpole that was flying a regular flag. I would walk along the flat curved streets to where our building site was located, where I would watch the men pour cement for the foundation, where I got to know the carpenters framing out the rooms, where I would mess around in the wood scraps with some glue, a hammer, and some nails. I would walk around on the springy plywood floors and in and out of the framed-out rooms — walk around in the space where my parents said my room would be. Then after a while, I would leave there and go and explore the other subdivisions farther down the highway that had names such as Dundee Hills, Edgewood, Glen Briar, Green Brier, Briarcliff, and Briarcliff Manor. Briarcliff Manor sat on a bluff overlooking the waterworks and the turnpike and the municipal airport.

At night I would go in by our sleeping mom's bed and drop down on my knees beside her pillow and whisper, "Mom, Mom, Mom. I can't sleep. I can't get any sleep." Then I would sit and wait, maybe get a glass of water from the bathroom, and I would wait and study her. Watch her for how she did it.

Then one night was the last; after that one night I never came in her room that same way again.

She could sleep. I could not.

Things happened. A small plane fell out of the sky and crashed nose-first into the open roof of a half-built split level. I ran and saw the perfect undamaged tail of the plane sticking up higher than the walls, and there was a wing I walked up and down on lying off with some rolled-up sod.

A farmhouse burned down to the ground — ancient electrical wiring — and our mom, Roberta, and I heard the sirens and all came running out of the kitchen, ran across the highway and on back behind the dance studio where we watched as fire trucks jammed up a pasture and boys dragged soggy, sooty mattresses and grimy sofas out into the yard, as a boiling fire took that dried wood house all the way down to the ground. Then below the ground.

There were other wonders. Rains that would snare-drum on the tin roof of the kitchen porch with the sun out, shining and hot. Also heavy, weighty rains that would flood the low spots in the yard, sopping rains where I could run out and dance myself around right across from the dance studio, then flop down by a ditch and let clear water run over my stretched-out legs, let rain-water paste my peasant blouse to my chest and back and shoulders, to turn it see-through to fine, thin lace, and I would, feeling myself "her," lift my chin up and stick my chest out and just sit there being beautiful.

Our dad and me, we were both of us up at night. If Winn were not so old, he would have lasted all night with us, but as it was, Winn was pretty much a transistor radio pulling a weak signal a long way off and real, real late at night. It was simple old age that saved Winn from that torture you need to be young like our dad and me, young and strong, to take. Anybody else would just collapse. And in the day, if you don't sleep at night, I found you cannot let down either. The whole problem is you cannot let down ever, so you must be able to work up a great jitteryness to get you going up and over your exhaustion in the mornings, and to keep up with a kind of shark-eating, frenzy-type energy throughout the day. Though I was still occasionally glancing in through our mom's door to see her sleep, and our dad did in fact stick real close by Winn in the BarcaLounger even though Winn was often asleep himself and not great company, our dad and I kept pretty much quiet with each other and everybody else about our nights. We would just include within us more and more of this problem, which became like any other thing we could not do a darn thing about. We were on our own, each of us alone, like I was beginning to think we all are anyway.

I would be coming out of my bedroom and pad on down the hall under a wedding veil of drifted cigarette smoke that hung in a swirled wasp nest around the overhead light fixture, and when I had made my way down the steep stairs to the parlor, there would be our dad, beanbag ashtray on knee, sitting in the BarcaLounger next to Winn's bed in the quiet of that old farmhouse where all you could hear was the refrigerator and our institutional freezer and the whole house that turned over from time to time in its deep sleep. He would be dressed in his flight suit from the war and be spooning ice cream out of a mixing bowl, scowling at numbers and figures that were listed out on a big tablet of paper.

At dawn I would finally just get dressed and go out of the house swinging my arms, turning cartwheels, going up and down the tree several times to get the blood going. I would slide under a forsythia bush for a heartfelt prayer (so what) that never changed one thing, never made the slightest difference, other than unlike our mom, I was let down every time I tried it. Prayer was only making me think again and again each time I tried it that I was the one that nothing worked for.

So carrying along on the side of the highway heading up toward our building site in the morning-milk-splashing-in-a-bowl-ofcornflakes sun, in the day-camp-bus-picking-up-the-little-kids-with-their-lunch-sacks sunshine, I would find Bic pens and number-two pencils and plastic barrettes lying along the side of the road. That is not true. That was only sometimes. Mostly I would find sticks and broken pop bottles and all kinds of wild flowering weeds that I would pick, the weeds, sometimes having to get down on my hands and knees and bite off the stalks with my teeth if twisting and turning and picking at them with my fingernails or sawing at them with a broken Coke bottle did not work.

I would see up ahead in the roadside debris a glint or flash, and I would walk faster; then I would see it was maybe only the inside wrapper from somebody's cigarettes causing the sun to flash, or the even thinner foil liner of a Nestlé Crunch bar. Once in a while it was the foil cover of an Eskimo Pie bar with our dad's name in small letters under the logo. Once it was a fifty-cent piece that bought me a small packet of something for my hair at the highway Rexall I had been in seeing what all they had. It smelled like vinegar when I mixed it with water, and when I rinsed it through my hair after washing, my hair shined so it was me who was the one causing the sun to flash.

In his big floaty Cadillac, our dad, with Winn and my brother packed inside, would sometimes come surging down the highway passing me by on those mornings. Sometimes, I would jump up and down and wave my bunch of flowery weeds at them, or throw a stick out in the road. Once I tried to kill them all by aiming a Coke bottle at their windshield. Once though, our dad slowed and crunched over onto the shoulder of the highway close to where I was standing, and as I went up to his side of the car, he made the most charming talk to me. He said, "And how are you, Mademoiselle Taylor?" and he said this in the French manner he learned from when he was in France having R and R from bombing the Germans, and I remember clear as day that "Mack the Knife" was playing on the Cadillac car radio and that our dad and Winn were together and smiling and happy.

No. *Really* happy. *Really, really* happy.

I had myself slung out along a tree branch looking down on top of my brother—I could see his head and the tops of his T-shirted shoulders shoving the push mower up and down the slopes of the yard, his arm reaching down from time to time to throw a stick or a rock out of the way, then hitching himself up again and shoving off to mow more grass, and I was thinking about how I would never want to be mowing the grass—and that obviously neither would my brother.

Our mom, who is in charge of me, I just wait out. I stay in the tree. Like the milk. Pouring the milk at dinner. Pouring milk for dinner is my job.

So slung on the branch overlooking my brother pushing the mower in rusty-blade-rotating shoves, I was busying myself with picking around and collecting acorns and small branches, things to drop down on his head as he would shove under my tree, things to ping off his flag-shirted shoulders, as I listened to him say, "Why? Why? Tell me why? Why is this such a big deal? I would just like to know what you think."

He was out across the yard in the dandelions and I could see the wheel nut fell off again or the mower was jammed up with a stick again. He tried getting it going by assuming different positions— like one foot braced up on the mower for extra push force, and then the other foot up on the mower and his shoulder braced on the handle and then picking up the entire mower and turning it over upside down, saying, "Why, why, why?" I watched him through a kaleidoscope of oak leaves as I was changing around my position in the tree, going from one side of the tree to the other, the arms flapping on my Hawaiian shirt, my hair, I suppose, flashing in the sun, and then I noticed him coming stolidly up the little slope, passing right under my tree, where I froze on my branch and took aim and bombed down on him a couple of the acorns. He headed into the garage where there are the tools.

Asking for more, my brother walked back under my tree (more acorns, twigs, some spit) and on back down a way to the push mower where he kneeled and dropped his ass low in the dande-lions. "Get me a Bomb Pop, Taylor," he said over his shoulder. "Get out of the stupid tree and go get me a Bomb Pop, or a Pop-sicle is okay."

I held still in the tree, flattened on my branch, my hair with the drugstore stuff hanging down to where even I could see the dif-ferent growing-out lengths, to where the ends thinned to a translu-cence from the sunlight that was laced in through the leaves.

My brother pulled off his Confederate flag T-shirt. He pulled it over his head and used it to wipe across his face, then glancing up at the bigger Confederate flag nailed on the barn, he worked at tying his shirt up around his head so it would flop down his back, flag out. Turning, he looked up at me. I flattened flatter.

"Popsicle, Taylor," he said. "Or I will come up there and kill you."

Grasses rustled from the little suppertime breeze. I was about ready to just go and get it for him, to get him his Bomb Pop or Popsicle. The sun, I noticed, was an egg yolk drooped over the fields as I shifted around on my branch, then monkeyed over to another branch, the back of my Hawaiian shirt floating out behind me, as my brother was watching and saying, "Go get me a Bomb Pop now, Taylor."

Then it was what I think must be sleep, that I was dreaming. The automatic reaction of, say, Mary Rogers Pearson happening in me; I froze. I was so quiet beside that delicate slipping through, a delicate slipping through is what it was, that I must have been sound asleep (finally) and dreaming this thing, this moving still-ness up there beside me, which after a brief pause set off my shoul-ders to press back, my rib cage to part wide for air, my lungs to grab for reaches of sound that I grabbed hold of, dug my heels in, and wrenched from my heart. Arm on its own volition reached out and grabbed hold of the moving stillness, and we fell, the two of us together, moving stillness now a garden hose with the water turned on full (but no water), we fell tangled around in the Hawai-ian shirt that flew up around my neck, we fell through the air together to land on my back out of the tree to there where my brother was standing with us rolling around, me screaming out, the garden hose all muscle now with trying to get away, undulating, coiling, and wrapping on me, my shoulders pressing forward, legs trying to stand up.

I got hold of, not the tail, but the whole rear third and unwound it off my body. Up in the air my arm went and straight up it went, but nothing. Nothing. So I did this, pretty calm too, I held it in one hand and found a better grip with the other, and then I did it, I cracked it again, but all that happened was it looped. It sketched a U shape in the air, so I did it again and let her fly, or he got away, or he got himself, herself, up in the air where she gave a bronco lunge and charcoaled several W's in the air and landed a way off deep in the dandelions over by where my brother was standing by the push mower. He, she, swished through the grasses, or she — she went — back to her babies. Or she *was* a baby and her mother was a mule-eating, Missouri-wheat-crop python waiting out there in the field for me when I went looking.

The picture window was a crowd of faces looking out, Winn in the middle sitting straight up in his hospital bed.

I fixed my shirt down from around my neck and went up the yard to get my brother his Bomb Pop. I got a couple of Bomb Pops out of the institutional freezer, our mom and dad calling out my name from the parlor, and then I ran back outside to my brother before the sun dropped its yolk completely into the field and the day was all over. We sat down together by the push mower and tore the wrappers off our Bomb Pops.

No one is in charge of me.

1992

Padgett Powell

THE WINNOWING OF MRS. SCHUPING

Mrs. Schuping lives on the edge of a five-acre swamp. According to the story, "Life was winnowing for Mrs. Schuping . . . 'I'm going beyond Walden,' she told herself," statements that send the reader to Webster's: *"Winnow (win'o) v. 1. To separate the chaff from (grain) by means of a current of air. 2. To examine closely in order to sort; sift. 3. To separate (a desirable or undesirable part); eliminate." The scintillating Mrs. S. accomplishes all of those definitions and, in the process, becomes (to use her word) "normal." The author of four books of fiction, the most recent of which is* Edisto Revisited, *Padgett Powell teaches at the University of Florida.*

Mrs. Schuping lived on a moribund estate that had once been grand enough in trees alone that a shipbuilder scouting live oaks in the eighteenth century had bought the tract for wood to make warships for the British navy. Oak of that sort, when fitted and shipped into six-inch walls, would not merely withstand or absorb cannonballs but repel them a good way toward their source. Mrs. Schuping did not know this, but she knew she had big old trees, and she patted their flanks when she strolled the grounds.

The house had died. So slatternly, so ratty was it that Mrs. Schuping was afraid to enter it again once she had worked up the courage to go out of it, which was more dangerous. She had been hit by boards twice while leaving the house but never when going in.

There was no such thing as falling-down insurance, an actuarial nicety that flabbergasted and enraged Mrs. Schuping. Falling down was what really plagued houses, therefore that was what you could not protect them from by lottery.

She called herself *Mrs.* Schuping arbitrarily. She had no husband nor had she ever found in the least logical the idea of having one man whom you so designated. Wholly preposterous.

She had a good toaster. It was a four-slice commercial stainless square job, missing its push-down knobs, so that you had to depress the naked notched metal thingies to lower the bread. It looked like you'd need a rag to protect your hand, but you did not. Perhaps if you were hustling breakfasts in a good diner you might, but not slowly, at home. Life was winnowing for Mrs. Schuping.

When she bought the house, she had found a huge collection of opera records, of which she knew nothing except that they sounded ridiculous. This collection she played dutifully, over and over, until it was memorized, until it could not be said that she was ignorant of opera. When she had mastered the collection, she wondered why, and she sailed the records, one by one, into the swamp behind the rotting house. She winnowed the collection of opera records until it was a collection of cardboard boxes, and eventually used those to set her first swamp fire.

Setting the swamp on fire was not a winnowing of her life, but it did winnow the swamp. The burnings seemed to her rather naughty and frivolous, and surprisingly agreeable to look at and to smell. She took an unadult pleasure in them, along with an adult fear that she might be somehow breaking the law even though the swamp was hers.

The second time she set the mangy tangled tract on fire the sheriff showed up, and she became sure it was the case that you could not burn your own swamp. The sheriff, whom she had not met before, confirmed her anxiety with his opening remark.

"Your *swamp* is on fire," he said, standing about fifteen feet off her right shoulder and slightly behind her.

She turned to him and said, not knowing what in hell else she might, "Yes, it is."

The sheriff stood there regarding first her and then the swamp and the fire, which gave his face a jack-o'-lantern orange sheen, and said again, "The swamp is *on fire*." The emphasis was meant to confirm his sympathies with having fires, and upon establishing that bond he walked briskly to Mrs. Schuping's side and planted his feet and crossed his arms and cocked back to watch the fire with her in an attitude that suggested he would be content to watch for a good long while. When he breathed, his belt and holster creaked.

Mrs. Schuping could not tell if his affection for the fire was genuine or a trap of the infamous misdirectional-innocuous-talk type favored by country police.

So she said two things. "Sheriff, I set my opera-collection boxes on fire; I confess they were in the swamp." Then, "Sheriff, I do not need a man."

The sheriff looked at the fire, followed it up into the high parts where it licked at the grapevines climbing on the tupelo gums. It was a hot yellow heat in the slack black-ass muddy gloom of a nothing swamp that needed it. He had been taking pure aesthetic enjoyment from the thing until Mrs. Schuping said what she said, which reminded him that they were not free to enjoy this mayhem and that he had to undo her concern with his presence. Concern with his presence was—more than his actual presence—*his job* ordinarily; it was how he made his living. This was the hardest thing about being sheriff: you could not go off duty. A city cop could. They even provided locker rooms and showers for them, and he imagined laundry and dry-cleaning takeout services for the uniforms. But a sheriff was the sheriff, and he was always, always up to something. That is why he had had to talk like a fool to this woman to get her to let him watch her fire with her. How else excuse standing in front of five burning acres and saying "on fire"? But it had not worked. And this *man* thing.

"Mizz Shoop, I just—"

"It's Schuping," Mrs. Schuping said.

"Yes'm. I know. I just like to call you Shoop, though."

With this the sheriff again squared off, with a sigh, to watch the fire, whatever he had been about to say cut off by Mrs. Schuping's correcting him. He hoped he had begun the dismantling of her concerns with his presence, both legal and sexual. He was aware

that he had not done much toward either end, but he did not want
to babble while watching a good fire. Unless she asked him off the
property, he'd hold his ground.

Mrs. Schuping was content, having posted her nolo contendere
on the fire and her *no desire* on the man, to let him stand there and
breathe and creak if he wanted to. She had been a little hard on the
sheriff, she thought. It was the legal part that worried her into
overstating the sexual part. Not *over*stating, *mis*stating: she did not
need a man, but wanting was another question. And if all you had
to do to get a big creaking booger like this one was set your backyard on fire, she was all for it.

Four months later the sheriff and Mrs. Schuping had their second date. He saw the smoke from the interstate, where he was
parked behind the Starvin' Marvin billboard at such a ridiculous
pitch that takeoff was nearly vertical and he resisted blasting off for
speeders unless provoked entirely. What had been provoking him
entirely lately was college kids with their feet out the windows of
BMWs, headed for Dade County, Florida, with their socks on.
That was making him strike, lift-off or no lift-off. He wondered
what it was like for a bass. How some lures got by and some did
not. For him it was *pink socks*. In the absence of pink socks, there
was smoke over the Fork Swamp.

Mrs. Schuping looked even more fire-lovely than she had at the
first fire. This time she saw him before he spoke.

"There won't be a problem with the permit," the sheriff said,
instead of the idiocies of last time. There was no problem with the
permit because there was no permit, but he thought this was a
good way to address those concerns of hers.

The sheriff had lost a little weight. Mrs. Schuping had been on
intellectual winnowing excursions, and she saw as a matter of vec-
tor analogy the trajectory of the sheriff toward her and the swale
of her sexual self. He had a swag or a sway—something—of gut
that suggested, even if a bit cartoonishly, a lion. This big fat tub
could get on *top* of her, she thought, with no identifiable emotion,

looking at the crisp, shrieking, blistering fire she had set with no more ado than a Bic lighter jammed open and a pot she didn't want anymore full of gasoline.

The sheriff took a slow survey of the fire, which was magnificent, and loyal—her little swamp was neatly set on a fork of creeks so that the fire could not get away—and turning back he caught a glance of Mrs. Schuping's profile as she watched the fire and, he thought, him a little, and down a bit he saw her breasts, rather sticking out and firm-looking in the dusky, motley, scrabbled light. Bound up in a sweater and what looked like a salmon-colored bra, through the swamp smoke stinging your eyes, on a forty-year-old woman they could take your breath away. He made to go.

"Good cool fire, Mizz Shoop," the sheriff said. "I've got to go."

"You're leaving, Sheriff?"

"It's business, purely business."

To the sheriff she seemed relaxed, legally, and there is *nothing* like a big Ford *pawboooorn* exit—a little air, a little air and a little time.

Mrs. Schuping had been through every consciousness and semi-consciousness and unconsciousness and raised- and lowered consciousness program contributing to every good conscience and bad conscience and middle struggling conscience there is. But now she was a woman in a house so falling apart that the children had taken it off the haunted register, and she was boiling an egg on a low blue flame. Outside were the large, dark, low-armed oaks.

Also outside, beyond the oaks, were the smoldering ignoble trees. The white, acrid, thin smoke drifting up their charred trunks was ugly. The swamp had powers of recovery that were astounding, though. It was this magical resilience that confirmed Mrs. Schuping as an avid swamp burner. When the swamp came back hairier than it had been before the burning, thicker and nastier, she found the argument for necessary periodic burning, which was of course a principle in good forestry. She was not a pyromaniac, she was a land steward. The trees stood out there fuming and hissing and steaming. Her life continued to winnow.

Beyond the disassembly of her opera holdings, Mrs. Schuping had gradually let go of her once prodigious reading. She had read in all topical lay matters. She had taught herself calculus, and could read *Scientific American* without skipping the math. She had taught herself to weld and briefly tried to sculpt in metal. She gave this up after discovering that all she wanted to sculpt, ever, was a metal sphere, and she could not do it.

She had dallied similarly in hydroponics, artificial intelligence, military science, and dress designing. She had read along Great Book lines and found them mostly a yawn, except for the Great Pornography Books, for which there seemed to be no modern equivalent. She had stopped going out to concerts and movies, etc., which she had done specifically to improve herself, because it got to where after every trip on the long drive back to the ruined estate she wondered what was so damned *given* about improving oneself. The opposite idea seemed at least as tenable. As her tires got worse, it seemed even more tenable, and she began to embrace the idea of winnowing: travel less, do less, it *is* more. She found a grocery that still delivered, and she picked up her box of groceries on the front porch — as far as the boys would go.

At first she regretted the winnowing, but then she did not: she had had a mind, but nothing had properly got in its way. That happens. The same for bodies: there were good athletes in this world who had never had the right field or the right ball get in their way. It was particle physics when you got down to it, and the numbers of people in the world today and the numbers of things to occupy them made the mechanics of successful collision difficult. So she'd burn her swamp, pat her good trees, cook her egg. She had one old clock radio, a GE in a vanilla plastic cabinet with a round dial for a tuner, which she played at night. If there were storms she listened to the static of lightning.

When the swamp had returned in its briary vitriolic vengeance, reminding her of a beard coming out of a face that was too close

to hers, she set it afire a fourth time. The fire went taller than
before, so she walked around to the front of the house to see if you
could see it from there and, if you could, if it looked like the house
was on fire, and there was the sheriff, parking his car.

He rolled down the window and said, "I've got you two puppies." She looked in at the front seat and saw that he did. All puppies are cute, but these seemed abnormally cute. She discarded,
immediately, protest. She was not going to be the sort, no matter
how holed up and eccentric, to refuse a dog because of the responsibility and other nonsense.

"What kind are they?"

"The kind dogfighters give me just before they have themselves
a convention." The sheriff opened the door and let the puppies out
and got out himself. They all walked back to the fire. At one point
the sheriff misjudged the ground and veered sharply into Mrs.
Schuping and nearly knocked her down. He was so big and tight
that he felt like the oak walls of the ships that flung cannonballs
back, which Mrs. Schuping did not know had made her trees,
under which they now walked, attractive to a shipbuilder two hundred years before.

The fire was a good one. There was a screaming, out of human
register, as oxygen and carbon clawed each other to pieces, going
through peat and leaf and the dirt that somehow stayed up in the
leaves, even when it rained, giving the swamp its dusty look that
would never be right for *National Geographic*. The dirt in the trees
presumably turned to glass, and maybe that was why, Mrs. Schuping thought, the fire always sounded like things breaking. Tiny
things breaking, a big fiery bull in the shop.

Without an inkling of premeditation, she turned to the sheriff,
who was breathing and creaking there in standard fashion, and
balled her fist, and very slowly brought it to his stomach and
ground it mock-menacingly into him as far as it would go, which
was about an inch. At this the sheriff put his hand on the back of
her neck and did not look from the fire. They regarded the fire in
that attitude, and the puppies romped, and in the strange orange

light they all looked posed for a family portrait at a discount department store.

Before going into the house, the sheriff knocked the mud off his boots, then decided that would not do and took his boots off and left them outside the back door on the porch. Mrs. Schuping put two eggs on to boil. The sheriff, who she thought might go three hundred pounds, should not eat an egg, she knew, but it was what you ate after a swamp fire — boiled hard, halved, heavy salt and pepper, and tasting somehow of smoke — and it was all she had, anyway.

They peeled the eggs at the metal table and put the shells in the aluminum pot the eggs had cooked in. Mrs. Schuping peeled hers neatly, no more than four pieces of shell, but the sheriff rolled his on the table under his palm until it was a fine mosaic. He rubbed the tiny bits of shell off with his thumb.

When the sheriff came out of the bathroom and stood by the bed, Mrs. Schuping became frightened beyond the normal, understandable apprehensions a woman can have before going to bed with a new man, especially the largest one it is conceivable to go to bed with. She also had a concern for the bed itself, and even for the structural capacity of the house — but that was hysterical; the sheriff was safely upstairs, and no matter what he did he would not get any heavier. Something else frightened her. It was as if a third party were in the room, a kind of silent presence, and then she realized what it was. The sheriff, naked, without his creaking leather, was quiet for the first time, a soundless man. It gave her goose bumps.

"Get in."

Mrs. Schuping decided it was best to trust a man this large in the execution of his own desire, and let him near-smother her. He made a way for air for her over one of his shoulders and began what he was about, which seemed to be an altogether private program at first but then got better, until she could tell that the sheriff was not simply a locomotive on his own track, and things got evenly communal, traces of smoky fire in the room, but enough air. Mrs. Schuping thought of winnowing and sailing records and her mother and of how long a gizzard has to cook to be tender, how much longer than a liver, and she lost track until she heard the sheriff breathing, about to die like a catfish on a hot sidewalk, and stop.

"Mizz Shoop," the sheriff said, when he could talk, "this is my philosophy of life and it proves it. Almost everything can happen. Yingyang."

"What would be an example, Sheriff?"

"Well— this," he said, his arms arcing in the space over them and reballasting the bed. "And did you hear about them boys killed that girl for p— excuse me. For sex?"

The sheriff then related the details of a rape case he had worked on. It was not the sort of talk she expected to follow a First Time, but she let him go on and found that she did not mind it. The sheriff had set in motion the pattern of rude and somewhat random speech that would follow their lovemaking in the high springy bed under the ripped ceiling. You would be allowed to say whatever was on your mind without regard to etiquette or setting. Once, it embarrassed her to recall, she declaimed apropos of nothing while they were still breathless, "Listen. I have a father and a mother. I'm a *real person*."

To this the sheriff firmly rejoined, "I think the whole goddam country has lost its fucking mind."

"I don't doubt it," Mrs. Schuping said.

They could talk like this for hours, their meanings rarely intersecting. The last thing the sheriff said before leaving that first night was, "Fifty pounds in the morning. They'll be all right under the porch." Mrs. Schuping slept well, wondering fifty pounds of what under the house before she drifted off.

The sheriff had initiated a pattern with this remark, too, but she did not know it. She would find that the sheriff was given to talking about things that he did not bother to preface or explain, and that she preferred not asking what the hell he was talking about. Whatever the hell he was talking about would become apparent, and so far the sheriff had delivered no unwanted surprises. She saw just about what she was getting.

In the river of her winnowing life, the sheriff represented a big boulder in the bed of the dwindling stream. It eventually would be eroded from underneath and would settle and maybe sink altogether. Mrs. Schuping, therefore, did not find the facts of her aggressively winnowing life and the solid, vigorous mass of her new man to be in conflict at all.

She had never known a man so *naturally* unrefined. Despite his bulk, the sheriff gave her a good feeling. That was as specific as she could be about it. He gives me a good feeling, she thought, marveling at the suspicious simplicity of the sentiment.

She had a dream of going into the swamp and finding her opera records unharmed and retrieving them and playing them for the sheriff, who, as his appreciation of them increased, began to dance with her in a ballroom that somehow appeared in her house, the operas having become waltzes, and began to lose weight, becoming as slender as a bullfighter; then, in the swamp again, she found the records hung in the trees and melted into long, twisted shapes that suggested, of all things, the severely herniated intestines of a chimpanzee she had once seen in a cheap roadside wild-animal attraction. She woke up glad to wake up. She would look for no records and wish no diet upon the sheriff. "Have my *head* examined," she muttered, getting out of bed.

In a very vague way Mrs. Schuping had decided — before the decisions and lack of decisions that set her life on its course of winnowing — that having her head examined was going to be the certain price if she did not begin to clear a few, or many, things out of it. She saw at the end of theories of consciousness and lay physics and broad familiarity with things topical and popular a wreck of the mind, her mind, on the rocks of pointless business and information. None of that knowledge, good or bad, simple or sophisticated, was ever going to allow her to do anything except more of *it:* drive another eighty miles to another touring concert or exhibition, read another article on the mating dynamics of the American anole.

She decided that a green lizard doing push-ups with his little red centerboard coming out of his throat was one thing, but if she *read* about it anymore, saw any more stylized drawings of "distensible throat flaps" on vectors heading for each other like units in a war game, she was going to be in trouble. This was a petty, flighty kind of fed-upness to reach, and not carefully thought out, she knew, but she did not care. If you looked carefully at bee No. W-128, who was vibrating at such and such a frequency, wagging his butt at 42° on the compass . . . God. Of all her prewinnowing interests, this arcane science was her favorite, yet, oddly enough, it was the first to go. It had looked insupportable in a way that, say, *Time* had not. Yet over the years she had decided, once *Time*, etc., had also been abandoned, that the lizards and bees and flow mechanics were supportable in the extreme by comparison—as were the weirdly eclectic opera records more justified than the morning classical-music shows on public radio—but once she had opted for winnowing there was no pulling back. "I'm going *beyond* Walden," she told herself, and soon thereafter began eying the cluttered swamp, which was not simple enough.

So she winnowed to prevent having her head examined. If it were to be, she wanted them to find nothing in it. She knew enough about the process. Her mother had had *her* head examined, many times. Mrs. Schuping did not like her mother, so that was all she needed to know about having your head examined. Not for her.

She looked out the window that morning and saw a man with a white stripe down each pant leg walk away from the house and get in a yellow truck, which then drove off. When she investigated she found a fifty-pound sack of dog food on the porch and the two puppies scratching at it very fast, as if they would dig in spoonfuls to China.

* * *

After their first night together, the sheriff arrived without Mrs. Schuping's having to set the swamp on fire. The sheriff had established the two things he would do for or to Mrs. Schuping. One was talk trash in bed and the other was supply her with goods and services that came through his connections as sheriff. After the dog food, which had belonged to the county police dogs until her puppies got it, a crew of prisoners showed up one morning and painted the entire porch, which surrounded her house, with yellow road paint, giving the house the look of a cornball flying saucer about to take off. The sheriff appeared that night — the fluorescent paint more than ever inspectable then — beaming with pride. He did not remark upon it directly or ask Mrs. Schuping how she liked it, but from his face, which in its pride nearly partook of the same yellow glow, it was obvious that he was sure she liked her hideous new paint job. She could not deny it.

She had watched the crew from a lawn chair, drinking coffee while they changed her haunted-looking, unpainted, unannounced house into something like ballpark mustard with mica in it, and never asked them what they thought they were doing. Nor had she asked the man with the shotgun what he was doing. And now it did not seem proper to ask the sheriff. The dog food was done, the porch under which the puppies were to live was done, and something else would be done, and it was in the spirit of winnowing to let it be done.

But in bed that night, before they got to the sheriff's spontaneous trash talking, she did let out one question.

"Listen," she said. "Isn't this, prisoners and . . ." She made a kind of scalloping motion with her hand in the air, where he could see it. "I appreciate it, but isn't it . . . *graft* or something?"

The sheriff took a deep breath as if impatient, but she already knew he would not, if he were impatient, show it; he was a man who could talk about rape in bed, but in other important ways he was a gentleman. He was breathing to compose.

"If you see something I have," he said, "there is something behind it I have given." He breathed for a while.

"Law is a series of *deals*," he said next, "and so is law enforcement." More breathing. "Nobody in law en*force*ment, unlike *law*, makes money *near* what the time goes into it."

They looked at the ceiling.

"If you don't do Wall Street, this is how you do it." A deep sigh.

"That dogfighter I got your puppies from made fifteen thousand dollars the next week in one *hour*, and I let him do it, and I did not take a dime. You have two good dogs he would have knocked in the head."

Mrs. Schuping was sorry she had asked and never did again. But if she saw the sheriff studying something about the place she might attempt to steer him off. He seemed to look askance at her mixed and beat-up pots and pans one night, and, fearful that he would strip the county-prison kitchen of its commercial cookware — perhaps inspired by the odd presence of her commercial toaster — and stuff it all into hers, she informed him casually that broken-in pots were a joy to handle.

She missed his citing for the deck and the boardwalk into the swamp, however. The one clue, mumbled in his sleep, "Ground Wolmanized, that'll be hard," she did not know how to interpret until the ground-contact-rated, pressure-treated posts were being put in the yard behind her house and on back into the swamp by black fellows with posthole diggers and the largest, shiniest, knottiest, most gruesome and handsome arms she had ever seen.

She watched them, as she had watched the housepainters, this time putting brandy in her coffee — something she had tried once before and not liked the taste of. Sitting there drinking spiked coffee, she felt herself becoming a character in the gravitational pull of the sheriff despite, she realized, efforts nearly all her life not to become a character — except for calling herself Mrs. Schuping.

The boardwalk through the thinned swamp looked miraculous, as if the burning had been a plan of architectural landscaping. The handsome, lean swamp, the walk suggesting a miniature railroad trestle going out into it, resembled a park. If you winnowed and got down pretty clean and were normal, she thought, and something happened — like a big-bubba sheriff and thousands of dollars of windfall contracting and a completely different kind of life than you had had — and you started becoming a character, and you paid nothing for it and did not scheme for it, and it reversed your winnowing, and you liked brandy suddenly, at least in coffee, while watching men who put classical sculpture to shame, was it your fault?

1993

Tony Earley

CHARLOTTE

Tony Earley nails the so-called New South in this story set in a Yuppie fern bar where a professional wrestler named Lord Poetry has been known to recite Yeats. For the bar manager/narrator and his girlfriend, Starla, the "Final Battle for Love"—a match between sentimental Lord Poetry and sexy Bob Noxious for the love of Darling Donnis—stands for their own battle. Tony Earley comes from Rutherfordton, North Carolina, and is the author of Here We Are in Paradise, *a story collection published in 1994.*

The professional wrestlers are gone. The professional wrestlers do not live here anymore. Frannie Belk sold the Southeastern Wrestling Alliance to Ted Turner for more money than you would think, and the professional wrestlers sold their big houses on Lake Norman and drove in their BMWs down I-85 to bigger houses in Atlanta.

Gone are the Thundercats, Bill and Steve, and the Hidden Pagans with their shiny red masks and secret signs; gone is Paolo the Peruvian who didn't speak English very well but could momentarily hold off as many as five angry men with his flying bare feet; gone are Comrade Yerkov the Russian Assassin and his bald nephew Boris, and the Sheik of the East and his Harem of Three, and Hank Wilson Senior the Country Star with his beloved guitar Leigh Ann; gone is Naoki Fujita who spit the mysterious Green Fire of the Orient into the eyes of his opponents whenever the referee turned his back; gone are the Superstud, the MegaDestroyer, the Revenger, the Preacher, Ron Rowdy, Tom Tequila, the

Gentle Giant, the Littlest Cowboy, Genghis Gandhi, and Bob the Sailor. Gone is Big Bill Boscoe, the ringside announcer, whose question "Tell me, Paolo, what happened in there?" brought forth the answer that all Charlotteans still know by heart—"Well, Beel, Hidden Pagan step on toe and hit head with chair and I no can fight no more"; gone are Rockin' Robbie Frazier, the Dreamer, the Viking, Captain Boogie Woogie, Harry the Hairdresser, and Yee-Hah O'Reilly the Cherokee Indian Chief. And gone is Lord Poetry and all that he stood for, his archrival Bob Noxious, and Darling Donnis—the Sweetheart of the SWA, the Prize Greater Than Any Belt—the girl who had to choose between the two of them, once and for all, during THE FINAL BATTLE FOR LOVE.

Gone. Now Charlotte has the NBA, and we tell ourselves we are a big deal. We dress in teal and purple and sit in traffic jams on the Billy Graham Parkway so that we can yell in the new coliseum for the Hornets, who are bad, bad, bad. They are hard to watch, and my seats are good. Whenever any of the Hornets come into the bar, and they do not come often, we stare up at them like they were exotic animals come to drink at our watering hole. They are too tall to talk to for very long, not enough like us, and they make me miss the old days. In the old days in Charlotte we did not take ourselves so seriously. Our heroes had platinum blond hair and twenty-seven-inch biceps, but you knew who was good and who was evil, who was changing over to the other side, and who was changing back. You knew that sooner or later the referee would look away just long enough for Bob Noxious to hit Lord Poetry with a folding chair. You knew that Lord Poetry would stare up from the canvas in stricken wonder, as if he had never once in his life seen a folding chair. (In the bar we screamed at the television, Turn around, ref, turn around! Look out, Lord Poetry, look out!) In the old days in Charlotte we did not have to decide if the Hornets should trade Rex Chapman (they should not) or if J. R. Reid was big enough to play center in the NBA (he is, but only sometimes). In the old days our heroes were as superficial as we were—but we knew that—and their struggles were exaggerated versions of our own. Now we have the Hornets. They wear uniforms designed by Alexander Julian, and play hard and lose, and make us look into our souls. Now when we march disappointed out of the new coliseum to sit unmoving on the parkway, in the cars we can't afford, we have to think about the things that are true: Everyone in Charlotte is from somewhere else. Everyone in Charlotte tries to be something they are not. We spend more money than we make, but it doesn't help. We know that the Hornets will never make the play-offs, and that somehow it is our fault. Our lives are small and empty, and we thought they wouldn't be, once we moved to the city.

My girlfriend's name is Starla. She is beautiful, and we wrestle about love. She does not like to say she loves me, even though we have been together four and a half years. She will not look at me when I say I love her, and if I wanted to, I could ball up those three words and use them like a fist. Starla says she has strong lust for me, which should be enough; she says we have good chemistry, which is all anyone can hope for. Late in the night, after we have grappled until the last drop of love is gone from our bodies, I say, "Starla, I can tell that you love me. You wouldn't be able to do it like that if you didn't love me." She sits up in bed, her head tilted forward so that her red hair almost covers her face, and picks the black hair that came from my chest off of her breasts and stomach. The skin across her chest is flushed red, patterned like a satellite photograph; it looks like a place I should know. She says, "I'm a grown woman and my body works. It has nothing to do with love." Like a lot of people in Charlotte, Starla has given up on love. In the old days Lord Poetry said to never give up, to always fight for love, but now he is gone to Atlanta with a big contract and a broken heart, and I have to do the best that I can. I hold on, even though Starla says she will not marry me. I have heard that Darling Donnis lives with Bob Noxious in a big condo in Buckhead. Starla wants to know why I can't be happy with what we have. We have good chemistry and apartments in Fourth

Ward and German cars. She says it is enough to live with and more than anyone had where we came from. We can eat out whenever we want.

Yet Starla breaks my heart. She will say that she loves me only at the end of a great struggle, after she is too tired to fight anymore, and then she spits out the words, like vomit, and calls me bastard or fucker or worse, and asks if the thing I have just done has made me happy. It does not make me happy, but it is what we do. It is the fight we fight. The next day we have dark circles under our eyes like the makeup truly evil wrestlers wear, and we circle each other like animals in a cage that is too small, and what we feel then is nothing at all like love.

I manage a fern bar on Independence Boulevard near downtown called P. J. O'Mulligan's Goodtimes Emporium. The regulars call the place PJ's. When you have just moved to Charlotte from McAdenville or Cherryville or Lawndale, it makes you feel good to call somebody up and say, Hey, let's meet after work at PJ's. It sounds like real life when you say it, and that is a sad thing. PJ's has fake Tiffany lampshades above the tables, with purple and teal hornets belligerent in the glass. It has fake antique Coca-Cola and Miller High Life and Pierce-Arrow Automobile and Winchester Repeating Rifle signs screwed on the walls, and imitation brass tiles glued to the ceiling. (The glue occasionally lets go and the tiles swoop down toward the tables, like bats.) The ferns are plastic because smoke and people dumping their drinks into the planters kill the real ones. The beer and mixed drinks are expensive, but the chairs and stools are cloth upholstered and plush, and the ceiling lights in their smooth, round globes are low and pleasant enough, and the television set is huge and close to the bar and perpetually tuned to ESPN. Except when the Hornets are on Channel 18 or wrestling is on TBS.

In the old days in Charlotte a lot of the professional wrestlers hung out at PJ's. Sometimes Lord Poetry stopped by early in the afternoon, after he was through working out, and tried out a new poem he had found in one of his thick books. The last time he came in, days before THE FINAL BATTLE, I asked him to tell me a poem I could say to Starla. In the old days in Charlotte you would not think twice about hearing a giant man with long red hair recite a poem in a bar, even in the middle of the afternoon. I turned the TV down, and the two waitresses and the handful of hardcores who had sneaked away from their offices for a drink saw what was happening and eased up close enough to hear. Lord Poetry crossed his arms and stared straight up, as if the poem he was searching for was written on the ceiling or somewhere on the other side, in a place we couldn't see. His voice was higher and softer than you would expect the voice of a man that size to be, and when he nodded and finally began to speak, it was almost in a whisper, and we all leaned in even closer. He said,

> *We sat grown quiet at the name of love;*
> *We saw the last embers of daylight die,*
> *And in the trembling blue-green of the sky*
> *A moon, worn as if it had been a shell*
> *Washed by time's waters as they rose and fell*
> *About the stars and broke in days and years.*
> *I had a thought for no one's but your ears:*
> *That you were beautiful, and that I strove*
> *To love you in the old high way of love;*
> *That it had all seemed happy, and yet we'd grown*
> *As weary-hearted as that hollow moon.*

P. J. O'Mulligan's was as quiet then as you will ever hear it. All of Charlotte seemed suddenly still and listening around us. Nobody moved until Lord Poetry finally looked down and reached again for his beer and said, "That's Yeats." Then we all moved back, suddenly conscious of his great size and our closeness to it, and nodded and agreed that it was a real good poem, one of the best we had ever heard him say. Later, I had him repeat it for me, line for line, and I wrote it down on a cocktail napkin. Sometimes, late at night, after Starla and I have fought, and I have made her say "I love you" like "Uncle," even as I can see in her eyes how much she hates me for it, I think about reading the poem to her, but some things are just too true to ever say out loud.

In PJ's we watch wrestling still, even though we can no longer claim it as our own. We sit around the big screen without cheering and stare at the wrestlers like favorite relatives we haven't seen in years. We say things like Boy, the Viking has really put on weight since he moved down there, or When did Rockin' Robbie Frazier cut his hair like that? We put on brave faces when we talk about Rockin' Robbie, who was probably Charlotte's most popular wrestler, and try not to dwell on the fact that he has gone away from us for good. In the old days he dragged his stunned and half-senseless opponents to the center of the ring and climbed onto the top rope, and after the crowd counted down from five (Four! Three! Two! One!) he would launch himself into the air, his arms and legs spread like wings, his blond hair streaming out behind him like a banner, and fly ten, fifteen feet, easy, and from an unimaginable height drop with a crash like an explosion directly onto his opponent's head. He called it the Rockin' Robbie B-52. ("I'll tell you one thing, Big Bill. Come next Saturday night in the Charlotte Coliseum I'm gonna B-52 the Sheik of the East like he ain't never been B-52ed before.") And after Rockin' Robbie's B-52 had landed, while his opponent flopped around on the canvas like a big fish, waiting only to be mounted and pinned, Rockin' Robbie leaped up and stood over him, his body slick with righteous sweat, his face a picture of joy. He held his hands high in the air, his fingers spread wide, his pelvis thrusting uncontrollably back and forth in the electric joy of the moment. Then he tossed his head back and howled like a dog, his lips a gleeful red O turned toward the sky. Those were glorious days. Whenever Rockin' Robbie walked into PJ's, everybody in the place raised their glasses and pointed their noses at the fake bronze of the ceiling and bayed at the stars we knew spun, only for us, in the high, moony night above Charlotte. Nothing like that happens here anymore. Frannie Belk gathered up all the good and evil in our city and sold it four hours south. These days the illusions we have left are the small ones of our own making, and in the vacuum the wrestlers left behind, those illusions have become too easy to see through; we now have to live with ourselves.

About once a week some guy who's just moved to Charlotte from Kings Mountain or Chester or Gaffney comes up to me where I sit at the bar, on my stool by the waitress station, and says, Hey man, are you P. J. O'Mulligan? They are never kidding, and whenever it happens I don't know what to say. I wish I could tell them whatever it is they need in their hearts to hear, but P. J. O'Mulligan is fourteen lawyers from Richmond with investment capital. What do you say? New people come to Charlotte from the small towns every day, searching for lives that are bigger than the ones they have known, but what they must settle for, once they get here, are much smaller hopes: that maybe this year the Hornets might really have a shot at the Celtics, if Rex Chapman has a good game; that maybe there really is somebody named P. J. O'Mulligan, and that maybe that guy at the bar is him. Now that the wrestlers are gone, I wonder about these things. How do you tell somebody how to find what they're looking for when ten years ago you came from the same place and have yet to find it yourself? How do you tell somebody from Polkville or Aliceville or Cliffside, who just saw downtown after sunset for the first time, not to let the beauty of the skyline fool them? Charlotte is a place where a crooked TV preacher can steal money and grow like a sore until he collapses from the weight of his own evil by simply promising hope. So don't stare at the NCNB Tower against the dark blue of the sky; keep your eyes on the road. Don't think that Independence Boulevard is anything more than a street. Most of my waitresses are college girls from UNCC and CPCC, and I can see the hope shining in their faces even as they fill out applications. They look good in their official P. J. O'Mulligan's khaki shorts and white sneakers and green aprons and starched, preppy blouses, but they are still mill-town girls through and through, come to the city to find the answers to their prayers. How do you tell them Charlotte isn't a good place to look? It is a place where a crooked TV preacher can pray that his flock will send him money so that he can build a giant water slide — and they will.

But PJ's still draws a wrestling crowd. They are mostly good-looking and wear lots of jewelry. The girls do aerobics like religion and have big, curly hair, stiff with mousse. They wear short, tight dresses — usually black — and dangling earrings and spiked heels and lipstick with little sparkles in it, like stars, that you're not even sure you can see. (You catch yourself staring at their mouths when they talk, waiting for their lips to catch the light.) The guys dye their hair blond and wear it spiked on top, long and permed in back, and shaved over the ears. They lift weights and take steroids. When they have enough money they get coked up. They wear stonewashed jeans and open shirts and gold chains thick as ropes and cowboy boots made from python skin, which is how professional wrestlers dress when they relax. Sometimes you will see a group of guys in a circle, with their jeans pulled up over their calves, arguing about whose boots were made from the biggest snake. The girls have long red fingernails and work mostly in the tall offices downtown. Most of the guys work outdoors — construction usually; there still is a lot of that, even now — or in the bodybuilding gyms, or the industrial parks along I-85. Both sexes are darkly and artificially tanned, even in the winter, and get drunk on shooters and look vainly in PJ's for love.

Around midnight on Friday and Saturday, before everyone clears out to go dancing at The Connection or Plum Crazy's, where the night's hopes become final choices, PJ's gets packed. The waitresses have to move sideways through the crowd with their trays held over their heads. Everybody shouts to be heard over one another and over the music — P. J. O'Mulligan's official contemporary jazz, piped in from Richmond — and if you close your eyes and listen carefully you can hear in the voices the one story they are trying not to tell: how everyone in Charlotte grew up in a white house in a row of white houses on the side of a hill in Lowell or Kannapolis or Spindale, and how they had to be

quiet at home because their daddies worked third shift, how a
black oil heater squatted like a gargoyle in the middle of their living room floor, and how the whole time they were growing up
the one thing they always wanted to do was leave. I get lonesome
sometimes, in the buzzing middle of the weekend, when I listen
to the voices and think about the shortness of the distance all of
us managed to travel as we tried to get away, and how when we
got to Charlotte the only people we found waiting for us were the
ones we had left. Our parents go to tractor pulls and watch "Hee
Haw." My father eats squirrel brains. We tell ourselves that we are
different now, because we live in Charlotte, but know that we are
only making do.

The last great professional wrestling card Frannie Belk put
together—before she signed Ted Turner's big check and with a dia-
mond-studded wave of her hand sent the wrestlers away from
Charlotte for good—was ARMAGEDDON V—THE LAST EXPLO-
SION, which took place in the new coliseum three nights after the
Hornets played and lost their first NBA game. ("Ohhhhhh," Big
Bill Boscoe said in the promotional TV ad, his big voice quaver-
ing with emotion, "Ladies and Gentlemen and Wrestling Fans of
All Ages: See an unprecedented galaxy of SWA wrestling stars col-
lide and explode in the Charlotte Coliseum. . . .") And for a while
that night—even though we knew the wrestlers were moving to
Atlanta—the world still seemed young and full of hope, and we
were young in it, and life in Charlotte seemed close to the way we
had always imagined it should be: Paolo the Peruvian jerked his
bare foot out from under the big, black boot of Comrade Yerkov
and then kicked the shit out of him in a flying frenzy of South
American feet; Rockin' Robbie Frazier squirted a water pistol into
Naoki Fujita's mouth before Fujita could ignite the mysterious
Green Fire of the Orient, and then launched a B-52 from such a
great height that even the most jaded wrestling fans gasped with
wonder (and if that wasn't enough, he later ran from the locker
room in his street clothes, his hair still wet from his shower, his

shirttail out and flapping, and in a blond fury B-52ed not one but *both* of the Hidden Pagans, who had used a folding chair to gain an unfair advantage over the Thundercats, Bill and Steve). And we saw the Littlest Cowboy and Chief Yee-Hah O'Reilly, their wrists bound together with an eight-foot leather thong, battle nobly in an Apache Death Match, until neither man was able to stand and the referee called it a draw and cut them loose with a long and crooked dagger belonging to the Sheik of the East; Hank Wilson Senior the Country Star whacked Captain Boogie Woogie over the head with his beloved guitar Leigh Ann, and earned a thoroughly satisfying disqualification and a long and heartfelt standing O; one of the Harem of Three slipped the Sheik of the East a handful of Arabian sand, which he threw into the eyes of Bob the Sailor to save himself from the Sailor's Killer Clam Hold — from which no bad guy ever escaped, once it was locked — but the referee saw the Sheik do it (the rarest of wrestling miracles) and awarded the match to the Sailor; and in the prelude to the main event, like the thunder before a storm, the Brothers Clean (the Superstud, the Viking, and the Gentle Giant) outlasted the Three Evils (Genghis Gandhi, Ron Rowdy, and Tom Tequila) in a six-man Texas Chain-Link Massacre Match in which a ten-foot wire fence was lowered around the ring, and bald Boris Yerkov and Harry the Hairdresser patrolled outside, eyeing each other suspiciously, armed with bull-whips and folding chairs, to make sure that no one climbed out and no one climbed in.

Now, looking back, it seems prophetic somehow that Starla and I lined up on opposite sides during THE FINAL BATTLE FOR LOVE. ("Sex is the biggest deal people have," Starla says. "You think about what you really want from me, what really matters, the next time you ask for a piece.") In THE FINAL BATTLE, Starla wanted Bob Noxious, with his dark chemistry, to win Darling Donnis away from Lord Poetry once and for all. He had twice come close. I wanted Lord Poetry to strike a lasting blow for love. Starla said it would never happen, and she was right. Late in the night, after it is over, after Starla has pinned my shoulders flat against the bed and held them there, after we are able to talk, I say, "Starla, you have to admit that you were making love to me. I could tell." She runs to the bathroom, her legs stiff and close together, to get rid of part of me. "Cave men made up love," she calls out from behind the door. "After they invented laws they had to stop killing each other, so they told their women they loved them to keep them from screwing other men. That's what love is."

Bob Noxious was Charlotte's most feared and evil wrestler, and on the night of THE FINAL BATTLE, we knew that he did not want Darling Donnis because he loved her. Bob Noxious was scary: He had a cobalt-blue spiked Mohawk, and if on his way to the ring a fan spat on him, he always spat back. He had a neck like a bull, and a fifty-six-inch chest, and he could twitch his pectoral muscles so fast that his nipples jerked up and down like pistons. Lord Poetry was almost as big as Bob Noxious, and scary in different ways. His curly red hair was longer than Starla's, and he wrestled in paisley tights — pink and magenta and lavender — specially made in England. He read a poem to Darling Donnis before and after every match while the crowd yelled for him to stop. (Charlotte did not know which it hated more: Bob Noxious with his huge and savage evil or the prancing Lord Poetry with his paisley tights and fat book of poems.) Darling Donnis was the picture of innocence (and danger, if you are a man) and hung on every word Lord Poetry said. She was blond, and wore a low-cut, lacy white dress (but never a slip), and covered her mouth with her hands whenever Lord Poetry was in trouble, her moist green eyes wide with concern.

Darling Donnis's dilemma was this: she was in love with Lord Poetry, but she was mesmerized by Bob Noxious's animal power. The last two times Bob Noxious and Lord Poetry fought, before THE FINAL BATTLE, Bob Noxious had beaten Lord Poetry with a folding chair until Lord Poetry couldn't stand, and then he turned to Darling Donnis and put his hands on his hips and threw his shoulders back, revealing enough muscles to make several lesser men. Darling Donnis's legs visibly wobbled, and she steadied herself against the ring apron, but she did not look away. While the crowd screamed for Bob Noxious to Shake 'em! Shake 'em! Let 'em go! he began to twitch his pectorals up and down, first just one at a time, just once or twice — teasing Darling Donnis — then the other, then in rhythm, faster and faster. It was something you had to look at, even if you didn't want to, a force of nature, and at both matches Darling Donnis was transfixed. She couldn't look away from Bob Noxious's chest and would have gone to him (even though she held her hands over her mouth and shook her head no, the pull was too strong) had it not been for Rockin' Robbie Frazier. At both matches before THE FINAL BATTLE, Rockin' Robbie ran out of the locker room in his street clothes and tossed the prostrate Lord Poetry the book of poetry that Darling Donnis had carelessly dropped on the apron of the ring. Then he climbed through the ropes and held off the enraged and bellowing Bob Noxious long enough for Lord Poetry to crawl out of danger and read Darling Donnis one of her favorite sonnets, which calmed her. But the night of THE FINAL BATTLE, all of Charlotte knew that something had to give. We did not think that even Rockin' Robbie could save Darling Donnis from Bob Noxious three times. Bob's pull was too strong. This time Lord Poetry had to do it himself.

They cleared away the cage from the Texas Chain-Link Massacre, and the houselights went down slowly until only the ring was lit. The white canvas was so bright that it hurt your eyes to look at it. Blue spotlights blinked open in the high darkness beneath the roof of the coliseum, and quick circles of light skimmed across the surface of the crowd, showing in an instant a hundred, two hundred, expectant faces. The crowd could feel the big thing coming up on them, like animals before an earthquake. Rednecks in the high, cheap seats stomped their feet and hooted like owls. Starla twisted in her seat and stuck two fingers into her mouth and cut loose with a shrill whistle. "Ohhhhh, Ladies and Gentlemen and Wrestling Fans," Big Bill Boscoe said from everywhere in the darkness, like the very voice of God, "I hope you are ready to hold on to your seats"— and in their excitement 23,000 people screamed *Yeah!*—"Because the earth is going to shake and the ground is going to split open"—*YEAH!*, louder now—"and hellfire will shoot out of the primordial darkness in a holocaust of pure wrestling fury"— they punched at the air with their fists and roared, like beasts, the blackness they hid in their hearts, *YEAH-HHHHH!* "Ohhhhhhh," Big Bill Boscoe said when they quieted down, his voice trailing off into a whisper filled with fear (he was afraid to unleash the thing that waited in the dark for the sound of his words, and they screamed in rage at his weakness, *YEAHHH-HHHH!*). "Ohhhhhh, Charlotte, ohhhhhhh, Wrestling Fans and Ladies and Gentlemen, I hope, I pray, that you have made ready"—*YEAHHHHHHHH!*—"for . . . the FINAL . . . BATTLE . . . FOR . . . LOOOOOOOOOVE!

At the end of regulation time (nothing really important ever happens in professional wrestling until the borrowed time after the final bell has rung) Bob Noxious and Lord Poetry stood in the center of the ring, their hands locked around each other's thick throats. Because chokeholds are illegal in SWA professional wrestling, the referee had ordered them to let go and, when they refused, began to count them out for a double disqualification. Bob Noxious and Lord Poetry let go only long enough to grab the referee, each by an arm, and throw him out of the ring, where he lay prostrate on the floor. Lord Poetry and Bob Noxious again locked on to each other's throats. There was no one there to stop them, and we felt our stomachs falling away into darkness, into the chaos. Veins bulged like ropes beneath the skin of their arms. Their faces were contorted with hatred, and turned from pink to red to scarlet. Starla jumped up and down beside me and shouted, "*KILL* Lord Poetry! *KILL* Lord Poetry!"

Darling Donnis ran around and around the ring, begging for someone, anyone, to make them stop. At the announcer's table, Big Bill Boscoe raised his hands in helplessness. Sure he wanted to help, but he was only Big Bill Boscoe, a voice. What could he do? Darling Donnis rushed away. She circled the ring twice more until she found Rockin' Robbie Frazier keeping his vigil in the shadows near the entrance to the locker room. She dragged him into the light near the ring. She pointed wildly at Lord Poetry and Bob Noxious. Both men had started to shake, as if cold. Bob Noxious's eyes rolled back in his head, but he didn't let go. Lord Poetry stumbled, but reached back with a leg and regained his balance. Darling Donnis shouted at Rockin' Robbie. She pointed again. She pulled her hair. She doubled her hands under her chin, pleading. "*CHOKE* him!" Starla screamed. "*CHOKE* him!" She looked sideways at me. "HURRY!" Darling Donnis got down on her knees in front of Rockin' Robbie and wrapped her arms around his waist. Rockin' Robbie stroked her hair but stared into the distance and shook his head no. Not this time. This was what it had come to. This was a fair fight between men and none of his business. He walked back into the darkness.

Darling Donnis was on her own now. She ran to the ring and stood at the apron and screamed for Bob Noxious and Lord Poetry to stop it. The sound of her words was lost in the roar that came from up out of our hearts, but we could feel them. She pounded on the canvas, but they didn't listen. They kept choking each other, their fingers a deathly white. Darling Donnis crawled beneath the bottom rope and into the ring. "NO!" Starla yelled, striking the air with her fists. "Let him DIE! Let him DIE!" Darling Donnis took a step toward the two men and reached out with her hands, but stopped, unsure of what to do. She wrapped her arms around herself and rocked back and forth. She grabbed her hair and started to scream. She screamed as if the earth really had opened up and hellfire had shot up all around her — and that it had been her fault. She screamed until her eyelids fluttered closed, and she dropped into a blond and white heap on the mat, and lay there without moving.

When Darling Donnis stopped screaming, it was as if the spell that had held Bob Noxious and Lord Poetry at each other's throats was suddenly broken. They let go at the same time. Lord Poetry dropped heavily to his elbows and knees, facing away from Darling Donnis. Bob Noxious staggered backward into the corner, where he leaned against the turnbuckles. He held on to the top rope with one hand and with the other rubbed his throat. "Go GET her!" Starla screamed at Bob Noxious. "Go GET her!" For a long time nobody in the ring moved, and in the vast, enclosed darkness surrounding the ring, starting up high and then spreading throughout the building, 23,000 people began to stomp their feet. Tiny points of fire, hundreds of them, sparked in the darkness. But still Bob Noxious and Lord Poetry and Darling Donnis did not move. The crowd stomped louder and louder (*BOOM! BOOM! BOOM! BOOM!*) until finally Darling Donnis weakly raised her head and pushed her hair back from her eyes. We caught our breath and looked to see where she looked. It was at Bob Noxious. Bob Noxious glanced up, his dark power returning. He took his hand off of his throat and put it on the top rope and pushed himself up higher. Darling Donnis raised herself onto her hands and knees and peeked quickly at Lord Poetry, who still hadn't moved, and then looked back to Bob Noxious. "DO it, Darling Donnis!" Starla screamed. "Just DO it!" Bob Noxious pushed off against the ropes and took an unsteady step forward. He inhaled deeply and stood up straight. Darling Donnis's eyes never left him. Bob Noxious put his hands on his hips and with a monumental effort threw his great shoulders all the way back. *No*, we saw Darling Donnis whisper. *No*. High up in the seats beside me, Starla screamed, "*YES!*"

Bob Noxious's left nipple twitched once. Twitch. Then again. Then the right. The beginning of the end. Darling Donnis slid a hand almost imperceptibly toward him across the canvas. But then, just when it all seemed lost, Rockin' Robbie Frazier ran from out of the shadows to the edge of the ring. He carried a thick book in one hand and a cordless microphone in the other. He leaned under the bottom rope and began to shout at Lord Poetry, their faces almost touching. *(Lord Poetry! Lord Poetry!)* Lord Poetry finally looked up at Rockin' Robbie and then slowly turned to look at Bob Noxious, whose pectoral muscles had begun to twitch regularly, left-right, faster and faster, like heartbeats. Darling Donnis raised a knee from the canvas and began to crawl toward Bob Noxious. Rockin' Robbie reached in through the ropes and helped Lord Poetry to his knees. He gave the book and the microphone to Lord Poetry. Lord Poetry turned around, still kneeling, until he faced Darling Donnis. She didn't even look at him. Five feet to Lord Poetry's right, Bob Noxious's huge chest was alive, pumping, a train picking up speed. Lord Poetry opened the book and turned to a page and shook his head. No, that one's not right. He turned farther back into the book and shook his head again. What is the one thing you can say to save the world you live in? How do you find the words? Darling Donnis licked her red lips. Rockin' Robbie began flashing his fingers in numbers at Lord Poetry. Ten-eight. Ten-eight. Lord Poetry looked over his shoulder at Rockin' Robbie, and his eyebrows moved up in a question: Eighteen? "YES!" screamed Rockin' Robbie. "EIGHTEEN." "Ladies and Gentlemen," Big Bill Boscoe's huge voice suddenly said, filled now with hope, "I think it's going to be Shakespeare's Sonnet Number Eighteen!" and a great shout of *NOOOOO!* rose up in the darkness like a wind.

Lord Poetry flipped through the book, and studied a page, and reached out and touched it, as if it were in Braille. He looked quickly at Darling Donnis, flat on her belly now, slithering toward Bob Noxious. Lord Poetry said into the microphone, "Shall I compare thee to a summer's day?" Starla kicked the seat in front of her and screamed, "NO! Don't do it! Don't do it! He's after your soul! He's after your soul!" Lord Poetry glanced up again and said, "Thou art more lovely and more temperate," and then faster, more urgently, "Rough winds do shake the darling buds of May," but Darling Donnis crawled on, underneath the force of his words, to within a foot of Bob Noxious. Bob Noxious's eyes were closed in concentration and pain, but still his pectorals pumped faster. Lord Poetry opened his mouth to speak again, but then buried his face in the book and slumped to the mat. Rockin' Robbie pulled on the ropes like the bars of a cage and yelled in rage, his face pointed upward, but he did not climb into the ring. He could not stop what was happening. *Please*, we saw Darling Donnis say to Bob Noxious. *Please*. The panicked voice of Big Bill Boscoe boomed out like a thunder: "Darling Donnis! Darling Donnis! And summer's lease hath all too short a date: sometime too hot the eye of heaven shines, and often is his gold complexion dimm'd!" But it was too late: Bob Noxious reached down and lifted Darling Donnis up by the shoulders. She looked him straight in the eye and reached out with both hands and touched his broad, electric chest. Her eyes rolled back in her head. Starla dropped heavily down into her seat and breathed deeply, twice. She looked up at me and smiled. "There," she said, as if it was late in the night, as if it was over. "There."

1993

Edward P. Jones

MARIE

*Marie is eighty-six, African-American, living in the most dangerous section of
our nation's capital, and wholly dependent on the Social Security Administration.
She has learned to always expect chaos and long waits in line. She speaks into a
historian's tape recorder: ". . . I never planned to live in Washington, had no idea
I would ever even step one foot in this city." Marie's story is as Southern as Marie's
heart, which, despite beating for decades in the city, remains one shaped by
the rural South. Edward P. Jones was born and raised in Washington, D.C. His
story collection,* Lost in the City, *won the 1993 PEN/Hemingway Award.*

Every now and again, as if on a whim, the federal government
people would write to Marie Delaveaux Wilson in one of
those white, stampless envelopes and tell her to come in to their
place so they could take another look at her. They, the Social Security people, wrote to her in a foreign language that she had learned
to translate over the years, and for all of the years she had been
receiving the letters the same man had been signing them. Once,
because she had something important to tell him, Marie called the
number the man always put at the top of the letters, but a woman
answered Mr. Smith's telephone and told Marie he was in an all-
day meeting. Another time she called and a man said Mr. Smith
was on vacation. And finally one day a woman answered and told
Marie that Mr. Smith was deceased. The woman told her to wait
and she would get someone new to talk to her about her case, but
Marie thought it bad luck to have telephoned a dead man and she
hung up.

Now, years after the woman had told her Mr. Smith was no

more, the letters were still being signed by John Smith. Come into our office at Twenty-first and M streets, Northwest, the letters said in that foreign language. Come in so we can see if you are still blind in one eye. Come in so we can see if you are still old and getting older. Come in so we can see if you still deserve to get Supplemental Security Income payments.

She always obeyed the letters, even if the order now came from a dead man, for she knew people who had been temporarily cut off from SSI for not showing up or even for being late. And once cut off, you had to move heaven and earth to get back on.

So on a not unpleasant day in March, she rose in the dark in the morning, even before the day had any sort of character, to give herself plenty of time to bathe, eat, lay out money for the bus, dress, listen to the spirituals on the radio. She was eighty-six years old and had learned that life was all chaos and painful uncertainty and that the only way to get through it was to expect chaos even in the most innocent of moments. Offer a crust of bread to a sick bird and you often draw back a bloody finger.

John Smith's letter had told her to come in at eleven o'clock, his favorite time, and by nine that morning she had had her bath and had eaten. Dressed by nine-thirty. The walk from Claridge Towers at Twelfth and M down to the bus stop at Fourteenth and K took her about ten minutes, more or less. There was a bus at about ten-thirty, her schedule told her, but she preferred the one that came a half hour earlier, lest there be trouble with the ten-thirty bus. After she dressed, she sat at her dining room table and went over yet again what papers and all else she needed to take. Given the nature of life — particularly the questions asked by the Social Security people — she always took more than they might ask for: her birth certificate, her husband's death certificate, doctors' letters.

One of the last things she put in her pocketbook was a knife that she had, about seven inches long, which she had serrated on both edges with the use of a small saw borrowed from a neighbor. The knife, she was convinced now, had saved her life about two weeks before. Before then she had often been careless about when she took the knife out with her, and she had never taken it out in daylight, but now she never left her apartment without it, even when going down the hall to the trash drop.

She had gone out to buy a simple box of oatmeal, no more, no less. It was about seven in the evening, the streets with enough commuters driving up Thirteenth Street to make her feel safe. Several yards before she reached the store, the young man came from behind her and tried to rip off her coat pocket where he thought she kept her money, for she carried no purse or pocketbook after five o'clock. The money was in the other pocket with the knife, and his hand was caught in the empty pocket long enough for her to reach around with the knife and cut his hand as it came out of her pocket.

He screamed and called her an old bitch. He took a few steps up Thirteenth Street and stood in front of Emerson's Market, examining the hand and shaking off blood. Except for the cars passing up and down Thirteenth Street, they were alone, and she began to pray.

"You cut me," he said, as if he had only been minding his own business when she cut him. "Just look what you done to my hand," he said and looked around as if for some witness to her crime. There was not a great amount of blood, but there was enough for her to see it dripping to the pavement. He seemed to be about twenty, no more than twenty-five, dressed the way they were all dressed nowadays, as if a blind man had matched up all their colors. It occurred to her to say that she had seven grandchildren about his age, that telling him this would make him leave her alone. But the more filth he spoke, the more she wanted him only to come toward her again.

"You done crippled me, you old bitch."

"I sure did," she said, without malice, without triumph, but simply the way she would have told him the time of day had he asked and had she known. She gripped the knife tighter, and as she did, she turned her body ever so slightly so that her good eye lined up with him. Her heart was making an awful racket, wanting to be away from him, wanting to be safe at home. I will not be moved, some organ in the neighborhood of the heart told the heart. "And I got plenty more where that come from."

The last words seemed to bring him down some and, still shaking the blood from his hand, he took a step or two back, which disappointed her. I will not be moved, that other organ kept telling the heart. "You just crazy, thas all," he said. "Just a crazy old hag." Then he turned and lumbered up toward Logan Circle, and several times he looked back over his shoulder as if afraid she might be following. A man came out of Emerson's, then a woman with two little boys. She wanted to grab each of them by the arm and tell them she had come close to losing her life. "I saved myself with this here thing," she would have said. She forgot about the oatmeal and took her raging heart back to the apartment. She told herself that she should, but she never washed the fellow's blood off the knife, and over the next few days it dried and then it began to flake off.

Toward ten o'clock that morning Wilamena Mason knocked and let herself in with a key Marie had given her.

"I see you all ready," Wilamena said.

"With the help of the Lord," Marie said. "Want a spot a coffee?"

"No thanks," Wilamena said, and dropped into a chair at the table. "Been drinkin' so much coffee lately, I'm gonna turn into coffee. Was up all night with Calhoun."

"How he doin'?"

Wilamena told her Calhoun was better that morning, his first good morning in over a week. Calhoun Lambeth was Wilamena's boyfriend, a seventy-five-year-old man she had taken up with six or so months before, not long after he moved in. He was the best-dressed old man Marie had ever known, but he had always appeared to be sickly, even while strutting about with his gold-tipped cane. And seeing that she could count his days on the fingers of her hands, Marie had avoided getting to know him. She could not understand why Wilamena, who could have had any man in Claridge Towers or any other senior citizen building for that matter, would take such a man into her bed. "True love," Wilamena had explained. "Avoid heartache," Marie had said, trying to be kind.

They left the apartment. Marie sought help from no one, lest she come to depend on a person too much. But since the encounter with the young man, Wilamena had insisted on escorting her. Marie, to avoid arguments, allowed Wilamena to walk with her from time to time to the bus stop, but no farther.

Nothing fit Marie's theory about life like the weather in Washington. Two days before, the temperature had been in the forties, and yesterday it had dropped to the low twenties, then warmed up a bit with the afternoon, bringing on snow flurries. Today the weather people on the radio had said it would be warm enough to wear just a sweater, but Marie was wearing her coat. And tomorrow, the weather people said, it would be in the thirties, with maybe an inch or so of snow.

Appointments near twelve o'clock were always risky, because the Social Security people often took off for lunch long before noon and returned sometime after one. And except for a few employees who seemed to work through their lunch hours, the place shut down. Marie had never been interviewed by someone willing to work through the lunch hour. Today, though the appointment was for eleven, she waited until one-thirty before the woman at the front of the waiting room told her she would have to come back another day, because the woman who handled her case was not in.

"You put my name down when I came in like everything was all right," Marie said after she had been called up to the woman's desk.

"I know," the woman said, "but I thought that Mrs. Brown was in. They told me she was in. I'm sorry." The woman began writing in a logbook that rested between her telephone and a triptych of photographs. She handed Marie a slip and told her again she was sorry.

"Why you have me wait so long if she whatn't here?" She did

not want to say too much, appear too upset, for the Social Security people could be unforgiving. And though she was used to waiting three and four hours, she found it especially unfair to wait when there was no one for her at all behind those panels the Social Security people used for offices. "I been here since before eleven."

"I know," the woman behind the desk said. "I know. I saw you there, ma'am, but I really didn't know Mrs. Brown wasn't here." There was a nameplate at the front of the woman's desk and it said Vernelle Wise. The name was surrounded by little hearts, the kind a child might have drawn.

Marie said nothing more and left.

The next appointment was two weeks later, eight-thirty, a good hour, and the day before a letter signed by John Smith arrived to remind her. She expected to be out at least by twelve. Three times before eleven o'clock Marie asked Vernelle Wise if the man, Mr. Green, who was handling her case, was in that day, and each time the woman assured her that he was. At twelve, Marie ate one of the two oranges and three of the five slices of cheese she had brought. At one, she asked again if Mr. Green was indeed in that day and politely reminded Vernelle Wise that she had been waiting since about eight that morning. Vernelle was just as polite and told her the wait would soon be over.

At one-fifteen, Marie began to watch the clock hands creep around the dial. She had not paid much attention to the people about her, but more and more it seemed that others were being waited on who had arrived long after she had gotten there. After asking about Mr. Green at one, she had taken a seat near the front and, as more time went by, she found herself forced to listen to the conversation that Vernelle was having with the other receptionist next to her.

"I told him . . . I told him . . . I said just get your things and leave," said the other receptionist, who didn't have a nameplate.

"Did he leave?" Vernelle wanted to know.

"Oh, no," the other woman said. "Not at first. But I picked up some of his stuff, that Christian Dior jacket he worships. I picked up my cigarette lighter and that jacket, just like I was gonna do something bad to it, and he started movin' then."

Vernelle began laughing. "I wish I was there to see that." She was filing her fingernails. Now and again she would look at her fingernails to inspect her work, and if it was satisfactory, she would blow on the nails and on the file. "He back?" Vernelle asked.

The other receptionist eyed her. "What you think?" and they both laughed.

Along about two o'clock Marie became hungry again, but she did not want to eat the rest of her food because she did not know how much longer she would be there. There was a soda machine in the corner, but all sodas gave her gas.

"You-know-who gonna call you again?" the other receptionist was asking Vernelle.

"I hope so," Vernelle said. "He pretty fly. Seemed decent too. It kinda put me off when he said he was a car mechanic. I kinda like kept tryin' to take a peek at his fingernails and everything the whole evenin'. See if they was dirty or what."

"Well, that mechanic stuff might be good when you get your car back. My cousin's boyfriend used to do that kinda work and he made good money, girl. I mean real good money."

"Hmmmm," Vernelle said. "Anyway, the kids like him, and you know how peculiar they can be."

"Tell me 'bout it. They do the job your mother and father used to do, huh? Only on another level."

"You can say that again," Vernelle said.

Marie went to her and told her how long she had been waiting.

"Listen," Vernelle said, pointing her fingernail file at Marie. "I told you you'll be waited on as soon as possible. This is a busy day. So I think you should just go back to your seat until we call your name." The other receptionist began to giggle.

Marie reached across the desk and slapped Vernelle Wise with all her might. Vernelle dropped the file, which made a cheap, tinny sound when it hit the plastic board her chair was on. But no one heard the file because she had begun to cry right away. She looked at Marie as if, in the moment of her greatest need, Marie had denied her. "Oh, oh," Vernelle Wise said through the tears. "Oh, my dear God . . ."

The other receptionist, in her chair on casters, rolled over to Vernelle and put her arm around her. "Security!" the other receptionist hollered. "We need Security here!"

The guard at the front door came quickly around the corner, one hand on his holstered gun and the other pointing accusingly at the people seated in the waiting area. Marie had sat down and was looking at the two women almost sympathetically, as if a stranger had come in, hit Vernelle Wise, and fled.

"She slapped Vernelle!" said the other receptionist.

"Who did it?" the guard said, reaching for the man sitting beside Marie. But when the other receptionist said it was the old lady in the blue coat, the guard held back for the longest time, as if to grab her would be like arresting his own grandmother. He stood blinking and he would have gone on blinking had Marie not stood up.

She was too flustered to wait for the bus and so took a cab home. With both chains, she locked herself in the apartment, refusing to answer the door or the telephone the rest of the day and most of the next. But she knew that if her family or friends received no answer at the door or on the telephone, they would think something had happened to her. So the next afternoon, she began answering the phone and spoke with the chain on, telling Wilamena and others that she had a toothache.

For days and days after the incident she ate very little and asked God to forgive her. She was haunted by the way Vernelle's cheek had felt, by what it was like to invade and actually touch the flesh of another person. And when she thought too hard, she imagined that she was slicing through the woman's cheek, the way she had sliced through the young man's hand. But as time went on she began to remember the man's curses and the purplish color of Vernelle's fingernails, and all remorse would momentarily take flight.

Finally, one morning nearly two weeks after she slapped the woman, she woke with a phrase she had not used or heard since her children were small: You whatn't raised that way.

It was the next morning that the thin young man in the suit knocked and asked through the door chains if he could speak with her. She thought that he was a Social Security man come to tear up her card and papers and tell her that they would send her no more checks. Even when he pulled out an identification card showing that he was a Howard University student, she did not believe.

In the end, she told him she didn't want to buy anything, not magazines, not candy, not anything.

"No, no," he said. "I just want to talk to you for a bit. About your life and everything. It's for a project for my folklore course. I'm talking to everyone in the building who'll let me. Please . . . I won't be a bother. Just a little bit of your time."

"I don't have anything worth talkin' about," she said. "And I don't keep well these days."

"Oh, ma'am, I'm sorry. But we all got something to say. I promise I won't be a bother."

After fifteen minutes of his pleas, she opened the door to him because of his suit and his tie and his tie clip with a bird in flight, and because his long, dark brown fingers reminded her of delicate twigs. But had he turned out to be death with a gun or a knife or fingers to crush her neck, she would not have been surprised. "My name's George. George Carter. Like the president." He had the kind of voice that old people in her young days would have called womanish. "But I was born right here in D.C. Born, bred, and buttered, my mother used to say."

He stayed the rest of the day and she fixed him dinner. It scared her to be able to talk so freely with him, and at first she thought that at long last, as she had always feared, senility had taken hold of her. A few hours after he left, she looked his name up in the telephone book, and when a man who sounded like him answered, she hung up immediately. And the next day she did the same thing. He came back at least twice a week for many weeks and would set his cassette recorder on her coffee table. "He's takin' down my whole life," she told Wilamena, almost the way a woman might speak in awe of a new boyfriend.

One day he played back for the first time some of what she told the recorder:

> . . . My father would be sittin' there readin' the paper. He'd say whenever they put in a new president, "Look like he got the chair for four years." And it got so that's what I saw— this poor man sittin' in that chair for four long years while the rest of the world went on about its business. I don't know if I thought he ever did anything, the president. I just knew that he had to sit in that chair for four years. Maybe I thought that by his sittin' in that chair and doin' nothin' else for four years he made the country what it was and that without him sittin' there the country wouldn't be what it was. Maybe thas what I got from listenin' to Father readin' and to my mother askin' him questions 'bout what he was readin'. They was like that, you see. . . .

George stopped the tape and was about to put the other side in when she touched his hand.

"No more, George," she said. "I can't listen to no more. Please . . . please, no more." She had never in her whole life heard her own voice. Nothing had been so stunning in a long, long while, and for a few moments before she found herself, her world turned upside down. There, rising from a machine no bigger than her Bible, was a voice frighteningly familiar yet unfamiliar, talking about a man whom she knew as well as her husbands and her sons, a man dead and buried sixty years. She reached across to George and he handed her the tape. She turned it over and over, as if the mystery of everything could be discerned if she turned it enough times. She began to cry, and with her other hand she lightly touched the buttons of the machine.

Between the time Marie slapped the woman in the Social Security office and the day she heard her voice for the first time, Calhoun Lambeth, Wilamena's boyfriend, had been in and out of the hospital three times. Most evenings when Calhoun's son stayed the night with him, Wilamena would come up to Marie's and spend most of the evening sitting on the couch that was catty-corner to the easy chair facing the big window. She said very little, which was unlike her, a woman with more friends than hairs on her head and who, at sixty-eight, loved a good party. The most attractive woman Marie knew would only curl her legs up under herself and sip whatever Marie put in her hand. She looked out at the city until she took herself to her apartment or went back down to Calhoun's place. In the beginning, after he returned from the hospital the first time, there was the desire in Marie to remind her friend that she wasn't married to Calhoun, that she should just get up and walk away, something Marie had seen her do with other men she had grown tired of.

Late one night, Wilamena called and asked her to come down to the man's apartment, for the man's son had had to work that night and she was there alone with him and she did not want to be alone with him. "Sit with me a spell," Wilamena said. Marie did not protest, even though she had not said more than ten words to the man in all the time she knew him. She threw on her bathrobe, picked up her keys and serrated knife, and went down to the second floor.

He was propped up on the bed, surprisingly alert, and spoke to Marie with an unforced friendliness. She had seen this in other dying people — a kindness and gentleness came over them that was often embarrassing for those around them. Wilamena sat on the side of the bed. Calhoun asked Marie to sit in a chair beside the bed and then he took her hand and held it for the rest of the night. He talked on throughout the night, not always understandable. Wilamena, exhausted, eventually lay across the foot of the bed. Almost everything the man had to say was about a time when he was young and was married for a year or so to a woman in Nicodemus, Kansas, a town where there were only black people. Whether the woman had died or whether he had left her, Marie could not make out. She only knew that the woman and Nicodemus seemed to have marked him for life.

"You should go to Nicodemus," he said at one point, as if the town were only around the corner. "I stumbled into the place by accident. But you should go on purpose. There ain't much to see, but you should go there and spend some time there."

Toward four o'clock that morning, he stopped talking and moments later he went home to his God. Marie continued holding the dead man's hand and she said the Lord's Prayer over and over until it no longer made sense to her. She did not wake Wilamena. Eventually the sun came through the man's venetian blinds, and she heard the croaking of the pigeons congregating on the window ledge. When she finally placed his hand on his chest, the dead man expelled a burst of air that sounded to Marie like a sigh. It occurred to her that she, a complete stranger, was the last thing he had known in the world and that now he was no longer in the world. All she knew of him was that Nicodemus place and a lovesick woman asleep at the foot of his bed. She thought that she was hungry and thirsty, but the more she looked at the dead man and the sleeping woman, the more she realized that what she felt was a sense of loss.

Two days later, the Social Security people sent her a letter, again signed by John Smith, telling her to come to them one week hence. There was nothing in the letter about the slap, no threat to cut off her SSI payments because of what she had done. Indeed, it was the same sort of letter John Smith usually sent. She called the number at the top of the letter, and the woman who handled her case told her that Mr. White would be expecting her on the day and time stated in the letter. Still, she suspected the Social Security people were planning something for her, something at the very least that would be humiliating. And, right up until the day before the appointment, she continued calling to confirm that it was okay to come in. Often, the person she spoke to after the switchboard woman and before the woman handling her case was Vernelle. "Social Security Administration. This is Vernelle Wise. May I help you?" And each time Marie heard the receptionist identify herself she wanted to apologize. "I whatn't raised that way," she wanted to tell the woman.

George Carter came the day she got the letter to present her with a cassette machine and copies of the tapes they had made about her life. It took quite some time for him to teach her how to use the machine, and after he was gone, she was certain it took so long because she really did not want to know how to use it. That evening, after her dinner, she steeled herself and put a tape marked Parents/Early Childhood in the machine.

> . . . My mother had this idea that everything could be done in Washington, that a human bein' could take all they troubles to Washington and things would be set right. I think that was all wrapped up with her notion of the gov'ment, the Supreme Court and the president and the like. "Up there," she would say, "things can be made right." "Up there" was her only words for Washington. All them other cities had names, but Washington didn't need a name. It was just called "up there." I was real small and didn't know any better, so somehow I got to thinkin' since things were on the perfect side in Washington, that maybe God lived there. God and his people . . . When I went back home to visit that first time and told my mother all about my livin' in Washington, she fell into such a cry, like maybe I had managed to make it to heaven without dyin'. Thas how people was back in those days. . . .

The next morning she looked for Vernelle Wise's name in the telephone book. And for several evenings she would call the number and hang up before the phone had rung three times. Finally, on a Sunday, two days before the appointment, she let it ring and what may have been a little boy answered. She could tell he was very young because he said hello in a too-loud voice, as if he was not used to talking on the telephone.

"Hello," he said. "Hello, who this? Granddaddy, that you? Hello. Hello. I can see you."

Marie heard Vernelle tell him to put down the telephone, then another child, perhaps a girl somewhat older than the boy, came on the line. "Hello. Hello. Who is this?" she said with authority. The boy began to cry, apparently because he did not want the girl to talk if he couldn't. "Don't touch it," the girl said. "Leave it alone." The boy cried louder and only stopped when Vernelle came to the telephone.

"Yes?" Vernelle said. "Yes." Then she went off the line to calm the boy, who had begun to cry again. "Loretta," she said, "go get his bottle . . . Well, look for it. What you got eyes for?"

There seemed to be a second boy, because Vernelle told him to help Loretta look for the bottle. "He always losin' things," Marie heard the second boy say. "You should tie everything to his arms." "Don't tell me what to do," Vernelle said. "Just look for that damn bottle."

"I don't lose noffin'. I don't," the first boy said. "You got snot in your nose."

"Don't say that," Vernelle said before she came back on the line. "I'm sorry," she said to Marie. "Who is this? . . . Don't you dare touch it if you know what's good for you!" she said. "I wanna talk to Granddaddy," the first boy said. "Loretta, get me that bottle!"

Marie hung up. She washed her dinner dishes. She called Wilamena because she had not seen her all day, and Wilamena told her that she would be up later. The cassette tapes were on the coffee table beside the machine, and she began picking them up, one by one. She read the labels: Husband No. 1, Working, Husband No. 2, Children, Race Relations, Early D.C. Experiences, Husband No. 3. She had not played another tape since the one about her mother's idea of what Washington was like, but she could still hear the voice, her voice. Without reading its label, she put a tape in the machine.

. . . I never planned to live in Washington, had no idea I would ever even step one foot in this city. This white family my mother worked for, they had a son married and gone to live in

Baltimore. He wanted a maid, somebody to take care of his children. So he wrote to his mother and she asked my mother and my mother asked me about goin' to live in Baltimore. Well, I was young. I guess I wanted to see the world, and Baltimore was as good a place to start as anywhere. This man sent me a train ticket and I went off to Baltimore. Hadn't ever been kissed, hadn't ever been anything, but here I was goin' farther from home than my mother and father put together. . . . Well, sir, the train stopped in Washington, and I thought I heard the conductor say we would be stoppin' a bit there, so I got off. I knew I probably wouldn't see no more than that Union Station, but I wanted to be able to say I'd done that, that I step foot in the capital of the United States. I walked down to the end of the platform and looked around, then I peeked into the station. Then I went in. And when I got back, the train and my suitcase was gone. Everything I had in the world on the way to Baltimore. . . .

I couldn't calm myself down enough to listen to when the redcap said another train would be leavin' for Baltimore, I was just that upset. I had a buncha addresses of people we knew all the way from home up to Boston, and I used one precious nickel to call a woman I hadn't seen in years, cause I didn't have the white people in Baltimore number. This woman come and got me, took me to her place. I 'member like it was yesterday that we got on this streetcar marked 13TH AND D NE. The more I rode, the more brighter things got. You ain't lived till you been on a streetcar. The further we went on that street-car — dead down in the middle of the street — the more I knowed I could never go live in Baltimore. I knowed I could never live in a place that didn't have that streetcar and them clackety-clack tracks. . . .

She wrapped the tapes in two plastic bags and put them in the dresser drawer that contained all that was valuable to her: birth and death certificates, silver dollars, life insurance policies, pictures of her husbands and the children they had given each other and the grandchildren those children had given her and the great-grands whose names she had trouble remembering. She set the tapes in a back corner of the drawer, away from the things she needed to get her hands on regularly. She knew that however long she lived, she would not ever again listen to them, for in the end, despite all that was on the tapes, she could not stand the sound of her own voice.

1994

Barry Hannah

NICODEMUS BLUFF

The narrator, Harris, tells this tale many years after the fact, after he's been "away" on drugs, trying (the reader is led to believe) to numb the effects of his father's past humiliation. When Harris was ten years old, he watched his father, an instinctive chess player, win an intense contest with a local banker to whom he owed a good deal of money. All the subtle factors of class in a small town are at work in this story about the varying levels of failure. Barry Hannah, a native Mississippian, is writer-in-residence at the University of Mississippi. His most recent collection is Bats Out of Hell.

That old woman has money, we know it, old withered dugs, used to teach high school. They say she even taught me thirty years ago but I'm not sure, I was mostly away on drugs. One thing about my body or bloodflow or whatall, I'm twice as put away as anybody else on a drug, always have been. I declare that I stayed away from the world thirty years and more. So when I saw the old woman on her porch chair as we ran by—running out the drugs of three decades—I just saw a new crone, not somebody I'd ever known. She was sitting up there taking up space and money, the leaves of the tree limbs reaching over her head looking like money itself, green. Say she used to teach me. I wonder what.

They stood me up and walked me when I was on those 'ludes and reds. No man ever liked a 'lude or red better than this man. They walked me around the high school halls and set me in the benches and showed me food, I guess, in the cafeteria. It is amazing what I never knew, amazing. I accompanied people. I was a devoted accomplice, accompanier, associate, minion, stooge. The term *et al.* was made for me. But I can't remember how. We would be in church or jail. I would just look around and take stock of the ten or so feet of box—a cube, I guess—around me and see what was in it, my "space," yes really. My space ended at ten feet wide, deep and high. Couldn't tell you further what was out there. It could be bars or a stained glass picture of Saint John baptizing Jesus Christ in the Jordan River, boulders and olive trees hanging over the water.

What was going on I wanted to be away from I believe was my father and his friends years ago at the deer camp in Arkansas. Something happened when I was out there. My father died that next week but it's like not only is he not dead but he is hanging at the border—the bars, the church window—of my space, that ten-foot cube—bloody and broken-up and flattened in the nose, a black bruise on his cheekbone because of what happened to him with those others years ago down in the swamps.

We used to be better folks even though my father's people had nothing. My mother was a better sort, a secretary to a wealthy lawyer in town. There seemed to be hope of our rising in the community. It's vague how you get to be "somebody" but mainly it has to do with marrying the right woman, then they honor you. Acts of kindness or neighborliness do not really count. I have seen people do acts of kindness over and over and although people smile, looking at them in their yard and thanking them, "much obliged"—this circle of doing for folks and making them "much obliged" is funny, don't you think? the way payback must forever continue amongst world citizens, kind to kind—they'd not think the man of any esteem. What made esteem was not acts of kindness but money, clothes, car, house, posture, lawn. You knew where you belonged in that time, and we were on the edge of being respected "gentlefolk" of the town (not my term but Dr. Debord's, the preacher-friend and chairman of the sociology department at the Methodist college in town who helped me for a while. He wouldn't like my thoughts about the old crone as we ran by, the old crone with her nice lawn, expensive auto, elegant house). That old woman is like time and my dog, how awful. My dog had its whole lifetime in my youth. Time was tearing it to pieces. Once out of one of my early drug stupors I looked at it and it was suddenly dilapidated and ancient and I started crying. Said she was a looker and I had a crush on her. Tried to write stories to get her attention. Now look at her. I am looking at all my drug time, decrepit, sitting on the porch. My mother had an easy gracious manner and dressed well naturally although she was not of moneyed people. She was a person of "modest understated grace," Mr. Kervochian told me once, wanting me not to forget what a valuable woman she was, so I'd have something to get up in the morning for. I run around the block again and again, gasping "success, success."

Dr. Debord had certainly tried everything else. However, getting me to admit the story was tough and deep, the story about my father—Gomar, he was called—so as to get up and be about my work at the animal shelter; my father that week among those new acquaintances who were going to be his new and lasting crowd—up from the failed farmers, the beer-for-breakfast mechanics, loiterers, and petty-thieving personnel who were his people. Yay for him, some people were saying. To bring himself up into genteel society. I think most people approved of his rise. In the old days the whole county knew each other, don't doubt it, and you might have thought there was some god placed in an office with account books where he let out the word on the social worth of all citizens hereabouts, keeping tab on these as rose, fell, or simply trod down the rut that was left by the prior generations; the word went around and was known.

But at ten years old what did I know when my father and the rest of them were out at that lodge? I did not know my father had borrowed heavily from Mr. Pool and that was why we had a nice house, lawn, two cars, even a yard man who rode a riding mower, a Negro man named Whit who was nice to me. Whit cut himself chopping down a tree for us and I recall thinking that his blood might be bluer and was surprised. Why do people live here at all,

I ask? They must know this is a filthy, wrong, haunted place. Even the trees that are left look wrong or wronged, beat-up. The red dirt is hopeless. The squirrels are thin and there is much—you can't get around it—suicide on the part of possums, coons, armadillos, and deer who tried to exist in the puny scratch but leap out on the highway. Also there are no stories of any merit to come out of this place. The only good woods are near the base of the little mountain. (Let me tell you something about all the drug pushers around here. They are no mystery to me. They are just country sorry, like my father's people. They aren't a new wave of punk. Country sorry.) Someone had a house and land and saved the woods at the west base of the little mountain (805 ft.). This person would shoot trespassers, hunters, and fishermen. (There was a deep black pond in the middle.) Nobody went in. The woods were saved. They were thick and dark with very high great oaks and ashes and wild magnolias, even bamboo, like nothing else around. Thicker, much, even than the woods over at the deer camp near the Mississippi River in Arkansas, with sloughs and irrigation ditches where the ducks come down too. Also you could catch winter crappie in the oxbow lakes if you could sit still in the cold. (Allow me to express myself about those woods near the mountain here. They were owned by a doctor who was an enormous dealer in drugs. Well I know.) In Arkansas it was sportsman's paradise. The only thing better I would see would be (later) the marijuana plantation at the state university where they grew it legal for government experimentation. I saw that once driving by with somebody when I was seventeen and almost came out of my cube of space to get them to stop the car. (No, I could never drive; didn't learn to drive until I was twenty and that is when I finished high school too. All of this delay, I believe, is because of what they did to my father.)

My father then had these acquaintances: a banker, an insurance man, a clothing store owner, a lawyer (employer of my mother), an owner of a small company that made oil pumps for aircraft engines, a medical doctor. Then there was Mr. Kervochian, a druggist, who turned out to be the kindest and the one who told me the whole story years later when he was dying of pancreatic cancer. My father—we had the lawn, the porch, the two cars, the nice fishing boat, the membership in the country club—I say again was lent heavily some money by three of these men. They told him it was a new kind of loan they were practicing with, a way to help really deserving men from the country who wanted to better themselves. It was agricultural rates interest, very low. It was "special" money on collateral of his personality and promise; and it entailed his being close by to aid these men at some business schemes; close by like at beck and call, said Mr. Kervochian. My father would get nice things immediately and pay it off so that he could enjoy the good life and pay along for it, not waiting until he was old like many men did, left only a few years to enjoy their station and bounty after a lifetime of work. They liked my mother and they thought my father was admirable the way he tried to sell real estate out in the country where the dead farms were. He knew them when they were dying and could be had.

He managed to get Mr. Pool and Mr. Hester a piece of land from a crazy man for almost nothing. The man went down to Whitfield, the asylum at Jackson. The land they used for turkey houses. That's where I came in: at age ten I went out there twice a day on my bicycle to feed and water the turkeys. I had a job, I was a little man. I was worthy of an invitation to the deer hunt. Everything was fitting together. My father had some prestige. He was arriving and I was well on the way to becoming a man of parts myself.

I can't remember why I was the only boy out at the deer camp in Arkansas. But I went along with my father, Gomar, and had my own gun, a little .410 single shot, for the delta squirrels, very fat, if I saw them, which I did but could not hit them much, at age ten. Something would happen when a live squirrel showed up in the bead at the end of the barrel. The squirrel would blur out and I'd snap the gun to the side, missing all of it. I think I embarrassed my father. A boy around here should be able to shoot at ten. The rest of them weren't hunting yet. They were in the lodge drinking and playing cards. I could hear the laughter getting louder and how it changed—louder and meaner, I guess—while I was out in those short stumps and wood chips on the edge of the forest. I remember seeing that cold oily-looking water in a pool in one stump and felt odd because of the rotten smell. They didn't know why I was frowning and missing squirrels out there and had gone back in to laugh harder, drinking. I could smell the whiskey from where I was and liked it. It smelled like a hospital, where I was once to have a hernia repaired.

The large thing I didn't know was that my father owed all this money to the three men, and he was not repaying it on time. I thought there were just his new friends, having them in this sort of club at the lodge, which was as good as a house inside or better with polished knotty pine walls and deer heads and an entire bobcat on a ledge. Also a joke stuffed squirrel with its head blown off, as I couldn't do out there smelling that rotten water, standing in the wet leaves in rubber boots made for a man, not my own, which I was saving for dry big hunting. I remember in December everything was wet and black. They said flash floods were around, water over the highway, and we were trapped in until the water went down. Then it began to get very cold. I went inside, without much to do. I came back outside with a box of white-head kitchen matches and started licking them on the head, striking them, and sailing them out so they made a trail like rockets, then hit and flamed up before the wet took care of them. I thought the future belonged to rockets—this had been said around—and I was very excited to get into the future. My father was providing a proud place for me to grow and play on our esteemed yard. One night I was watching television, an old movie with June Allyson. Her moist voice reached into me and I began crying I was so happy— she favored my mother some. But my father owed all this money, many years of money. It seemed the other two, Mr. Hester and Colonel Wren, weren't that anxious about it. But the banker, Mr. Pool, who owned the lodge, was a different kind.

The trouble was, Mr. Kervochian told me, as he died of pancreatic cancer, that my father thought he had considerably reduced the debt by getting that piece of land from that insane man for almost nothing. This provided grounds for a prosperous turkey farm for the men. Twenty or more houses of turkeys it would be. My father supposed that he had done them a real turn, a very handy favor, and he felt easy about his lateness of payment. He assumed they had taken off several thousand dollars from it and were easy themselves. He thought things had been indicated more than "much obliged." It was riling somebody, though. Just the money—considerable—wasn't all of it. Something else very terrible was mixed in.

I didn't catch on to much except their voices grew louder and here and there a bad word came out. My father asked me to go back to my bunk in another room. There wasn't anything to do back there but read an *R* encyclopedia. I could read well. Almost nothing stopped me. My father could read but it was like he learned the wrong way. He took forever and the words seemed to fly off on him like spooked game. He held his finger on the page and ran it along like fastening down the sounds. My mother taught me and I could not see the trouble. I was always ahead of the teacher. I felt for my dad when I saw him reading. I knew this feeling wasn't right, but I wanted to hold his hand and read for him. It almost made me cry. Because it made me afraid, is what it did. He wasn't us.

The terrible thing mixed in it was that my dad was good at the game of chess and vain about it. He had no degree at all—I don't believe he had finished high school, really, unlike Mr. Pool, who had college and a law degree. He had never played Mr. Pool but he had whipped some other college men and he was apt to brag about it. He would even call himself "country trash," winking, when he boasted around the house, until Mother asked him to quit, please, gloating was not character. But Mother did not know that my father, when he played chess, became the personality of a woman, a lady of the court born in the eighteenth century (said Mr. Kervochian). The woman would "invest" Dad and he would win at chess with her character, not his own man's person at all. Mr. Kervochian took a long time explaining this. The chess game, as it went on, changed him more and more into a woman, a crafty woman. He began sitting there like a plain man, but at the end of the game he couldn't help it, the signs came out, his voice went up, and his arms and hands were set out in a sissy way. He was all female as the climax of his victory neared. He would rock back and forth nervously and sputter in little giggles, always pursing his lips. It wasn't something you wanted to look at and those he defeated didn't want to remember it. It unnerved them and made them feel eerie and nervous to have been privy to it, not to be talked about. I didn't know what was going on, with the noise out there in the great "den" of the lodge. Mr. Hester and Colonel Wren, the doctor (Dr. Harvard) and the oil pump company owner (Ralph Lovett), with Mr. Kervochian just leaning near them, drinking, were playing poker that night. Only two of them had gone out to hunt a little in the rain and vicious cold but come back. My father and Mr. Pool were at the other end playing chess very seriously. My father's feet became light, tapping on the floor as with princess slippers. All through the other quiet I heard them.

Mr. Kervochian, dying of cancer, told me it was not clear how my father's change came about or even where he learned to play chess, which was a surprise—his chessmanship—unto itself. He was not from chessly people. They were uneducated trash and sorry—even my grandmother Meemaw, a loud hypochondriac, a screamer—had failed on the farm and in town both and lived between them, looking both ways and hating both of what they saw. But Gomar, my dad, knew chess, maybe from one month in the army at the time of the Korean conflict, after which he came back unacceptable because of something in his shoulders (is what he said when I asked him once). My mother looked at the floor. She hated war and was glad he'd never been in one. But I wanted him to have been in the war. Mr. Kervochian believed somebody in the service taught him, but where he came in contact with the "woman" he does not precisely know. But early on he was playing chess with the circuit-church riding minister at the church near Meemaw's home. Some time somewhere the woman in him appeared. It was a crafty, clever, "treacherous" woman; a "scheming, snooty, snarling" woman, rougher than a man somehow in spitefulness. She knew the court and its movements and chess was a breeze for her. She'd take him over about mid-game or when things got tough. It would lurch into him, this creature, and nobody could beat him. He beat a college professor, a hippie who was a lifetime chess bum that lived at a bohemian café; a brilliant Negro from New Orleans; two other town men who thought they were really good. Something was wrong, terrible about it. He wasn't supposed to be that good.

He might have picked up the woman who inhabited him from somebody in the army, or from that preacher, whose religion had its strange parts, its "dark enthusiasms," Mr. Kervochian said, weakly speaking from his cancer. We don't know, but it led to that long rain of four days at the deer camp, the matter of the owed money, and Mr. Pool, the banker, who professed himself a superior, very superior chess player.

Voices were short but loud and I heard cursing from the "den" where the men were. They were drunk and angry about the rain. When I peeped out I saw the banker looking angrily into my father's face. My father's face was red, too. He saw me at the door and told me to go back in the room.

I said, Daddy, there's nothing to do. He brought our guns over to me and said, Clean them, without looking at me. Then he shut the door. It was only me, the R encyclopedia, and the guns with their oil kit. I went on reading at something, I think Rhode Island, which was known for potatoes. The doctor, Dr. Harvard, I could hear complaining and very concerned about the rain cutting us off, although we had plenty of food. I recall he wasn't drinking and was chubby with spectacles, like an owl, looking frightened, which wasn't right. I didn't like a doctor acting frightened about the weather. My father and Mr. Pool were in a trance over the board of pieces. Mr. Kervochian was drinking a lot, but he wasn't acting odd or loud. This I saw when I cracked the door and peeked again. Mr. Kervochian had a long darkish foreign face with heavy cheek whiskers. He stared out the window at the white cold rain like a philosopher, sad. He liked Big Band music—there was some he had brought on his tape machine—and I learned later that he wrote some poetry and might be a drug addict. He seemed to be a kind man, soft, and would talk with you (me), a kid, straight ahead. He never made jokes or bragged about killing game like the others, my father too. I remembered he had given me a box of polished hickory nuts. They were under the bed and I got them out and started playing with them.

The thing was, Mr. Pool did not believe any of my father's chess victories. Something was wrong, or fluked, he thought. It couldn't be that a man from my father's circumstances could come forth with much of a chess game, to Mr. Pool, who, with his law degree and bankership, hunting, golf, and chess, thought of himself as a "peer of the realm," Mr. Kervochian said later. "A Renaissance man, a Leonardo of the backwater." There was a creature in Mr. Pool, too, Mr. Kervochian said, hoarse and small because of his cancer. Mr. Pool owned the lodge and midway (*"media res,"* said Mr. Kervochian) in his affairs he began thinking to own people too. He had a "dormant serfdom" in his head. His eyes would grow big, his tongue would move around on his teeth, and he would start demanding things, "like an old czar." Thing was, there was nobody to "quell" him when he had these fits. He did pretty much "own" several people, and this was his delight. People were "much obliged" to him left and right. Then he would have a riot of remembering this. He would leer "like Rasputin leching on a maid-in-waiting." Mr. Kervochian knew history. Pool was "beside himself" as the term had it: "himself outside the confines of his own psyche." Like he was calling in all his money and the soul attached to it. I could hear they had been talking about money and Mr. Pool was talking over all the conversation. My father's point was that the purchase transfer from the old loony man was worth a great deal as a piece of work and should make some favorable patience about the loan on Mr. Pool's part. But I didn't know all that, what their voices were saying. I knew hardly anything except for the strange loudness of their voices with the whiskey in them which was an awful thing I'd never heard.

I knew my father wasn't used to drinking and did not do it well. Once the last summer when he was coming up in the world, he had bought a bag and some clubs, some bright maroon-over-white saddle oxford golf shoes, a cart, and took me with him to try out the country club. I remember he had an all-green outfit on. This was the club where those men who were his new group played; but this was a weekday, a workday, and he wanted to come out alone (only with me) because he'd never played. So he rolled his cart into the clubhouse and we sat in a place with a bar. He began ordering glasses of whiskey almost one after the other. I went around here and there in the chairs and came back and sat, with him looking straight at me, his ears getting red and his eyes narrowing. I didn't know what was happening but the man behind the bar made me think everything was all right, saying "sure" and "certainly" when Daddy wanted another glass of whiskey. But then he, my father, wouldn't answer me at all when I asked wasn't it time to play golf. I wanted to chase the balls and had several on the floor, playing.

"You know, really. You're not supposed to bring your bag in here," said the barman, kindly.

My father looked like he didn't know what the man was talking about. I pointed at the golf bag and said, He means your club bag, Daddy.

"What?" He looked at me, whininglike at me.

Then he drank another whole glass and something happened. I watched my father fall to the side off the chair, knock over the golf cart and bag, and hit the floor, with his golf hat falling off. I got up and saw he was really down, asleep, at the other end of his saddle oxfords maroon and white. He had passed out.

My mother came from the office of the lawyer to pick him up after the barman called. I sat in the chair and waited for him to wake up while other people came in, not helping, just shutting their eyes and looking away. I was awfully scared, crying some. It wasn't until a long time later I learned (from Mother) that he was afraid to start playing golf and embarrass himself, although there were just a few people at the course. He wasn't sure about the sticks or the count. My mother whispered this to me but I never understood why he'd go out there at all. My father, I say, had no whiskey problem, he just couldn't drink it very well and hardly ever did. My mother I don't think had any problems at all and she had high literacy and beauty.

At the deer camp the weather would not quit. I can't recall that kind of cold with that much rain. One or the other usually stops but on top of the roof the roar of water kept up and my window outside was laid on by a curtain of white, like frost alive. They were quiet in the "den" for a long, long time. I imagined they were all asleep from drinking the whiskey. I liked imagining that because what was out there was not nice, I'd seen it, even if they were only playing chess, a game I knew nothing about, but it looked expensive and serious, those pieces out there, made of marble, a mysterious thing I knew my father was very good at.

Mr. Kervochian knew the game and had watched Mr. Pool (Garrand, his first name) defeat many good ones around the town and in big cities. Mr. Pool wore a gray mustache and looked something like an old hefty soldier "of a Prussian sort," said Mr. Kervochian. You could picture him ordering people around. You could feel him staring at you, bossing. He'd hardly looked at me, though. I was not sure, again, why I was the only child out there.

It got late at night but the lights were still on out there. I had gone to sleep for a while, dreaming about those polished hickory nuts and squirrels up to your hips. When I peeped out I saw all the others asleep, but Garrand Pool and my father, Gomar, were staring at the board without a sound. They had quit drinking but were angry in the eyes and resolved on some mean victory, seemed to me. It was fearsome. The others in the chairs snoring, the rain outside. Nothing seemed right in the human world I knew. Then Mr.

Pool began whispering something, more hissing maybe, as grown men I knew of never did. Pool was saying, "Stop it, Stop that. Stop that, damn you!" This made my father's body rise up and he put his hand down and moved a piece. He stiffened to a proper upright posture with shoulders spread back, and then this light queer voice came from him. I didn't know, but it was the woman overcoming him. Even in his wrist—thinking back you could see a womanly draped thing. His fingers seemed to have become longer. Now this was another evil: Mr. Pool knew nothing about the woman and thought my father was mimicking him. He seemed to be getting even angrier and I shut the door. Let me tell you, it was odd but *not* like a nightmare. Another kind of dream maybe even more wicked and curious, a quality of dream where the world was changed and there was a haze to it, and you couldn't get out by opening your eyes. It made you weird and excited, my father's voice and posture and hands.

"Now hunt, old toad," he had said actually to Mr. Pool, jangling high-voiced like a woman in a church choir.

So I had to open the door a crack again.

Mr. Pool stood up and cursed him and told him something about "deadbeat white trash." But my father said something back shrilly and Mr. Pool I thought was coming out of his skin.

"Don't you mock me with that white-trash homo voice! I won't stand for it!"

The other men woke up and wanted to know what was happening. Nobody had had any supper. They ate some crackers and cheese, commented on the steady rain, then went back to their rooms to sleep. My father and Mr. Pool had never halted the chess and paid no attention to anybody else. I was very sleepy and lost-feeling (in this big lodge, like something in a state park made for tourists). I lay there in the bunk for hours and heard the female voice very faintly and was sick in my stomach through the early morning hours. Ice was on the inside of the window. I could feel the cold gripping the wall and a gloomy voice started talking in the rain, waving back and forth. It wasn't any nightmare and it was very long, the cold wet dark woods talking to me, the woman's voice curling to the room under the doorjamb.

Another whole person was out there playing chess, somebody I never knew. A woman and I thought, somehow, sin, were in the lodge. Without a dream I was out of the regular world and had prickly sparking feelings like they had put you in a tub of ice and then run you through a wind tunnel.

At daybreak they were still at the game. Garrand Pool had started drinking again. He was up looking out a kitchen window and my father was leaned over studying the board, cooing and chirping. Mr. Pool was going to say something, turning around, but then he saw me in the doorway and stopped, coughing. When my father turned in the chair, I didn't recognize his face. It was longer and his mouth was bigger. His eyes were lost behind his nose. I was very glad he didn't say anything to me. He hurled back then as if my eyes hurt him. I shut the door again. Soon there was a knock on the door. I felt cold and withered.

But it was Mr. Kervochian. He told me to dress up, it was cold out, had quit raining, and he was going to take me out, bring my gun. In a few minutes the two of us walked by Mr. Pool and Daddy, frozen at the board, not looking up. Mr. Kervochian brought me some breakfast out on the porch—some coffee (my first), a banana, and some jerky. It was hurtfully cold while we sat there on the step. I could smell whiskey on Mr. Kervochian, but he had showered and combed his hair and had on fresh clothes. My boots were new and I liked them, bright brown with brass eyelets. I felt manly. I think Mr. Kervochian was having whiskey in his coffee.

"Let's go about our way and see what we can see, little Harris," he said.

"Don't you want your gun?" I asked him.

"No. Your big shooter's all we need."

I picked up the .410 single, which was heavy. He told me how to carry it safely. We walked a long time into the muddy woods, down truck tracks and then into deep slimy leaves with brown vines eye-high. I tripped once, went down gun and all with shells scattered out of my coat pocket. Mr. Kervochian didn't say anything but "That happens." We went on very deep in there, toward the river, I guess. How could cobwebs have lived through that rain? They were in my face. Mr. Kervochian, high up there with his Thermos, could float on the leaves and go along with no danger, but I was all webby. He began talking, just a slight muddiness in his voice because of the drink.

"He used to have a colored man out here with us, like successful Southern white men have at a deer camp. A happy coon, laughing and grinning, step and fetch it. Named Nicodemus, you know. Factotum luxury-maker. Owing so much to Pool Abe Lincoln's proclamation didn't even touch him. Measureless debt of generations. Even his pa owed Pool when he died."

"Mr. Kervochian, what's happening with my daddy and Mr. Pool back in the lodge?"

"Old Pool's calling in his debts. He always does, especially with some whiskey in him. He's that kind, perfect for a banker, gives so gladly and free, then when you don't know when, angry about the deal and set on revenge. Gives and then hates it. One of those kind that despises the borrower come any legal time to collect."

"Are they playing for money? Is that why they're so mad?"

"They could be, a lot of money if I heard right, whatall through their whispering. I don't know for sure. It's a private thing and you can be sure Pool's not going to let it go."

"It's like nobody else's in the lodge."

"Let's hunt. Tell you what: there's got to be big game down by the river."

We walked on and on. Cold and tired, stitch in the side, sleepy, was I.

We were on a little bluff and then there was just air. He caught me before I walked out into the Mississippi River. It was like a sea and I'd almost gone asleep into it, that deep muddy running water. "Watch ho, son!" he said. Then I was pulled back, watching our home state across the big water.

"You've got to watch it around here. Something's in that bluff under us. It's haunted here. This would be a very bad place to fall off."

The river was huge like a sea and angry, waves of water running. "Why is it haunted?"

"Nicodemus is under the bluff, son."

"That colored man? Why?"

"Old Pool and Colonel Wren."

"Are you drunk now, Mr. Kervochian?"

"Yes, son, I am."

"Please don't scare me."

"I'm sorry. Pay no attention to me. I can get sober in just three minutes, though, boy."

We walked back toward the lodge very slowly, the Nicodemus place behind me and the chess game going on, I guessed, ahead. We saw two squirrels, but again, I missed them. I didn't care. Mr. Kervochian said I was all right, he wasn't much of a hunter either.

"You know, all under our feet are frozen snakes, moccasins and rattlers, sleeping. All these holes in the ground around us. Snakes are cold-blooded and they freeze up asleep in the cold winter."

I didn't like to think of that at all.

Then it began raining all of a sudden, very hard, as if it had just yawned awhile to come back where it was. We were already stepping around ditches full of running water.

"Little Harris, there is a certain kind of woman," he all at once said, for what? "a woman with her blond hair pulled back straight from her forehead, a high and winsome forehead, that has forever been in fashion and lovely, through the ages. And that is your mother. Like basic black. Always in fashion. Blond against basic black and the exquisite forehead, for centuries."

I said nothing. We stopped and saw through the forest where Mr. Hester and Colonel Wren went across a cut with their guns, out trying to hunt but now caught by the rain, heading back to the lodge. We didn't say anything to them, like we were animals watching them.

"She used to come in the drugstore for her headaches. A woman like that in this town, I predicted, would always have some kind of trouble. That nice natural carriage, big trusting gray eyes."

"It's raining hard, Mr. Kervochian."

When we at last returned to the lodge my eyes were hanging down out of their holes I was so tired. There were empty plates on the bar of the kitchen and nobody in the chess seats, just empty glasses and cups on the table. Dr. Harvard said they had left off the game and finally gone to bed, thank God. He peered at the rain past us beyond the doorway and commenced fretting, almost whining about the weather and the thunder and when were we ever going to get out of here, the way the roads were flooded over. There was no telephone, and so on. To see a grown medical doctor going on like this, well, was amiss. It changed me uglily. I went right on to bed and was out a long time.

When I woke it was late into the day and going out I saw Mr. Pool and my father were sitting there again, at it after their nap. They looked neither left nor right. My father suddenly gave a yelp, shrill, and I thought Garrand Pool had done something to him. But he was only making a move with a chess piece that must have been a good and mean one, because Mr. Pool cursed and drank half a glass of whiskey.

Mr. Kervochian took his place at the window with a new glass. He looked out into the weather as if he could see a number of people, all making him melancholy. Colonel Wren and Mr. Hester were all wet. They threw more logs on the fire and got it really blazing. They talked about more poker. Nobody knew quite what to do with all their big grownup bodies and eyes and ears trapped in by the rain these days. Dr. Harvard nagged himself asleep again. The insurance man, Mr. Ott, came tumbling in the door holding his hand. He had cut it on an ax out there chopping wood. The blood was all over it and when he put his hand in the sink it dripped down in splotches around the drain. They woke up Dr. Harvard and he was in the kitchen with Mr. Ott a long time. Then he went out in the rain to get his bag. Mr. Ott needed stitches. I was fascinated by this, sewing up a man. Dr. Harvard worked over Mr. Ott for a long time. Every now and then Mr. Ott would cry out, but in a man's way, just a deep *uff!* I looked over at my father and Mr. Pool. They had never even looked up during the whole hour.

Then Colonel Wren said he was going to have something, damn it all, and went outside with his gun, where in late evening it was just sprinkling rain. Everybody had read all the magazines. I found an old *Reader's Digest Condensed Books* and went back to read something by Somerset Maugham.

It put me to sleep although I liked the story. I guess it was after midnight when I heard them making more sound than usual out there. I went out in my pajamas. The men at the poker table were high on beer, maybe, but they were very concerned about Colonel Wren. It was raining, thundering and lightning, and he hadn't returned. One of them called him a crazy Davy Crockett kind of fool. Mr. Kervochian, sipping at the fireplace, put in, "Closer to it, Kaiser Wilhelm the Second. Shot ten thousand stags, most of them near-tame. Had a feeble arm he was trying to make up for."

Then who comes in all bloody and drenched, with a knife in one hand and a spotlight in the other, but Colonel Wren. He was tracking mud in and shouting.

"There's breakfast out on the hook, by God!"

We went to the door past Mr. Pool and my father, frozen there, and saw a cleaned deer carcass hanging on the board between two trees. It showed up sparkling in the spotlight beam in all the rain.

"That's just a little doe, isn't it?" said Mr. Kervochian.

"That's all the woods gave up, help of this spotlight," said Colonel Wren, very loudly. "It'll eat fine. Come that liver and eggs in the morning, partners, we'll have an attitude change here!"

I won't say any more that my father and Mr. Pool paid no attention to any of this, and didn't do anything but play and take little naps for the next two days straight.

After breakfast around eleven that day, I drove out with Mr. Kervochian and Dr. Harvard to check the roads. We looked out of the truck cab and saw wide water much bigger than it used to be, the current of the creek rushing along limbs and bushes. It was frightening, not a hint of the road. Dr. Harvard was white when I looked at him. Later Mr. Kervochian explained that every man has a deathly fear and that Harvard's just happened to be water.

There was more poker and Big Band music on Mr. Kervochian's tape player, now and then a piece of radio music or weather announcement. But the next two days they argued mainly about Kilarney Island. Colonel Wren said he knew the deer were all gathered there from all the flooding. And that there was an old boat, they could go out in the Mississippi and shoot all the deer they wanted. The rain shouldn't stop them. This wasn't a goddamned retirement lodge, they were all hung over and bitchy from cabin fever. He wanted to start the expedition.

"Our old boat should be right under Nicodemus Bluff," he said. There would be nothing to rowing out there.

I looked over at Mr. Kervochian. The others were arguing about whether that old boat was any good anymore, the river would be raging, it was stupid and dangerous. Mr. Kervochian, looking with meaning at me, said that was hardly any hunting at all. The deer on that island, which was only fifty yards square, would just be standing around and it would be nothing but a slaughter.

"You couldn't shoot your own foot anyway, Cavort-shun," said Colonel Wren meanly. "You're an old thought-fucked man." Then Wren looked down at me. "Sorry," he said.

But early the next morning we were all ready to get out of the place. Except for you know who, at it, in another world. Mr. Pool suddenly won a game, but he just got tight-lipped and red in the face to celebrate. I didn't want to look at my father's face. When Mr. Pool said "Checkmate, Gomar!" it sounded like a foreign name in the house.

I went along with them, taking my gun. Mr. Kervochian took a gun and his Thermos. The rain was very light now in the early morning. The plan was, when they got to the island, Colonel Wren was going to scare a deer off the island just for me. It couldn't swim anywhere but almost right to me on the shore and I could blow it down. I wanted to do this. A deer was larger than the squirrels and I wasn't likely to miss. So there I was at ten all bloody in my thoughts, almost crazy from staying in that lodge around that chess tournament that who knows when it would end, both of them looking sick when I could stand to look at them.

We tracked that long way out to the bluff. They went down and found the boat and set out with the paddles, three of them. Mr. Kervochian stayed with me. He seemed to either care for me or wanted a level place to drink. With all these people the bluff didn't seem that fearsome, so I asked him what about Nicodemus, what happened?

"You can't tell this around, little Harris."

"I wouldn't."

We watched them flapping and plowing the water, heading left and north to the island, just a hump out there a half mile away.

"Looking at it several ways, it's still a wretched thing. The man was full of cancer. Owed Pool a lifetime's money. Couldn't afford a hospital. He asked Pool to shoot him and so they did. I don't know which one."

"He'd been with them—"

"His whole life. You could blame Pool for the cancer too. The way he gave, then hounded. Nicodemus, that man, still, wanted 'to keep it in the family.'"

They were hollering now out in the tan water, paddles up in the air. Something was wrong with the boat. They turned it around and headed back in. You could see the boat was getting lower in the water. The going was very slow and there was a great deal of grief shouted out. They must've been up to their knees. But my sense of humor was not attuned correctly. I heard Mr. Kervochian laughing. The river to me, though, looked like the worst fiercest place to drown. They came back under the bluff, their guns underwater and their throats stuffed with rage.

Then of course the rain came on, half-strong but mocking, and you could feel the sleet in it. The wet men said almost nothing flapping back through the woods. It took forever.

There was a shout ahead, a cackling. Down the cut I could see some motion in those stumps in the edge of the lodge clearing. The cackling and now a yipping called at us through the last yards, a stand of walnuts where on the ground you crunched the ball husks of the nuts with your boots.

Mr. Pool was beating my father on the neck with a pistol. It was a long gun. He kept whacking it down. But my father, holding his hands over his head and trying to dodge, kept cackling and yipping. Thing was, he was laughing, down on his knees, fingers on the top of his head, kneewalking and sloshing through the pools. It was there where the water lay rotten-smelling in the tops of the stumps, putrid and deep back in your nostrils.

"It's all mine, free and clear. I won it! I won it!" my father was shrieking, in that woman's voice.

He couldn't know we were standing all around him. He was shrieking at the ground. Mr. Pool didn't know we were there either. He hit my father, Gomar, again. The gun made an awful fleshy thunk on him.

"You trash scoundrel. Stop it, stop it!"

Then Mr. Pool drew around and saw us all, then me especially. He hauled my father around facing me, on his knees. Garrand Pool was a big man and my father had gone all limp. His face was cut, his nose was smashed down. He looked horrible, the rain all over his face, and his face long, his mouth hung down gaping like frozen in a holler.

"Show him. Talk for your son. Let him see who you are."

I went up close to stop Mr. Pool. I was right in front of my father. He came up with his face, and you could tell he didn't want to, but couldn't help it. He spilled out in that cracking cackling female voice.

"I won! I won!"

Then Mr. Pool just thrust him off and he fell on his face out there in that stinking water.

What Garrand Pool had done seemed awful, but my father almost cancelled it out. Nobody could make a direction toward either one. I know how they felt.

The next morning we left. Dr. Harvard was terrified, but the water had receded some and the tall trucks whipped right out through it and to the highway.

He couldn't even look at me for days when we got home. He was all bandaged up and sore. I never saw my father full in the face again. His face would start to turn my way, then he'd shake it back forward.

Nobody, I heard from Mother, ever bothered us about payments of any sort ever again while she was a widow. We had the house, the nice lawn, the two cars, a standing membership in the country club, which I only used to get loaded at and fall in the pool over and over again, swimming underwater long distances full of narcotics until my wrungout lungs drove me to the surface.

My father never got it right at the country club either, you see. The next week after the deer lodge he was walking at twilight down the road next to the golf course. The driver of the car says he swerved out of a sudden right into the nose of his car. They didn't find any alcohol in his blood, and none of it made much sense unless you had seen his eyes trying to call back that terrible woman's voice, pleading right at me.

The extra money my mother had, her legal secretary's salary free and clear, was in a way my downfall. She did not know how not to spoil me, and I always had plenty of money, more money than anybody. And Mr. Kervochian felt for me deeply, truly, I will never blame him. He was of that certain druggist's habit of thought that drugs are made to help people through hurtful times. You wouldn't call him a pusher because he meant only the kindly thing, he saw I was numbed, shocked, and injured, so he provided plenty of medicine for me. He gave some to my mother too. She wouldn't take hers. So I got hers and took it. I went back and he was always a cheerful giver.

Later, he even came down to the jail and brought me out after

I'd be taken in, accompanying somebody, some group, some-how an accomplice, just lugging there and near keeling over in that racing little sleep I loved. Never did I fight or even com-plain much. My mother never remarried. Her looks, her high brightness and carriage, you would have thought she could have a number of prominent handsome men, but she was a woman, I found out—maybe there are a few of them—who don't want but just the one marriage. They are quite all right going along alone. I was shocked, I believe when I was eighteen or there-abouts, only slightly Nembied in the kitchen, when she told me she actually had loved my father very much. Then I was con-fused even a bit more when she said, "Your father was a good man, Harris."

"He *was?*"

This confused me, as I say. I'd hated him for being on his knees with that voice at the lodge, I'd hated him for being killed, and I was angry at him through his brother, his own country-trash brother, when I saw him at Dad's funeral in a longsleeved black silky shirt with a gold chain on his chest. His own brother in not even a suit.

Soon I needed some more drugs and went by Kervochian's.

"My mother said my father was a good man. Is that how you saw him, Gomar Greeves?"

"Gomar? . . . Well, Harris. Frankly, I just don't know. I hadn't known him that well. But he was probably a good man."

Later, but before he got sick, Mr. Kervochian, sharing a 'lude with me, began trying to have a theory, like so: "This state is very proud of its men's men. Its football-playing, tough, rough, whiskey-drinking men. But I tell you, you calculate those boys at the Methodist college who come by the store here. At least *half* of them are what you call epicene—leaning toward the womanly too. The new Southern man is about half girl in many cases, Harris. Now that means their mothers raised them. Their fathers didn't get into it at all. So these men, maybe Gomar was a country ver-sion, the woman came—"

"I don't want to hear that, any of that." I was thinking of that awful Meemaw.

"But it was—I watched and heard closely, closely—a brilliant courtly woman invested him, a spirit—"

I just walked off from him.

Of course I returned for drugs. He told me two things about Mr. Pool and one about Colonel Wren, but I hate to repeat them because here my testimony gets pushy toward life's revenge, but I'll say the real fact is, Kervochian didn't have to tell me, I saw Pool plain enough around town. The man began losing his face. It just fell down and he got gruesomer and gruesomer and at last just almost unbearably ugly. He went and had galvanized electric facial therapy—$500—at the beauticians, but nothing would save him. The last time I saw him in a car windshield he was driving with nought but two deep eyeholes hanging on to a slab of red wrinkled tissue. He had got strange too. He had women out to the deer lodge. His wife found out about it and went over and burned it down. Then Colonel Wren, whom I never saw again, did a thing that got him "roundly mocked," said Mr. Kervochian. Wren was a veteran of Wake Island, where the U.S. soldiers had bravely held off a horde of Japanese before they were beaten down, the survivors going to a prison in China until the end of the war. Wren wrote a long article for an American history magazine, telling the true story, in which he figured modestly and with "much self-deprecation." Then in the next issue in the letter section of that magazine there was a long letter from a man who was a private at Wake with the others. He went on to say how modest the then Captain Wren was, too modest. He had exposed himself to danger over and over, carrying wounded in one arm and firing his .45 with the other, etc. The letter was signed "Pvt. Martin Lewis, Portland, Oregon." All was fine until somebody found out Wren had written the letter himself.

"In his seventies, old Wren. Pathetic," smacked Mr. Kervochian. None of these happenings raised my spirits and I am putting them in only in memory of Mr. Kervochian, who died such a long painful death, but had explained nearly the whole town to me before he passed on.

When we lap that old woman's house and see her sitting there, on her porch, grand car to the side, safe and nestled in, blasted dry with age, I still say over and over "success, success" to my running buddy. Forever on—maybe I'll get over it—I hate a good house, a lawn, the right trees, I despise that smart gloating Mercedes in the drive, all of it. Early on, I moved out of our house, way back there, thirteen or fifteen or something like that. I believe I moved into a shack, maybe even I lived once in a chicken shack. I have missed a great deal, but as the drugs run out with each kick and step, I am beginning to see the crone, once my teacher, go back in time. My legs are pushing her back to a smoother face, a standing position, an elegant stride, a happy smile, instructing the young cheerfully and with great love.

Now there is something for tomorrow. What are women like? What is time like? Most people, you might notice, walk around as if they are needed somewhere, like the animals out at the shelter need me. I want to look into this.

1994

Melanie Sumner

MY OTHER LIFE

This story, set in Senegal, is told by a Peace Corps volunteer from Stipple, Tennessee. Fantasizing about marrying her East African boyfriend (one of his father's twenty-one children), she imagines the Stipple First Baptist Church members craning their necks to see her "say 'I do,' and kiss a man as black as Satan." Melanie Sumner's wonderfully funny story about the many colors, sizes, and shapes of bigotry is included in her first book of stories, Polite Society, *published in 1995. Sumner grew up in Georgia and lives now in Chapel Hill, North Carolina.*

In Africa, I often imagined that my parents were dead. Although my mother sent me long letters and my father wrote on the backs of her pages, signing his name beside a martian face that he colored in with his highlighter, Jesse Ray and Dean had receded so far back into my mind that I pictured them as midgets. They had the bluish white skin of zombies, and like the people in my dreams, they spoke with their mouths closed. When I pretended they were dead, I got drunk and cried for hours. Then, lying on the cool black-and-white tiles of my living room floor with the batiks and wooden masks spinning slowly around me, I fantasized about my wedding with Yousouf Ibrahima Diop.

We would be married at the First Baptist Church in Stipple, Tennessee. Since Yousouf was the son of a man with three wives and twenty-one children, our engagement announcement would take up a full page of the *Stipple Star News*. Everyone would be horrified. They would flock to the wedding and crane their necks to see Darren Parkman say, "I do," and kiss a man as black as Satan.

His beauty would outrage them. He was slender, long-limbed, and high-gloss black all over except for his palms and the soles of his feet, which were pink. His lips were a deeper pink, cut into a wet, exquisite curve. He had a straight nose, flaring delicately at the nostrils, and enormous eyes so thickly lashed that they appeared to be lined with kohl. I pictured him walking down the aisle—smooth, catlike—and hoped someone would faint.

Even in my wildest moments, I could not imagine my parents at this ceremony. Two years ago at the Memphis airport, Dean had made me promise him that I would not come home with a Senegalese man.

"I haven't asked you for many things in your life," he said, "but promise me this. Promise your Dad that you won't marry a black man."

"Peace Corps volunteers aren't allowed to fraternize with the natives," I said, but he looked all the way into me with those blue eyes, and I promised.

I don't remember how I met Yousouf, but when I realized that I loved him, I stopped answering my door. He came to my apartment at different times of the day and night, trying to catch me at home. I always waited until I heard his footsteps growing faint on the stairs before I bent down to pick up his note. Then one day I opened the door. It had never been locked.

Although he kept a room on the outskirts of Dakar, where rent was cheaper, Yousouf spent most of his time at my apartment. I made it clear to him that I would never give him a key, and it took him three months to get one off of me. After a year, we began to talk about marriage.

"The reason I won't marry you," I told him, "is that I would hate your second wife." He was sitting on a Moroccan cushion, one skinny leg crossed over the other one, clipping his toenails into the palm of his hand. He was naked except for a pair of black bikini briefs and the string of leather talismans he wore around his waist.

"Mais, non," he said, lifting his head so that I could see the strong, clean line of his jaw. *"Quelle deuxième femme?"* He flashed

his white teeth and assured me that it was entirely too expensive to keep more than one wife on a banker's salary in Dakar.

Once I showed him a newspaper photo of the Ku Klux Klan marching down Main Street in Stipple. *"Bilaay!"* he exclaimed in Wolof. *"Xoolal góór-ni!"* I leaned over his shoulder to look at the men. Their white robes and pointed hoods resembled the costumes that nine-year-old Senegalese boys wore after their circumcisions, when they paraded through the streets. "Will these men kill me?" asked Yousouf. "Will they come to our wedding and shoot me with pistols like the American cowboys?" He rolled his eyes to the ceiling, pretending to be afraid, and then wrapped his sinewy arms around me and buried his head in my neck. "But my *Boy* will save me," he said in my ear. "My *Boy* will say, I love one African man. Let him live!" He kissed me on the ear and whispered, *"N'est-ce pas?"*

Then one day I received a letter from Jesse Ray informing me that she and Dean were coming to Dakar to spend Christmas with me. Enclosed with this letter was a package of letters written by ten-year-old girls in the First Baptist Church, commending me for my work as a missionary in Africa.

I read the letters on my windowsill, with one leg dangling over the side of the building, and a fifth of Four Roses bourbon beside me. In the parking lot, seven stories down, the guardian turned his wrinkled face up and squinted. To Muslims, bare legs are more provocative than bare breasts. I waved and poured more bourbon into my Coke. I unfolded the letter again and imagined that it read:

"It is with great sadness that I inform you that your mother and father were not among the survivors of this plane crash. . . ."

I had not told my parents that I had a Senegalese lover, and I had not told Yousouf that I had parents. *"Merde!"* I said to the empty room. Then I staggered to my feet, took a mask off the wall, and fitted it over my face. I stood in front of the mirror and practiced explaining to Yousouf, in French, the sudden appearance of a woman and a man I called Mom and Dad.

* * *

The right moment to give this speech never arrived. I ended up blurting out my confession in bed, two days before my parents' arrival.

"*Tu rêves*," Yousouf mumbled, pulling the blanket back over his head. Since I insisted on keeping the windows open, and he shivered in the seventy-degree winters, this is how he slept.

"I'm not dreaming." I pulled the cover away from his face. His hair was cut short, and his ears were small and round, fitted close to his head. I traced them with my finger. "My parents are coming on Christmas Eve. You have to move your clothes out of my closet."

He sat up, crossed his arms over his chest, and shivered. "*On ne t'a pas trouvé dans une poubelle?*"

I winced. "No, I wasn't found in a trash can. I lied."

"*Donc, tu n'es pas orpheline?*" I would miss the sound of that word. Who could help but love someone called "*orpheline*"?

I took a gulp from the wine glass on my nightstand and said, "No. I'm not an orphan. I'm just an asshole."

"What's an asshole?"

I pointed to my rear end. He raised his eyebrows and carefully repeated the word. When I stood up to refill my glass, he said, "Bring a mango juice. Asshole."

When I got back into bed, Yousouf said, "You know, Darren, in Africa we say that if there are two paths, and on the shorter path there is a man who waits to kill you, then it is faster to take the longer path. I am surprised that now you tell me you are not an *orpheline*, but I am not angry. To Americans, words seem very important, but in Senegal the words are not the meaning."

Then, apparently remembering that I had told him he is supposed to hug me when I cry, he put one arm awkwardly around me and patted me on the head. "You drink too much," he said. "You are young and pretty and intelligent. You have a man who doesn't drink, and now you have parents. Why are you wanting to die?"

"I want to live," I said. "I just have too many lives."

"You are too complicated, Darren. I know you do not like my advices, but listen to me this one thing. When your parents come here, show them our African hospitality. Show them *Teranga.*" I stared out the window. *"Boy. Ss, boy-bi."* He caught my chin in his hand and turned my face toward him. Then he rapped his knuckles lightly on my head, as though testing its hardness, and said, *"Têtue."* Our child, he had told me, would be beautiful and stubborn.

The next night Yousouf packed up his toothbrush, razor, and shaving cream and took all of his suits out of my closet. "My mother is not concerned about your color," he told me as he examined my pink Polo shirt and then added it to his suitcase. "But she asks me not to live with you, and she says I should not marry you except on the condition that you convert to Islam. I answer her that the American girl is too independent. *N'est-ce pas?*"

"That's my shirt," I said.

"Our shirt. Why do you put your parents to a hotel? They should sleep here in your bed. You can sleep on the floor. You should not drink all the time alone in your apartment. It is Jesse Ray and Dean who are the orphans." He paused in front of the mirror to pat his hair smooth. "Hello, Mr. Parkman," he said, holding his hand out to the glass and smiling. "Hello, Papa."

On Christmas Eve, he drove me to the airport and waited in the car while I went inside to find my parents. I am half the size of the average gazelle-legged Senegalese, and I used this to my advantage. I bent low as I sped through the crowd, clasping my purse to my belly and sticking my elbows out.

"Mademoiselle!" hissed a boy. He sidled up beside me and spread his long black fingers across my arm. *"Mademoiselle, attends!"* I ducked and turned, slick as a greased ball in water.

I spotted Dean and Jesse Ray before they got through the gates. They were wearing London Fog trenchcoats and stood next to a pile of matching leather luggage. Their cheeks were pink with excitement, and like all Americans in foreign countries, they looked absurdly friendly. I waved. They looked right through me.

Dean walked away from Jesse Ray and stared intently into the crowd of black bodies around me. He wore a tweed cap. Beneath his open trenchcoat he wore starched, creased khaki pants, a V-neck sweater the color of corn silk, and a blue button-down shirt. He had replaced his gold watch with a plastic one, as I had instructed in my last letter, but neither he nor Jesse Ray had followed my suggestion to remove their wedding rings.

"Dad!" I called, waving my arm. "Dad, I'm here!" He looked frantically all around me.

When he saw me, his eyes glowed, and his arm shot into the air and stayed there, waving. "Darren!" he cried. "Hi, Darren!" There was a huge, silly grin on his face, and he kept waving. Tears rolled out of my eyes, and I tried to squeeze them back. Still waving, he called out, "Jesse Ray!" The Tennessee accent reverberated through the airport, and people stared at him. "She's over here! I found her! Here she is!"

Jesse Ray spun around. For a moment she tossed her head this way and that, and then she threw her arm up in a wave. She had once held the title of Miss Western Tennessee, and she still walked as though she wore a banner across her chest. She had never learned how to smile, but her eyes shone with soft lights. They were sea green, shadowed with an intelligence that would have been unnerving if one could stare into them longer than the second she permitted.

"Now hold on to your bags," I said as I led them outside. "Watch your rings. These guys will pull them right off your fingers."

"Baayileen suma yaay," I yelled to the two boys leaning in close to Jesse Ray.

In greasy English, one of them was saying, "Madame! Hello, Madame. Are you from Los Angeles, California?"

"Hello," she said. "No, we're from Stipple—" One of the boys was already untying her shoelace so she would look down while the other one went for her pocket.

"Thief!" I shouted. "Get lost." A man pulled on Dean's suitcase, crying, *"Taxi! Venez monsieur!"* Dean pulled back on the handle, smiling all around with his Rotary Club smile. "This is the welcoming committee," he said. A leper planted himself in front of him and rattled a coffee can of coins.

"Aycaleen," I yelled. As I looked for Yousouf's car, I waved my hands at the tightening circle around us.

"Why are they hissing?" asked Jesse Ray. "I don't know why I minored in French. I don't remember a word of it." To the delight of the crowd, she hissed back. "They sure are black," she said, as a man pushed an African mask in her face. "And tall."

Suddenly, a boy scooted into our circle on a homemade skateboard. He had no legs and rode the board on his belly, propelling himself with both hands, on which he wore flip-flops. He wheeled right up to Jesse Ray, raised himself off the board with his hands, and said, *"Bonjour, Madame."* He smiled. *"Donnes-moi cent francs."*

"Lord a mercy," said Jesse Ray. "Dean, look at this one."

"Babeneenyoon," I said to the boy. "Tomorrow." He paddled around with his hands and turned his sly face up to me. "Oh, you speak Wolof," he said. *"Mayma xaalis."* His voice was unctuous, wheedling, and hard as the cement beneath his hands. When I didn't give him the money, he demanded it in French.

"I told you to go away." I turned my back to him and looked for Yousouf.

"You told me to go away?" he repeated, as though amazed by my rudeness. "I beg your pardon, Mademoiselle. I'm not talking to you anyway."

When he wheeled around to Dean, I jumped between them. *"Aycaleen, Demuleen,"* I shouted. *"Baay u suma Pàpp! Baay u suma Mama!"* I yelled this so harshly that my voice broke. I waved my arms at all of them, rasping, "You're rude! You're not normal!"

"Nous sommes corrects!" the legless boy yelled back. "You're the one who is rude!" The smooth mask of charm had dropped from his face. He laughed in a long hiss and called me a whore.

"Go to hell!" I screamed. I wanted to kick his head and send him flopping off the sidewalk.

My parents were watching me with wide eyes. "Why Darren," said Jesse Ray, "I believe you're acting uglier than they are."

Then Yousouf hopped out of his car, parting the crowd as he walked up to greet us. Dean gave him the same noncommittal smile he was giving all the black men around him and pulled back on the suitcase. "Dad!" I said in a low voice. "This is my friend. This is Yousouf. He wants to put your suitcase in the car."

Yousouf smiled. He looked sharp in his suit, a navy blue one that he wore with my pink Polo shirt and the tie I had given him last Christmas.

"Excuse me," said Dean. He let go of the suitcase to shake Yousouf's hand. He had told me once that he judged a man by his fingernails. As I watched the white hand clasp the black one, I checked Yousouf's manicure; it was perfect. *"Don Jour,"* Dean said.

Without a second's hesitation, Yousouf replied, *"Bonjour, Monsieur."* In English he said, "You have only been in Senegal for half an hour, and you are already speaking French."

"Just one word of it," said Dean, following him to the car.

"It's *Bond Jour,* Dean," said Jesse Ray, "Not *Don Jour. B* as in Boy."

"You sit in the backseat with your parents," said Yousouf. In the car, Dean patted my knee and beamed at me. "It's been seven hundred and nineteen days since I last saw you," he said. "I counted each one."

"What beautiful weather," said Jesse Ray. "It's just like Hawaii." On Avenue Pompidou, they laughed at the giant Santa Claus revolving on a rooftop.

"I guess the Africans would think Santa Claus is black," said Dean. "I never thought of that."

"We didn't think the Muslims celebrated Christmas," Jesse Ray said. "We brought you a tape of Christmas carols and a Christmas tree, a miniature one with miniature lights and ornaments and even miniature tinsel."

"I plugged the lights in to make sure they work," said Dean. Each time he spoke to me, he touched me, as though he feared I wasn't really there. They thanked Yousouf for carrying the luggage up to the apartment but barely noticed when he left.

Still wearing her trenchcoat, Jesse Ray stood in the center of my living room and said, "Darren, I have missed you. You may not think so." Her nose turned red, the way it did when she was going to cry.

"Hug your mother's neck," said Dean. "She loves you." I gave her a bear hug.

"Your Dad missed you," said Jesse Ray, digging in her black pocketbook for a Kleenex. "Went through a depression. Just sat in that chair every night. Moped. Sometimes he'd go in your room and just stand there. I got to where I had to leave the house."

When we both looked at him, Dean smiled bashfully. He was sitting on the vinyl couch where no one ever sat. "This couch must have a loose screw in it somewhere," he said. He bounced twice in his seat and then got down on his knees to look beneath the frame.

Dean's hair was completely white, and his pink scalp showed through the strands he combed over his bald spot. Jesse Ray's hair was a color she called bronze. She wore a red dress covered with lions and zebras and a chunky necklace of wooden beads she had bought in Memphis. Both of them looked so white.

"Here," said Jesse Ray. "I brought some of my work to show you. I'm doing African art now." She rummaged through a suitcase and handed me a sheaf of prints she had made with cut potatoes and ink. As I flipped through the primitive images of lions, tigers, and turtles, she said, "My art teacher thinks I should change my name. Jesse Ray doesn't sound like an artist's name. She suggested I use my maiden name, Darren, but I told her that was your name now. You wouldn't like that, would you?" When I didn't raise my head, she said, "I didn't think so. Do you want one of these prints? They're not very good. The potatoes were a little soft." I took the turtle and studied her signature in the corner.

"I like your name," I said.

"It's country. Everybody had a double name back then. We didn't have much, but we got two names."

Through the open windows, the sound of drums beat in the room.

"The natives are rising," said Dean.

"It's probably a wrestling match," I said.

"Your apartment sure is clean." He gave the couch two shakes, dusted the wooden frame off with his handkerchief, and then walked to the window.

"It's bare," said Jesse Ray, "But she likes it that way. Spartan."

Yousouf and I had recently redecorated the apartment. After we hung the black curtains figured with white fish skeletons, he had stepped back to admire them and said, "This is our home." Then he pulled out his key, winking at me before he slipped it back into his pocket.

"So this is your color scheme," said Jesse Ray. "Black and white."

"Is Use-off one of your students at the university?" asked Dean.

"He said he works at a bank," said Jesse Ray. "You don't listen."

"He's a real good-natured fellow."

"He's a good-looking boy," said Jesse Ray. "Cute personality."

Dean tested the window on its hinge until he was satisfied that it didn't need oiling. Then he looked out. "You've got an ocean-side view," he said. "This is good real estate property. I thought you'd be living like a pauper over here in Africa. Does the Peace Corps pay the rent?"

"The Senegalese government stole it for me."

"We've got to get that sunset," said Jesse Ray. She set up the Camcorder, but the light wouldn't come on, and long after the sun had dropped into the sea, she and Dean were still arguing about it.

"Well, dad-blame it then, you read the directions yourself," she said. She handed him her owl-eyed glasses, which he set firmly on his face. Then he opened the instruction booklet and snapped the pages between his fingers.

"It's all in Japanese," he said.

I suspected that the print was just too small for him to read, but I said, "How silly of them to write in their own language."

"She's getting crabby," said Jesse Ray. "We should go to our hotel and let her rest." As we walked out the door, she glanced at the pack of Marlboros in my hand and said, "Still smoking, I see. I brought you a picture of a black lung."

"That was thoughtful of you," I said. Then I felt mean. I put my arms around her rigid back and dropped my head on her shoulder. She gave me a quick hug and pushed me away saying, "I just don't want to go to your funeral. Children should outlive their parents."

"I don't guess this place would burn down to the quick," said Dean, "with all this cement." He watched me lock the door and waited until I had stepped away from it before he tried the handle to make sure it was locked.

"There's no fire escape," said Jesse Ray. "Don't take the elevator if there's a fire."

Dean stopped. "Goodness gracious, no!" He looked hard at me. I was trying to untie my goatskin bag to get some matches.

"I can never untie your knots, Dad. Why did you tie my bag?"

"I was trying to help you. I didn't want everything to fall out. Here, I'll get it. Don't ever get in the elevator if there's a fire."

"I know that."

"She knows that," said Jesse Ray.

"She's a smart girl." He patted me on the back. "I guess she'd get out pretty quick." When the gray walls of the elevator closed around us, he said, "I guess they don't have fire drills in Africa."

As I walked them down the street to their hotel, I held their hands. "Don't go outside," I said. "Don't talk to anyone. I'll be here in the morning to get you."

"Now you know what we went through when you were a kid," said Jesse Ray. "Every time I turned my back, you had wandered off somewhere." I had already decided that if they showed up at my apartment during the night, Yousouf would have to crawl out the window and stand on the ledge. Since he was afraid of heights, I didn't know how I would get him out there, but I intended to try.

When I got back to my apartment, I found Yousouf in bed with the Ziploc bag of brownies Jesse Ray had brought me. He was trying to sing along with "Frosty the Snowman." The lights of the Christmas tree scattered like sequins over his black arms. *"C'est cool ça,"* he said, examining the zipper of the bag. "These clever Americans."

I stretched out beside him with a glass of bourbon. "Do white people look funny to you?"

"Toubab." He drew out the word, the way children did on street corners, and tossed my hair in his hands, saying, *"Toubab* hair! Ha, ha." Then he was serious. "Your family is handsome. Dean and Jesse Ray seem wise. *Ils sont* 'nice' *quoi."* As he ran his hand along my thigh, I watched the colored lights of the Christmas tree slide over our skins. *"Eh, orpheline?"* I pressed my face in his shoulder, and he took the glass out of my hand, saying softly, *"Suma Boy, kooku daal,"* which was a phrase from a song about a woman leaving a man.

On Christmas Day, at nine A.M. sharp, I sat Jesse Ray and Dean on the rickety wooden bench beside the parking lot of my building. This gave Yousouf some extra time to get out of the apartment.

"Now make sure you don't leave your pick on the sink," I had told him, "or a sock on the floor, or your . . ." I stopped. I sounded exactly like Dean and Jesse Ray.

"I am going to lean out the window and yell, 'Hello, Papa Dean; hello, Mama Jesse Ray,'" Yousouf said. He took my chin in his hand and kissed me.

After dark, the whores did their business in this thin strip of trees along the edge of the street, but in the morning it belonged to a bent little man in a red stocking cap who sold coffee and bread.

"They served a breakfast buffet at the hotel," said Jesse Ray, narrowing her eyes as the man rinsed out a dirty plastic cup and began stirring Nescafé and hot water into it. "Are we drinking after people?"

We opened gifts in my apartment. Islamic chants screamed out of the mosque's loudspeakers in a static roar, drowning out Handel's "Messiah." As Dean unwrapped the grinning wooden mask rolled in one of my old curtains—yellow *legos* printed with violet squiggly creatures—he said, "This will be yours someday. You'll inherit all of the African things."

"She won't inherit everything," said Jesse Ray. "The other children will get their share, too."

"She'll inherit all the African things. These are hers."

"Stop talking about dying," I said. I checked my watch to see if it was too early for a drink. It was midmorning.

"Open another present," said Dean. He had a smile on his face, and with his eyes he was telling me to smile now. I tore the red paper from the package and removed the Polo shirts I planned to rewrap and give to Yousouf after my parents went home.

"These are going to swallow you whole," said Jesse Ray, "But I got the size you wanted. I guess you like them big." As I gently set the shirts on top of the heap of other gifts they had given me, I considered telling them the truth, but Dean was still trying to make me smile, and Jesse Ray had taken out her camera.

I wanted to take my parents to a Catholic monastery where bongo drums were played in the service, but Jesse Ray insisted on going to the Baptist mission. She had contacted the missionaries from Tennessee.

"Most of the Senegalese are devout Muslims," I said. "The rest are devout Catholics or devout Animists. Do you know how many converts the Baptists have snatched up in the last five years?"

"I don't care for your language," said Jesse Ray.

"Two," I said. "And those were Methodists from Sierra Leone."

"Ha, ha," said Dean. "Everybody get along."

The service was terrible. It was centered around a duet given by the missionary couple's two daughters—lanky girls with stringy blond hair and pink combs sticking out of their back pockets. Neither of them could sing a note. One of them forgot the words. I rolled my eyes at Jesse Ray, who stared straight ahead and pretended not to notice.

Afterward, she cornered the preacher and made a big deal about how we were all Americans here in Senegal and all Baptist to the bone. "How many people in your fellowship are Senegalese?" she asked, glancing at me to make sure I was listening.

"Well," he drawled, "I don't know. They all look alike to me."

"Darren can tell them apart," said Jesse Ray.

When we were back in the taxi she said, "You're right. He was a dumbbell." Then she leaned out of the window with the Camcorder and shot everything on the street, something I had asked her not to do. Someone threw a rock at the taxi.

Later that night when I heard Yousouf's knock on my door— two long raps, and then a short one—I stayed in the window. I wanted to know if he would use his key. When I heard his footsteps moving away, I ran to the door and opened it.

He stood very straight in the doorway and kept his arms by his sides. *"Qu'est-ce qu' il y a, Darren?"*

"Don't leave me, Yousouf. Please don't leave me."

"My *Boy*. You feel solitary." Then he saw the bottle in the window. He frowned. Loosening his tie, he walked to the bedroom, saying, "Really, you are difficult sometimes. I want to use the key, because I am thinking, maybe she is sitting in the window drinking bourbon and will fall. Then I am thinking, maybe Dean and Jesse Ray are here. They will ask, why does this boy have a key?" He sat down on the edge of our bed and removed his socks and shoes. Without looking at me, he shined each shoe with a sock and set the pair neatly against the wall. "You see, Darren, the pains you give me."

"Why do I have to pretend that you are just my friend? The man I love is none of my parents' business. They can't run my life."

He was silent as he undressed and hung his clothes in my closet. When he was lying naked on the bed, he folded his arms behind his head. "You must respect your parents. I notice that you do not do this enough." As I climbed in beside him, he pressed me against his chest and pulled the sheet over our heads. His smooth, supple skin smelled of indigo. I tightened my arms around him and licked the silky hollow in his neck.

"What afraids you, Darren?"

"Nothing."

"But there are many things to be afraid of in Africa. Three o'clock in the morning is the worst time. Then you can see a white horse, or even a woman. You know, if you see a white woman at this hour, she is the devil. She will make you make love to her, and then you will be schizophrenic."

Long ago I had stopped trying to convince Yousouf that there is no such thing as magic. Like most black Muslims in Senegal, he ranked witch doctors with religious men and insisted that genies are mentioned throughout the Koran.

"What scares you?" I asked, expecting another horror story about the *kangkurang,* a spirit dressed up as a tree that chases newly circumcised boys, or the genies that come through open windows at night and jump inside of your chest to eat your heart.

"I am afraid that you will go back to the United States and forget me here." When he kissed me, his face was wet.

In the middle of the night, I woke up to the crack of bone against bone. Outside, under the low curse of a man, a whore wailed. Yousouf was leaning out of the window. The faint light from the streetlamps exposed the delicate ribs moving beneath his skin and cast a purple sheen on his smooth, round buttocks. Somewhere in the trees, the whore laughed, then sobbed, then laughed again—high and wild. Again, the man hit her, and again she screamed.

"Stop him," I said, sitting up in bed. "Do something!" When he didn't answer, I thought he might have walked in his sleep. I ran to the window and screamed, "Leave her alone, you black son of a bitch."

"*Viens-toi!*" Yousouf pulled me away from the window.

"Why is she here? Why doesn't she leave him?"

"She's a whore," he said, holding my wrists. "She has no mother. Where would she go?"

"I'm sorry. Yousouf, I'm sorry I said that."

"You have stress. This is very obvious." For a moment, it was so quiet outside that we could hear the ocean washing up on the sand. Beyond the streetlamps, all around the city, drums beat in and out like the heart of a beast holding Dakar against his chest.

The next morning Jesse Ray came to my apartment. Yousouf had left ten minutes earlier to hire a taxi to take us to his mother's village. When I saw my mother standing at the door my heart jumped, and then my head began to hurt. "What's wrong?" I demanded.

"Nothing is wrong. You look tired. Did you stay up late? Dean is coming. He wanted to take the stairs. He's all in a dither because there's not a fire escape in your building."

"I told y'all not to leave the hotel without me." I glanced around the room to make sure Yousouf hadn't left anything lying about. To me, the whole apartment smelled like sex. "Last week a seventy-year-old Peace Corps volunteer was beaten up and mugged in broad daylight. I don't know why you won't listen to me."

"We're not seventy yet," she said. "Two fellows did follow us real close, trying to sell us some watches, but I told them we weren't interested. They snickered about it but didn't bother us after that. I'd like some coffee."

I followed her into the kitchen where she put a pan of water on the stove and found the Nescafé. I leaned against the sink, blocking her view, but Yousouf had already washed and dried our two coffee cups and put them away.

"I don't know how you live without hot water," she said. "I guess you've got some things to look forward to when you come back home." She made a face as she sipped her instant coffee and then said, "So you want a white house with a picket fence and a German shepherd. No husband?" I had written about the house and dog in a letter. "No grandchildren?"

"You'll have grandpups."

"Thank you." She wet the corner of a dish towel and rubbed a spot off of her vest. "I got this out of your closet at home," she said. "I hope you don't mind. You left it."

"It looks nice on you." It was a fringed suede vest, embroidered with cowgirls; I had worn it when I was sixteen.

"I can still wear young clothes," she said. "Whenever I show my senior citizen discount card at the grocery store, the cashier can't believe that I'm sixty-one." As she twisted the towel in her veined hand, I watched the diamond glint on her finger. Dean had given her the ring when she was twenty, and she had never removed it.

Now she looked around my kitchen as if she might find a machine gun leaning against the wall, or a black man peering out from a cabinet. I knew that she had made this unannounced visit to see what I was really doing in Senegal, and in a way I admired her for that. Jesse Ray was tough.

"More coffee?" I asked.

She cleared her throat and said, "You aren't planning to marry Yousouf, I hope."

"He's just a friend."

"You better make that clear to him. He sure does seem to like you."

"I'll keep us white."

"It's not that. Yousouf is a good-looking man, and just as nice as he can be, but there are cultural differences that you should be aware of. Religious differences. A man is so different from a woman to begin with that you don't want to start out with somebody as different as a . . . martian."

I brushed past her, took a beer out of the refrigerator, opened it with my army knife, and drank. She stared. "I have a headache," I said.

"Louise Darren Parkman." When she pressed her lips together, the wrinkles around her mouth cut into deep lines. The rest of her face seemed to sag. "Why do you need alcohol at eight o'clock in the morning?"

"My head hurts." For a split second, she looked me in the eye. Then she turned away. I finished the beer in silence while she looked for an aspirin.

In the parking lot, as the driver tied our luggage on the roof of his taxi, Dean explained our change of plans to Jesse Ray. "Yousouf's father is spending the holidays with his third wife here in Dakar, so Yousouf is lending his car to them." He spoke as though he had been dealing with the nuisances of polygamy all of his life. "We're going to take a taxi to the village. Yousouf's mother is the first wife." If Yousouf drove his Peugeot into the village, he would be hounded for money the rest of his life.

"Where's the taxi?" asked Jesse Ray.

"This is it," said Dean, pointing to the blue-and-yellow van painted with pictures of African women carrying bowls of fruit on their heads, African men dancing around them, palm trees, and big yellow suns. One window was covered with cardboard, and the front window appeared to have been put back in with tape. Across the back of the van, in heavy black letters, there were supplications to Allah.

The driver was arguing with Yousouf about the price. He had apparently thought Yousouf would be traveling with Africans, and now that he saw the leather luggage and the cameras, he insisted that we all pay the *Toubab* price.

"*Déédéét!*" said Yousouf. He pressed his hand to his breast and flapped his arm like a chicken wing, twice, to emphasize his refusal. Each time the driver pulled a bag off the roof, Yousouf returned it.

"Board," he told me. I jerked open the door, which almost came off the hinges, and held it for Jesse Ray.

"Put the camera away and get in the car," I said. "Please, Mom. Don't take the driver's picture. It's not polite. He isn't an animal in a zoo."

"Yousouf lets us take his picture," she said. She climbed in the car and made a face through the cracked window. "What I can't understand is how you can tell us that we are being impolite when you are so rude to your parents."

After we were all in the van, the driver cursed, jumped in his seat, and jammed a piece of wire into the ignition. The prayer beads and the blond Kewpie doll hanging from his rearview mirror swung against each other as we bounced down the road. He drove like Evel Knievel, slamming around cars that stopped for lights, bearing down on goats crossing the road, skidding to stops in front of children. Once, for no apparent reason, he drove down a street in reverse.

"I'm just not going to look," said Jesse Ray, widening her eyes as another van, top-heavy with rams, careened toward us. We were out of the city, and the desert stretched out on both sides of the road, vast and empty.

The taxi dropped us off at a *marché* where we piled onto a donkey cart driven by a gaunt man with dust in his hair. He lashed a whip across the donkey's ribs, and we bumped down a rutted path into the dry millet fields. The millet was just stubble poking up through the sand. There was nothing else on the ground but enormous anthills.

"We've got to get pictures of these," said Dean. Yousouf told the driver to stop, and Dean and Jesse Ray got out with the Camcorder and two handheld cameras, one for slides and one for prints, to photograph the anthills. While the donkey nosed around in the sand for something to eat, the driver cleaned his teeth with a chew stick.

"Why are they looking at those?" he asked Yousouf. It was as odd as if an African had been riding along in a taxi through New York City and asked to stop so that he could photograph the fire hydrants.

As the sun rose higher in the sky, my eyes began to hurt behind my sunglasses. There was nothing between us and the sun — no building, no tree, no cloud. The sky was a white glow. It was easy to see pools of blue water in the distance, but there were none. There was nothing around us but dirt and light. "Imagine living way out here without a car," said Dean. "What if you needed a doctor?"

An hour later, we came to a circle of mud huts that looked like forts children might build. The tin roofs shimmered like water. A woman with a baby strapped to her back stood over the well rapidly throwing one hand over the other as she drew up a leaking bag of water. Nearby, a girl pounded millet with a pestle as long as an oar. She sang, threw the pestle up in the air, and clapped her hands twice before she caught it. Her arms were beautifully toned.

The children had seen us coming and were running toward us. They wore ragged Goodwill clothes, and their bellies were swollen up like balloons.

"Jërëjëf waay," I said to the driver as I reached into my purse for the fare.

"I'll pay for it," said Dean.

"Don't open your wallet. You have more C.F.A. in your pocket than the average Senegalese man makes in a year."

He put his arm around my shoulder and said, "You're going to make it." The love in his eyes embarrassed me. I reworked the latch on my purse. "I was worried about leaving you alone when I die. I can't leave this earth without knowing that you're all situated. You've grown up out here, though. I think you can fend for yourself now. That gives me peace of mind."

"All she needs is money," said Jesse Ray. Before we were even out of the cart, she had the camera rolling. The children halted a short distance away from us and bunched together, giggling and falling against each other as they called out, *"Toubab! Toubab! Toubab!"*

"What are they saying?" asked Dean.

"Honkey."

"Play ball!" cried Jesse Ray. She hastily tore the Christmas paper from a red ball and threw it to them. Shrieking, they began to fight for it. In a robotic voice, she said into the Camcorder, "We are now in Yousouf's village. Yousouf is Darren's friend in Senegal, West Africa. He is working on his Ph.D. in economics and works for the present time at a bank. These are the village children." Then she handed the camera to Dean and ran into the crowd, clapping her hands and crying, "Ball! Throw the ball!"

The men, who had risen from their mats to greet us, didn't know what to make of this spectacle. "Please, Mom," I said with my teeth clenched. "Please put the camera down. We're supposed to greet the village elders. This is rude. You're embarrassing me."

"Oh, hush," said Jesse Ray. She threw the ball back into the crowd of screaming children, crying, "Whee! Whee! Play ball!" An old man wearing a ragged brown robe and a fake leopardskin cape looked at my mother in amazement. *"Kii borom ker le,"* said Yousouf, and he went to greet the head of the village.

"Dad," I said. "The chief is staring at Mom. Make her behave." He put his arm around me. "She's just excited," he said. "We've never been in a village before. Show me what you want me to do."

We shook hands, first with the men, then with the women who stood behind them retying the *pagnes* around their waists, and finally with the children rounded up by a woman who switched their ankles with a stick. They edged shyly toward us and held out their limp hands.

I studied all of the women's faces, looking for Yousouf's mother, whom I had never met. At last, she emerged from a dark doorway in a billowing white cloud of gauze. Instantly, I recognized Yousouf's face. On her, the jawbone was softened, and the cheekbones were not quite as sharp, but those were his eyes.

Her upper lip was painted a deep red, and her gums were dyed blue. Gold earrings glinted from her ears. She was a big woman, but she curtsied nimbly before Dean. When he curtsied back, the other women laughed.

Dean enjoyed the attention. He glanced away from the buxom young woman in the black bra, who couldn't stop giggling, and held his hand out to Yousouf's mother. "Dean Parkman," he said loudly. *"Don Jour."*

She looked just to the side of his head, which was level with her own, and said, *"Bonjour, Monsieur."* This was the extent of her French. Yousouf translated our greetings.

When he introduced her to me, she looked me dead in the eye. I had asked Yousouf once how she felt when his father married a second wife.

"My mother is a good Muslim," he said. "She turned to the education of the children. She gave to us all of her love."

"Did she love your father?" I asked.

"Very much. I used to hear them laughing in bed. They were in love. But she got old. She had her children, and we still needed her."

Now she looked about forty. Her face was smooth and glossy, but I could see the years in her eyes.

She spoke in Mandinka, a soft language from the jungles of the Casamance, as indecipherable as the sound of rain. As she talked, she continued to look me in the eye. The sun burned down on us, and flies gathered around my eyes and mouth and nose. I let them land on my face without trying to brush them away—she stood so still. I tried to show my respect by glancing away now and then, but I wanted to see everything in her eyes. She was the most serene person I had ever met. Finally, she finished speaking and was silent.

Yousouf turned his head to look at Jesse Ray, who had picked up a naked baby with talismans tied around its neck and belly. Then he looked down at Dean's white loafers and translated, "My mother says that since she does not speak French or Wolof, and you do not speak Mandinka, you cannot talk to each other." She smiled at me. There was nothing coy or malicious in it. It was a beautiful, kind, wise smile, and I understood that she would never give me her son.

"I'm her mother," said Jesse Ray, stepping in front of me to shake her hand. "Mo-ther," she said loudly, stretching her lips to exaggerate each syllable. The fringe on her vest swung as she turned to point at me and back to herself. The sun bore down on us with the hot white intensity of a spotlight. When I began to see red, I closed my eyes.

With my nostrils full of the smell of sweat and milk and dung, I looked past the shifting red dots behind my eyelids and saw myself in America, laying flowers on my parents' graves and walking back to a white picket fence, through the gate, past a German shepherd, and into my house.

"Darren," said Yousouf. "*Ça va?*"

"*Ça va,*" I replied, opening my eyes.

James Lee Burke

WATER PEOPLE

*As a young man growing up on the Texas-Louisiana coast, James Lee Burke
worked on the oil rigs in the Gulf. His admiration for the hardworking, often
inarticulate men he worked with is obvious in this story about a smoldering feud
between two such men and the guilt it engenders. He has said of these characters,
". . . even at age twenty, I knew their story was that of Chaucerian pilgrims." James
Lee Burke lives now in Montana. He is the author of a very successful series of
novels that feature the Cajun detective, Robicheaux. The most recent of these is*
Burning Angel.

O ur drill barge was moored out in the middle of this long
flat bay, like a big rectangle of gray iron welded onto a
cookie sheet, I mean it was so hot anything you touched scalded
your hands, and the sun was a red ball when it rose up out of the
water, and you could smell dead things on the wind out in the
marsh, amongst all those flooded willows and cypress and gum
trees. That was right before Hurricane Audrey hit the Louisiana
coast in 1957. The thundershowers we got in the afternoon weren't
anything more than hot steam, and when lightning hit on the
sandbars you could see it dancing under the chop, flickering, like
yellow snakes flipping around in a barrel full of dark water.

Skeeter was our shooter, or dynamite man, and was about forty
years old and thought to be weird by everybody on board, partly
because he was a preacher over in Wiggins, Mississippi, but also
because he had a way of coming up behind you and running his
hands down your hips. In other words, he wasn't apt to make a
skivvy run to Morgan City, although that could have been because

he was a religious man. The truth is doodle-buggers did the dirtiest work in the oil field and it was no accident other people referred to us as white niggers.

I watched Bobby Joe, our driller, drop the last six-can stick of explosives down the pipe and feed the cap wire off his palms. Bobby Joe's chest looked like it was carved from a tree stump, it was lean and hard and tapered, swollen with muscle under the arms, tanned the gold-brown color of worn saddle leather. He had a BCD from the Crotch for busting up a couple of S.P.'s. He told me once his little boy drowned in a public swimming pool that was full of colored people and Puerto Ricans in Chicago. The next day he told me he'd lied because he was drunk and I'd better not tell anybody what he'd said. Like I'm on board to write the history of Bobby Joe Guidry.

I wrapped the cap wire around the terminals on Skeeter's detonator and screwed down the wingnuts and said "You're lit, pappy," and everybody went aft or got on the jugboat that was tied to the stern, and when Skeeter gave it the juice those eighteen cans of hot stuff went off with a big *thrummmmmp* deep down in the earth and fish jumped all over the bay like they'd been shocked with an electric current; the force of the explosion kicked the drill barge's bow up in the air and slapped it back against the surface, then a second later brown water and sand and cap wire came geysering out of the pipe the way wildcat wells used to come in years ago and a yellow cloud of smoke drifted back across the jugboat and filled the inside of your head with a smell like a freshly tarred gravel road.

Skeeter wore a long-sleeve denim shirt and a cork sun-helmet and steel-rim glasses that caused him to crinkle his nose all the time. His face was round, puffed with the humidity, always pink with fresh sunburn, and his eyes blue and watery and red along the rims, like they were irritated from the smoke that seeped out of the water after he'd zapped the juice into the hole and given things down below a real headache. Bobby Joe was wiping the drilling mud off his chest with a nasty towel he'd gotten out of the engine room. His hair was the color of dry straw under his tin hat and there was a green and red Marine Corps tattoo on his upper arm that was slick and bright with sweat.

"Y'all put too many cans down, Bobby Joe," Skeeter said.

Bobby Joe went on wiping at his hands with that rag and didn't even look up.

"I tell you how to do your job, Skeet?" he said.

"We're killing fish we ain't got to. You can blow the casing out the hole, too," Skeeter said.

"You study on things too much." Bobby Joe still hadn't looked up, he just kept on wiping at those big, flat hands of his that had scars like white worms on the backs of his fingers.

"Hit don't say nowhere we got to blow half the damn bay into the next parish," Skeeter said.

"Skeet, you put me in mind of an egg-sucking dog sniffing around a brooder house," Bobby Joe said. "I declare if you don't."

We knew it was a matter of time before one of those two ran the other off. The party chief would abide any kind of behavior that didn't hurt the job; that's why he'd let a liberty boat head for the hot pillow joints in Morgan City the fifth night out on the hitch, about the time some guys would start messing around in the shower and pretend it was just grab-assing; but he wouldn't put up with guys hiding vodka in their seabags or fighting over cards or carrying a personal grief out on the drill barge, it got people hurt or killed, like the time this Mexican boy I'm fixing to tell you about fell off the bow and got sucked under the barge just when the skipper kicked over the screws, and not to be overlooked it cost the company a shitload of money.

His nickname was Magpie because he was missing two teeth up front and he had black hair with a patch like white paint in it. He weighed about three hundred pounds and traveled around the country eating light bulbs and blowing fire in a carnival act when he wasn't doodle-bugging. Bobby Joe said he saw him cheating in the bouree game and told him to his face. Magpie might have looked like a pile of whale shit but I saw him pick up a six-foot gator by its tail once, whip it around in the air, and heave it plumb across the barge's deck and leave two or three drillers with wee-wee in their socks. Magpie told Bobby Joe they were going to have a beer and learn some helpful hints about behavior when they got off the hitch, and Bobby Joe replied he knew just the spot because the dispenser for toilet seat covers in the can had a sign on it that said *Pepperbelly Place Mats*.

A week later we were way down at the mouth of the Atchafalaya, with storm winds capping the surface, and Magpie fell off the drill into the current and was swept down under the hull just as I was running at the bridge, waving my arms and yelling at the skipper who was looking back over his shoulder at the jugboat with a cigarette in his mouth. This retarded kid on the jugboat was the first to see Magpie surface downstream. He vomited over the rail, then started screaming and running up and down on the deck till his father put him in the pilot house and wiped his face and held his head against his chest. Think of water that runs by the discharge chute on a slaughter house. The thunder and wind were shrieking like the sky was being ripped loose from the earth. I don't care to revisit moments like that.

The quarterboat was moored with ropes to a willow island and at sunset Skeeter would stand out on the bow in the mosquitoes by himself, where all the sacks of drilling mud were stacked, or sometimes get in a pirogue and paddle back through the flooded trees. I used to think he was running a trot-line but I found out different when he didn't think anybody was watching him. He had a paper bag full of these little plastic statues of Jesus, the kind people puts on their dashboard, and he'd tie fish twine around the feet with a machinist's bolt on the other end and hold it to his head with his eyes squinted shut, then sink it in the water and paddle on to the next spot.

"You been out here long, W.J.?" he said when he was tying the pirogue back up.

"Not really."

I felt sorry for him; it wasn't right the way some guys made fun of him behind his back. He was at Saipan during the war. That was a lot more than most of us had done.

"You got something fretting you, Skeet?"

"A Mexican boy gets shredded up in the propeller and don't nobody seem bothered."

"Bobby Joe says Magpie was fooling around and hanging off the rail taking a whiz. It's just one of them things."

"Nobody else seen hit."

"Them ain't good thoughts, Skeet."

"Bobby Joe wasn't watching his little boy when he drowned in that swimming pool. He blames them other people for not saving him. I was in that bouree game. That Mexican boy wasn't cheating."

At breakfast on the quarterboat we got anything we wanted; you just had to pass through the galley and tell the cook: pancakes, eggs, stacks of bacon and fried ham, grits, coffee, cereal, white bread and butter and jam. Dinner was even better: steaks, fried chicken, meatloaf, gumbo and catfish on Fridays, mashed potatoes, rice and milk gravy, sweating pitchers of Kool-Aid and iced tea, cake or ice cream for dessert.

Lunchtimes though we were out on the drill barge and usually cooked up something pretty putrid, like Viennas and rice, in the small galley behind the bridge and ate it in the lee of the pilot house. The sky was the color of scorched brass when Bobby Joe sniffed at the air and said to Skeeter, "Is there something dead out where you keep your dynamite at?"

"Could be," Skeeter said.

"It's mighty strong. You ought to do something about it, Skeet, wash it off in the shallows, slap some deodorant on it."

"I might have hit on my clothes. I ain't got hit on my conscience."

Bobby Joe puffed on a filter-tipped cigar without missing a beat.

"I wish I was smart," he said. He leaned forward and tipped ashes off the side of the deck. "Then I could figure out how come

I like girls and I didn't turn out to be a faggot. I'm here to tell you, boys, it's a pure mystery."

Skeeter stared at Bobby Joe and rolled a wood match back and forth across his false teeth. You could flat hear that match clicking it was so quiet.

At quitting time that day the party chief said anybody who wanted could go into the levee on the crewboat as long as they were back in the galley sober at 0600 the next morning. The upper deck of the quarterboat was divided into two rows of tiny one-man cabins, with the showers and a can at one end of the gangway and a recreation room with a big window fan, where we played cards, at the other. The rain had just stopped and the air was cool and smelled like fish and wet trees, with yellow and purple clouds piled out on the Gulf, wind blowing through the willow islands and mullet jumping where the sunlight still shone above the dead cypress; everybody was in a good mood, whistling, combing their hair with Lucky Tiger and butch wax, putting on starched khakis, skin-tight jeans, snap-button shirts, and hand-tooled belts with chrome buckles as big as Cadillac bumpers and Indian stitching along the edges.

Bobby Joe was sitting on the edge of his bunk, buffing the points of his black cowboy boots till the leather was full of little lights. Skeeter leaned against the hatchway with his arms folded across his chest, crinkling his nose under his glasses.

"What you want, Skeeter?"

"You ain't got to carry hit."

"Carry what? What the fuck are you talking about?"

"What happened to your little boy."

"I hate guys like you. You're always feeding off somebody's grief. You quit pestering me."

"I don't mean you no harm."

You could hear Bobby Joe breathing. Another guy had just cut his hair for him out on deck, and there was a white stretch of skin half-mooned under the hairline on his neck. His hands opened and closed into rocks, his knuckles swelling up the size of quarters. Then he just about knocked Skeeter down tearing out the door into Skeeter's cabin. He ripped the mattress back off Skeeter's bunk and grabbed the paper bag with all the little statues of Jesus in it, wadded it up in his hands, and pushed the screen out on the stick and flung the bag straight out into the willow and cypress trees. You could see it spinning in an eddy just before the paper turned dark with water and went under.

"Now you leave me alone," Bobby Joe said, his hands trembling at his sides, the veins in his forearms purple and thick as soda straws.

"All right, Bobby Joe. I promise I won't bother you no more," Skeeter said.

He wasn't expecting that.

I'd been to Claudette's before and always thought the girls were pretty nice, no worse or better than us, anyway, people don't always get to choose what they are, that's the way I figured it. Most of them came from mill or farm towns in Texas and Louisiana and Mississippi, the kind of towns where people worked in ammunition or roach paste factories, places where hanging out at the Dairy Queen or down at the filling station was the biggest thing going on Saturday night, which wasn't the reason they got in the life, I think, although that's what they tried to tell you when you asked how they ended up in a hundred-year-old two-story house next to colored town with a blue light over the door and the paint eaten off the wood by the salt and a pimp in the front room who once knocked the glass eye out of a girl for sassing him.

You want to get one of them mad? Ask her about her father, what kind of guy was he, did he ever take her to a kid's show or a county fair, did he know what happened to her, did he *care* what happened to her, something like that, and tell me about it.

I never thought they were bad girls, though. As long as you bought a beer, it was six-bits for a little-bitty Schlitz, you could talk to them, or listen to the jukebox and you didn't have to take one of them upstairs, nobody'd bother you, really.

But I saw something that changed my thinking. It was a weekday afternoon and business was slow except for a roughneck who'd just been paid off his rig and three kids with boogies, flat-tops with ducktails on the sides, and black jeans and boots with steel taps and chains dripping off the leather, the kind of stomp-ass stuff juvenile delinquents wore back in those days. The roughneck was juiced to the eyes, by himself, no crew to take care of him, and kept splitting open his billfold and showing off his money to the girls, like this would have them lining up to glome his twanger.

One of the three kids said something about rolling the guy. Then a girl pulled the kid over by the jukebox, you could see them wreathed in cigarette smoke against the orange and purple light from the plastic casing, their heads bent together like two question marks, her hair like white gold, her mouth glossy and red, she was pretty enough to make you hurt, I'll never forget what she said to him because it wasn't just the words, it was the smile on the kid's face when she said it, like a twisted slit across bread dough, "Y'all take him somewhere else and do it, okay? Then come back and spend the money here."

It was pretty depressing.

After most of the others took off for the levee, I went out on the jugboat with Skeeter to move his dynamite caps and primers to a new sandbar. The caps and primers were a lot more sensitive than the actual dynamite, and he kept them in a big steel lockbox on a sandbar and he had to move the box every week or so to keep up with the drill barge.

"I wouldn't let it bother me, Skeet," I said. "Bobby Joe's got a two-by-four up his butt sometimes."

"Hit ain't him."

"So what's got you down?"

"My ministry ain't gone nowhere. Same back in Wiggins. I might as well be out talking in a vacant lot."

We unloaded the box, then heaved it empty up on the deck. The water was capping in the south and you could smell salt in the wind and see birds flying everywhere.

"Maybe if you went about it a little different," I said. "Sinking those little dashboard statues is a mite unusual."

"I done something I never could make up for," he said. "A bunch of Japs was down in a cave, maybe seventy or eighty of them. I blew the mountain in on top of them. You could hear a hum through the coral at night, like thousands of bees singing. It was all them men moaning down there."

He scratched a mosquito bite on his face and looked at the willow islands and the leaves that were starting to shred in the wind.

"Sometimes people have to do bad things in a war," I said.

"I almost had myself convinced they wasn't human. Then I seen them people going off the cliffs at Saipan. Women threw their babies first, then jumped after them, right on top of the rocks, they was so scared of us."

I pulled the anchor and we drifted out into the current. The sun's afterglow made a dark red light in the water.

"What's that got to do with statues?" I said.

"I bring Jesus to them people who jumped into the sea. The same water is wrapped all the way around the earth, ain't hit? Hit ain't that way with land. You could drive this boat from here to Saipan if you had a mind."

"I say don't grieve on it. I say let the church roll on, Skeeter."

But there was no consoling him. He sat on the deck rail, his face like an empty pie plate, and I kicked the engines over and hit it hard across the bay. The sky in the south had gone white as bone, the way it does when the barometer drops and no birds or other living things want to be out there.

Hurricane Audrey flat tore south Louisiana up. It killed maybe five hundred people in Cameron Parish, just south of Lake Charles, and left drowned people hanging in trees out in the marsh. We rode it out though, with the wind screaming outside, houseboats spinning around upside down in the current, and coons climbing up the mooring ropes to hide from the rain on the lee side of the deck.

Then the third day the sun rose up out of the steam like a yellow balloon over the cypress trees and we were climbing back on the crewboat and headed for the drill barge again. The night before I'd been out looking for a bunch of recording jugs that got washed overboard, and till we picked up the dynamite caps and primers at the lockbox out on the sandbar, I didn't even notice Skeeter was gone and we had a new shooter on board, a man with a steel-gray military haircut and skin the color of chewing tobacco who didn't have much to say to anybody and worked a crossword puzzle. Everybody was enjoying the ride out to the barge, smoking hand-rolls, drinking coffee, relaxing on the cushions while the bow slapped across the waves and the spray blew back over the windows, when I asked, "Where's Skeeter at?"

Suddenly nobody had diddily-squat on a rock to say.

"Where's he at?" I said.

"He drug up last night," one fellow finally said.

"That don't make sense. He would have told me," I said.

"He got run off, W.J.," another guy said.

"The hell he was," I said. Then I said it again, "The hell he *was*."

All I could see were the backs of people's heads staring at the windows. The engines were throbbing through the deck like an electric saw grinding on a nail.

At first I thought the party chief decided it was either Bobby Joe or Skeeter and it was easier to hire a new shooter than a driller who had to keep a half dozen other men who hated authority in line and make them like him for it at the same time.

But that evening, when I talked to Ray, the party chief, he cut right to it. So did I, just as soon as I found Bobby Joe up in his cabin, playing solitaire on his bunk, biting a white place on the corner of his lip.

"You sorry sonofabitch."

"I don't let a whole lot of people talk to me like that, W.J. "

"He won't be able to work anywhere. That was a lousy thing to do, Bobby Joe."

"A man oughtn't have to work with a queer."

"You told Ray Skeeter came on to you."

"How you know he didn't?"

"'Cause I know you're a damn liar, Bobby Joe. I know you lied about Magpie cheating, too."

"You're in my light."

"Too bad. You're going to hear this," I said, and sat down on his bunk, right on top of his cards. His face twitched, like a rubber band snapping under the skin. Then I told him everything I knew about Skeeter, the coral rocks humming with the voices of Jap soldiers trapped down below, women with their babies dropping off the cliffs into the sea, all the guilt he was carrying around twelve years after we set fire to the air over their cities and had parades and got back down to making money.

"I ain't got nothing to say to you, W.J."

"I bet you ain't."

I was too hard on Bobby Joe, though. Two nights later he started acting weird, almost like Skeeter, paddling the pirogue out in the swamp, raking a pile of silt up on the paddle and staring at it, walking along the edge of a sandbar like he'd lost something while cicadas droned in the sky and the sun's last light looked like electric blood painted on the trees.

"The hurricane blew them sloughs slick as spit," I said to Bobby Joe.

"Where you figure Skeeter headed to?" he asked. He bit on his thumbnail and looked at it.

"Back to Wiggins, I expect."

"You think?"

"They'd know where he's at."

Bobby Joe drug up the next day, told Ray to mail his check general delivery, New Iberia, Louisiana. I never saw him or Skeeter again. But I sure heard about them; they must have been looking for each other all over the oil patch, one man trying to forgive the other so he could lay his own burden down.

Sometimes when it's hot and the barometer starts falling and the bottom of the sky turns green in the south, the way it does right before a storm, I start to think about Bobby Joe and Skeeter, or the girls in the hot pillow joint who'd set up a drunk to get rolled, or the guys who didn't speak up when the party chief ran Skeeter off, and I commence to get a terrible headache, just like when you'd breathe that awful cloud of yellow smoke boiling off the water when we'd zap the juice into the hole and blow carp and catfish belly-up to the surface, never worrying about it or asking a question, like it was all a natural part of our old war with the earth and whatever was down there.

APPENDIX

A list of the magazines currently consulted for the *New Stories from the South* series with addresses, subscription rates, and editors.

Agni
Boston State University
236 Bay State Road
Boston, MA 02215
Semiannually, $12
Askold Melnyczak

Alabama Literary Review
253 Smith Hall
Troy State University
Troy, AL 36082
Semiannually, $10
Theron Montgomery, Editor-in-
    Chief; James G. Davis, Fiction
    Editor

American Short Fiction
Parlin 14
Department of English
University of Austin
Austin, TX 78712-1164
Quarterly, $24
Laura Furman

The American Voice
The Kentucky Foundation for
    Women, Inc.
332 West Broadway, Suite 1215
Louisville, KY 40202
Triannually, $15
Frederick Smock, Editor
Sallie Bingham, Publisher

Antietam Review
7 West Franklin
Hagerstown, MD 21740
Once or twice a year, $5.25 each
Susanne Kass

The Antioch Review
P.O. Box 148
Yellow Springs, OH 45387
Quarterly, $30
Robert S. Fogarty

Apalachee Quarterly
P.O. Box 20106
Tallahassee, FL 32316
Triannually, $15
Barbara Hamby and Bruce Boehrer

The Atlantic Monthly
745 Boylston Street
Boston, MA 02116
Monthly, $17.94
C. Michael Curtis

Black Warrior Review
The University of Alabama
P.O. Box 2936
Tuscaloosa, AL 35486-2936
Semiannually, $11
Leigh Ann Sackrider

Blue Mesa Review
Creative Writing Center

University of New Mexico
Albuquerque, NM 87131

Carolina Quarterly
Greenlaw Hall CB# 3520
University of North Carolina
Chapel Hill, NC 27599-3520
Triannually, $10
Amber Vogel, Editor

The Chariton Review
Northeast Missouri State University
Kirksville, MO 63501
Semiannually, $9
Jim Barnes

The Chattahoochee Review
DeKalb College
2101 Womack Road
Dunwoody, GA 30338-4497
Quarterly, $15
Lamar York, Editor; Anna
    Schachner, Fiction

Cimarron Review
205 Morrill Hall
Oklahoma State University
Stillwater, OK 74078-0135
Quarterly, $12
Gordon Weaver

Concho River Review
c/o English Department
Angelo State University
San Angelo, TX 76909
Semiannually, $12
Terence A. Dalrymple

Confrontation
Department of English
C. W. Post of L.I.U.
Brookville, NY 11548
Semiannually, $10
Martin Tucker, Editor-in-Chief

Crazyhorse
Department of English
University of Arkansas at
    Little Rock
2801 South University
Little Rock, AR 72204
Semiannually, $10
Judy Troy

The Crescent Review
P.O. Box 15069
Chevy Chase, MD 20825-5069
Semiannually, $10
J. Timothy Holland

Crosscurrents
2200 Glastonbury Road
Westlake Village, CA 91361
Quarterly, $18
Linda Brown Michelson

Crucible
Barton College
College Station
Wilson, NC 27893
Terrence L. Grimes

CutBank
Department of English
University of Montana
Missoula, MT 59812
Semiannually, $12
Francesca Abbate and C. N.
    Blakemore

Epoch
251 Goldwin Smith Hall
Cornell University
Ithaca, NY 14853-3201
Triannually, $11
Michael Koch

Esquire
1790 Broadway
New York, NY 10019

Monthly, $15.97
Will Blythe, Literary Editor

Fiction
c/o English Department
The City College of New York
New York, NY 10031
Triannually, $20
Mark J. Mirsky

The Florida Review
Department of English
University of Central Florida
Orlando, FL 32816
Semiannually, $7
Russ Kesler

The Georgia Review
The University of Georgia
Athens, GA 30602
Quarterly, $18
Stanley W. Lindberg

The Gettysburg Review
Gettysburg College
Gettysburg, PA 17325-1491
Quarterly, $18
Peter Stitt

Glimmer Train
812 SW Washington Street,
   Suite 1205
Portland, OR 97205-3216
Quarterly, $29
Susan Burmeister-Brown and Linda
   Davis

GQ
The Condé Nast Publications, Inc.
350 Madison Avenue
New York, NY 10017
Monthly, $20
Thomas Mallon

Granta
2-3 Hanover Yard
Noel Road
Islington
London N1 8BE
England
Quarterly, $32
Ian Jack

The Greensboro Review
Department of English
University of North Carolina
Greensboro, NC 27412
Semiannually, $8
Jim Clark

Gulf Coast
Department of English
University of Houston
4800 Calhoun Road
Houston, TX 77204-3012
Semiannually, $22 for two years
Glenn Blake

Harper's Magazine
666 Broadway
New York, NY 10012
Monthly, $18
Lewis H. Lapham

High Plains Literary Review
180 Adams Street, Suite 250
Denver, CO 80206
Triannually, $20
Robert O. Greer, Jr.

Image
3100 McCormick Avenue
Wichita, KS 67213
Single issue, $10
Gregory Wolfe

Indiana Review
316 North Jordan Avenue
Bloomington, IN 47405

Semiannually, $12
Cara Diaconoff

The Iowa Review
308 EPB
The University of Iowa
Iowa City, IA 52242-1492
Three times a year, $18
David Hamilton

Iris
P.O. Box 7263
Atlanta, GA 30357
Quarterly, $12
Dennis Adams

The Journal
The Ohio State University
Department of English
164 West 17th Avenue
Columbus, OH 43210
Biannually, $8
Michelle Herman and Kathy Fagan

Kalliope
Florida Community College
3939 Roosevelt Blvd.
Jacksonville, FL 32205
Mary Sue Koeppel

Karamu
English Department
East Illinois University
Charleston, IL 61920
Annually, $5
Peggy Brayfield

The Kenyon Review
Kenyon College
Gambier, OH 43022
Quarterly, $22
Marilyn Hacker

The Literary Review
Fairleigh Dickinson University

285 Madison Avenue
Madison, NJ 07940
Quarterly, $18
Walter Cummins

The Long Story
11 Kingston Street
North Andover, MA 01845
Annually, $5
R. P. Burnham

Louisiana Literature
P.O. Box 792
Southeastern Louisiana University
Hammond, LA 70402
Semiannually, $10
David Hanson

Mid-American Review
106 Hanna Hall
Department of English
Bowling Green State University
Bowling Green, OH 43403
Semiannually, $12
Robert Early, Senior Editor; Ellen
    Behrens, Fiction

Mississippi Quarterly
Box 5272
Mississippi State, MS 39762
Quarterly, $12
Robert L. Phillips, Jr.

Mississippi Review
Center for Writers
The University of Southern
    Mississippi
Box 5144
Hattiesburg, MS 39406-5144
Semiannually, $15
Frederick Barthelme

The Missouri Review
1507 Hillcrest Hall
University of Missouri

Columbia, MO 65211
Triannually, $15
Speer Morgan

Negative Capability
62 Ridgelawn Drive East
Mobile, AL 36608
Triannually, $15
Sue Walker

New Delta Review
English Department
Louisiana State University
Baton Rouge, LA 70803
Semiannually, $7
Catherine Williamson and Nicola
    Mason

New England Review
Middlebury College
Middlebury, VT 05753
Quarterly, $23
David Huddle

The New Yorker
20 West 43rd Street
New York, NY 10036
Weekly, $36
Bill Buford, Fiction Editor

Nimrod
Arts and Humanities Council of
    Tulsa
2210 South Main Street
Tulsa, OK 74114
Semiannually, $10
Francine Ringold, Editor; Geraldine
    McLoud, Fiction Editor

The North American Review
University of Northern Iowa
Cedar Falls, IA 50614
Six times a year, $18
Robley Wilson

North Carolina Literary Review
English Department
East Carolina University
Greenville, NC 27858
Semiannually, $15
Alex Albright

Northwest Review
369 PLC
University of Oregon
Eugene, OR 97403
Triannually, $14
John White

Ohioana Quarterly
Ohioana Library Association
1105 Ohio Departments Building
65 South Front Street
Columbus, OH 43215
Quarterly, $20
Barbara Maslekoff

The Ohio Review
290-c Ellis Hall
Ohio University
Athens, OH 45701-2979
Triannually, $16
Wayne Dodd

Old Hickory Review
P.O. Box 1178
Jackson, TN 38302
Semiannually, $12
Dorothy Stanfill and Bill Nance

Ontario Review
9 Honey Brook Drive
Princeton, NJ 08540
Semiannually, $12
Raymond J. Smith and Joyce Carol
    Oates

Oxford American
114A South Lamar

Oxford, MS 38655
Bimonthly, $24
Marc Smirnoff

Other Voices
Department of English
UNIL Box 4348
601 S. Morgan Street
Chicago, IL 60680
Semiannually, $20
Lois Hauselman and Sharon
    Fiffer

Outerbridge
College of Staten Island
English Department
2800 Victory Blvd.
Staten Island, NY 10314
Annually, $5
Charlotte Alexander

The Paris Review
Box S
541 East 72nd Street
New York, NY 10021
Quarterly, $24
George Plimpton

Parting Gifts
March Street Press
3413 Wilshire Drive
Greensboro, NC 27405
Robert Bixby

Pembroke Magazine
Box 60
Pembroke State University
Pembroke, NC 28372
Annually, $5
Shelby Stephenson, Editor;
    Stephen E. Smith, Fiction Editor

Pfeiffer Review
Pfeiffer College
Box 3010

Misenheimer, NC 28109
D. Gregg Cowan

Playboy
680 N. Lake Shore Drive
Chicago, IL 60611
Monthly, $29
Alice K. Turner, Fiction Editor

Ploughshares
Emerson College
100 Beacon Street
Boston, MA 02116
Triannually, $19
DeWitt Henry, Editor; Don Lee,
    Fiction Editor

Prairie Schooner
201 Andrews Hall
University of Nebraska
Lincoln, NE 68588-0334
Quarterly, $20
Hilda Raz

Puerto del Sol
Box 3E
New Mexico State University
Las Cruces, NM 88003
Semiannually, $10
Kevin McIlvoy

Quarterly West
317 Olpin Union
University of Utah
Salt Lake City, UT 84112
Semiannually, $11
M. L. Williams

Reckon
Center for the Study of Southern
    Culture
University of Mississippi
University, MS 38677
Quarterly, $21.95
Ann Abadie and Lynn McKnight

River Styx
14 South Euclid
St. Louis, MO 63108
Triannually, $20
Jennifer Tabin

Santa Monica Review
Santa Monica College
1900 Pico Blvd.
Santa Monica, CA 90405
Semiannually, $12
Jim Krusoe

Sewanee Review
University of the South
Sewanee, TN 37375-4009
Quarterly, $15
George Core

Shenandoah
Washington and Lee University
Box 722
Lexington, VA 24450
Quarterly, $11
Dabney Stuart

Snake Nation Review
110 #2 West Force Street
Valdosta, GA 31601
Quarterly, $20
Roberta George

The South Carolina Review
Department of English
Strode Tower Box 341503
Clemson University
Clemson, SC 29634-1503
Semiannually, $7
Richard J. Calhoun

South Dakota Review
Box 111
University of South Dakota
Vermillion, SD 57069

Quarterly, $15
John R. Milton

Southern Exposure
P.O. Box 531
Durham, NC 27702
Quarterly, $24
Pat Arnow, Editor; Jo Carson,
    Fiction

Southern Humanities Review
9088 Haley Center
Auburn University
Auburn, AL 36849
Quarterly, $15
Dan R. Latimer and R. T. Smith

The Southern Review
43 Allen Hall
Louisiana State University
Baton Rouge, LA 70803-5605
Quarterly, $18
James Olney and Dave Smith

Sou'wester
Southern Illinois University at
    Edwardsville
Edwardsville, IL 62026-1438
Triannually, $10
Fred W. Robbins

Southwest Review
6410 Airline Road
Southern Methodist University
Dallas, TX 75275
Quarterly, $20
Willard Spiegelman

Stories
Box Number 1467
East Arlington, MA 02174-0022
Triannually, $12
Amy R. Kaufman

Story
1507 Dana Avenue
Cincinnati, OH 45207
Quarterly, $22
Lois Rosenthal

StoryQuarterly
P.O. Box 1416
Northbrook, IL 60065
Quarterly, $12
Anne Brashler, Diane Williams, and
    Margaret Barrett

Tampa Review
Box 19F
University of Tampa
401 W. Kennedy Blvd.
Tampa, FL 33606-1490
Semiannually, $10
Richard Mathews, Editor; Andy
    Solomon, Fiction

The Threepenny Review
P.O. Box 9131
Berkeley, CA 94709
Quarterly, $16
Wendy Lesser

TriQuarterly
Northwestern University
2020 Ridge Avenue
Evanston, IL 60208
Triannually, $20
Reginald Gibbons

Turnstile
Suite 2348
175 Fifth Avenue
New York, NY 10010
Semiannually, $12
Mitchell Nauffts

The Virginia Quarterly Review
One West Range
Charlottesville, VA 22903
Quarterly, $15
Staige D. Blackford

Voice Literary Supplement
VV Publishing Corp.
36 Cooper Square
New York, NY 10003
Monthly, except the combined
    issues of Dec./Jan. and
    July/Aug., $17
Lee Smith

Weber Studies
Weber State College
Ogden, UT 84408-1214
Triannually, $10
Neila C. Seshachari

West Branch
Bucknell Hall
Bucknell University
Lewisburg, PA 17837
Semiannually, $7
Karl Patten and Robert Taylor

Wind Magazine
P.O. Box 24548
Lexington, KY 40524
Semiannually, $10
Steven R. Cope and Charlie G.
    Hughes

ZYZZYVA
41 Sutter Street
Suite 1400
San Francisco, CA 94104
Quarterly, $28
Howard Junker

PREVIOUS VOLUMES

Copies of previous volumes of *New Stories from the South* can be ordered through your local bookstore or by calling the Sales Department at Algonquin Books of Chapel Hill. Multiple copies for classroom adoptions are available at a special discount. For information, please call 919-967-0108.

NEW STORIES FROM THE SOUTH: THE YEAR'S BEST, 1986

Max Apple, BRIDGING

Madison Smartt Bell, TRIPTYCH 2

Mary Ward Brown, TONGUES OF FLAME

Suzanne Brown, COMMUNION

James Lee Burke, THE CONVICT

Ron Carlson, AIR

Doug Crowell, SAYS VELMA

Leon V. Driskell, MARTHA JEAN

Elizabeth Harris, THE WORLD RECORD HOLDER

Mary Hood, SOMETHING GOOD FOR GINNIE

David Huddle, SUMMER OF THE MAGIC SHOW

Gloria Norris, HOLDING ON

Kurt Rheinheimer, UMPIRE

W. A. Smith, DELIVERY

Wallace Whatley, SOMETHING TO LOSE

Luke Whisnant, WALLWORK

Sylvia Wilkinson, CHICKEN SIMON

New Stories from the South: The Year's Best, 1987

James Gordon Bennett, DEPENDENTS

Robert Boswell, EDWARD AND JILL

Rosanne Coggeshall, PETER THE ROCK

John William Corrington, HEROIC MEASURES/VITAL SIGNS

Vicki Covington, MAGNOLIA

Andre Dubus, DRESSED LIKE SUMMER LEAVES

Mary Hood, AFTER MOORE

Trudy Lewis, VINCRISTINE

Lewis Nordan, SUGAR, THE EUNUCHS, AND BIG G.B.

Peggy Payne, THE PURE IN HEART

Bob Shacochis, WHERE PELHAM FELL

Lee Smith, LIFE ON THE MOON

Marly Swick, HEART

Robert Love Taylor, LADY OF SPAIN

Luke Whisnant, ACROSS FROM THE MOTOHEADS

New Stories from the South: The Year's Best, 1988

Ellen Akins, GEORGE BAILEY FISHING

Rick Bass, THE WATCH

Richard Bausch, THE MAN WHO KNEW BELLE STAR

Larry Brown, FACING THE MUSIC

Pam Durban, BELONGING

John Rolfe Gardiner, GAME FARM

Jim Hall, GAS

Charlotte Holmes, METROPOLITAN

Nanci Kincaid, LIKE THE OLD WOLF IN ALL THOSE WOLF STORIES

NEW STORIES FROM THE SOUTH: THE YEAR'S BEST, 1989

NEW STORIES FROM THE SOUTH: THE YEAR'S BEST, 1990

Tom Bailey, CROW MAN

Rick Bass, THE HISTORY OF RODNEY

Richard Bausch, LETTER TO THE LADY OF THE HOUSE

Larry Brown, SLEEP

Moira Crone, JUST OUTSIDE THE B.T.

Clyde Edgerton, CHANGING NAMES

Greg Johnson, THE BOARDER

Nanci Kincaid, SPITTIN' IMAGE OF A BAPTIST BOY

Reginald McKnight, THE KIND OF LIGHT THAT SHINES ON TEXAS

Lewis Nordan, THE CELLAR OF RUNT CONROY

Lance Olsen, FAMILY

Mark Richard, FEAST OF THE EARTH, RANSOM OF THE CLAY

Ron Robinson, WHERE WE LAND

Bob Shacochis, LES FEMMES CREOLES

Molly Best Tinsley, ZOE

Donna Trussell, FISHBONE

NEW STORIES FROM THE SOUTH: THE YEAR'S BEST, 1991

Rick Bass, IN THE LOYAL MOUNTAINS

Thomas Phillips Brewer, BLACK CAT BONE

Larry Brown, BIG BAD LOVE

Robert Olen Butler, RELIC

Barbara Hudson, THE ARABESQUE

Elizabeth Hunnewell, A LIFE OR DEATH MATTER

Hilding Johnson, SOUTH OF KITTATINNY

Nanci Kincaid, THIS IS NOT THE PICTURE SHOW

Bobbie Ann Mason, WITH JAZZ

Jill McCorkle, WAITING FOR HARD TIMES TO END

Robert Morgan, POINSETT'S BRIDGE

Reynolds Price, HIS FINAL MOTHER

Mark Richard, THE BIRDS FOR CHRISTMAS

Susan Starr Richards, THE SCREENED PORCH

Lee Smith, INTENSIVE CARE

Peter Taylor, COUSIN AUBREY

NEW STORIES FROM THE SOUTH: THE YEAR'S BEST, 1992

Alison Baker, CLEARWATER AND LATISSIMUS

Larry Brown, A ROADSIDE RESURRECTION

Mary Ward Brown, A NEW LIFE

James Lee Burke, TEXAS CITY, 1947

Robert Olen Butler, A GOOD SCENT FROM A STRANGE MOUNTAIN

Nanci Kincaid, A STURDY PAIR OF SHOES THAT FIT GOOD

Patricia Lear, AFTER MEMPHIS

Dan Leone, YOU HAVE CHOSEN CAKE

Karen Minton, LIKE HANDS ON A CAVE WALL

Reginald McKnight, QUITTING SMOKING

Elizabeth Seydel Morgan, ECONOMICS

Robert Morgan, DEATH CROWN

Susan Perabo, EXPLAINING DEATH TO THE DOG

Padgett Powell, THE WINNOWING OF MRS. SCHUPING

Lee Smith, THE BUBBA STORIES

Peter Taylor, THE WITCH OF OWL MOUNTAIN SPRINGS

Abraham Verghese, LILACS

NEW STORIES FROM THE SOUTH: THE YEAR'S BEST, 1993

Richard Bausch, EVENING

Pinckney Benedict, BOUNTY

Wendell Berry, A JONQUIL FOR MARY PENN

Robert Olen Butler, PREPARATION

Lee Merrill Byrd, MAJOR SIX POCKETS

Kevin Calder, NAME ME THIS RIVER

Tony Earley, CHARLOTTE

Paula K. Gover, WHITE BOYS AND RIVER GIRLS

David Huddle, TROUBLE AT THE HOME OFFICE

Barbara Hudson, SELLING WHISKERS

Elizabeth Hunnewell, FAMILY PLANNING

Dennis Loy Johnson, RESCUING ED

Edward P. Jones, MARIE

Wayne Karlin, PRISONERS

Dan Leone, SPINACH

Jill McCorkle, MAN WATCHER

Annette Sanford, HELENS AND ROSES

Peter Taylor, THE WAITING ROOM

NEW STORIES FROM THE SOUTH: THE YEAR'S BEST, 1994

Frederick Barthelme, RETREAT

Richard Bausch, AREN'T YOU HAPPY FOR ME?

Ethan Canin, THE PALACE THIEF

Kathleen Cushman, LUXURY

Tony Earley, THE PROPHET FROM JUPITER

Pamela Erbe, SWEET TOOTH

Barry Hannah, NICODEMUS BLUFF

NEW STORIES FROM THE SOUTH: THE YEAR'S BEST, 1995